FEAR GOD AND
DREAD NAUGHT

FEAR GOD AND DREAD NAUGHT

(ARK ROYAL, BOOK VII)

CHRISTOPHER G. NUTTALL

ISBN-13: 9781535119849
ISBN-10: 1535119845

http://www.chrishanger.net
http://chrishanger.wordpress.com/
http://www.facebook.com/ChristopherGNuttall

Cover by Justin Adams

http://www.variastudios.com/

All Comments Welcome!

AUTHOR'S NOTE

Fear God and Dread Naught is the direct sequel to *Vanguard*, but it calls upon a handful of characters from the previous two trilogies - and one of them, Prince Henry, plays a fairly major role. All you really need to know about him is that he was a starfighter pilot during the First Interstellar War (with the Tadpoles) who got captured and played a major role in peace talks. Since then, he has been assigned to Tadpole Prime as Earth's Ambassador.

As always, reviews, comments and suchlike are warmly welcomed. Please feel free to forward spelling corrections and suchlike to me.

Finally, please follow my blog and/or mailing list for future releases. I've discovered that Facebook doesn't share my posts with all of my followers.

Thank you

CGN

PROLOGUE

Published In *British Space Review*, 2216

Sir.

In their recent letters, the Honourable Gordon Cameron and General Sir David Anilines (ret) both asserted that Britain - and humanity - has no legal obligation to go to the aid of the Tadpoles, even though human ships were attacked and destroyed during the Battle of UXS-469. They claim that we can pull back and allow the Tadpoles to face the newcomers on their own.

I could not disagree more.

The blunt truth is that the newcomers attacked a joint task force composed of ships belonging to both ourselves and the Tadpoles. They made no attempt to open communications; they merely opened fire (which is, in itself, a form of communication). Their attack came alarmingly close to capturing or destroying over thirty warships from five different nations, including the Tadpoles. They followed up by invading a number of Tadpole-held star systems, culminating with a thrust at a major colony that would, if captured, have opened up access to tramlines leading towards Tadpole Prime. Those are not the actions of the innocent victims of unthinking aggression. They are the actions of an aggressor.

We do not know - we have no way to know - what our new opponents are thinking. They may be so xenophobic that an immediate offensive is their only possible response to any alien contact, although the proof that we are in fact facing two unknown races seems to render this unlikely. Or they may merely be an aggressive, expansionist race taking advantage of the contact to snatch as much territory as possible. Given their technical advantages, we dare not assume that the whole affair is a simple misunderstanding. Nor do we dare assume that communications have merely been poorly handled and the matter will be solved through simple negotiation. We are at war.

From a cold-blooded perspective, fighting the war well away from the Human Sphere has a great deal to recommend it. Human colonies and populations will not be at risk. We can and we will trade space for time, if necessary; there will certainly be no messy political repercussions from military missteps so far from Earth. Keeping the war as far from our major worlds as possible cannot do anything, but work in our favour.

But there is another point - one of honour. We gave our word to the Tadpoles that we would uphold the Alien Contact Treaty. Are we now to welsh on the treaty we proposed and drafted? Are we now to confirm to the Tadpole Factions that humans are truly untrustworthy? And should we write off the deaths of over thirty thousand human spacers we can ill afford to lose? Their deaths cry out to be avenged.

No one would be more relieved than I, should we find a way to communicate with our unknown foes. But I have seen nothing that suggests that communication - meaningful communication - is possible. We may be dealing with a mentality that will refuse to negotiate until they are given a convincing reason *to* negotiate or we may be dealing with a race that we *cannot* talk to, whatever we do. The only way to guarantee the safety and security of the Human Sphere is to assist our allies and make it clear, to our new foes, that human lives don't come cheap. And if we are unable to convince them to talk to us, then we must carry the offensive forward and strike deep into their territory.

The galaxy is a big place. But it may not be big enough for both of us.
Admiral Sir Tristan Bellwether, Second Space Lord (ret).

CHAPTER
ONE

"Henry," the First Space Lord said. He rose to his feet as Henry was shown into his office and held out a hand in greeting. "It's been a long time."

"Longer for you than for me," Ambassador Henry Windsor said. He hadn't visited Nelson Base since the endless series of debriefings, after he returned from Tadpole space. "It's been quite some time since we served together on *Ark Royal*."

"True," the First Space Lord agreed. He shook Henry's hand, then motioned him to take a comfortable chair. "I remember when you were just a fledgling fighter pilot."

"And I remember when you were a mere captain," Henry said. He smiled, rather tiredly, as he took his seat. "It's definitely been a very long time."

He studied his former commanding officer thoughtfully as the First Space Lord ordered tea and biscuits. Admiral Sir James Montrose Fitzwilliam had been a dark-haired young man - some would say an over-ambitious young man - when he'd talked his way into the XO slot on HMS *Ark Royal*. His dark hair had shaded to grey and there were new lines on his face, but Henry still had no trouble seeing the face of the man he'd liked and respected, even when he'd been called out on the carpet for hiding his true identity from his lover. And yet, there was a strain there that Henry found somewhat disconcerting. Admiral Fitzwilliam had commanded the task force that had recovered the Pegasus System and defeated the Indians seven years ago, but it had been too long since he'd stood on a command deck.

"You've been back on Earth for a month," the First Space Lord said. "How are the kids?"

"Safe on my estate," Henry said, bluntly. "They're complaining about being prisoners, but at least they're safe from the parasites outside the walls."

"The media," the First Space Lord agreed. "And to think I thought the King intended to welcome them at court."

Henry shook his head. "Over my dead body," he said. "None of the girls are going to grow up in a goldfish bowl, certainly not without any real reward at the far end."

"A commendable attitude," the First Space Lord said. "But what are you going to do about their education?"

"I'll hire tutors," Henry said. He looked up as the aide reappeared, carrying a tray laden with tea and biscuits. "They're certainly not going to boarding school."

He sighed inwardly as the aide poured them both a cup of tea then retreated, as silently as she had come. Paeans had been written to the British Boarding School - he had a sneaky feeling that the people who'd written them had never actually been there - but his three daughters were not going to attend. He didn't remember his school years very fondly and he'd had the advantage of being a strong boy, with unarmed combat training from a couple of his bodyguards. Being sent away from home had left scars that had never truly healed.

And it was worse for my sister, he thought. *No wonder she clings so hard to the throne.*

He took a sip of his tea - it was excellent, of course - and then leaned forward, resting the cup on the armrest.

"I assume you know why I'm here," he said. "It certainly took a while to secure an appointment."

The First Space Lord didn't bother to dissemble. "Susan Onarina."

"Correct," Henry said. He met the older man's eyes, reminding himself - sharply - that they were no longer senior officer and junior officer. "My contacts inform me that no final decision has been reached on her case."

"That is correct," the First Space Lord said. He shifted, uncomfortably. "There have been issues…"

"It's been a month," Henry interrupted.

"Collecting evidence for the Board of Inquiry can sometimes take much longer, as you well know," the First Space Lord said. "This is a question of mutiny in the face of the enemy."

"Bullshit," Henry said.

The First Space Lord lifted his eyebrows. "I beg your pardon?"

Henry stared back, evenly. "Should I have said bovine faecal matter?"

He plunged on before the First Space Lord could say a word. "Let us be blunt, Admiral," he insisted. "Susan Onarina assumed command of HMS *Vanguard* in the middle of a battle. I do not believe that fact is in dispute. But it is also clear that the battleship's former commander, Captain Sir Thomas Blake, froze up in the middle of *two* consecutive combat operations. If she had not taken command, in the manner she did, we would be mourning an additional fifteen *thousand* spacers."

"That's one interpretation of the data," the First Space Lord said, icily.

"It isn't just *my* interpretation of the data," Henry noted. "The Yanks have...*requested*...permission to award her the Navy Cross for her actions, which saved the lives of several thousand American spacers too. Captain Owen Harper - they've bumped him up to Rear Admiral now - has considerable reason to be annoyed at her, but his report - which *accidentally* found its way across my desk - praises her to the skies. You *know* how touchy the Americans are about placing their ships under outside command."

He took a breath. "I believe the only other naval officer with that honour, in recent memory, was Theodore Smith."

Something *flickered* in the First Space Lord's eyes. "The Americans do not dictate what we do - or don't do - with our personnel."

"No, they don't," Henry agreed. "But sooner or later, they're going to actually want to award her that medal - and it will be pretty *fucking* embarrassing if we have to explain to the media cockroaches that she's in Colchester awaiting court martial."

He picked up one of his biscuits and dunked it in his tea as he spoke. "And, by law, formal court martial proceedings have to be public," he added. "It will set the government up for a disastrous political catfight at the worst possible time."

"She does have the option of retiring quietly," the First Space Lord pointed out.

"Which is as good as an admission that there's no real case against her," Henry snapped. "I have the recordings, sir; I have the data records. Blake was a crawling sycophant who should never have been promoted above Midshipman, let alone put in command of our largest and most powerful battleship! He was damn lucky that Admiral Boskone didn't realise just how badly he screwed up during the war games or he would probably have been brutally strangled on his own command deck."

"Blake was a good officer, once," the First Space Lord said, quietly.

"He wasn't when he assumed command of *Vanguard*," Henry said. He made an effort to moderate his tone. "I'm not going to second-guess the officers who put him in charge, sir, but my reading of the situation is that his former XO was covering for him. It would have taken a toll on anyone. I'm not surprised that he deserted.

"And if *that* gets out," he added, "all hell is going to break loose."

"It may still break loose," the First Space Lord admitted. "Blake…had a number of friends in high places."

Henry groaned. "And they're the ones pressing for court martial," he guessed. "Because heaven forbid that such illustrious personages ever make a fucking mistake!"

"You're an illustrious personage," the First Space Lord snapped. "You are still first or second in line to the throne…"

"I took myself out of the line of succession," Henry said. "And I have *never* knowingly promoted someone above his level of competence."

"Neither did they," the First Space Lord countered. "This was a terrible surprise to them too."

"So they're going to destroy an innocent woman, a woman we should be hailing as a hero, to cover their arses," Henry snarled. "And you are going to let them get away with it."

He felt anger rising and choked it down, savagely. It was the arrogance of the aristocracy that had driven him away from it, the arrogance of people who knew they held very real power and the will to use it. And he, the Crown Prince of Great Britain and her Colonies, would have inherited nothing, if he'd taken the throne. His role had been to be nothing more than a figurehead. He honestly didn't know why his father had chosen to stay on the throne for over thirty years. Henry knew *he* would have gone stir-crazy within the month.

"I have very little choice," the First Space Lord said. "I…"

"Bullshit," Henry said, again. "What happened to you?"

It was a struggle to keep his voice even, but he managed it. "What happened to the commander who saw fit to ignore his instructions and save his superior's career? What happened to the captain who stood up to his admiral and told him to keep his nose out of command business? What happened to the admiral who plotted the defeat of the Indian Navy and then carried it out?"

The First Space Lord slapped his desk, making the teacups rattle. "I will not be spoken to like this."

"Then it's high time you remembered your duty," Henry said, sharply. "Your duty is to the men and women under your command, the men and women wearing naval uniform and risking their lives in combat. Or have you been behind a desk long enough to forget what is really important?"

He leaned back in his chair, deliberately presenting a relaxed demeanour. "The facts of the whole affair *will* get out, sir," he warned. "And when they do, the government will wind up with a shitload of rotten egg on its collective face."

"I see," the First Space Lord said. "Is that a threat?"

"Merely a statement," Henry said. "There isn't a naval force in the Human Sphere that doesn't have copies of the combat records. I'm surprised they haven't leaked already. And those combat records include statements from Captain Harper and myself. Once they leak…"

He leaned forward. "Once they leak, everyone will see the government covering its arse at the expense of a genuine naval heroine's career," he added. "God damn it, sir; you *know* how fragile the government's position is right now. The Opposition will not hesitate to take the whole affair and use it as a stick to beat the government to death. And then we will run the risk of losing the right to promote our own officers without obtaining governmental permission, in triplicate.

"And you, the person who should be defending her, is sitting on the sidelines muttering about politics!"

"I cannot afford to risk my position, not now," the First Space Lord snapped. "If I…"

"And what," Henry asked, "would Admiral Smith think of *that*?"

The First Space Lord glared at him, his jaw working incoherently. Henry watched him, wondering absently if he was about to be kicked out of the older man's office. The First Space Lord was no coward, whatever Henry might have implied. His pride might lead him into a damaging political fight with no clear winner - with no *possible* winner - if he listened to it, rather than Henry.

"I suspect he might have changed, if he'd had to do battle with this job and its excessive paperwork," the First Space Lord said, rather coldly. He picked up his cup and took a long sip, clearly calming himself. "What do you propose?"

Henry carefully hid his smile. He'd won.

"I assume you know who backed Blake for command of *Vanguard*," he said. "Get them up here and explain, as thoroughly as you can, that Blake screwed up twice - and, the second time, he got a great many people killed. There's no way they can pin it on poor Susan Onarina. They may destroy her career, if they try, but the facts *will* come out and Blake *will* be turned into a scapegoat for the entire battle."

"They may not go for that," the First Space Lord said.

"A handful of them will be former naval personages themselves," Henry said. It was *traditional* for the aristocracy to send at least one or two of their children into the military, normally the Royal Navy. "They'll understand. And the ones who aren't will have someone to explain it to them, even if they have to use words of one syllable. They may not grasp the complexities of a naval engagement, but they will understand looming political disaster."

"I confess I don't share your faith in their rationality," the First Space Lord mused.

Henry shrugged. There was no shortage of inbred idiots amongst the British Aristocracy - in his nastier moments, he wondered if his sister had only one or two working brain cells - but the ones who managed to reach high rank tended to be very competent indeed. And they would be ruthless enough to drop Blake like a hot rock, if patronising him raised the spectre of watching helplessly as their own positions were undermined.

"We will see," he said.

He took a breath. "At that point, you will inform them that the Board of Inquiry has decided that *Captain* Susan Onarina acted in the finest traditions of the Royal Navy, etcetera, etcetera and that it has recommended that she be confirmed as *Vanguard's* commanding officer. You will, of course, accept this recommendation. And when they protest, as they will, you will *also* tell them that the Board of Inquiry has recommended that Captain Blake be given a medical discharge from the Royal Navy. They will, I am sure, regard it as a way out of the mess they've managed to get themselves into."

"And grab it with both hands," the First Space Lord observed. "Do you think the Board of Inquiry will cooperate?"

"A fair-minded Board of Inquiry will definitely produce a report that backs my conclusions," Henry pointed out. "Right now, I suspect they're worried about the effects on their careers if they produce the *wrong* report, without actually knowing which one *is* the wrong report. And if they seem reluctant, you can merely order them to come to the right conclusions."

"Boards of Inquiry hate being leaned on," the First Space Lord said.

"But it is a defensible position," Henry said. "And if it blows up, it will blow up in your face, not theirs."

"I'm starting to think you don't like me anymore," the First Space Lord commented. He smiled, rather thinly. "You've changed, Henry."

"I was an ambassador for over a decade," Henry said. He bit down the urge to ask just how much respect an admiral who was prepared to throw one of his subordinates under the shuttlecraft deserved. His former commander was caught between two fires. "I still am, technically. And I have learned a great deal about how the universe works in that time."

The First Space Lord smiled, again. "And what about Blake himself?"

"My impression of him, towards the end of the voyage home, was one of relief," Henry said, honestly. "I think he will accept his pension and fade into obscurity."

He sighed, inwardly. Captain Blake hadn't impressed him, but the First Space Lord was right. Blake *had* been a good officer once, before he'd lost his nerve. Henry would have been sorry for him if he'd been smart enough to request relief before the shit hit the fan, but he understood. No officer would request relief if there was any way it could be avoided, knowing that it meant the near-certainty of never seeing command again.

You wouldn't have done it either, he told himself, dryly. *Would you?*

He shook his head, dismissing the thought. He'd been a starfighter pilot. Even towards the end of the war, he'd never progressed beyond Squadron Commander...and only *then* because everyone above him had been killed. The Admiralty had promoted him to captain when he'd retired, but he'd never commanded a warship and probably never would.

"I will trust that you are right," the First Space Lord said. He cocked his head. "Might I ask why you chose to beard me in my den?"

"The new aliens attacked us," Henry said. "They made no attempt to contact us; they made no attempt, either, to sound us out before opening fire. Even the Tadpoles watched us from stealth before the war began. But these new aliens? Their behaviour is insane, which worries me. Either they were waiting for us to enter their system before attacking or they merely attacked us on sight..."

"That's nothing new," the First Space Lord said, sharply.

"No, it isn't," Henry agreed. He'd spent most of the last month closeted with the xenospecialists as they struggled to make sense of what few scraps had been recovered from damaged or destroyed alien ships. If politics - damnable politics - hadn't drawn him away, he would be there still. "But we are at war, sir. We need every capable officer we have..."

He leaned forward. "And destroying a young officer's career for saving her ship - and a dozen others - is a dangerous mistake," he added. "What sort of message does *that* send to the navy? Or have you been off the command deck for too long?"

"*Touché*," the First Space Lord said. He nodded, slowly. "It will be done as you suggest, Henry. And I suggest" - his voice hardened - "that you don't speak to me like that again."

"Of course, sir," Henry said. Why would he? He'd won the argument. "It was a pleasure meeting you again."

"I'm sure it was," the First Space Lord said. He rose, terminating the meeting. "My aide will show you back to your shuttle, Henry."

"Thank you," Henry said. He rose, too. "And you will tell Susan - Captain Onarina - the good news in person?"

"I suppose I should," the First Space Lord said. The hatch opened; his aide hurried into the chamber. "Be seeing you, Henry."

"I'm sure you will," Henry said. He shook his former commander's hand, then turned to the hatch. "But right now you have a war to fight."

CHAPTER TWO

The chamber was a prison. A comfortable prison, to be sure, but still a prison.

Susan Onarina - who wasn't sure if she was a captain or a commander or on the verge of being put in front of a court martial board - lay back on the comfortable bed and sighed, heavily. The suite was luxurious, easily more luxurious than her cabin on *Vanguard*, but there was a lock on the hatch and - she suspected - an armed guard on the far side. She could amuse herself, between debriefings that often became interrogations, by watching hundreds of movies and television episodes stored in the room's processor, taking long baths with seemingly unlimited water supplies or writing letters she knew would pass through a dozen hands before they reached their destinations, if they ever did. But she couldn't leave.

She sighed again as she tried to force herself to relax. It had been a month, a month when the only human company she'd encountered had been her guards and a number of high-ranking officers, none of whom had bothered to give their names before launching into the same questions, repeated over and over again. She wasn't sure if they were desperately trying to pin something - anything - on her or if they were merely stalling for time, unsure just how to proceed. She'd tried pointing out that regulations entitled her to both a clear statement of her position and legal advice, if she wished it, but they'd ignored her. It suggested that her fate, whatever it would be, wasn't going to be decided on Titan Base.

Giving up on relaxing, she sat upright and swung her legs over the side of the bed, dropping neatly to the deck. Titan's low gravity had been a shock at first - she wasn't used to working in low-gee environments - but she'd gotten used to it, after a few embarrassing incidents when she'd just arrived. Striding over to the middle of the chamber, she launched herself into a series of calisthenics that - she hoped - would burn up a little energy. She couldn't help feeling flabby after a month of inactivity, even though she'd tried hard to keep up with her exercise routines. Not *knowing* what was going to happen to her was the worst.

But I would do it again, she told herself, firmly. *Whatever the price, I would do it again.*

The thought made her scowl. Thanks to the unnamed officers, she'd gone through the whole deployment, from her assignment to *Vanguard* to her ship's return to Sol, and she knew she would do the same thing twice, even despite knowing it might see her put in front of a wall and shot. It was hard to be sure how many lives she'd saved, but she *knew* that Captain Blake - wherever he was now - wouldn't have saved *anyone*. She wondered, idly, if Captain Blake was currently bad-mouthing her to the Admiralty or if he'd taken advantage of the opportunity to quietly resign. It was what she would have done, in his place.

And he lost a ship to something that might well be termed a mutiny, she thought, darkly. *He won't get another command.*

She smiled at the thought as she felt sweat running down her back. Captain Blake hadn't been a monster, not like the legendary Captain Bligh, but she didn't regret her actions. Blake had frozen up in combat, something that could easily have gotten the entire ship destroyed before he recovered himself or his superiors ordered him removed from command. She might have pitied him, once upon a time, if he'd simply resigned when he realised he had a problem, but he'd stayed in the command chair. And his reluctance to admit his own weakness had nearly cost him the ship. It had certainly cost him his command - and any hope of flag rank.

There was a tap on the hatch. Susan straightened up, glanced down at her sweat-stained underwear, then shrugged as she tapped the switch to open the hatch. There was no point in trying to be modest, not in a prison suite. She would have been astonished if there weren't pick-ups scattered all over the compartment, monitoring her every move. She'd rarely had any real privacy since she'd joined the navy - she'd certainly never had a private cabin until she'd been promoted to lieutenant - but it galled her. She was, at base, a prisoner.

The hatch hissed open, revealing a grim-faced military policeman. Susan turned to face him, absently admiring the man's professionalism. But then, Titan Base had to be heaven when redcaps normally spent their days wrestling drunken squaddies in garrison towns or rooting spacers out of spaceport bars an hour before their shuttles were due to leave. Susan might be in hot water, but she was neither drunk nor dangerous. And even if she did decide to escape, getting off Titan Base would be damn near impossible. No one had escaped since the base had been founded, over a century ago.

"Onarina," the redcap said. He didn't address her by rank. They never did. "You have been ordered to meet a visitor in thirty minutes. Shit, shower and then knock on the hatch for relief."

He turned without waiting for an acknowledgement and strode out of the chamber, the hatch hissing closed behind him. Susan frowned, thinking hard. A visitor? The representative she'd requested? Or a government lawyer coming to lay down the law? It was nice to think that her friends or family would be clamouring to see her, but she knew it was extremely unlikely. Her civilian friends - and her father - wouldn't be permitted on Titan Base, while her military friends had probably been advised to have as little contact with her as possible until her fate was decided. She'd done everything she could to ensure that the blame could only fall on her, but she knew - all too well - that others would probably be smeared too. A single person turning on her would have been enough to keep her contingency plan from going into operation.

And it would have killed us, she thought, as she walked into the washroom and turned on the shower, discarding her sweaty underwear in the basket. *Captain Blake would have lost the ship to the newcomers.*

She pushed the thought aside as she washed herself clean, then dried herself thoroughly before donning her uniform. They hadn't taken *those*, somewhat to her surprise. She wasn't sure if it was a sign they knew they had no case against her or preparation for tearing off her rank badges and awards before throwing her arse in Colchester. As soon as she was dressed, she glanced in the mirror. The dark-skinned girl looking back at her, eyes tired and old, was almost a stranger. She'd worked hard to claw her way up the ladder by sheer ability, but she might well lose everything, just for doing the right thing. Bitter resentment welled up within her, mingled with quiet relief. She'd saved the ship and much of the Contact Fleet. It was something to remember when Admiralty REMFs tried to pin something - anything - on her.

The hatch hissed open when she tapped it, revealing two redcaps waiting for her. There were no handcuffs, nothing to mark her as a prisoner, but she couldn't help feeling trapped as she fell in between them and walked through a series of unmarked hatches. She'd tried to memorise the interior of the base, when she'd first arrived, but she was starting to think that the entire complex was designed to confuse the inmates. She hadn't seen any other inmates either.

They stopped in front of a hatch, which hissed open. Susan glanced at one of the impassive redcaps, then stepped into the tiny compartment. A large metal table, bolted solidly to the deck, dominated the room; two chairs, one on each side, waited for her. A tea machine and water dispenser sat against the far wall, which *was* a surprise. She'd been allowed to drink water during the endless debriefings, but they'd always provided her with the water themselves. Did they honestly think someone could kill with a plastic cup of water?

The hatch at the far side of the room hissed open. Susan straightened automatically, even though she suspected it would be pointless. Mutiny *and* disrespect for senior officers? She'd never get a job with a record like that. And then she saluted, sharply, as she recognised the man stepping into the room. She'd never met the First Space Lord in person - and she doubted he remembered her from his speech at the academy - but he was unmistakable.

"Please, be seated," the First Space Lord ordered. He glanced past her to the redcaps. "Dismissed, corporal."

"Sir," the redcap said.

Susan felt her head spinning as she heard the hatch opening and closing behind her. The First Space Lord in person? What did *he* want? She sat down, carefully, then fought to keep her astonishment off her face as her superior - her *ultimate* superior - carefully poured them both a cup of tea. It felt utterly surreal, as if she'd shifted into an alternate universe. Surely he had minions for pouring tea. As the junior, *she* should be pouring the tea!

"I need to talk bluntly," the First Space Lord said. He passed her the cup, then sat down facing her, resting his hands on the table. "And you should understand, right now, that this conversation is *not* to be repeated."

Susan nodded, curtly. He was going to advise her to retire, she was sure. There would be no need to bother with the performance if they were going to put her in front of a court martial board. No, she'd be told to retire quietly with an unblemished record and be grateful. If nothing else, she'd have a good chance at getting a post on a civilian ship...

"The Board of Inquiry took longer than I had expected to come to a decision," the First Space Lord said. His voice was very even, but there was an undertone that bothered her. "On one hand, you are guilty of mutiny against your senior officer; on the other hand, your actions made the difference between life and death for thousands of British and allied personnel. It is fortunate that Captain Blake has foregone the chance to bring charges against you and has, instead, quietly resigned."

It was hard, very hard, to keep the surprise from her face. Susan's mind whirled as she considered the implications. There was no way that Blake's resignation would be seen as a honourable act, not now. It would be seen as an admission of responsibility, a confession that he bore some - perhaps all - of the blame for matters getting out of hand. His patrons had to be stunned, she considered. Or perhaps they'd advised him to jump, hoping to bury the whole affair as quickly as possible. It was what *she* would have done, if she'd been a patron.

And if Blake had demanded a court martial, she thought, *the Admiralty would have found it hard to deny him.*

"You therefore pose something of a problem," the First Space Lord continued. "Mutiny is not something we can condone, but you *did* save the ship and countless lives. Therefore" - he gave her a frosty smile - "your actions have been retroactively authorised. This is not something I would advise you to bank on in future."

"Yes, sir," Susan said, stunned.

14

"That isn't the only question over your conduct," the First Space Lord added, after a long moment. "According to your debriefing, you stated that you were aware of...issues...with Captain Blake shortly after you boarded *Vanguard*. Is that correct?"

"Yes, sir," Susan said.

The First Space Lord eyed her thoughtfully. "Why didn't you bring them to the attention of your superiors?"

Susan met his eyes. "And what would have happened, sir," she asked sharply, "if I'd done that?"

She pressed on, grimly. "At best, I would have secured Captain Blake's removal, but my career would have dropped like a stone," she answered. "No CO worthy of the title would want an XO who'd knifed her *previous* CO in the back, even if her actions had been officially condoned. I would have been lucky to secure a post on an asteroid mining station in the middle of nowhere. And at worst, Captain Blake would have retained his position and I would be dishonourably dismissed from the navy."

The bitterness and frustration welled back up, forcing her to pause long enough to gather herself. "I hoped the plan wouldn't be necessary, sir," she said. "If we hadn't faced a major engagement with unknown enemies, we wouldn't have *needed* to relieve Captain Blake of command. We would have returned to Earth without anyone ever having to know that the plan had been devised at all."

"But Blake would have been left in command," the First Space Lord observed.

"Yes, sir," Susan confirmed. "What would *you* have done?"

"My commander nearly fell off the wagon," the First Space Lord said. It took Susan a moment to realise he was talking about Admiral Smith. "I had written orders authorising me to assume command of the ship, if necessary. And in the end, I chose to help him rather than put a bullet in his career."

"And if you had," Susan asked, "what would have happened to *your* career?"

She scowled. "Permission to speak freely, sir?"

"It's a little late for that," the First Space Lord noted. "But yes, you may speak freely."

"I was caught in a no-win situation," Susan said. "Whatever I did, I risked losing my career - and perhaps my life. There were no good options, sir, and no one sitting on a comfortable chair in a ground-based office can magically pull one from his rear end. Our regulations may claim to protect men and women who blow the whistle, but our culture does not. Betraying one's superior, even in a good cause, is a bad thing."

"One might argue that choosing to do so shows significant moral courage," the First Space Lord said.

"One might also argue that significant moral courage doesn't pay the bills," Susan pointed out, tartly. "And that, after the accolades are gone, everyone that person works with will *remember*."

"One might," the First Space Lord agreed.

He leaned forward. "As I said, the Board of Inquiry has retroactively authorised your actions on HMS *Vanguard*," he stated. "A copy of their final report will be made available to you, if you wish; for the moment, all you need to know is that you are *officially* in the clear."

Susan nodded. "What about my crew?"

The First Space Lord looked pained. "Yes, you covered that nicely," he said. "Just about everyone involved cannot be charged with anything, as you painted yourself as the sole mover behind the...*contingency* plan. Given the situation, the Board of Inquiry has quietly decided to drop the issue. I believe they will be advised to try to avoid plotting against their next commanding officer."

Because there won't be a second chance, Susan thought.

"You have been formally confirmed as commanding officer of HMS *Vanguard*, retroactively from the date you assumed command," the First Space Lord continued. "You'll take a shuttle from Titan Base to L4, where you will..."

Susan stared at him. "I'm in command again?"

"Yes," the First Space Lord said. "Under the circumstances, it was either confirm you as *Vanguard's* commanding officer or try to court martial you. The former allows us to bury as much as possible of the affair before the media starts asking too many questions. As far as anyone is concerned - and I suggest you stick with it - you spent the last month in a top-secret military base, assisting the analysts in studying the records from the battle."

"Understood, sir," Susan said. She was in command? She hadn't dared to hope she'd be allowed to return to *Vanguard* - or anything bigger than an asteroid mining base. "Sir...what is the ship's condition?"

"Your presumptive XO has also been promoted and will brief you, upon your return to command," the First Space Lord said. "For now, suffice it to say that we will be sending a major task force to assist the Tadpoles."

He rose. "The guards will assist you in packing up before you leave this place," he added, dryly. Clearly, he knew as well as she did that she had nothing to pack. "And one other thing?"

Susan rose, too. "Yes, sir?"

"I understand that you were trapped in a hellish situation," the First Space Lord said. "And that it had political implications that were not immediately obvious to you. And I do not blame you for the decisions you took."

"Yes, sir," Susan said.

"*But*...the decisions you took could easily have been seen in a worse light," the First Space Lord added. "I suggest - very strongly - that you don't do *anything* to blot your copybook over the next few years. You've made a number of political enemies, Captain, and those enemies will stop at nothing to see your scalp being pinned to their walls."

"I understand, sir," Susan said, tiredly. She understood more of the political and naval realities than she cared to admit. She had no patrons of her own, no friends in high places. If someone with a title wanted her gone, it wouldn't be long before they found a suitable excuse to dismiss her from the navy. "It won't happen again."

"I should hope not," the First Space Lord said. "And remember, as far as anyone is concerned, this month never happened. The records are sealed and will remain so until everyone involved is safely dead."

"Of course, sir," Susan said. Behind her, the hatch hissed open. "I won't say a word."

CHAPTER
THREE

"Welcome back, Your Excellency," Doctor Katy Murray said. "It's been too long since we were last blessed with your presence."

Henry sighed, inwardly, as Doctor Murray turned to lead him through the network of secure airlocks that led into the asteroid facility. She was middle-aged and strikingly pretty, with red hair tied up in a neat little bun, but she was no research scientist. Her file had made it clear that she was a political operator first and foremost, struggling desperately to secure as much funding and backing for the Wells Research Facility as possible. Henry would have thought that funding wasn't in question - it wasn't as if their work wasn't important - but he did have to admit that the government sometimes had odd ideas about the correct way to allocate funds. Doctor Murray might just have a point, even if she *was* a crawling sycophant.

And at least her heart's in the right place, he thought. There wasn't even a single hint that Doctor Murray was doing anything, but supporting her subordinates. *She isn't prostituting herself for anything personal.*

He pushed the thought aside as he followed her into her office, which was strikingly bare. A large hologram floated in one corner, projecting an image from the oceans of Tadpole Prime, but the walls were bare, save for a single diploma in xenological research. He wasn't surprised, really, that she hadn't chosen to practice afterwards, not when there were only a handful of genuine research slots to fill. Instead, she'd moved into data analysis and then into management.

"I can get you tea or coffee, Your Excellency," Doctor Murray said. "Or would you rather something stronger?"

"Tea would be quite suitable," Henry said. He'd been forced to pose as a trencherman during innumerable ambassadorial dinners - he had a sneaking suspicion that several countries deliberately served the vilest food they could and claimed it was a local delicacy - but it wasn't something he cared for. Alcohol led to bad decision making, a lesson he'd learned the hard way. "And I'm afraid I don't have much time."

Doctor Murray looked disappointed. It was genuine, as far as he could tell.

"We don't see many visitors out here," she said, as she called her aide and ordered tea. "My staff would be delighted to know they haven't been forgotten."

"I would be surprised if *anyone* has forgotten about this place," Henry said. "Even before the recent engagement at UXS-469, this facility was hardly *unimportant*."

"We're orbiting on the far side of the sun," Doctor Murray pointed out. "Well out of sight and probably quite out of mind."

Henry shrugged. So far, humanity *hadn't* found any alien bacteria that could infect human beings - or vice versa - but no one was inclined to take chances. Doctor Murray and her team knew, all too well, that there was a *slight* chance that something would mutate and pose a threat to human life - and, if it did, that the thermonuclear warhead buried at the centre of the facility would blow it into dust if medical science couldn't stop the outbreak in its tracks. Just *getting* to the base required an intensive medical screening…

…And, when he left, Henry knew he'd have to go through the whole unpleasant procedure again.

"There are strong reasons for your isolation," he said, as the aide returned with a tray of tea and biscuits. "And you're not the only ones carrying out such research."

"No," Doctor Murray agreed. She scowled. "I understand the political realities, Your Excellency, but they are quite annoying at times."

Henry nodded, shortly. He'd hoped, after First Contact, that human research into alien biology could be consolidated, but none of the human powers had been particularly enthusiastic about sharing their notes. Given what the Russians had tried to pull…he shook his head, irritated. Genetically-engineered viruses had posed a major threat, back during the Troubles, and still would if someone came up with an adaptive disease that defeated all current inoculations. Henry would have preferred to ban all such research, but he knew it was impossible. The only way to research cures was to research the diseases themselves.

He sipped his tea and listened, quietly, as Doctor Murray talked about her facility. Much of what she said wasn't new to him, but there were details he hadn't heard before, including expanded security and under-the-table attempts by various scientists to share notes on alien biology with their foreign counterparts. All such attempts had been reported, of course, raising the question of just who had authorised them. Were the Russians attempting to share notes without *appearing* to share notes… or were they just trying to get a handle on British progress? There was no way to be sure.

"We did make some interesting discoveries regarding Unknowns #1 and #2," Doctor Murray added. Henry straightened up. *This* was the important part. "And I believe you requested to be briefed personally."

"By the person who did the research," Henry said. He trusted Doctor Murray, but he'd fought enough political battles to know that data could be…massaged between source and destination. The bureaucracy was loathe, as always, to push bad news up the chain of command. "Can you arrange for her presence?"

"Of course, Your Excellency," Doctor Murray said. She tapped her wristcom once, then looked back at him. "I quite understand."

Henry concealed his amusement behind a practiced mask. He would have been surprised if Doctor Murray *did* understand - or, if she did, if she accepted it. Bypassing her weakened her position in the bureaucratic hierarchy. But he hadn't given her a choice, not really. The new aliens were too important to allow bureaucratic bullshit to get in the way.

Particularly if I am to make it back to the estate before being dispatched back to Tadpole Prime, he thought. *I don't want to leave before saying goodbye.*

He scowled at the thought, silently cursing - again - the fate that had made him a prince, first in line to the throne. His daughters - and his wife - were an object of intensive media attention…and he wouldn't be there to protect them, once he was on his way back to the front. The cockroaches who called themselves reporters might not be able to get into the estate - his bodyguards were armed and had authority to engage anyone crossing the inner wall with lethal force - but some toad of a political representative would probably try to pressure them into making an appearance or two. And without him, who knew *what* would happen? He was damned if he was letting the media ruin his daughters like they'd ruined his sister.

The hatch opened. "Doctor Song," Doctor Murray said. "Thank you for coming."

Henry rose and held out a hand. Doctor Song looked to be East Asian, with an oval face, almond eyes and long dark hair that fell to her shoulders. She took his hand and shook it with a surprisingly firm grip, then held up a datachip. Doctor Murray nodded to the room's processor and motioned for her to plug it in. Henry lifted his eyebrows - didn't they trust their internal communications network - and then sat back down. Doctor Murray could run her little fiefdom in whatever way she wanted, he knew, as long as she got results.

"Unlocking the alien DNA-analogue has proved challenging," Doctor Song said. She had an enchanting voice. Henry reminded himself, firmly, that he was a married man. "We don't believe we have put together enough of Unknown #2's DNA to make any credible guesses as to their appearance, but we have learned a great deal about Unknown #1."

She tapped a switch. A holographic image - the internal structure of the fox-like aliens - appeared in front of them. Henry felt a flicker of disquiet, knowing - at some level - that the aliens were far from human. The similarities - the newcomers were more like humanity than either the Tadpoles or the Vesy - made it harder to accept the differences. This, he was certain, was *genuine* competition. Humanity could co-exist with the Tadpoles, but *these* aliens?

The galaxy might not be big enough for the two of us, he thought. *And isn't that worrying?*

"Until we get a live specimen to examine," Doctor Song informed him, "all of our conclusions are tentative. However, we can say certain things with a great deal of certainty."

She paused. "The oddest aspect of these aliens," she added, "is that they are functional hermaphrodites. We've identified both penis-analogues and womb-analogues in some of the more intact alien bodies. Unlike every other known race, there is no separation into male and female; there is only one sex, which combines the two."

Henry frowned. "Are you sure?"

"As sure as we can be," Doctor Song said. "As you can see" - she zoomed in on the alien pelvis - "this particular specimen has both a penis and a vagina-analogue. My best guess is that they copulate doggy-style, perhaps taking turns to bend over. I *assume* that pregnancy does something to their hormones, perhaps rendering sex impossible, but - again - there's no way to be sure without a live specimen. It's also possible that pregnancy doesn't keep them from performing their jobs."

"Odd," Henry said. He leaned forward, studying the display. "What does this do to their society?"

"Impossible to say," Doctor Song told him, gently. "One of my researchers wrote up a detailed list of possibilities, which you are welcome to read, but they are rough guesses at best. The aliens may alternate between siring or bearing children or they may determine who serves as the mother and who serves at the father when they mate. We have no way to be sure."

"I see," Henry mused. Would *he* have birthed one of his children, if he'd had a womb? The whole concept felt profoundly unnatural. Medical science had yet to find a way to give a man a proper womb. "We'll have to ask them, if we convince them to talk to us."

Doctor Song nodded. "Their hearing is markedly better than an unenhanced human's," she noted. "I'd go so far as to say that a loud noise would hurt them more than it hurts us. But they shouldn't have any problems communicating with us. I *think* they will have problems speaking our languages - their mouths aren't designed to pronounce most of our words - yet they shouldn't have any problems understanding us, once we build up a working database of their tongue. There's no obvious reason why they shouldn't be able to communicate with us."

She sighed. "Particularly as they clearly *do* communicate with another intelligent race."

Henry nodded. "They're both intelligent?"

"It would seem so," Doctor Song said. "And they're clearly not related to each other. You have more in common with a chimpanzee than our two unknowns have with one another. I am ninety percent sure they're from different star systems."

"But you're not certain," Doctor Murray said.

"No, director," Doctor Song agreed. "But we've only encountered four other forms of intelligent life. The odds against even *one* race reaching intelligence are staggering; the odds against two doing it in the same star system are beyond calculation. I would bet half my salary that one race travelled to the other's star system and made a conquest."

"I wouldn't bet against you," Henry said. "I assume you don't know which race is in charge?"

"We know *nothing* about their social structure," Doctor Song said. "All we have is speculation - and unproductive speculation at that."

Henry nodded. "What else can you tell me about them?"

"The Foxes - for want of a better word - are probably very fast," Doctor Song said, reluctantly. "It's impossible to be absolutely sure" - Henry hid his irritation with an effort - "but we found traces of something that resembles an organic booster drug within their bloodstreams. I think that, if challenged, they will be able to boost themselves automatically, probably without the side effects noted by our military. They'll be used to the drugs."

"I see," Henry said. He'd heard a great deal about combat drugs, but all of them had dangerous drawbacks that rendered them unsuitable for deployment. A soldier might be boosted for a short period, yet afterwards he'd be lucky to survive long enough to reach medical treatment. "How long will the boost last?"

"Probably no more than thirty minutes, which may be a very conservative estimate," Doctor Song told him. She altered the display, showing him the drug glands buried within the alien's neck. "I suspect the drug also affects their liver-analogue, forcing it to cleanse their blood at a truly frightening speed. But I think if they were pushed, they'd be in deep trouble when they finally came off the drug."

23

"They'll know it too," Henry mused.

"I don't see how they *couldn't* know it," Doctor Song said. "But *we* were surprised when someone dropped an orgy bomb in Birmingham."

Henry winced. Someone - and years of investigation had never isolated a suspect, according to the files - had created a hormonal cocktail during the height of the Troubles and released it in a shopping mall in Birmingham, UK. The result had been an absolute nightmare, with hundreds of shoppers driven wild with lust. And the first responders, unsure just what they were about to encounter, had been affected too. Dozens of people had been killed and the remainder had been badly traumatised. Pheromone manipulation had been theoretically possible for years, but it was the first time anyone had experienced the potential on a large scale. It had shocked Britain to the core.

Doctor Song went on, ruthlessly. "Their hearing is probably better than ours, as I said," she added, "and so is their sense of smell. However, I'd bet that their eyesight isn't as effective as ours, at least in the daytime. At night…things may be different. However, I'd be surprised if they didn't have the technology to even the odds. We certainly do."

"True," Henry agreed. "Did you spot anything to suggest genetic or technological enhancement?"

"No to the latter," Doctor Song said. "We didn't find a trace of implants or anything along the same lines. There didn't even seem to be a basic neural link. But genetically" - she shrugged, expressively - "we simply don't understand their genetic code well enough to make any comments. It took over a century to unlock many of the mysteries of the *human* gene code and…well, we still make mistakes."

Henry nodded. The dream of enhanced humans, for better or worse, had yet to materialise. It was easy enough to improve individual traits - his immune system was far tougher than that of his ancestors - but enhancing the entire human race? There was no shortage of people who wanted to do just that; thankfully, they'd never actually gotten anywhere. He had no doubt that 'superior' humans would eventually have turned on 'inferior' humans.

"I understand," he said.

"I trust that you got what you came for," Doctor Murray said. "Our work here is important."

"It is," Henry agreed. He looked at Doctor Song. "Doctor, would you care to accompany the task force?"

Doctor Song stared at him. "I am not a military officer," she protested. "I've never been on a warship in my life."

"I need her here," Doctor Murray added, sharply. "Your Excellency..."

"The country needs her expertise on the front lines," Henry said, firmly. "We don't have *time* to send back biological samples, let alone live aliens. Doctor Song will be assigned to an escort ship and, hopefully, have the first look at any captives we take."

Doctor Murray scowled. "And could you guarantee her safety?"

"No," Henry said. There was no point in trying to lie. "But she would have a chance to make a very real difference. This war...this war may hinge on learning how to communicate with the newcomers."

"Or learning how to kill them more effectively," Doctor Song said, quietly.

"Exactly," Henry said. He took a breath. "I can't force you to accompany the task force" - technically he could, but the last thing anyone wanted was a resentful xenospecialist - "but your presence would be very welcome. It might make a considerable difference."

Doctor Song looked at Doctor Murray, then back at Henry. "Can I write a letter to my parents first, explaining why I'm leaving the system?"

"Of course," Henry said. "You'll have at least a week to pack your supplies, including all the data and tools you think you'll need, then you'll be transported to the RV point to link up with the rest of the task force. If you change your mind" - honour demanded he tell her, even though part of him suspected Doctor Murray would try hard to change her mind - "you need to let us know before the end of the week, so someone else can be invited in your place."

"I understand," Doctor Song said. She took a breath. "And I will come, if you need me."

"We need *someone*," Henry confirmed. "I suggest you go write your letters now, then start planning for the trip."

He waited until she had left the office, then looked at Doctor Murray. "Don't try to talk her out of this."

"I need her," Doctor Murray said, flatly. "She isn't a military officer, Your Excellency. Her expertise took years to develop."

"That's why we need her too," Henry said. "How long does it take to get a message from Earth to Tadpole Prime?"

"Two months," Doctor Murray said.

"And this time the task force will be operating further from Earth," Henry warned. He knew she wouldn't understand, but he had to try. "Having an expert on the spot, Doctor, may make the difference between life and death."

"And so you're taking a valuable researcher away from me," Doctor Murray said.

"I'm taking her to where she can make an important contribution," Henry said. He rose, checking his watch. There should be time to make it back to Nelson Base before the next round of briefings. "And there will be plenty to be done back here, too."

CHAPTER
FOUR

"We're approaching *Vanguard* now, Captain," the pilot said. "Do you want to come up front?"

Susan nodded and scrambled to her feet, hurrying forward until she was standing right behind the pilot and peering towards the L4 Shipyard. Hundreds of starships, shuttlecraft and worker bees were buzzing around the complex - the human race was, once again, preparing for war - but her attention was helplessly drawn towards a cluster of lights waiting at the edge of the shipyard. Illuminated by spotlights mounted on the spacedock, HMS *Vanguard* slowly took on shape and form as the shuttle approached. Susan stared, memorising each feature anew.

My ship, she thought. It was a hell of a reward - a sign, perhaps, that she *did* have friends in high places after all. Even if her promotion to Captain was confirmed, she'd be a long way down the line to command a *battleship. And yet she's all mine.*

She pressed against the cockpit as the battleship grew larger. The damaged hull plates had been removed, she noted; the destroyed turrets had been replaced, hopefully with their weak points heavily armoured or removed altogether. No one had taken a battleship into combat until the war - the Second Interstellar War - had broken out; no one had realised, absent that very real combat experience, the true strength and weaknesses of the design. HMS *Vanguard* had been through the fire, enduring more than any of her predecessors would have been able to handle, but the unknowns had come very close to destroying her.

And if we had been a mite less lucky, she thought, *we would have been destroyed.*

The shuttle pilot circled the battleship once before shaping a course towards her officers dock, positioned towards the prow of the giant battleship. It was traditional for a new commanding officer to arrive in the main shuttlebay, where her crew could greet her formally, but Susan had already been in command of the battleship. There was no time to waste on pointless formalities, particularly formalities that did nothing beyond stroking her ego, when there was work to be done. She strode back to her seat and collected her knapsack as a low thud echoed through the shuttle, followed by a hiss as her hatch opened slowly.

"Thank you for the flight," she said, as she walked to the hatch. "Are you heading straight back to Titan?"

"I have orders to report to Nelson Base," the pilot said. "Good luck, Captain."

Susan nodded and stepped through the hatch, feeling the gravity quiver around her as she left the shuttle's gravity field and entered *Vanguard's*. It felt harsh, after the lighter gravity of Titan, but she was damned if she was admitting any kind of weakness. Besides, it wasn't as if a month was enough to cause muscle degradation, not with the enhancements spliced into her genetic code. A week or two and she'd probably have forgotten that she'd ever felt...uneasy...with the higher gravity.

The inner hatch hissed open. "Captain," a familiar voice said. "Welcome back."

"Paul," Susan said. Commander Paul Mason was an old friend - and a co-conspirator when she'd plotted her contingency plans. "Congratulations on your promotion."

"Congratulations on *yours*," Mason said. He saluted, smartly. "We only got the word a couple of hours ago. I'm afraid we haven't *quite* dusted everywhere yet."

"I'm sure the finishing touches can wait an hour or two," Susan said. She felt an odd lump in her throat as she surveyed her crew. "I hope...I hope matters were not too hard on any of you."

"You took all the blame, it seems," Major Christopher Andreas said. The Marine CO leaned forward to shake her hand. "It didn't stop General

Ramón from bawling me out, Captain, but I think most of us were in the clear."

Mason cleared his throat. "This is Lieutenant-Commander Jean Granger," he said, introducing a redheaded woman. "She's been assigned as our tactical officer."

"Captain," Jean Granger said. "It is a pleasure to meet you."

"And you," Susan said. She supposed that not *all* of her former crew could be bumped up a rank or two, although she'd expected Lieutenant David Reed to get the tactical slot. But then, the Admiralty would probably want *someone* in place who hadn't been contaminated by any...*contingency planning*. "I'll speak to you later, if you don't mind."

"Not at all, Captain," Jean said. Very few officers would *mind* talking to their commanding officer - and if they did, they should know to hide it. "I also have a tactical brief from the Admiralty for your attention."

Susan nodded, quietly making a mental note to ensure she spoke to Jean within the day. "I thank you all for this," she said, raising her voice to address her officers. "It's very good to be back. And I would like to invite you all for dinner tonight, at 1900. We have much to discuss."

She paused. "Commander Mason, remain behind," she ordered. "The rest of you, dismissed."

"We cleared Captain Blake's gear out of his cabin," Mason told her, quietly. "It's open for you now, if you wish it."

"Good," Susan said. She'd left his cabin alone after she'd assumed command - it had been as good a place as any to put him - but now it was hers. "You can come with me. I imagine we have a great deal to discuss."

She kept her face expressionless as she strode through the corridors, silently noting the ongoing work to prepare the battleship for war. Crewmen - many of them unfamiliar - were unpacking boxes, installing components and checking and rechecking their work. A handful of her junior officers snapped to attention as she passed, then relaxed as she strode on to her cabin. It wouldn't be long before word got around the ship, if it hadn't already. Captain Onarina had returned.

"Well," she said, once they had entered the bare cabin. Someone had put a bottle of whiskey on the captain's table, along with a pair of glasses, but there was nothing else in the compartment. "How was it for you?"

"They asked a great many questions," Mason said. He relaxed as soon as the hatch had hissed closed. "And I answered them to the best of my ability. There was a week in pokey and then they sent me back to the ship with a promotion and orders to get her ready for combat as soon as possible."

"That's good," Susan said. It was hard not to feel envy, but she *had* been the one who had worked hard to ensure she took most of the blame. Her subordinates could claim they'd followed orders, although she had no idea how well *that* would have stood up in a court martial hearing. "Have you heard anything else?"

"Your father sent me a number of emails, which I have strict orders to pass on to you at the most convenient moment," Mason told her. "He appears to believe we're lovers."

Susan would have blushed, if her skin had allowed it. Mason and she had been barrack mates, back at the academy. She *couldn't* have been his lover, not when it would have landed them both in hot water. And besides, it would have felt like kissing her brother.

"I'll v-mail him tonight," Susan said. "Or perhaps we can have a real conversation."

"You should be able to," Mason said. He reached for the bottle and poured them both a generous dollop of alcohol. "You *are* the Captain, Captain."

He sobered. "I think he was trying to round up political support," he added. "You'd probably be better emailing him now, before he does something foolish."

Susan winced. Her father was a stubborn old man - hell, he wasn't really that old. He'd been strict with her, pointing out that he expected her to excel at everything she did, but he'd also fought hard for her. She had a feeling she might have been expelled from Hanover Towers if her father hadn't driven up to the school to argue her case personally with the headmistress, citing chapter and verse to make sure her suspension couldn't become an expulsion. The thought of the conversation they'd had afterwards made her cringe, but she'd never doubted her father was on her side. He'd proved it too many times.

"I will," she said. She took a sip of the whiskey as she sat down, silently promising herself that she'd get some more comfortable furniture moved into the suite before they left the spacedock. "How is the ship?"

A shadow crossed Mason's face. Susan couldn't help feeling a flicker of guilt. She would have hated it if a senior officer had come in and taken command, after she'd spent days repairing the damage and preparing the ship for war. Mason was a friend, but he would have been more than human if he hadn't felt *some* resentment. Yesterday, he'd been commanding officer in all but name; now, he was nothing more than her XO.

"Most of the major damage has been repaired," Mason said. He stared down into his glass as he spoke. "We've altered the control links to the turrets, ensuring we cannot be cut off from them if - when - we go back into battle. And we've hardened the armour and added additional plating in places, as well as a number of extra point defence weapons. I dare say we should be able to give the aliens quite a surprise in our next encounter."

Susan nodded. "And the bad news?"

"Two-thirds of the crew were rotated out during the first week," Mason said. He sounded pissed. She didn't blame him. "The CO who got dumped in your chair while we were being interrogated…he didn't kick up a fuss when the Admiralty went looking for trained and experienced personnel. It took me a week of arguing, pleading and kissing several buttocks before they dispatched replacement crew - and, even now, we're understrength."

"Fuck," Susan said.

"Quite," Mason agreed. "Thankfully, we haven't had any disciplinary problems so far - nothing the senior chiefs couldn't handle, in any case. But we've lost nearly all of our middies - Georgina Fitzwilliam is the only one who stayed with us, although heaven alone knows why."

"She's the First Space Lord's niece," Susan recalled. "I imagine he wouldn't want to pull her out when it might make him look bad."

"Perhaps, Captain," Mason said. "In any case, she's been given leave - along with half of the experienced crew - and should be returning to us in the next two days…"

Susan blinked. "We're short on crew and you gave them leave?"

Mason met her eyes, evenly. "They were pushed right to the limits, Captain," he said. "The number of mistakes caused by tiredness was rising sharply. I made the call to give them some leave, which they desperately needed."

"And it was your call to make," Susan conceded. "Do we have any other problems?"

"The Admiralty wants us at the RV point within the week," Mason said. "I suspect they might want us to be there, ready or not. There was a... *finality* about the message."

"As long as we don't run off with the shipyard workers," Susan said. "That might get us in some trouble."

She smiled in genuine amusement. Stellar Star had done that, but Stellar Star had an overflowing shipsuit and a friendly scriptwriter. She didn't want to *think* about what the Admiralty would say if she kidnapped a few dozen shipyard workers. They'd probably shoot her first and worry about the charges later.

"Yeah," Mason agreed. "It would probably get us into very deep shit."

He tossed back his drink, then placed the glass on the table. "I think we can make it, Captain, but we're going to be pressed for crew. I've got an application in for additional crewmen, yet...from what I'm hearing through the grapevine, there aren't many crewmen left who can be diverted to *Vanguard*. Right now, the Admiralty is hard-pressed to keep up with demand. I suspect that reservists are being mobilised, but...well it will be weeks before they're ready to take up positions and we'll be gone well before then. The only good news is that we should have an *almost* complete roster of midshipmen, when they actually arrive, but most of them are either green or have very limited experience."

"They'll have to be tossed in at the deep end," Susan said. She sighed. There was no shortage of ways for greenie midshipmen to screw up and, without proper supervision, there was a good chance that one of those ways would be disastrous. "Make sure you keep a close eye on them - ask Lieutenant Fraser to do the same."

"The First Middy won't like that," Mason reminded her. "She's supposed to be supreme within the wardroom."

"It will just have to be endured," Susan said, crossly. "And you can make that point to her, if necessary.

She ran her hand through her dark hair, knowing it wouldn't be easy. Traditionally, what happened in Middy Country *stayed* in Middy Country, at least unless it got far out of hand. If the First Middy couldn't keep control - or appeared to be leaning too much on her superior officers - it could cost her any chance of promotion. It was a delicate balancing act and too many promising young officers had fallen off.

"As you wish, Captain," Mason said. He pulled a small datapad from his belt. "As you can see" - he passed the datapad to Susan - "we are within five days of being ready to depart. I think we could leave now, if necessary, but I would prefer to avoid combat in that case. And in *any* case, we're going to have a great deal of work to do while we're in transit."

"Joy," Susan said. She *wanted* to get back out into deep space, where she didn't have to worry about desk-bound officers peering over her shoulder, but if any problems developed it would be better to handle them near a shipyard. "Did you run a full shakedown test?"

"Levels one and two," Mason said. "I decided to leave the level three test for a couple more days. We should have everything in place to make it successful by then."

"Very good," Susan said. "And we'll have three days to fix anything that goes badly wrong."

She glanced at the datapad, running her eye down the list of neat little reports. Her ship wasn't *quite* ready to depart, but she *was* close enough. The storage compartments were being filled with spare parts and additional ammunition, as well as...

"Paul," she said, holding out the datapad. "What's this?"

"Supplies for a portable biological research chamber," Mason said. He didn't seem surprised that she'd noticed it. "Or, put a little more bluntly, a prison cell for any alien captives."

Susan stared at him. "On my ship?"

"In theory, the research team - which is headed by Prince Henry, by the way - will be transferring to a support ship once we reach the front," Mason told her. "In practice, we may be keeping them for longer."

"Wonderful," Susan said. She had nothing against Prince Henry - he'd insisted he was nothing more than an Ambassador - but she didn't like the idea of untrained civilians on her ship. "What happened to the researchers from Tadpole Prime?"

"I don't know," Mason said. "But they won't be coming with us."

Susan rubbed her forehead. "Are there any more surprises?"

"Apparently, there will be a formal briefing once we reach the RV point," Mason said. "I imagine they're saving the nasty surprises until then."

"Quite," Susan agreed. "It is the sort of thing they tend to do."

She scanned the rest of the datapad, then looked back at him. "I'm going to call my father, if we're close enough for a direct conversation," she said. "And then I'll meet you on the bridge for the formal assumption of command. And *then* we will go over the ship in cynical detail."

Mason nodded. "Make sure your father knows you're safe," he said. "I was quite worried he'd start pressuring his MP."

Susan sighed. Maybe he *had* started pressuring his local MP. No one took democracy - and freedom - more seriously than a man who had fought and bled to preserve it. She had no idea just what had happened, over the last month; she doubted she would ever know. But at least it had worked in her favour. She had command of a warship, her actions had been officially approved…as far as anyone outside the charmed circle knew, she'd done nothing even remotely wrong. But it would remain in her file for the rest of her life.

"I'll ask him," she said, reluctantly. "I'll see you on the bridge."

Mason nodded and left the compartment, the hatch hissing closed behind her. Susan sighed and tapped her console, requesting a direct link to the planetary surface. There was a good chance she wouldn't get it - the military communications network was presumably very busy - but it was worth a try. And luck was with her. Five minutes later, her father's face appeared in the terminal. He looked older than she recalled, his face carved with new lines that worried her. He'd clearly been *very* worried about her.

"Father," she said, feeling another lump in her throat. "I'm fine."

"Susan," her father said, gruffly. "What happened?"

"It's a long story," she said, tapping her ears to indicate that they might be overheard. If the Admiralty had doubts about her, they might just be listening to the call. "But I'm fine now."

Her father looked at her for a long moment - the same look, she realised with a shock, he'd given her when she'd asked his blessing to apply to the Academy. He'd known she was an adult, he'd known she was responsible...and yet, she was still his little girl.

"I hope you're right," he said, finally. He trusted her, she knew. He might have his doubts - and his fears for her - but he trusted her. "Now, who's been feeding you and why haven't they done a good job of it?"

Susan sighed and settled in for the long haul.

CHAPTER
FIVE

Mars, Midshipwoman Georgina Fitzwilliam thought, was meant to be *red*.

And it *was* red, she knew, outside the dome. Outside the areas that had been steadily - and ruthlessly - terraformed into a new home for the human race. There were no Martians to object, no native life to be displaced...the humans who might have objected, once upon a time, had bowed to the harsh truth that the human race had only one true homeworld in the entire galaxy. And even after the tramlines had been discovered, the terraforming project had continued, combining genetically-engineered plants with asteroid water and a giant orbital mirror to heat the planet.

And there are even humans who are adapted to live on the surface, she thought, as she stared up at the dome. *They're the real natives now.*

She smiled to herself as the fake sunlight beat down on her nude body. It couldn't pass for the Maldives, where she'd spent a couple of happy summers during vacation from school, but it was close enough. Water - warm water - washed against a sandy beach, framed by palm trees and illuminated by sunlamps bright enough to give her a tan. It looked like a piece of heaven, removed from its rightful place and embedded in the red dust of Mars. And, best of all, no one knew who she was. To the resort staff, she was just another midshipwomen splurging on a fancy holiday before returning to her ship.

And we will have to go back soon, she thought, as she sat upright. *We can't stay here forever.*

The thought made her scowl as she peered out over the fake ocean. A couple of young men were swimming through the water, both ignoring her presence. Mars, surprisingly, had a more hedonistic population than Earth, although perhaps that was no surprise. The early colonists had all been nationalistic, part of a rush to claim as much of the planetary surface as possible, but the later colonies had a more independent bent. And several of them were even giant experiments in alternate living. She'd even heard that one of them was a solely nudist colony. Visitors left their clothes - and their dignity - at the airlock. She'd been tempted to visit, but apparently they were very careful about just who they allowed through the doors.

"George," a voice called. She turned, just in time to see Peter Barton striding towards her, carrying a pair of fancy drinks. The resort couldn't match the aristocratic parties she'd been forced to attend - some of her elder relatives preferred to get drunk as quickly as possible, just to make the time go swiftly - but at least it was trying. "They're trying to up the price again."

"I'm not surprised," George said. She looked him up and down, openly admiring his unclad body. Peter Barton couldn't match an aristocratic fop for sheer handsomeness - they normally had a little plastic surgery when they turned eighteen - but there was a crudeness about his muscular body that she found attractive. "You *did* tell them we had a deal?"

"They're probably regretting it now," Barton said. He passed her the drink, then sat down next to her. "I'm sure they expected more from their heroes."

George shrugged. She'd heard - through the grapevine - that she'd been marked down for a medal, along with several of the other officers and crew on *Vanguard*, but she hadn't heard anything else before she'd joined Barton for a joint leave. The Admiralty wasn't normally so slow about recognising bravery and awarding medals, according to her uncle. She was tempted to write to him and ask what had happened, but she knew better. Her uncle would not be pleased and her father would be furious.

Either be the best officer you can be, she told herself as she sipped her drink, *or resign yourself to a lifetime trapped in a gilded cage.*

"They probably thought we could be talked out of requesting privacy," she said, finally. "I'm not going to budge on that, Peter."

"Me neither," Barton agreed. "They'll probably hit us with another bill as soon as we try to check out."

George shrugged. She had an expense account - if she wished to use it - with a credit limit that would allow her to buy a new shuttlecraft, *if* she didn't mind her family looking over her shoulder. Her naval account was separate, private; they wouldn't know what she chose to spend her wages on. Or so she hoped. Naval accounts were supposed to be secure, at least without a court order, but she doubted that an accountant would deny the First Space Lord a glimpse at his niece's accounts, if he thought to ask.

"We paid what they demanded in advance," she reminded him, dryly. "They don't have a right to anything else."

She glanced at him, watching as his gaze wandered over the ocean. He *wasn't* what her family wanted for her, not when he was *just* a Gunnery Officer. And as much as she'd enjoyed what they'd been doing together over the past few days, she knew better than to think they had anything permanent. Their affair would be a minor scandal, on Mars, but on *Vanguard* it would be a gross breach of regulations. She knew, all too well, just what her uncle would have to say about it, if they were caught in a privacy tube. She'd be lucky if she was allowed to resign without a major fuss.

The swimmers were making their way back to their encampment, followed by a pair of equally nude women. George wondered, idly, if they were their lovers or merely resort staff, eager to make sure their guests were catered to in *every* way. She hadn't been able to believe the number of options on the menu, even if they were all technically legal on Mars. But then, given the amount of money visitors splashed around, she could understand why the staff went out of their way to please. A single bad report could be disastrous.

She watched as the young men scrambled out of the water, feeling oddly unconcerned about their nakedness - or hers. Nudity was nothing special, she supposed, when everyone was nude. Even the staff wore nothing but their birthday suits. The two girls followed the men out of the water, their bodies glistening under the sunlight. They were so perfect that she couldn't help thinking that they too had had a little plastic surgery. And their contracts presumably prevented them from putting on weight.

"There're no distractions here," Barton said, quietly. "No worries, no concerns..."

"Until the money runs out," George said. She scowled. Just because she had a trust fund didn't mean she had to abuse it. "And we go back to the ship."

She leaned back, feeling the sunlight grow hotter. She'd been worked to the bone, along with the other midshipmen, over the last three weeks. And then they'd been reassigned, leaving her as the *only* middy. It had been nice to have Middy Country to herself for a week, but there had been something unnatural about sleeping on her own. And yet, if she'd mentioned that to *anyone*, they would have called for the men in white coats to take her away. Privacy and solitude were so rare for midshipmen that every last fragment of them was precious.

"You're thinking," Barton accused, mischievously. "I can tell."

"I'm surprised you can recognise the symptoms," George said. "Do you actually do any thinking at all."

"I let my little head do all the thinking for me," Barton said. He sat upright, then brought his lips to hers for a long kiss. "And right now, there's nothing else to do."

George smiled as she opened her legs, allowing him to slip gently into her. She hadn't been a virgin when she'd boarded *Vanguard* - she hoped, desperately, that her family didn't know anything about her last few days at Hanover Towers - but Barton had been her first serious partner. The things he did to her made her body purr, even though she *knew* there could never be anything permanent between them. She leaned back as he thrust deeper, gasping as his hands played over her breasts. And then she was lost in the sensation...

Afterwards, they showered under the waterfall before walking along the beach to the cafe, holding hands. A handful of other couples were sitting there, as naked as the two of them; they took a seat and ordered dinner, then held hands as they waited. The food was very good, she'd discovered, even though much of the meat was vat-grown rather than imported from Earth. But then, importing real steak and ribs from Earth would have driven the price up into low orbit.

The waiter returned, carrying a tray of steak and mashed potatoes in one hand and a datapad in the other. "Messages have arrived for both of you," he said. "They're both marked low priority."

George exchanged a glance with Barton. Messages? Messages from whom? Her family didn't know where she was, as far as she knew. She took the datapad and tapped the scanner, allowing it to read the naval ID chip implanted in her palm. Moments later, the message unlocked itself. She read it quickly and scowled.

"They want me back at the ship a day early," she said. It wasn't *really* a surprise - she'd been lucky to get five solid days of off-ship leave approved - but it was annoying. She'd hoped for another night together. "And you too, I guess."

Barton took the datapad and read his message. "A very good guess," he said. "I'm expected to report to my new department head tomorrow morning."

George sighed as she took back the datapad and checked the travel schedules. The resort didn't have a proper airport or spaceport and it wasn't on the high-speed monorail network that linked the various settlements together. They'd have to get a tripod, paying through the nose for passage to the nearest spaceport. And they'd have to get a shuttle from there to L4.

"We're going to be pushing it," she said. There was no way the Royal Navy would devote an interplanetary shuttle to a very junior officer and a crewman, no matter who she happened to have for relatives. "We'll have to leave in less than a couple of hours if we want to make it there for the deadline."

"Then we need to be out of here in one," Barton said. He cut up his steak, then started to chew it piece by piece. "Eat up quickly, George. There'll be a delay at the shuttleport or my name's not Peter Barton."

"You'll be renamed *Mud* if you're wrong," George said, warningly. "I don't want to get back *too* early."

She shook her head. He was right. She knew he was right. Getting back to the ship early would get them commended for their devotion for duty, getting back to the ship late would earn them both shit duties for the rest of the week. And if *Vanguard* had to leave without them…they might as well resign before their careers were blown out of the water. A soldier might just be able to catch up with his unit, at his own expense, but even *her* expense account wouldn't be enough to hire an interstellar starship to follow the battleship.

They ate their food quickly, then hurried back to their suite to dress and pack up their bags before departure. It felt odd to wear clothes again, but George rather doubted she'd be allowed to walk about naked on a battleship. She'd slept in her underwear during normal operations and fully dressed during the long crawl home, knowing that they might have to snap awake and run to their duty stations at any moment. She took one last look at the huge room - the bed had been more than large enough for some of their more exotic experiments - and then scooped up her knapsack and headed for the door. Barton followed her, shaking his head slowly. To him, she realised dully, the four nights had to have been paradise.

And they were pretty good for me too, she thought, as they hurried down to the airlock. The tripod was already there, waiting for them. *It's almost a shame our time here has to end.*

"Thank you for your stay," the manager said. He was an oily little man who somehow gave the impression of wearing a suit and tie, even though he was as naked as his staff. "The remainder of your bill will be forwarded to you."

George bit down on the response that came to mind. Most - perhaps all - of his normal clientele wouldn't notice a few tens of thousands of pounds going missing, one way or the other. They'd pay the bill without thinking about it. But *she* knew better than to waste her money paying bills she didn't *have* to pay. She'd take a good look at the bill, when it arrived, just to make sure they didn't have a legitimate claim. And then she'd ignore it, secure in the knowledge they wouldn't try to force her to pay.

"Thank you," she said, instead. "We enjoyed our stay."

The interior of the tripod was nothing more than a small canopy, rather like an oversized starfighter. It lurched to life as soon as the airlock was sealed, disconnecting from the resort and heading across the dusty red landscape. George sat on one of the seats and stared out of the canopy, leaning against Barton as he wrapped his arm around her shoulder. There were patches of Red Weed - genetically-engineered plants designed to boost the oxygen levels in the air - everywhere, but otherwise there were few signs of the terraforming effort. Mars still looked remorselessly alien.

"There are people engineered to live outside the domes," she mused, as the tripod picked up speed, hurrying across the red landscape with a rollicking gait that reminded her of her first pony. "What will happen to them as the oxygen levels rise towards Earth-norm?"

"They're supposed to be engineered to survive on Earth," Barton said. "But I don't know how well it will work in practice when the oxygen levels get higher."

George leaned into his arm and forced herself to relax, watching a pair of shuttles screaming through the air and heading towards the space-port. They couldn't do anything intimate as soon as they reached their destination, not when there would be hundreds of other naval personnel around. The thought hurt, more than she cared to admit, but it wasn't as if they were going anywhere anyway. They had just set out to have fun in a patch of unreality...

...And now they were returning to the real world.

"Peter," she said, slowly. "We have to talk."

She sensed his body stiffen and deliberately pulled away, knowing she didn't dare push any closer. "What we did - what we did here - it has to stay here."

Barton met her eyes as she turned to look at him. "Because you're an officer and I'm not."

He didn't sound accusing. George couldn't help thinking that that didn't make her feel any better. She would almost have preferred to have him shouting at her.

"Yes," she said. She remembered his touch on her - in her - and flushed. No one would have cared, if they'd been civilians, but they weren't civilians. "It will destroy our careers if anyone finds out about it."

"And that Fraser may use it against you," Barton said. "He doesn't like you, does he?"

George shrugged. Fraser - formerly the First Middy - and she had been getting on a great deal better since his promotion, but he was *still* supervising her career. She wasn't sure what *he* got out of it, unless it was an unspoken apology for the way he'd treated her when she'd joined the crew, yet she found it hard to care. Fraser might be a prickly asshole, but much of what he said was good advice.

"It doesn't matter," she said. "What does *matter* is that everything we did together has to remain strictly between ourselves."

"I do understand," Barton said. He rose slowly and moved backwards, letting go of her completely. "And if you want to share the next shore leave…"

"Assuming we survive the coming deployment," George said. She hadn't heard anything, but it didn't take a genius to work out that the Royal Navy was preparing for war. "If we do, I would be honoured to share it with you."

Barton leaned forward and gave her a quick kiss, then made a show of settling down at the other side of the cab. George turned to stare out over the landscape, blinking away tears she knew she shouldn't be crying. They didn't have anything, they couldn't have anything…they were just two adults, enjoying each other's company. But it still hurt.

They said nothing as they arrived at the spaceport and boarded a shuttle back to the L4 shipyard. George took advantage of the long flight to take a nap, then catch up with her email. There was almost nothing important, save for a long message from one of her old academy chums telling her that he'd been assigned to HMS *Impervious*, a *Theodore Smith*-class fleet carrier and that he'd be shipping out in two days. George wondered, absently, if that made him a lucky bastard or not. The year of seniority he'd been granted for his role in the early engagements - along with herself and a number of other midshipmen - gave him a reasonable chance of being First Middy.

But he'll be on a brand new ship, she thought. *The XO might have other ideas.*

She shook her head, then glanced at her wristcom. They'd be back on *Vanguard* within three hours…

…And she just couldn't wait to be home.

CHAPTER SIX

"Midshipwoman Fitzwilliam," a familiar voice said. "Welcome back."

George stiffened, then hastily saluted as she saw Lieutenant Charles Fraser standing by the airlock, looking grim. He was a big bruiser of a man - if anything, he was bigger than she remembered - wearing a lieutenant's uniform like he was born to it. She couldn't believe she'd challenged him to a fight, or that he hadn't smashed her into a bloody mess. He returned her salute, then motioned for her to follow him down the passageway. She saw his face twist in disapproval as he saw Barton making his way out of the shuttle and sighed inwardly. Fraser might not be out to ruin her - not any longer - but he had good reason to be concerned.

He said nothing until they reached his cabin, a small space that was undoubtedly *his*. George couldn't resist looking around, even though she knew she should stay at attention until he released her. The bulkheads were covered with certificates - martial arts, squadron fighting awards - and a large photograph of a younger Fraser with two people she assumed were his parents. Fraser had been more accomplished than she'd known, she realised. He'd definitely gone easy on her during their bout.

"You were with him," he said, flatly. "Weren't you?"

George was tempted to lie, but there was no point. "Yes, sir."

"I *suggest* that you make sure that you have *nothing* to do with him that isn't strictly professional," Fraser said. His tone made it clear that it was an order. "Your career could wind up in the crapper if someone puts two and two together."

"Yes, sir," George said. She considered, briefly, pointing out that Fraser was no longer First Middy, then abandoned the suicidal thought. "I have already made it clear to him."

"That's good to hear," Fraser grunted. He sat down on the bunk and waved her to the sole chair. "Stand at ease, Middy, and sit down."

"Yes, sir," George said. She didn't relax. Fraser and she might have come to an understanding, but it was hard to relax around him. "You have a very nice cabin."

Fraser's lips twisted. "And you have turned into a liar," he said. "And not a very good liar at that."

George shrugged. Fraser's cabin would have vanished without trace on her father's estate, but compared to the middy bunkroom it was paradise incarnate. Fraser actually had some *privacy!* No one who'd shared a wardroom with eight or so sweaty midshipmen would turn up his nose at such a cabin, regardless of its size. The private washroom alone was sheer heaven. And she would have been surprised if he didn't get a bigger water ration as a lieutenant.

"Still, we're not here to discuss your fragile grip on the truth," Fraser added. "I have been...asked...to involve myself in supervising the midshipmen, reporting directly to the XO. This is, as you can imagine, an awkward situation."

"Oh," George said. "That's...bad."

She felt a flicker of sympathy, both for him and the new First Middy. It *was* an awkward situation. Technically, *she'd* been the last First Middy... although, given that there hadn't *been* any other midshipmen, the title had been a little pointless. But the First Middy was supposed to have a free hand in the wardroom. His predecessor was certainly not supposed to be looking over his shoulder.

"One trusts it can be handled without aggro," Fraser added, dryly. "I don't think the XO will be very pleased if he has to involve himself in the affairs of the wardroom."

"No, sir," George said, wondering why he was talking to *her.* She was his only subordinate officer, arguably, but that wouldn't last. And they'd never been close friends before his promotion. "It would be very bad for us."

"Yeah," Fraser agreed. His lip twisted, sourly. "Particularly as *you* will be First Middy."

George blinked. "I am? I mean…I will be?"

"Yes," Fraser said. He picked a datapad from his desk and passed it to her. "Manpower, as you are perfectly aware, is quite limited. We're receiving four midshipmen: two transferring from other ships, two being shipped directly from the Academy. And, thanks to the year's seniority you were given, you are the senior midshipman."

He smiled. "Congratulations, First Middy."

George thought rapidly. She wasn't very senior at all - she'd had about seven months as a midshipman - but her seniority *had* been boosted. *And* she was the sole experienced midshipman left on *Vanguard*, the only one who was already familiar with the ship and her crew. Still…nineteen months, give or take a few days. There were midshipmen who had - should have had - two or three years on her before their careers started to stagnate. She couldn't help thinking that there was trouble ahead.

"You're *sure* about this?" She asked. "Really?"

"I *do* know how to count the years," Fraser said, dryly. "And you're meant to call me *sir* when you're speaking to me."

George coloured. "Sorry, sir."

"That's better," Fraser said. He cleared his throat. "Midshipman Simon Potter is only a couple of days short of being First Middy himself, so you should probably keep an eye on him. The last thing you need is to be beached for a week with an ambitious toad in the background. His record is suspiciously blank, which worries me. Chances are his commander let him go without a fight for reasons that were never written down."

"I see," George said. "How do you know that, sir?"

"Long experience," Fraser said. "Potter is, in theory, on the fast-track to promotion. But if his CO let him go, there's something wrong with him that was never written into his file."

George scowled. There were files - and subsections of files - that neither she nor Fraser could access. If something had been written down there, she wouldn't be able to see it, unless she convinced a senior officer to allow her access. And merely *making* the request would be enough to get her in trouble, unless she came up with a very convincing reason.

"Maybe he has a powerful family, sir," she mused. "Does he?"

"Not as far as I can tell," Fraser said. "But you'd know more about that than I would."

"Yes, sir," George said. He was right. The world of the aristocracy was larger than most people imagined, but she knew - either personally or by reputation - everyone in the same age bracket as herself. She'd never heard of a Simon Potter. "It could be a false name, I suppose."

"Perhaps," Fraser said. He gave her a nasty, sharp-edged smile. "But he's your problem now, *First Middy*."

George felt her scowl deepen. She *could* ask for advice, if she wished, but it would be taken as a sign of weakness. Fraser might not report her to the XO - she had no idea how he'd react - yet she knew it would be held against her. And, oddly, she found that she wanted his respect. Winning him over would be a coup in its own right.

"The other experienced midshipman - midshipwoman - is Paula Spurgeon," Fraser explained, after a long moment. "Her file is rather interesting, with just enough written down to convince me that there's something else hidden in the classified sections. From what I *have* been able to glean from the open sections, she was beached for two years after an...*incident*... on HMS *Queen Elizabeth*. I'm honestly surprised she didn't resign, given that much of a beaching. Her chances of promotion have to be non-existent."

"And it would take years to rebuild her seniority, sir," George mused. She couldn't help wondering if Fraser felt any sympathy for the older woman. "She might live and die a midshipwoman."

"Probably," Fraser agreed. "You should keep an eye on her too. She might well be bitter and resentful - and we have no idea what actually *happened* on *Queen Liz*. It's possible she might have had an illegitimate affair" - he gave George a sharp look - "or it could be something a great deal more serious."

"Perhaps she rammed an asteroid, sir," George said. Fraser's comments were hitting a little too close to home. "Or maybe she forgot to wear her dress uniform when the admiral was inspecting the ship."

"Ramming an asteroid would be a remarkable feat," Fraser pointed out, rather dryly. "And I can't see them letting her stay in the navy afterwards, even if she avoided court martial."

He cleared his throat. "The two newcomers are Clayton Henderson and Felicity Wheeler," he added. "Unsurprisingly, there's very little in their files; they passed through the Academy without attracting many comments, positive or negative, from their tutors. Henderson had quite a low ranking in his senior years, but *someone* has to be on the lower end of the scale."

George grimaced. If she was ever put in command of the Academy, she intended to make sure that the tutors didn't grade on a curve. Fraser was right. *Someone* had to be at the lower end of the scale - and that person might be heads and shoulders ahead of a civilian who couldn't pass the tests necessary to gain admittance to the Academy. A person smarter than her, during a particularly bad year, might gain a reputation for stupidity that was thoroughly undeserved.

"You said they didn't have many comments, sir," she mused. "What *did* they say?"

"Nothing of great interest," Fraser said. "They would have passed their evaluations or they would never have been permitted to graduate, but…"

He shrugged. "They're due to board tomorrow, whereupon you will greet them to the ship and show them around," he added. "And, as First Middy, you get the honour of working out the timetables. I'm afraid they'll have to hit the deck running."

George took the datapad, forcing herself to think. The midshipmen would have to be assigned to the different departments, then rotated around…they'd have to get their certifications before they could be trusted to take watch duty or command a small detachment…it was going to be a major headache. She didn't know how Fraser had done it, but she could guess. He'd only had to deal with one or two newcomers at a time, relying on the other midshipmen to handle themselves without constant supervision. *She* had four newcomers…

…And their conduct would reflect upon her.

"Give them a day to orientate themselves," Fraser advised, as she began to work. "And then assign them to the departments most in need of extra manpower."

He frowned. "I'd check with tactical and helm, if I were you," he added. "They both need additional staff, but they might not have time to train up complete newcomers. Potter and Spurgeon both have excellent tactical ratings, so they might be assigned there without causing any problems that will make you look bad."

"Thanks, sir," George said, sourly.

Fraser gave her a brilliant smile. "You're welcome."

George worked her way through the timetable, then looked up at him. "Do you have any other words of advice?"

"Two," Fraser said. "First, remember that *you* are in charge, You're not their friend, you're not their comrade, you're not their den mother. You're the First Middy and you're expected to *act* as though you are in charge. A hint of weakness at the wrong time and the knives will come out."

"You make it sound as though they are animals, sir," George protested.

Fraser lifted his eyebrows. "And you never thought I was an animal?"

George felt her cheeks heat, but said nothing.

"You know as well as I do that competition for promotion is intense," Fraser added, after a long moment. "And you do *not* have the advantage of spending two years in uniform, gaining experience before you take on true responsibility. Two of your subordinates are well-positioned to take advantage of any problems you have, while the other two are unlikely to see you as a superior officer. You must take control right from the start and if that means acting like a bitch, you act like a bitch."

"Yes, sir," George said. "And the second piece of advice?"

"Be tough, be firm…but also be fair," Fraser said. "Yes, you will have to chew them out when they screw up - and they will. But you will also have to realise that not every screw-up is the result of malice or stupidity. You don't need them to like you, let alone to love you, but you do need them to *trust* you. They won't come to you with their problems if they feel they cannot trust you to actually *listen* to them."

He paused. "And one other piece of advice?"

George nodded, wordlessly.

"Two of them are young women, one a couple of years older than you, the other a year younger," Fraser noted. "*Don't* allow them to suck you into a female clique. You are their superior officer and you cannot run the risk of allowing cliques to form, certainly not along those lines. It would be disastrous."

49

"Yes, sir," George said.

Fraser took a breath. "If you need advice, you can come to me," he said. "I also expect you to find time to continue your physical training with me. Let me know when you are available."

George nodded. Fraser was a slave-driver, but he knew his stuff. And she'd grown under his tuition. She'd never be a martial artist, not like him, but she knew enough to take care of herself. And her shooting was getting much - much - better.

You're still getting outpointed by the marines, her thoughts reminded her. *Don't get cocky.*

She pushed the thought aside as Fraser dismissed her, then made her way back to Middy Country. It felt eerily empty, as if she was the only person on the ship; the lockers had been emptied and the beds had been stripped, leaving her the only occupant. A large care package, addressed to her, sat on the deck. She sighed, recognising the return address. Her sister's heart was in the right place, but she had no idea just what it was like to serve on a warship - or just how embarrassing it had been to receive a piece of naughty underwear that wouldn't have been out of place in a brothel. None of the others had ever let her forget it.

I have to write to Anne, she reminded herself as she tore open the box. *Someone* must have had a word with her - probably their uncle - because she'd crammed the box with chocolate bars, rather than anything more awkward. There was still rather more of it than she would have preferred, she decided, but it was certainly more practical. *I'll have to thank her.*

She put a chocolate bar aside for later consumption - she could afford to eat one, she told herself - and then stowed the others in the locker. She'd have to share them with the other middies - and she should probably give a few to Fraser and the other officers - once they got accustomed to serving on a battleship. It would be awkward - chocolate bars were traded at two or three times market value once the ship was underway - but better than keeping the chocolate all for herself. A piece of paper fell out of the box as she finished emptying it and dropped onto the deck. Her sister was expressing - again - her hope that George would find a handsome man and come home.

George crumpled up the paper, feeling a flicker of angry frustration. Anne should never have gone to that damned Swiss finishing school, not after leaving Hanover Towers. She wasn't precisely stupid, but the finishing school was more concerned with moulding young girls into perfect little ladies instead of developing their minds. Anne looked stunning in a long blue dress - George knew that hardly anyone considered *her* a true lady - but she was *very* good at giving the impression that she had nothing between her ears. And there were times when George had been inclined to believe that Anne was truly stupid. Maybe she'd bribed the tutors to give her the answers before entering the examination chambers.

She's your sister, she reminded herself, as she checked the duty roster. Unsurprisingly, the shipboard management program hadn't realised she'd come back from leave a day early. She had no assigned tasks until the other midshipmen arrived, the following day. *And she's trying to be helpful.*

But she isn't being helpful, her own thoughts answered. The chocolate was a more practical gift than underwear, but it would still cause her problems. *And all she's doing is driving me mad.*

She pushed the thought out of her mind and undressed, enjoying the privacy for the final time. Thankfully, there were no water rations in spacedock; she stepped into the shower, luxuriated under the warm stream for ten minutes and then dried herself, checking her appearance in the mirror. Her hair had grown out, a little, but she didn't need to have it hacked back to the roots *just* yet. Anne would probably have a heart attack if someone had suggested chopping off her blonde locks and wearing an ill-fitting uniform. And she would probably react badly if she knew what George had been doing with Peter Barton. No doubt she'd be disgusted at the thought of kissing someone worth less than five hundred thousand or so a year.

Forget him, she told herself firmly. She climbed into the bunk, feeling oddly cold and alone as she clicked off the light. She'd grown too used to falling asleep in his arms after two or three rounds of lovemaking. *Enjoy the peace. Tomorrow is going to be a very different day.*

CHAPTER
SEVEN

"Welcome back, Your Excellency," Captain Susan Onarina said. "I trust you had a pleasant flight?"

"It could have been worse, Captain," Henry said. "And please allow me, Captain, to offer my congratulations for your promotion. It was very well deserved."

He studied Susan with interest as a small team of crewmen materialised from nowhere to help his staff move their equipment and supplies down to their quarters. She was darker than he remembered, although there was an odd pallor to her skin that probably came with too little sleep - and a great deal of stress. Her dark hair was tied up in a bun - he was mildly surprised she hadn't cut it short, unlike many other crewmen - and she wore her uniform very well. Thankfully, she'd honoured his request for a complete lack of actual ceremony.

"Thank you," Susan said. She sounded tired too. According to the briefing notes, she'd only been back on her ship for two days. "If you would care to accompany me to my cabin, Your Excellency…"

Henry nodded and followed her, wondering if she knew he'd gone to bat for her. The First Space Lord was unlikely to mention it to anyone, but she didn't have many other friends in high places. Captain Blake's resignation might have taken the wind out of her enemies' sails, yet they were still formidable - and very well connected. Henry just hoped she could build up a reputation - and contacts of her own to offset the balance - before they rallied and found another way to harm her career. And he was sure she would.

There's nothing small-minded people hate more, he thought morbidly, *than having their arses saved by someone who doesn't even care to lord it over them.*

"I have several datachips for you," he said, as soon as they were in her cabin. She'd hung a portrait of a smiling couple - a black man and a white woman - on one of the bulkheads, but the remainder of the compartment was remarkably bare. Given how much expensive crap Captain Blake had somehow stuffed into his quarters, he couldn't help finding it something of a relief. "And the latest from the front too."

"That's something, at least," Susan said. She motioned for him to sit on the sofa as she poured them both a glass of shipboard rotgut. Henry wondered, absently, if the choice of alcohol was a backhanded compliment or a subtle insult. Probably the former, he decided; Captain Susan Onarina didn't have a nasty bone in her body. "We're due to depart in two days."

Henry nodded in agreement. "My team and I will do our best to stay out of your way," he said, as he took the glass and sniffed it carefully. Shipboard rotgut ranged from remarkably smooth to a guaranteed choking fit, if one drank hastily. "And I trust the same will be true of the other additions."

Susan snorted. "We're taking on nearly a thousand soldiers," she said. She sounded annoyed, although he was relieved to note she didn't sound bitter. "And we're having to bed them in the corridors, because we don't have anything like enough bunks for all of them. Do you know how many things could go wrong?"

"Yes," Henry said. He'd argued against it - the soldiers could have been sent on military transports - but the brass had been adamant. Britain needed to make it clear that it was making a major commitment to the campaign, now the politicians had finally realised that the country - and the world - was at war. "It won't make your voyage any easier, even if things go according to plan."

Susan gave him a droll look. "And when have things *ever* gone according to plan?"

She shook her head. "Do you have any idea where we're even *going*?"

"Unity," Henry said. He watched her closely, wondering just how much she'd already guessed, but her dark face betrayed nothing. "Admiral

Harper is expected to take a multinational task force to reinforce the defences, with *Vanguard* as one of his ships."

"At least I know him," Susan said. She smiled, rather sardonically. "I would have thought he never wanted to see me again."

"He recommended you for the Navy Cross," Henry told her. "Politics may impede you actually receiving it, Captain, but his citation makes impressive reading."

He sighed, inwardly. The First Space Lord might hope that parts of the story - or at least the embarrassing parts - could be buried, but Henry knew too much to expect the cover-up to endure indefinitely. The story was really too good to be left untold. Thankfully, very few people knew the full story - and most of them had been warned to keep their mouths shut - but rumours were already leaking out. He could only hope that no one would put the full story together until *Vanguard* was already on her way to Unity.

Susan smiled for the first time since he'd boarded her ship. "So he doesn't bear a grudge?"

"He'd have some problems explaining to his superiors why he did, given that you saved the fleet," Henry reminded her. "And he's honest enough to admit that you *did* save the fleet."

"That's good," Susan said. She took another sip of her drink. "So... what are the mission orders?"

Henry took a moment to organise his thoughts. "Intelligence believes - everything they know is two months out of date, unfortunately - that our new enemies are going to launch a major offensive towards Unity," he said. "Given that they *do* seem to be restricted to standard tramlines, it does seem to be their best option...assuming, of course, that they managed to capture a database from one of the disabled starships."

He scowled at the thought. Hundreds of analysts had gone over the recordings of the battle with a fine-toothed comb, but - in the end - none of them had been prepared to say, with complete certainty, that *no* databases had fallen into enemy hands. In theory, every database was supposed to be rigged to automatically wipe itself and then self-destruct, if the ship was too badly damaged to escape the enemy, but in practice...he knew, all too well, just how much could go wrong. And while naval crews knew better than to carry private computers and databases with them, one of the civilians might have done just that.

And a portable encyclopaedia would be enough to point them to Sol, he thought. *And they're designed for children.*

"And that they won't duplicate the improved Puller Drive for themselves," Susan mused, thoughtfully. "That would give them a whole host of options."

"Intelligence is unable to give us any timetable on when - if - they will," Henry confirmed, bluntly. "We took six months to understand the principles behind it, but we had a working model to examine. They...may not have been so lucky."

"It would be unwise to count on it," Susan warned.

Henry nodded. "Assuming the enemy successfully takes control of the Unity System," he said, "they will have access to tramlines leading into human space as well as the chance to outflank the Tadpole defences and punch towards Tadpole Prime. Joint Headquarters has decided that humanity should make its first major contribution to the war by securing Unity and preventing the unknowns from taking the system."

"Because it's also the easiest way to withdraw from Tadpole space," Susan said, cynically.

"Correct," Henry acknowledged. He met her eyes, warningly. "Joint Headquarters is aware, Captain, that we have an obligation to support our allies. But, at the same time, they're concerned about the prospect of major fleet losses. We took heavy losses in the opening engagements of the war and they're understandably concerned about the danger they represent."

Susan nodded, curtly. "Does that mean we will have orders to break contact and retreat if the odds swing too heavily against us?"

"Yes," Henry said. He nodded to the bulkhead. "How long does it take to put a battleship together?"

"*Vanguard* took five years," Susan said, shortly. "Her sisters took two years - but by then, we understood what we were doing."

"And had ironed out the glitches in the design," Henry said. Even with *his* level of access he hadn't been able to read *everything* about the *Vanguard*-class, but he knew that Commodore Naiser and his team had run into all sorts of problems as they struggled to finalise the design and turn the diagrams into reality. "The point is, Captain, that major fleet losses in the coming battles could *shorten* the war. We have space to trade for time and we're going to need it."

"I understand," Susan said. "But will the Tadpoles?"

"They are a remarkably practical species," Henry said. "I think they will understand."

He kept the rest of the thought to himself. Joint Headquarters hadn't forgotten *all* of the lessons of the First Interstellar War, but they'd clearly forgotten some of them. Their elaborate orders, designed to cover every imaginable scenario, gave very little leeway to the commanders on the spot. And the moment they ran into something the orders didn't cover, they were going to be in deep trouble.

"I hope you're right," Susan said. "We don't need *two* wars on our hands."

Henry nodded in agreement. The Tadpoles didn't think like humans, a lesson he'd had pounded into his skull time and time again. Some of their laws made sense, but others were frankly incomprehensible...and there were gaps in their legal system that constantly horrified their human allies. But Henry had no doubt that they felt the same way about humanity. He'd once spent two hours trying to explain *rape* to them and discovered that they reacted with horror and incomprehension.

But their child mortality rates are through the roof, he thought. *And that horrifies us too.*

"Assuming we get there before the enemy, we are to take up defensive position and evacuate as many of the colonists as possible," he said. "Once the enemy arrive, we are to drive them out of the system by any means necessary. JHQ would be delighted if we captured an enemy ship or two - and a few of their personnel - but the main priority is to score an outright victory over the newcomers. Admiral Harper has authority to launch a counterattack if he feels it justified..."

He shook his head. "Protecting Unity is the key," he added, softly. "That's politically important for our lords and masters, I think."

Susan nodded in silent agreement. Henry understood. Unity had been discovered shortly after the First Interstellar War and, given its position in the heart of the neutral zone between the Human Sphere and the Tadpoles, the question of settlement rights had always been a touchy one. He had been involved in hammering out the agreement to share the world, despite strong feelings on both sides that colony worlds should *not* be shared. But then, it wasn't as if the two races really impinged on one another.

"I heard that funding was almost cancelled twice," Susan said. "And that settlers were few and far between."

"It wasn't the settlers that posed a problem," Henry said, "even though there was some fear that we were risking another Terra Nova. But funding…that was threatened more than once."

Susan frowned. "Do they have any defences at all?"

"Just a handful of automated orbital weapons platforms," Henry said. "They never had the level of investment they needed, even though Unity was quite a promising star system. Too many question marks over who owned the system, really."

"Wonderful," Susan said. She took a final swig from her glass and put it down on the table, then looked at him. "There was no way to arrange for some kind of return on investment?"

Henry shook his head. A colony world was a *very* good long-term investment, if someone got in on the ground floor, but Unity had too many caveats to make it a very good investment for anyone. The Tadpole economic system was so different from humanity's that he doubted they understood the *concept* of ownership, let alone a return on investment. Perhaps it was possible to work out a deal with the human settlers, but even that would be chancy. The investors Unity needed were unwilling to take the risk unless the governments guaranteed their investments…

…And, with far too many other demands on their budgets, governments had been unwilling to make that commitment.

And the treaty stipulated that the system had to be largely undefended, he thought, sourly. *I don't think anyone wants to invest billions of pounds when they could lose their investment overnight.*

"Which means that the colonists will probably not be inclined to listen to us," Susan said, finally. "Strong-minded independent types?"

"Mostly," Henry said. "Each of the Great Powers provided a cadre of settlers, but it wasn't easy to find suitable volunteers without offering massive inducements. There are just too many other potential destinations. The ones who *did* volunteer were people who wanted to be away from the government or had some…reason…for wanting to leave the Human Sphere permanently. I think they were seriously considering deporting small-time criminals to make up the numbers."

"God help them," Susan said. "Did they ever try?"

"Not to Unity, thankfully," Henry said. "Someone pointed out that it would be bad if the Tadpoles got a good look at what sort of bastards we could be."

"They captured a database or two of our popular entertainment," Susan pointed out. She smiled, rather thinly. "I'm surprised they didn't insist on fighting the war to the bitter end."

Henry shrugged. The Tadpoles hadn't understood much of the entertainment files they'd captured - and, even with human cultural experts trying to bridge the gap, they'd never really made progress. Much human entertainment was as incomprehensible to them as their entertainment was to human observers. Trying to explain the ninth season of *Star Trek* had wasted a couple of hours, even though the *tenth* season had featured a Tadpole officer on the *Enterprise-Z*. They just hadn't understood what they were seeing.

He put the matter aside as he leaned forward. "The planetary settlers, we think, will help us, but they may also resent us," he warned. "That's another problem for me."

Susan lifted her eyebrows. "You've been there?"

"Not for five years," Henry said. He'd visited twice, once when the first colony was landed and again when the third batch of settlers arrived, but he hadn't had much time to look around. The handful of settlers he'd met had struck him as the usual hardy outdoors type, eyeing him with disdain for being born with a silver spoon in his mouth. "I imagine things will have changed a great deal in that time."

"Probably," Susan agreed.

Henry gave her a long look. "Can I ask a more personal question?"

Susan lifted her eyebrows, but nodded shortly.

"Tell me," Henry said. "When was the last time you slept?"

"I caught a couple of hours sleep last night," Susan said. She seemed surprised by the question, which nagged at his mind until he remembered she'd been bombarded with sharp questions, all prying into her innermost thoughts and feelings, over the last month. "There's too much to do, Your Excellency."

"I would still advise a sounder sleep," Henry said, delicately. *He* wouldn't have liked to be told anything of the sort, back when he'd been a starfighter pilot…and he knew, all too well, that Kurt Schneider would not have hesitated to tell him to go to his bunk - and ground him from flying, if he refused to take proper care of himself. "There's still a day or two before the fleet has to move to the RV point, right?"

"Yes," Susan said. She cleared her throat. "I've been away from this ship for a month, Your Excellency. I have to command her in battle, but I don't have anything *like* a complete understanding of her new capabilities - not yet. The new weapons mix is largely unfamiliar to me, as are the repairs and modifications made to her hull. I have to know what I have in my hand before I try to use it."

"And you are on the verge of falling asleep," Henry said, gently. "You'll have two months, in transit, to get to know your ship. I'm sure your crew will have brought any significant concerns to your attention by now."

"We may not *know* they are significant concerns," Susan said. She looked, just for a moment, as if she was fighting back a yawn. "But you may have a point."

"It's no good getting back in the command chair," Henry said, "if you put yourself in sickbay through overwork."

Susan gave him a sharp look, which - in itself - proved just how tired she was. Glaring at an ambassador, even one she probably considered a friend of sorts, was never a good idea. He resisted the urge to point it out and waited, knowing he couldn't go any further. Calling the ship's doctor *might* be technically within his power, depending on how one looked at it, but it would utterly destroy their working relationship. She'd see it as a betrayal.

And she doesn't know I spoke up for her, he thought, numbly. He was sure of that, now. *She isn't used to having anyone stand up for her.*

59

"I'll catch some sleep," Susan said, finally. "And I'll expect a full copy of your department's findings before you transfer - if you transfer."

"I'll do my best to stay out of your hair," Henry promised. He rose and bowed politely as she rose too. "And you'll be first in line to hear what we discover."

"Try and find a way to talk to them," Susan said. "Fighting the war would be a great deal easier if we knew what they *wanted*."

CHAPTER
EIGHT

The shuttle hatch didn't *look* ominous - it was a standard hatch, no different from countless others installed on countless starships - but George couldn't help feeling a flicker of nervousness as she stared at the blank metal and waited. She'd received the update only ten minutes ago, informing her that the shuttle carrying the new midshipmen was on its way and hurried down to the hatch, without even bothering to change into her dress uniform. She still wasn't sure if that had been a wise move or not.

You were a prefect, she told herself, as she clasped her hands behind her back. *You shouldn't be concerned about bossing younger students around.*

But these aren't younger students, her own thoughts answered her. *Two of them are older than me - and one of them would be in command, save for a fluke chance.*

She sucked in her breath as the indicator over the hatch turned from red to green. She'd gone through the files, as Fraser had suggested, but they'd left her with more questions than answers. There was no clear reason why Paula had been beached for so long, no suggestion as to what horrible crime she'd committed. It was possible, George supposed, that she'd accidentally been rude to the Captain's wife, but surely *that* would have been included in the files. Her commander would have had to give *some* reason why he was issuing such a harsh punishment. Transferring her sideways - to an asteroid mining station - would have been easier.

The hatch hissed open. She stood straighter as four young officers filed into the compartment and snapped to attention, saluting the flag and then saluting her. George returned the salute, taking advantage of the opportunity to study them carefully. Both Simon Potter and Paula looked older than her, the latter so crisp in her white uniform that she could have stepped off a recruiting poster. Her blonde hair was cut short in a determined attempt to render her features masculine, much like George herself. She couldn't help wondering if she'd found a kindred soul.

"Welcome aboard," she said, allowing her eyes to roam over them. "I am Midshipwoman Fitzwilliam, First Middy."

Simon Potter's handsome face was a mask, but she saw a flicker of irritation crossing his features before he managed to hide it. A handful of extra days and *he* would have been First Middy…that *had* to sting. His uniform was neat, but not crisp; it was clear, even to the untrained eye, that he'd been a midshipman for over a year. He lacked the freshness of a midshipman who'd only just left the Academy.

Beside him, Clayton Henderson looked…odd. George studied him thoughtfully, trying to put her finger on it. There was nothing wrong with his uniform, nor his stance, but there was *something* wrong with him. It nagged at her mind, suggesting that she'd seen something like it before, yet no matter how hard she thought, she couldn't see it. There was a blandness about his features that surprised her, even in naval uniform. She resolved to keep a sharp eye on him and turned her attention to his companion.

Midshipwoman Felicity Wheeler was a slight girl, wearing a naval uniform that looked a size or two too big for her. George had no idea how she managed to give that impression - it was beyond belief that the quartermaster wouldn't have provided her with a uniform that fitted perfectly - but it was hard to escape the sense that she was under eighteen. George knew for a fact that she was twenty-two - it was rare for someone to enter the Academy before turning eighteen, although George herself had managed it - and yet she looked utterly unsure of herself, utterly out of place. She should be grateful, George supposed, that she didn't have to deal with Fraser as First Middy.

George cleared her throat. "Follow me," she ordered, keeping her voice calm. It wasn't *that* unlike being a school prefect. "Once we're in Middy Country, we'll sit down and have a long talk."

She led the way through the maze of corridors, wondering if she should have tasked one of them with leading the way. Their orientation packet would have included a shipboard diagram, a map of the giant battleship; it would be interesting, she supposed, to see how many of them had actually studied it. But then, she knew from bitter experience that the orientation packet didn't include *all* the details. She'd managed to get lost more than once, even though she'd memorised the original set of deck plans. Fraser had been very sarcastic after she'd nearly been late to her duty assignments a couple of times.

And he told me to make sure I always arrived early, she thought, as they passed through the hatch into Middy Country. *He never gave me any better advice.*

"Put your knapsacks in the lockers and choose a bunk, then join me in the wardroom," she ordered. "If any of you need to go to the toilet, go now."

She watched, feeling growing concern, as the four newcomers bickered over the bunks. *She* hadn't fought over the lockers, had she? But then, she'd been one of two new midshipmen and the pecking order had already been established. Potter laid claim to the locker closest to hers, pushing Henderson aside; Paula and Felicity seemed torn over who should have the locker furthest away from the bunks. Technically, it should have been Felicity's, but Paula seemed to want it. And to think she could claim the one right after Henderson, if she wished.

"That will do," she snapped at Potter, when he pulled Felicity back from claiming the upper bunk. They'd always been seen as *better* than the lower bunks, although objectively she knew there was no real difference. "There's more than enough room for all of us."

"She should be at the bottom," Potter argued. There was a glint of irritation in his eyes, mixed with an unspoken challenge. "She's just left the academy."

"And you are expected to be an officer and a gentleman," George said, feeling a flicker of sympathy for Fraser. No wonder he'd been so tempted to settle matters with his fists. "Take one of the lower bunks, then join me in the wardroom."

George sighed as she turned and left the compartment. Henderson and Paula, thankfully, had taken their bunks without complaint, although she caught Henderson looking at the upper bunks a little wistfully. No doubt he was looking forward to being First Middy himself, she thought, even though it would take several years before he was the senior midshipman. *She* might be promoted, but other midshipmen might be brought onboard…

"Take a cup of something and sit down," she ordered, once all four midshipmen had assembled in the wardroom. "And take a bar of chocolate from the fridge too."

She smiled, inwardly, at the flicker of astonishment on Potter's face, although Paula showed no visible reaction. The two younger middies didn't realise just how odd it was to hand out chocolate bars, certainly not *real* chocolate. They were in for a shock when someone gave them a cheap mass-produced navy-issue quasi-chocolate bar. George had heard that they cost the government a pound apiece, but no one knew what happened to the remaining seventy-five pence. She wouldn't have been surprised to hear that it vanished into a top secret black project on the other side of the Human Sphere.

"First, welcome to Middy Country," she said, once they were all sitting down. Felicity and Henderson were munching their chocolate, while the older - and wiser - midshipmen had concealed their bars in their pockets. "This is going to be your home for the next six months, at the very least. If you should happen to want to leave…well, it isn't going to happen unless you can talk the doctor into a medical discharge."

She smiled, rather humourlessly. The doctor would take a dim view of any malingering, particularly amongst the officers. God knew George had seen quite a few girls, back at school, claiming to be ill - or homesick - and almost all of them had bucked up after a quick visit to the matron. Personally, she suspected their conditions had improved so rapidly because hardly anyone wanted to visit the matron. The woman had been widely believed to be a war criminal from a Russian gulag. She'd certainly been unpleasant enough.

"Second, I'm afraid you're going to have to hit the ground running," she added. "Normally, there would be one or two newcomers and five or six experienced hands. Now, you have me, two midshipmen with experience on other vessels and two newcomers. I'm afraid that means there will be a great deal of work and hardly any downtime."

"We can take it," Potter said, cheerfully.

"I'll be relying on you and Paula to handle yourselves as much as possible," George said, firmly. "You already have a number of badges, so I've assigned you to duty posts where you can actually be of use. If you have problems, of course, let me know."

"We won't have any problems," Potter said. He gave Paula a suggestive wink, but she didn't show any trace of a reaction. "You can count on us, really."

George eyed him darkly, then nodded. "Clayton and Felicity will have to start the standard program from scratch, which won't be easy because the crew is already overworked," she added. "I've put together a training program for both of you, including a great deal of time in the simulators. You won't receive your first set of badges until you're actually checked out on the various consoles and departments, but we'll get you as far along as possible before you're expected to perform."

"It's no substitute," Potter said.

"No, it isn't," George said. She would have been more impressed if that wasn't common knowledge. Their instructors had hammered into their heads, time and time again, that there was no substitute for actual experience. She'd known promising cadets who'd flunked out when confronted with a *real* problem. "Do you have any better suggestions?"

"I do have several badges," Potter said. "It wouldn't be hard for me to introduce them to the systems…"

"Except you're not cleared to *train*," George said. She had no idea what the XO would say, if she tried, but she suspected it would be very bad. Allow a junior midshipman to train his subordinates? She'd be lucky if she only got beached long enough to put her right back at the bottom of the pecking order. "Or do you have a training certificate that isn't included in your file?"

She scowled at Potter, who looked back at her with an irritating firmness. "I'm just trying to help."

"Then keep your help *reasonable*," George snapped. She forced herself to calm down. "We will concentrate on simulations as much as possible, at least until we can get some proper training done."

Standing, she keyed the wall-mounted terminal. "You have the rest of the day to explore the ship and orientate yourself," she said. "If you *have* memorised the deck plans, you would be well-advised to go through the ship and make sure you know what's different. Quite a few things have changed in the last month and the deck plans in the orientation packet are probably out of date."

"Probably," Paula repeated.

"Probably," George said. Paula should have enough experience to know, by now, just how easily such things could get out of date. The bureaucracy took weeks or months to catch up, by which time the interior designs could have changed again. "You can download copies of your timetables, assignment schedules and the ship's files from the database. If you have any problems, or you think you can't handle your tasks, let me know. This is not the time and place to pretend that you are super-competent."

"Or Stellar Star," Felicity said, with a shy smile.

"You don't have the bust for it," Potter said. "Or the hair…"

"Or the scriptwriter," Paula added. She smiled, rather humourlessly. "Stellar Star has the most powerful weapon of all - a friendly man writing the lines."

"It isn't as if she has a bad technique," Potter objected. "Fall out of her uniform every twenty minutes…who's going to say no to her?"

George cleared her throat. "And in the *real world*, Stellar Star would be arrested and put in front of a court martial board," she said. "Trying her techniques would land you in the brig too."

She smiled, recalling an incident from the Academy. One of her instructors, after catching George and a few of her friends watching the latest movie, had ordered them to work out a charge sheet for Stellar Star, assuming she was actually a real person. They'd concluded that she could be dishonourably discharged for everything from conduct unbecoming to an officer to theft and misuse of naval resources. And the instructor had added a dozen other charges without even trying.

But she couldn't help noticing Felicity's face fall at the gentle ribbing.

She'll have to toughen up, she told herself, sternly. *How did she pass four years at the Academy without a thick skin?*

"Potter, Henderson, Wheeler, you are dismissed," she said, firmly. "Potter; report to the tactical department at 0900 tomorrow, as stated in your timetable. Henderson, Wheeler; report to the Chief Engineer. Spurgeon, remain behind."

George watched the three midshipmen leave, then turned to look at Paula. The older woman gazed back at her impassively, her face utterly unreadable. George couldn't help thinking that she might have been carved from ice, for all the expression she showed. And yet, there was something about Paula that bothered her on a very primal level. Nothing like Fraser, she thought, but something equally dangerous.

She pushed the unease out of her thoughts with an effort. "Spill," she ordered.

Paula quirked an eyebrow. "Spill?"

"You were stripped of three years of seniority," George said. She'd heard of midshipmen being retroactively beached all the time, but never for more than a couple of months. An offense so serious as to require more punishment surely deserved court martial…unless, for some reason, Paula had decided not to contest the NJP. "Three *years*. What did you do to deserve that?"

"I believe, with the greatest respect," Paula said, "that my former life is none of your business."

"I'm the First Middy," George said. She was damned if she was going to let Paula intimidate her. "And something that happened in your…*former life*…may cause problems for me."

"If you had a need to know," Paula told her coolly, "your superiors *would* have told you."

She held up a hand before George could come up with a response. "Rest assured, it will not pose any problems for you," she added. "And you can have my word on that, if that is enough for you."

George met her eyes, refusing to look away. "What did you do?"

Paula sighed heavily. "If you insist on knowing…"

"I do," George said.

"I was caught in bed with a lieutenant," Paula said. Her voice was very flat. "It was…strongly suspected…that he had been fiddling with my efficiency reports, in exchange for sex. He threw himself on his sword for me, insisting that he hadn't done anything to help my career. I believe he was dishonourably discharged from the navy."

George winced. "What the hell were you thinking? What was *he* thinking?"

She looked at Paula and knew the answer. Cut from ice or not, Paula was beautiful in a way that made George feel decidedly frumpy. She could have worked at the resort on Mars without any plastic surgery at all. Yes, she could easily see some fool of a lieutenant inviting her into bed, despite the risk. Some men - and some women too - were too fond of allowing their smaller heads to do their thinking.

"I was told that I could go right back to the start," Paula added, "or be discharged myself. I chose to remain in the navy, even though promotion seemed unlikely."

George considered it for a long moment. There was something about the story that didn't quite add up. Paula didn't have a hope in hell of further promotion and she had to know it, not with her record...unless she did something so heroic that the promotions board decided she'd paid for her sins. But there *was* a war on. Paula might *just* have a chance.

And if she was discharged, she'd find it hard to gain employment, George thought. *A sealed record wouldn't look much better than a dirty one.*

"I see," she said, finally.

"I would be grateful if you didn't share the story with anyone else," Paula said. "I...intend to focus on my career, rather than..."

"Get into bed with senior officers," George finished. She was sure Paula had learned her lesson. Hell, she'd been very lucky to be allowed to remain in the navy. And yet, there were still unanswered questions. "Might I suggest a chastity belt?"

Paula essayed a faint smile. "Do *you* wear one?"

George gave her an unpleasant look. *That* had hit a little bit too close to home. She'd been separated from Barton for just under two days and her body already missed him dreadfully. It wouldn't be so bad, she was sure, once the ship finally got underway, but until then...she shook her head, crossly. She was going to be very busy managing the middies as well as handling her own duties and bucking for promotion.

And Potter is eying my back for the knife, she thought, tiredly. *A week of being beached would be enough to make him First Middy.*

"No," she said, sharply. She swallowed the urge to make a catty remark - or assign punishment duty. "I keep my panties on. And I expect you to do the same. Dismissed."

CHAPTER
NINE

"It's a pleasure to see you again, Captain," Admiral Harper said. "I'm glad to hear that your government made your promotion permanent."

"I believe I have you to thank for some of it," Susan answered. She shook his hand, silently relieved that he hadn't taken the chance to ruin her career. He would have been more than human if he hadn't felt some annoyance over her brief assumption of command. "Your citation did my ego good."

Harper smiled, cheerfully. "And it was all true too," he noted. "It makes a pleasant change from the days we had to download whole dictionaries to find new ways to say 'can walk on water and piss wine.'"

He nodded to a dark-skinned officer standing next to him. "Can I introduce you to Keith Glass, my flag captain?"

"Charmed," Susan said. Glass could easily have passed for her elder brother or her uncle, although she'd only met her father's side of the family a couple of times. "We must share notes on commanding battleships when we have the time."

"Of course," Glass said. He had a southern accent, although he'd lost some of the tenor during his service. "*New York* is an impressive ship, but she hasn't seen actual combat just yet."

Susan frowned as an American yeoman pushed a glass into her hand. "She'll have her chance," she said, grimly. "Did you learn anything from our experience?"

"The yard dogs insisted on slapping more armour on the hull," Glass told her. "Apparently, it's good for our survival."

"But lousy for our speed," Susan said. "Getting here took longer than I had expected."

She scowled at the thought, relieved that Admiral Harper hadn't made an issue of their late arrival. *Vanguard* had practically *crawled* to the RV point as the engineers tested and retested the drive. Her armour was supposed to be solid - stronger even than the legendary *Ark Royal's* - but she paid one hell of a mass penalty. The aliens would have no trouble *catching* the ship, if they wanted to give chase, yet would they *want* to catch up? Anything strong enough to go toe-to-toe with *Vanguard* would have serious problems actually getting into weapons range.

Unless they aim themselves at a target they know we have to defend, she thought. *Or force us to punch our way through them to reach the tramline.*

Glass chatted to her as they circled the giant room, introducing her to the sixteen other commanding officers of Task Force Unity and the ground-force commanders. General Kershaw, USMC, explained that he had every confidence that his light infantry could make an impression on the aliens, although Susan had her doubts. If the task force controlled space, the aliens wouldn't be able to land; if the task force was driven away from Unity, the aliens could drop KEWs on any human military force foolish enough to show itself. The ground-based weapons stowed away on the giant American freighters *might* make a difference, but Susan wasn't convinced. If nothing else, the aliens could simply throw rocks from a safe distance and batter the planet into surrender.

"There is, of course, a very simple question," Captain Boreyev Yegorovich said. The Russian officer leaned forward, his eyes glimmering with suppressed amusement. "Why *did* the unknowns open fire as soon as they saw us?"

"We don't know," Susan said, irked. The Russian had clearly had more than a few glasses of wine. "We may never know until we learn how to communicate with them."

"Ah," Yegorovich said. "But, you see, the *Tadpoles* opened fire without bothering to communicate - at least as far as we knew. We thought they'd just come out of nowhere and invaded our space. But there *had* been a prior encounter between humans and Tadpoles and *we* were the aggressor."

"A problem that could have been resolved if they'd just *talked* to us," Glass pointed out, tartly. Heinlein had technically been an independent colony, but there had been no hiding the fact that the vast majority of the settlers had come from America. "It isn't as if we would have risked war over a honest mistake."

"You would certainly have been alone, if you had," the Russian said. He finished his glass and placed it on the table. "Was there a prior encounter between the Tadpoles and the unknowns?"

"Not as far as we know," Susan said. She sighed, wishing that Prince Henry had accompanied her to the dinner. "They hunted us - they *stalked* us - and then they opened fire."

"We *were* trespassing on their territory," Yegorovich pointed out. "How pleased would we be if *someone* sent a large fleet into the Terra Nova System?"

"Terra Nova, despite political problems, is a developed star system," Captain Jeanette Pierre countered. The Frenchwoman smiled, rather dryly. "It would be obvious from the moment someone popped through the tramline that it was home to a spacefaring race. They'd have to be blind not to see the freighters moving around the system, or the cloudscoops, or even the lights on the planet's surface. UXS-469 was - is - a completely empty star system. There was no trace of any technological presence until they dropped their cloaks and opened fire."

She tapped her glass, meaningfully. "I'm sure we would have taken more precautions if we'd *known* we were being watched."

"Yes," Susan agreed. "And if a large fleet *did* happen to appear at Terra Nova, wouldn't we try to communicate with it?"

"Terra Nova isn't expendable," Yegorovich said. "It's practically the gateway to Earth."

"The Tadpoles had no trouble sending their fleet through the system," Glass said. "It wasn't as if they bothered to bombard the planet or occupy the surface."

"They didn't have to," Yegorovich said. "Terra Nova's total industrial might is *puny*."

So is yours, Susan thought. The Russians had taken a beating during the war and even now, ten years later, they had yet to recover completely.

Sending a carrier to serve with the task force was one hell of a risk, even though they presumably wanted to re-establish themselves as serious players. *And losing New Russia hurt you badly.*

Admiral Harper cleared his throat. "I'm glad to hear that we are establishing a working relationship," he said, cheerfully. "But for the moment, the cooks are serving the meal and they will be very disappointed if we don't eat it."

Susan nodded and followed the other officers into the giant dining compartment. The Americans had put out a long table, with Admiral Harper sitting at one end and his flag captain taking the other. She took her assigned seat - they seemed to be handed out at random - and smiled as the yeomen appeared, carrying trays of food. Being so close to Earth had its advantages. They could - and did - have *real* food shipped to the RV point, rather than being forced to eat reconstituted dinners.

Don't get used to it, she told herself firmly. *You'll be eating recycled crap soon enough.*

"It isn't that far from Thanksgiving," Admiral Harper explained, as he started to carve a giant roast turkey. "And I thought I'd treat you all to a traditional American dinner."

"How *kind* of you," Yegorovich said. He was *still* drinking. "And will we require stomach pumps afterwards?"

"I dare say they can be provided," Harper said. "But really, if you don't want to eat the food, just say so. The junior officers will appreciate it."

Susan nodded to herself as she took a plate of turkey, then piled it high with potatoes, vegetables and gravy. It didn't look *that* different from the dinners she'd eaten as a younger girl, although she knew the cooks would have worked hard to prepare it. The Americans were determined that their crews should have a proper Thanksgiving dinner - just as the Royal Navy tried hard to make sure that everyone had turkey for Christmas - but it wasn't easy. Keeping a few hundred turkeys in the freezer took up space that could be more efficiently used to store rations or pre-packaged meals.

The conversation at the dinner table, as they munched their way through the meal, was decidedly irrelevant to the war. Susan was surprised at just how many subjects were covered, ranging from football to chess, but she supposed it was a way to learn more about their fellow officers. Yegorovich explained, as the yeoman refilled his glass yet again, that Russia's chances in the World Cup were extremely good - indeed, the Russians had spent a large fortune preparing the stadium in Moscow for the anticipated crowds. She couldn't help wondering if the war would interrupt their plans.

Glass had the same thought. "Do you think thousands of people will flock to Russia when there's a war on?"

"There's *always* a war on," Yegorovich replied, bluntly. "It makes no difference."

Susan supposed that was true, for him. Russia's southern border was almost completely lawless, with criminals, bandits and terrorists running tiny kingdoms that lasted until a kill-team came to call. The chaos regularly threatened to move north into Russia and the Russians responded brutally, hammering villages from orbit and sending in commandos to finish off the survivors.

"This isn't yet another brushfire along the border," Glass needled. "We're staring down the barrel of another interstellar war."

"Yes, but it is hundreds of light years away," Yegorovich said. "The average man in the street has far more reason to worry about terrorism - and putting food on the table - than he does about the war. As far as he is concerned, we're heading off into the great unknown."

"The entire world was bombarded, ten years ago," Susan pointed out. "It is a little more serious than a random terrorist attack."

"Yes, but it is less important to a man concerned with surviving," Yegorovich said. "Just because something is important to *us* doesn't mean it's important to *everyone*."

"That's true," Jeanette said. "My government was reluctant to commit *anything* to the task force. The President had to argue hard to get authorisation to deploy my ship and crew to the front line."

"And they sent a carrier, rather than a battleship," Glass said. "Do they consider you more expendable?"

Jeanette shrugged. "There's still room for a fleet carrier in this day and age," she said. "Yes, we *did* take hideous losses in the Battle of New Russia. There's no point in trying to argue that we *didn't* get our heads handed to us. And yes, all of our pre-war carriers might as well be giant floating targets in the modern age. But now...we have more armour on our carriers and better weapons too. And our starfighters have enhanced range. Rest assured, we will more than pull our weight."

"That's right," Yegorovich agreed. "My government would hardly have dispatched *my* ship if they didn't expect us to make a difference."

And let's just hope, Susan thought, *that you don't make it seventeen destroyed ships instead of sixteen.*

It was odd, she had to admit. The Royal Navy had *always* deployed its interstellar carriers to the war zone, although that *had* led to a major disaster at New Russia. But now, there were two carriers in the task force and neither of them were British - or American. The Royal Navy had worked closely with the French - she had no doubt that Jeanette and her ship would fit smoothly into the task force - but she had no idea how well anyone would cope with the Russians. It had been ten years since the Russians had exercised with *anyone*, let alone sent a capital ship to a war zone.

"We have two months to work on our planning," Harper said, answering her unspoken concerns. "I think that's plenty of time to work out the kinks in our system."

He motioned for them to rise and move back into the reception compartment, where more drinks and cigars were waiting. Susan politely declined the offer of a Cuban cigar, even though they were staggeringly rare after Cuba had been battered with monstrous tidal waves during the Bombardment of Earth. There might be vaccines against tobacco damage these days, but her father had always considered smoking a filthy habit. She'd never really understood why it was so popular.

"I'm sure you've all had a private briefing from your governments," Harper said, once they were all seated. "And the basic ops plan has not changed. If we get to Unity ahead of the aliens, we land troops, evacuate the population and then scout out the nearby systems, watching for the inevitable offensive. If we don't, we evaluate the situation and then either harass the enemy or make a full-fledged attempt to evict them from the system. Given the nature of the tramlines in that region, JHQ would obviously prefer we evicted the enemy before they manage to turn the Tadpole flank."

"Which does prove they weren't prepared for war," Captain Steve Stewart pointed out. "If they're having to scramble to get forces in place to secure their flanks, they clearly weren't *expecting* to have to fight."

"Neither were we before the first war," Glass countered. "It didn't stop us assembling a multinational force."

"Which is what they wanted us to do," Yegorovich said. "We could be sailing right into another trap."

Susan had to admit he had a point. The Tadpoles had *deliberately* held back after the early engagements of the First Interstellar War, giving the human race plenty of time to assemble the multinational force that had confronted them - and then they'd slaughtered the entire force, leaving only a handful of survivors. It was possible, just possible, that the new enemies had something similar in mind, if they understood that they were waging war against two separate interstellar powers. But she didn't see why they *wouldn't*. If nothing else, they would probably have recovered plenty of bodies after the first savage battle.

Harper nodded. "The possibility has crossed JHQ's mind," he said. "And that's why their commitment is actually quite small, for the moment. There won't be a larger commitment until we are truly ready for war."

"If we ever are," Jeanette said. "To us, the loss of thousands of spacers is tragic, but it may have made little impact on the general public."

"I hope you're wrong," Susan said.

"Our population understands that we - they - have to make sacrifices," Yegorovich thundered. "And your populations should know it too."

Harper tapped his glass. "We depart tomorrow," he said. "My staff will be forwarding copies of the first exercise scenarios to you once we pass through the tramline to Terra Nova - we'll commence simulations and starfighter drills shortly afterwards. Depending on what news we receive from the front, particularly as we cross the border, we may have time for some proper exercises as well. Before then..."

He looked from face to face. "Does anyone have any concerns that should be raised?"

"A secondary commanding officer has to be named," Yegorovich said, bluntly. Susan would have been surprised if he *wasn't* angling for the position himself. "Right now, both you and your flag captain are on the same vessel."

"*New York* is a tough ship," Glass snapped.

"So were the Tadpole dreadnaughts," Yegorovich sneered. "It didn't stop them being blown to rubble, did it?"

"Captain Onarina will serve as my second," Harper said. He nodded to Susan, who stared at him in shock. "She's junior to all of you, but she has both combat and fleet command experience. Captain Trodden will serve as *her* second, if things go badly wrong. Right now, I would prefer to keep the chain of command on the battleships. They're tougher than the carriers."

"*Chernozhopi*," Yegorovich muttered.

Susan ignored him. She'd been called worse. And while she'd hated being mocked for the colour of her skin, she couldn't help feeling that she'd done better than many of the spoilt brats she'd known and detested at school. The little bitches would never know what it was like to command a warship in combat...

"We are being sent out, among other things, to uphold the honour of the human race," Harper warned. If he'd overheard Yegorovich's comment, he gave no sign of it. "JHQ would prefer, however, if we were careful during our engagements. We have plenty of space to trade for time, if necessary."

"Tadpole space," Jeanette said. "If we have to retreat, Admiral, which way do we go?"

"Back towards Earth," Harper said. "JHQ's orders admit of no ambiguity, Captain. We are not to risk getting bottled up in Tadpole space."

Yegorovich snorted. "Let me guess," he said. "The person who wrote these orders was not a serving naval officer."

"They're trying to please their political masters," Harper said. Susan rather suspected he privately agreed with Yegorovich. "And they are leery about taking major losses if it can be avoided."

"Of course they are," Yegorovich sneered.

Susan kept her face expressionless. Yegorovich might be a jerk - and he'd clearly hoped for a position he could use to make himself look good - but he had a point. Being bottled up in Tadpole space was not going to happen unless the enemy pounded the fleet into scrap metal first. And if that happened they were screwed anyway.

And retreating back to human space would tell them where to go, she reminded herself. *They can just follow us into the Human Sphere.*

"They're the orders we have," Harper said, patiently. Susan was quietly impressed at his diplomacy. *She* would have found it hard to handle Yegorovich for more than an hour or two without considering grievous bodily harm. "If you want to have them altered, I suggest you petition your government. They might just be able to talk JHQ into changing its mind."

Yegorovich snorted. "They just want a victory," he said. "They don't care about how it comes."

"Just like everyone else," Stewart commented.

"Quite," Harper said. He looked around the compartment as the yeomen refilled glasses before withdrawing once again. "Shall we now discuss tactical variables?"

CHAPTER
TEN

"You didn't do too badly," Lieutenant David Reed said. "And you managed to miss all the asteroids in your path."

George nodded in relief. It would be a year or more, she suspected, before she was allowed to actually take the helm - unless the ship was in deep trouble anyway - but praise from the helmsman was rare. She'd heard he didn't intend to *stay* on the command track, even though he would eventually be beached anyway. He enjoyed flying the battleship more than he enjoyed giving orders.

"Thank you, sir," she said. "Is there anywhere in space with such a... *crowded*...asteroid field?"

"No," Reed said. "But if you can ace *this* simulation, you shouldn't have any trouble with a more *realistic* situation."

He cleared his throat. "If you continue at your current rate, you should be ready to take the exam within the next month," he added. "Are you considering a sideways transfer into the helm department?"

"No, sir," George said. "I'm aiming for command."

"You'll still need to know how to fly the ship," Reed noted. He didn't seem offended, merely amused. "And you'll definitely need to know what she can do."

George nodded as she rose from the console and stretched, feeling tired and stiff. She'd been sitting down for nearly two hours, but it felt longer. She would have killed for a bath, if one had been available. But not even the captain had a bath in her quarters. She'd just have to make do with five minutes under the shower before she took a quick nap.

"Dismissed," Reed said, after passing her a datachip. "Make sure you register it before we leave the system or it won't be added to your permanent record."

"Thank you, sir," George said. It wouldn't do her any good - it wasn't as if there were bonuses for passing the simulations - but it would prove to her uncle that she was actually trying. "I'll be back here tomorrow?"

"Probably," Reed said. "And well done."

George smiled as she walked through the hatch and down towards middy country, carefully stepping over a handful of soldiers sleeping on the decks. It was an accident waiting to happen, she thought; officers and crew rushing to their duty stations when the alarms sounded were going to be tripping over the soldiers and crashing to the deck. But no one had asked *her* opinion. She was a midshipman. Her opinions wouldn't be considered important until she was promoted to lieutenant or even higher up the chain.

Her wristcom bleeped. "Midshipwoman Fitzwilliam?"

She keyed the device automatically. "Fitzwilliam."

"Midshipman Henderson has not reported for his duty shift," Lieutenant-Commander Jean Granger said. The tactical officer sounded annoyed. "Is there a *reason* he hasn't arrived?"

"I don't think so, Commander," George said. She checked her datapad hastily. If Henderson had gone into sickbay, there would be a note in his file. But there was nothing. "He should have been with you ten minutes ago."

"I am *aware* of that, Midshipwoman," Granger said. "Find out what happened to him, then report back to me."

"Yes, Commander," George said.

She cursed under her breath as the connection broke. She'd told the new midshipmen, time and time again, to make damn sure they aimed to reach their duty stations ten minutes before they were actually due there. Even with the corridors crammed with soldiers, they shouldn't have had any trouble reaching their stations. And Henderson should have had punctuality hammered into his head at the Academy. Getting to a classroom late *once* would have been grounds for a sharp lecture by the tutor - and doing it repeatedly would have been enough to get him kicked out.

"Computer," she said. "Locate Midshipman Henderson."

"Midshipman Henderson is in the Midshipman's Bunkroom," the computer said.

George blinked in astonishment, then turned and hurried down to Middy Country. She *knew* Henderson had been sleeping when she'd left the compartment, but he should have been smart enough to set his alarm. It was hardly rocket science! Gritting her teeth - it was *just* possible there was a reasonable explanation for the whole affair - she made her way through the hatch and stuck her head into the bunkroom. Henderson was lying in his bunk, snoring loudly. George stared at him in shock, then poured herself a glass of water from the dispenser and tipped it over his head. He sat up so sharply, water dripping from his hair, that he cracked his head against the overhead bunk.

"What..."

"You are ten minutes late for your duty assignment," George snarled. She had to fight to resist the urge to just grab his arm and drag him out of his bunk. Only the awareness that she might not be strong enough to budge him kept her from doing just that. "And Lieutenant-Commander Granger contacted me to find out what happened to you."

She clenched her fists as Henderson stared at her, blinking his eyes in shock. This was going to reflect badly on *her*. Never mind that she'd been at her own duty station, never mind that Henderson was hardly a child... it was going to reflect badly on her. Lieutenant-Commander Granger wasn't the sort of person to let such a problem slide, not when she was new to the ship herself. George had a nasty feeling that the XO would give her a stern lecture himself once he heard the news.

"Get up," she snapped. "Now."

Henderson sat upright, swinging his legs over the side of the bunk. She found it hard to resist the urge to scream at him as he pushed back the blanket. He hadn't even had the sense to wear his uniform! It was the only way to catch a few extra moments of sleep before running to one's station, although Fraser had never let *her* get away with it. She forced herself to watch as he grabbed his trousers and jacket, then donned them with practiced ease. If he hadn't looked sleepy, she wouldn't have known he'd only just woken up.

"Get to your duty station," she ordered. "And don't even *think* about trying to get away with it."

She watched him go, then slowly - reluctantly - keyed her wristcom. "Commander, he's on his way," she said. "He overslept."

"I see," Granger said. George winced. She would have preferred an explosion of rage. "I'll have to report this to the XO."

"I understand, Commander," George said.

"And I shall be assigning punishment duty for Mr. Henderson," Granger added. "I trust you will have no objection?"

George resisted the urge to roll her eyes, even though she knew Commander Granger couldn't see her. It was a bad habit. But really...as if she *could* have any objection! And she didn't have any objection. Hell, she intended to hand out a few punishment duties of her own too, once Henderson returned. A fortnight spent cleaning the head should teach him a lesson - and, if it didn't, there were worse possibilities.

"No, Commander," she said, fighting to keep her voice even. "I have none."

"Good," Granger said.

She closed the connection. George stared at the wristcom for a long moment, then swore venomously, using a whole string of nasty words she'd learned from Fraser. There was no point in beaching Henderson - he had barely three days of seniority - but *she* could be beached. And if she *was* beached, she was in deep shit. The XO had every reason to make sure she *was* beached too, just to make it clear that her family name wouldn't protect her from consequences. But it hadn't been her fault.

The topmost bunk rustled. Potter poked his head out. "I didn't know you knew such words."

George felt her temper flare. "And I didn't know you were up there," she snapped. "Aren't you meant to be in the lower bunk?"

Potter gave her a maddening smile. "Felicity was kind enough to agree to a trade."

He shrugged. "And you really *should* have made sure that he was up and dressed before you headed to *your* duty station."

"I'm not a bloody prefect," George swore at him. The prefects at her school *had* been responsible for getting the girls and boys out of bed, but they'd slept in the same dorms and shared the same timetables. It hadn't been a responsibility she'd enjoyed. Hell had no fury like a boarding school pupil trying to snatch a few extra minutes of sleep. "And he isn't a bloody schoolchild."

"You should probably tuck him up at night too," Potter added. "And read him a bedtime story to make sure he actually goes to sleep."

"Shut up," George ordered. Her stomach growled, reminding her that she hadn't eaten for four hours. "And if you want to read him a fucking bedtime story, you *can* read him a fucking bedtime story."

Potter ignored her. "And the wardroom isn't too clean," he added. "You really should…"

"Shut up," George repeated. She *knew* he was pushing her, but she found it hard not to give in to the urge to snap back. Maybe she could ask the XO to beach him…no, that would make her look bad, particularly now that there was a risk of getting beached herself. "And as your duty shift starts in two hours, make damn fucking sure that you're there twenty minutes before it is due to start."

She turned and stormed out of the wardroom, passing Paula as she returned from her own duty shift. Somehow, the older woman managed to look as if she'd just stepped out of the shower, rather than working in the engineering department. George scowled at her and paced down towards the mess, wondering if the cooks would be interested in some help. Assigning a midshipman to the gallery would be seen as a slap across the face, but Henderson deserved it. And he couldn't complain without admitting to his own failings.

There was no sign of Fraser in the mess, much to her disappointment. She would have liked to talk to him, perhaps ask his advice. It wasn't as if *he* wanted to take her place. Hell, she was sure he would have sooner slit his wrists than go back to being a midshipman. But there was no sign of him or anyone else she could have legitimately talked to, not without eyebrows being raised. Perhaps Potter had stumbled on something after all. In so many ways, the caste system that pervaded the Royal Navy was *very* much like school.

But everyone here is expected to act like an adult, she thought, as she took a plate of sausages, chips and beans and found a small side table. *You can't act like an idiot in space.*

She chewed her food slowly, concentrating on calming herself. The world always felt better after a good dinner - or so her father had always maintained. He'd been a great trencherman when she'd been young, although a lifetime of fine dining and heavy drinking had taken its toll. He would have been horrified at the food in the mess - she had a sneaking suspicion what he would have suspected had gone into the sausages - but that wouldn't have stopped him eating. If his wife - George's mother -hadn't put her foot down after the bombardment, she had a feeling he would have eaten himself to death.

We had to look as though we were tightening our belts, she remembered. She'd been too young to truly understand what was happening, but she recalled, all too clearly, the food riots shown on live TV. *Or the proles might have revolted.*

She pushed the thought aside as she finished her meal, picking up the tray and dumping it in the cleaner before heading to the hatch. Her next duty assignment started in two hours, plenty of time to get some exercise before going back on duty. She walked slowly down to Middy Country, then frowned as she heard banging and clattering from the wardroom. Who was in there? Bracing herself, she peered through the hatch and frowned. Felicity Wheeler was on her hands and knees, scrubbing the deck.

George cleared her throat. "What are you *doing?*"

Felicity jumped, nearly knocking over the pail of water. George couldn't help thinking she looked like Cinderella, if Cinderella had worn a naval uniform rather than a ragged dress and remarkably fetching hairdo. She pushed the thought aside as Felicity stood and snapped out a salute, remembering that Felicity's next duty assignment was just after hers. What the hell was she doing scrubbing the deck?

"I'm cleaning the compartment," Felicity said. "Mr. Potter ordered me to make sure the floor was so clean he could eat his dinner off it."

George felt her temper flare. "And by what right," she demanded, "does *he* issue orders?"

Felicity looked perplexed. "He is senior to me, isn't he?"

"It doesn't work that way," George snarled. She was going to kill him. It was hard, so hard, to resist the urge to storm back into the bunkroom and tear Potter a new arsehole. "I'm the senior midshipman - that makes me the First Middy. *I* am in charge. How the hell did you get through four years at the Academy without knowing *that*?"

She had to fight to resist the urge to shake the younger girl. *She'd* been drilled extensively on rank, seniority and questions of precedence. There was no way *that* particular part of the curriculum would have been removed, not when it was far too important to the chain of command. Potter might be senior to Felicity, but that meant nothing as long as Potter wasn't the First Middy. And yet, he was trying to assert his authority...

Bastard, she thought. There were limits to what she could do to him, limits she dared not cross. It would just get her in hot water. And yet, she couldn't go to the XO or anyone higher up the food chain either. It would make her look weak. Potter...might just have contrived a situation where she practically *had* to let him get away with it, if she wanted to keep her position. *Fucking bastard*!

Her palms hurt. She realised, numbly, that she'd been squeezing her fists and driving her nails into her skin hard enough to draw blood. Fraser would probably have settled the matter with his fists, taking Potter into the ring for a one-sided bout, but that wasn't an option for *her*. She might lose...

...And if she did, she would be honour-bound to concede the position to him.

Felicity looked nervous, as if she was on the verge of breaking into loud sobs. George stared at her in disgust. How the hell had she survived four years at the Academy? *George* had found it hard going and *she'd* been a goddamned tomboy! She'd practiced everything from getting up at the crack of dawn to multitasking while an officer was screaming at her. God knew boarding school was *excellent* preparation for the naval academy...

"Clear up this mess," George ordered, sharply. She was tempted to comfort the younger girl, as she'd comforted her sister, but Felicity had to learn to stand on her own two feet. "And if he gives you any more orders, feel free to treat them as *suggestions*."

She turned and stormed out of the room, heading down to the bunk-room and opening the hatch. Paula was lying on her bunk, snoring gently; Potter was sitting on the lower bunk, smiling thinly to himself. She opened her mouth, then bit down hard. Whatever she said to Potter, she knew she couldn't wake Paula. She needed her sleep too.

"Come with me," she ordered. "Now."

Potter rose - so slowly she *knew* he was trying to annoy her - and followed her into the next compartment. It was normally used to allow midshipmen to record v-mails for their families, but now - thankfully - it was empty. She closed the hatch - absurdly, she wished suddenly that she could slam it - and turned to glare at him. Potter met her rage with the same maddening smile.

"You are *not* in charge of this compartment," George snapped. "You are *not* First Middy."

"For now," Potter said.

George wished, just for a moment, that Fraser had stayed as First Middy. *He* would never have tolerated Potter, not for a second. But there was no point in wishing for things she knew she couldn't have.

"You have been a midshipman on two different ships," she said, instead. "You *know* how to act" - although she couldn't help wondering if Potter had caused trouble elsewhere - "so fucking do it. If you become First Middy, you can issue orders all you please…but for the moment, take orders instead of giving them!"

Potter smirked. "What if I have to tell them what to do?"

"Then explain why it has to be done," George said.

"There might not be time to explain," Potter said. "They might need to be given orders."

George placed iron controls on her temper. She knew what he was trying to do and she was damned if she was letting him. Potter reminded her, all too much, of the little brats at school who'd been practicing for a career in law by finding all the loopholes and exploiting them ruthlessly. But at least she'd had more options for dealing with them.

"You will not issue orders unless absolutely necessary," she said. "And if the orders are *not* necessary, in *my* opinion, you *will* have punishment duties. Do you understand me?"

"Of course, Your Supremacy," Potter said.

"And, seeing you seem to believe the compartment needs to be cleaned, you can clean out the bunkroom after you get back from your next duty station," George added. "And make damn sure you don't disturb anyone while you work. Do you understand me?"

Potter, just for a second, looked irked. She counted it as a small victory.

"Yes," he said. "I understand."

George gritted her teeth. She knew, all too well, that the whole affair was far from over.

CHAPTER
ELEVEN

The command chair felt...different.

Susan settled into it as the crew ran through the final checks, silently relieved that they were about to leave without any further problems. She'd sat in it dozens of times, from the hours she'd spent on watch duty to the time she'd served as *Vanguard's* commanding officer, but this was different. This time, the ship was *hers*. There were no rocks waiting to fall on her head, no grim awareness that she might be sent to Colchester - or worse - after she brought the ship home. *Vanguard* was hers. And no one could ever take it from her.

She surveyed the bridge, quietly noting how the crew had taken up their positions and were readying the ship to depart, then moved her eyes to the near-space display. The massive battleship, flanked by USS *New York* and USS *Indianapolis*, dominated the scene, a collection of firepower that could comprehensively thrash any formation from the First Interstellar War without breaking a sweat. Two giant carriers hung in space behind the battleships, their starfighters running long-range recon flights around the task force. No one had any reason to expect that the new enemies might be watching Earth, but there was no point in taking chances. Besides, JHQ might decide to slip a stealth ship into firing range, just to test their defences.

And they probably would, if we had more time, Susan thought. Seventeen warships and twenty-seven transports...it was a formidable force, but tiny compared to the massed power of humanity's fleets. *They're concerned with getting us out as quickly as possible.*

She glanced at her console as status reports started to come in from all over the ship, each one reporting a complete lack of problems. Susan was torn between relief and concern; she knew, all too well, just how many problems would only appear when the fleet went to full military power. And, by then, they might be halfway to their destination. It wouldn't do her reputation any good if her ship had to limp back to Earth, having lost half her drive rooms to an unexpected emergency.

"Captain," Mason said. "All departments have reported in. All systems are green. I say again, all systems are green."

"Very good, Mr. XO," Susan said, with equal formality. She watched as he turned his head back to his console. "Communications, raise the flag. Inform Admiral Harper that we are ready to depart on schedule."

"Aye, Captain," Lieutenant Theodore Parkinson said.

Susan gazed at the back of his head, silently relieved that Parkinson had been left on *Vanguard*. He was a Tadpole expert - too rare and valuable to be charged with anything, unlike the rest of the crew - but she had a feeling she'd be glad of his expertise when they finally reached their destination. Prince Henry's small crew of experts were decent people, she was sure, yet they were *civilians*. They wouldn't understand the importance of putting military matters first, when there was a war on.

"Signal from the flag," Parkinson said. "The task force is to proceed as planned."

"Understood," Susan said. "Helm?"

"All drives are online and ready to go," David Reed said.

Susan sucked in a breath. "Take us out," she ordered. "And make sure we hold combat position."

A low thrumming echoed through the hull as the giant battleship slowly started to move, picking up speed as she headed towards the tramline. The two American battleships seemed to fall behind for long seconds - Susan couldn't help noticing that their drives were either less efficient or their hulls were too heavily armoured - before they picked up speed and returned to their flanking positions. She wasn't too surprised to note that the carriers didn't seem to be having any trouble keeping up with the battleships, although the smaller units were definitely leading the way. But then, destroyers and frigates had unsurprisingly sharp acceleration curves.

"We are holding position, as planned," Reed reported. "We will cross the tramline in forty minutes."

"Copy our final records to the Admiralty," Susan ordered. "And then remind the crew that they have thirty minutes to upload any messages into the planetary datanet."

She smiled, inwardly, at the thought. The only person *she* wanted to talk to was her father - and she'd uploaded a long v-mail to him the previous night. It was a shame they couldn't talk in person, or even hold a proper conversation without an increasingly annoying time-delay between messages and replies, but wishful thinking couldn't change the laws of nature. Until someone managed to find a way to send messages at FTL speeds, humanity would just have to adapt to the universe.

And besides, he might ask too many questions if we were face-to-face, she thought, sardonically. She'd given her father the official story, but she'd never been able to lie to him as a young girl. He would know that *something* was wrong, although - as an experienced military officer himself - he would probably understand that such matters were classified well above his former pay grade. *And what would he say if he found out the truth?*

She pushed the question aside as she monitored her ship's performance. Apart from a brief spike in messages being beamed off the ship, back to the communications hub orbiting Earth, everything seemed to be normal. All of the starship's fusion reactors were online and supplying power - more power, in fact, than the battleship actually *needed*. But then, there *was* a strong prospect of losing one or more of the reactors during a particularly savage engagement. *Vanguard* could - in theory - run and fight on a single reactor.

But no one has actually tested the concept, she reminded herself. The thought sent a chill running down her spine. *We might find out, if the war goes on long enough.*

"Signal from the flag," Parkinson informed her. "Admiral Harper wishes us to proceed to the tramline with no further delay."

Susan's eyes narrowed. They *were* going to the tramline and Harper knew it. Was he trying to sound efficient...or was one of his other subordinates questioning his orders? She tossed the possibilities around in her head for a long moment, then shrugged. It wasn't her concern, not right now. If she had to assume command of the task force, it would be in the thick of a battle and no one in their right mind would dispute her claim to authority.

"Acknowledge the signal," she ordered. "And then keep us on our current course."

"Aye, Captain," Parkinson said.

Susan nodded, then glanced at the final string of messages appearing in her inbox. None of them were marked urgent - officers who abused the classification system had short and unpleasant careers - but it was astonishing just how much worthless crap the REMFs expected her to study during the voyage. Did they think she was on a pleasure cruise? It wasn't as if she was lying on a four-poster bed, a drink in one hand and a book in the other, sunning herself under the cabin lights. The only update of interest was a short note stating that enemy activity had been observed in three new systems, but as the titbit was out of date by two months she was fairly sure it was largely useless.

It might not be completely useless, she thought, darkly. *By the time we get there, they might just have secured the systems and moved to cut Unity off from reinforcements.*

She contemplated the problem for a long moment, despite both training and experience telling her it was pointless. It didn't take an ace captain - or a patriotic scriptwriter - to run a blockade, at least as long as they didn't try to get close to the planet. Hell, the SAS had managed to land on Pegasus during the Anglo-Indian War, despite a strong enemy presence and enough ground-based planetary defence units to make Haig weep. The newcomers might have better weapons and sensors, but they didn't seem to have anything too far ahead of the Royal Navy. If they had, the war would already be over.

"Captain," Reed said. "We will be crossing the tramline on schedule."

"*Jones* is moving ahead to sweep the transit point," Parkinson added.

"Good," Susan said. "Make sure we pull a live feed directly from their sensors."

She leaned forward, feeling her heart starting to pound in her chest. Sending a destroyer to sweep the space around the tramline for cloaked starships smacked of paranoia - it wasn't as if they were hopping directly into unexplored territory, where entire enemy fleets might be lying in wait - but it was good practice. Half of history's naval disasters, she'd been told, could have been averted if someone had taken basic precautions before it was too late. And if the enemy *did* manage to get a point-blank shot at *Vanguard* or one of the other capital ships, it would be very embarrassing indeed. The operation might be over before it had even begun.

"Local space is clear," Lieutenant Charlotte Watson said. The sensor operator worked her console with practiced skill, never taking her eyes off the feed of raw data washing into her systems. "If there's anything watching us, Captain, it's *very* well hidden."

Which proves nothing, Susan thought. *A single destroyer, lying doggo with all of her sensors and drives stepped down to the bare minimum, would be able to get a hard lock on all of us before we knew she was there.*

"Signal from the flag," Parkinson said. "All ships are to make transit as planned."

"Helm, take us through," Susan ordered. "And then maintain course."

"Aye, Captain," Reed said.

Susan closed her eyes as a dull quiver echoed through the ship, marking the moment the ship jumped through the tramline. She opened them again, just in time to see the tactical display blank out and then hastily start reformatting itself, drawing data from the starship's sensors and the remainder of the squadron. Her worst nightmare - every commanding officer's worst nightmare - was running straight into the teeth of enemy fire, but there didn't seem to be any surprises lying in wait, merely the steadily-growing interplanetary infrastructure pervading the Terra Nova system.

"Jump complete," Reed reported.

"All systems read clear," Charlotte added.

Susan nodded. It would be hours before they received any signals from Terra Nova itself - or any of the smaller settlements scattered around the system - but it didn't *look* as though there was any reason to panic. Terra Nova might be one of the most lawless systems in the Human Sphere - the planet was still politically fragmented, making it harder for its governments to try to assert authority outside the gravity well - yet there was still enough of an outsider naval presence to make sure that any alien ships that poked their noses into the system got them cut off. Or so she hoped...

There's also enough activity within the system to make it easier for the enemy to sneak around, if they were careful, she thought. *And that could be very bad.*

She rose. "Mr. XO, you have the conn," she said.

"Aye, Captain," Mason said. "I have the conn."

Susan nodded, then strode through the hatch into her office. There was paperwork to do, ranging from unimportant matters that still needed the captain's personal touch to an emailed request from a reporter, asking to speak with her at her earliest convenience. Susan eyed the latter darkly for a long moment, then deleted the message, discarding it into the terminal's recycle bin. Normally, Public Relations would be nagging her to speak to the press - after making sure she was primed with the navy line on all matters - but for once PR seemed to believe that it was better to be silent. Besides, with the reporters trapped on *New York*, they'd have some problems pestering her.

Poor Harper, she thought. *He'll have the bastards camping outside his cabin just for a chance to shout questions at him.*

She sighed, then returned to sorting through the paperwork. There was no getting away with it. She'd just have to get it all done as quickly as possible.

And with two months between us and Earth, once we reach Unity, she reminded herself, *they'll find it hard to demand corrections before we get home.*

"I was expecting something more, Your Highness," Doctor Song said. They stood together in the observation blister, staring out at the unblinking stars. "All of the movies show flashing starlight or waves of eerie light."

"The media knows nothing and the film producers know even less," Henry said. He had to admit he'd been disappointed too, when he'd made his first jump through the tramlines, but his superiors had kept him too busy to complain. "Reality" - he waved a hand at the stars outside the blister - "isn't dramatic enough for them."

Doctor Song eyed him, thoughtfully. "Is there a reason for that?"

Henry shrugged. "Shipboard lasers are invisible to the naked eye," he said. "And missiles move so quickly that the human mind has difficulty tracking them. Only plasma cannons produce spectacular blast effects and, even then, they're not *quite* the death rays that Hollywood finds attractive. And most of the time, the hard realities of naval combat defeat the producers. They just don't understand them."

He smiled, rather thinly. "And so you have movies where starships explode with beams of light that should be visible halfway across the solar system and starfighters perform feats that should be impossible, without completely rewriting the laws of physics."

"And Stellar Star's breasts," Doctor Song added. "They defy the laws of physics too."

"It's the most common superpower," Henry said, dryly.

"I thought that was Royal Blood, Your Highness," Doctor Song said. "Or was I wrong?"

Henry winced. "Call me *Your Excellency*, if you must," he said, pained. "I try to forget that I was ever a prince."

He braced himself for the usual barrage of questions and was surprised when Doctor Song merely nodded and peered back out into the darkness. He'd suggested she go to the observation blister after she'd started to get a little cabin fever - it wasn't uncommon, even on a battleship - despite the risk she'd think he was flirting with her. Doctor Song was pretty, he would happily admit, but he was a married man. And his wife had put up with a great deal, even sacrificing her career.

But she couldn't have had a normal career, after marrying me, he thought. *And I never warned her before it was too late.*

His wristcom bleeped. He glanced at it, half-expecting a message from his subordinate asking when he was due back in the compartment and lifted his eyebrows when he realised it was an invitation to dine with the captain. Doctor Song glanced at her own wristcom, then looked at him. She'd received the same invitation too.

"I don't have anything to wear," she said. She paused. "What *do* I wear? What do I *do*?"

Henry blinked. "You were never taught the rules of formal dining at school?"

Doctor Song shook her head. Henry wondered at that for a long moment, then shrugged and composed his thoughts. Formal dining had been taught at his school, but it was possible that other schools didn't touch on the subject. Any officers attending a regimental dinner - or a dinner with their commanding officer - would be briefed on how to behave beforehand.

"You don't have a uniform," he said, after a moment. "Did you bring a decent civilian outfit?"

"No," Doctor Song said. "Just my normal clothes."

"Draw something from the quartermaster," Henry said. They'd have something Doctor Song could wear, even if they had to take the rank stripes and badges off a naval uniform. "And remember to speak with everyone you can, even if you don't like them."

He ran through the same advice he'd been given, although formal dinners had never been a big part of his naval career. "Be there early; that's when they start serving the booze. If you're not a big drinker, make sure you get a glass of juice or water. Check where you'll be sitting, then make the acquaintance of the man sitting to your right. He'll be escorting you to your chair, when the mess call is played. Eat what you are given; if there is anything you don't like, just leave it on your plate…"

Doctor Song was looking faintly shell-shocked by the time he finally came to a halt. "Is there anything *more*?"

"Don't buttonhole the captain," Henry said, after a moment. "My uncle was fond of telling me about an…incident during a regimental dinner, but I don't think anyone else found it funny. There was a young officer, who'd drunk enough of the port to make him mildly tipsy, who captured his superior officer - his *very* superior and told him everything that was wrong with his regiment. And it was a very silly list."

"I see," Doctor Song said. "What happened to the young man?"

"I believe he was reassigned to a monitoring post in the Falklands," Henry said. He smiled at her expression. "But I don't think the captain will be *that* concerned about you."

"That's a relief," Doctor Song said. "But what about you?"

"I'm a lost cause," Henry said.

He smiled at her, then turned towards the hatch. "The dinner is at 1900 for 1930," he added, pausing. "Make sure you're there for 1900. An officer will be delighted to show you the way, if you don't want me escorting you there. And try not to get drunk."

"I don't drink," Doctor Song said. "And after what you've said, I don't know why anyone drinks."

"It helps to make parties merry," Henry said. If he had a pound for every glass of wine he'd had at diplomatic dinners, he'd have at least a hundred thousand pounds. "And sometimes it makes them too merry."

CHAPTER
TWELVE

Whoever had designed the Royal Navy's dress uniform, George thought for what had to be the thousandth time, had been an absolute sadist. The jacket was too tight, the shirt was too white and the trousers felt unnaturally stiff against her skin. She had the ominous feeling that a sudden hasty movement would result in her clothes splitting open, something that would probably get her busted all the way back to cadet. But there was nothing she could do about it. Midshipmen were encouraged to alter their day uniforms to suit their needs, if necessary, but the dress uniforms were untouchable. All she could do was endure.

She felt an odd pang as she led the other midshipmen into the officers wardroom, feeling more than a little out of place. She'd endured a number of formal dinners during her childhood - sitting at the table for longer than half an hour was one of the skills her parents had hammered into her young head - but this was different. This time, she was responsible for four other midshipmen, one of whom wanted her job while another seemed remarkably lazy.

"Mingle," she ordered, quietly. "And be *polite*."

"I am always polite," Potter muttered.

George resisted the urge to glare at him as he hurried over to chat to one of the civilian specialists - a woman who looked to be half-Chinese - and then made her way over to the wall-mounted seating plan. It looked as though the captain had invited every officer and civilian on the ship, including the marines and all of the civilian specialists. She breathed a sigh of relief as she discovered she'd be sitting next to Prince Henry, then looked around for him. He was standing against the bulkhead, chatting to Lieutenant Reed. George hesitated, knowing it would be unwise to interrupt their conversation. Whoever said there was no rank at the mess - or during an officer's party - had clearly never served in the military.

She frowned as she saw Felicity standing against one wall, looking utterly out of place despite a uniform that somehow managed to make her look good. The girl seemed to be shy, too shy. George could understand the value of solitude, but she honestly didn't understand how Felicity had managed to get through basic training without either losing the shyness or at least learning how to fake an interest in someone else. But then, Felicity had no experience talking to someone who outranked her, at least in a social setting. George might be a midshipman, but she took *social* precedence over just about everyone else in the room.

Depends if you count Prince Henry, she thought, as she walked over to Felicity. The younger girl looked relieved to see her, which had to be a first. *He might just be heir to the throne.*

"Come with me," she ordered. Prince Henry had finished his discussion with Lieutenant Reed, much to her relief. "I'll introduce you to His Excellency."

Prince Henry showed no visible irritation as George introduced him to Felicity. He even kissed her hand, which made her giggle and blush. George concealed her amusement with an effort, then chatted freely to him about the new aliens, inviting Felicity to chat too. He was good at bringing her out of her shell, George noted. But then, he'd been expected to be nothing more than a figurehead for most of his life. Being *good* to people was all he'd been taught to do.

"That's the mess call," Prince Henry said, as a low whistle echoed through the compartment, cutting off the buzz of conversation. He held out an arm to George. "Shall we go?"

"Yes, Your Excellency," George said.

She took the opportunity to glance around for the other midshipmen. Frasier, it seemed, was sitting next to Felicity. She looked tiny against his massive frame, too intimidated to speak even as he walked her into the compartment. Henderson had been placed next to Lieutenant Watson, which had to be awkward; Paula was sitting next to one of the marine officers. And Potter, it seemed, was sitting next to the Chinese scientist. He was going to be unbearable for the next few days.

"Your uncle sends his regards," Prince Henry said. "I had a long chat with him last week."

"I haven't spoken to him since our last departure," George said. She'd half-hoped he'd speak with her when he'd visited *Vanguard*, a week after they'd returned to Earth, but he hadn't called for her. "What did he say?"

"We chatted about the war," Prince Henry said. "And politics. And family."

"You have children," George recalled. "How are they coping with Earth?"

"Complaining about the weather, mainly," Prince Henry said. He pulled out her chair, allowing her to seat herself, then took his own chair. "It's freezing cold as far as they are concerned."

George nodded. Tadpole Prime was hardly her idea of a prime vacation destination, but she could see why a gaggle of small children would love it. Endless beaches, bright sunlight…the ice cream never running out…she'd have loved it too, if she'd been eight when she'd gone there. And it was safe in a way that Earth could never be, even though the oceans were teeming with deadly animals.

"Maybe you should send them to Jamaica," she said, after a moment. "Or the Maldives."

"It has its attractions," Prince Henry said. He straightened up as the XO called for attention, his voice echoing around the compartment. "But it's really too far from Britain."

———

Susan had never been fond of formal dinners, although Hanover Towers had drilled comportment into her until she was incapable of making a mistake. And yet, she had never hosted one of her own until now. She'd passed most of the duties on to the mess officers, but she still found it stressful. There was an odd edge running through the room that bothered her, even though she couldn't put her finger on it.

"The midshipmen are a little stroppy," Paul Mason muttered. Her XO had clearly picked up the same vibes. "And I'd say they really need more supervision."

Susan frowned, her gaze easily picking out the midshipmen amongst the room. George Fitzwilliam looked...tense, while Clayton Henderson looked bored and Paula Spurgeon looked impassive. And Simon Potter seemed to be enjoying himself, laughing and flirting with one of the civilians, while Felicity Wheeler looked terrified.

"It isn't easy with four new midshipmen," she mused. "I only ever had to integrate two into middy country."

"Two of them should be making it easier for her," Mason observed. "But it doesn't look as though they are, does it?"

Susan nodded, slowly. She would have thought that a life in the aristocracy would have prepared George Fitzwilliam to issue orders, if nothing else, but it seemed that her preconceptions were ill-founded. George looked like a particularly harried mother, one whose teenage children routinely ignored her even though *she* suffered when they got into trouble. The dynamics of life as a midshipman could be harsh, at times - Susan had lost count of the number of times she'd had to fight to maintain her position - but matters definitely seemed to be getting out of hand.

Perhaps it was a mistake to promote Fraser, she thought, as the stewards brought the first course, a thick chicken and vegetable soup. *But he'd more than earned his promotion.*

She considered the options as she sipped her soup, quietly noting that all five of the midshipmen had decent table manners. But then, they'd had them battered into their heads at the Academy. Their instructors would not have hesitated to point out any mistakes as loudly as possible, just to show others just what mistakes *could* be made. This...this was different.

"We can't interfere openly," she muttered. "Can we?"

"No, Captain," Mason said. "It would be bad."

Susan nodded. A First Middy *could* call upon help from her superiors, if she needed it, but making the call could easily be seen as an admission of weakness. George Fitzwilliam was meant to wield authority, not go running to superior authority at the first hurdle. She might be right, she might need help...and yet it would cost her any real chance at promotion. If she couldn't handle a middy compartment, people would ask, why should she be trusted with an entire ship?

"Keep an eye on the situation," she ordered, finally. "And let me know if it gets any worse."

She felt her lips thin with disapproval as she eyed Midshipman Henderson. He might not be *interested* in his dinner companion, but he didn't seem to have the wit or the ability to feign interest in whatever she might say. There were commanding officers, she knew, who wouldn't hesitate to call a young officer on the carpet for such behaviour, along with his immediate superior. But George Fitzwilliam couldn't tell him off from halfway across the room, could she?

"We could always fiddle with the sleeping rotations," Mason suggested. "Put a couple of marine officers in Fraser's cabin and move him back to Middy Country. He'd still be a lieutenant, but he'd definitely be in charge."

"No," Susan said. It would be seen as a demotion for *both* Fraser and George Fitzwilliam, no matter what excuse they used. "She really needs some extra support."

She scowled as the stewards removed the soup bowls and brought out plates of roast beef and vegetables. She'd been First Middy...and she'd known she could trust the rest of the midshipmen to handle themselves, leaving her with the task of supervising one or two newcomers at a time. George Fitzwilliam...didn't have that luxury. She had to run around supervising all four of the newcomers, even though two of them had prior experience. No wonder she was looking ragged. If the handful of complaints Susan had heard were just the tip of the iceberg, her career was on a knife-edge.

"Put Potter in the tactical compartment full-time," Mason offered. "Jean can take care of him - and make sure he's worked to the bone."

"Maybe," Susan said. Perhaps she could rotate one of the midshipmen to *Edinburgh* or *Pinafore*, although she doubted that either Captain Stewart or Captain Garret would be happy with a midshipman in bad odour. "I'll give it some thought."

The rest of the meal went surprisingly well, much to her relief, until the toasts finally rolled around. Susan pretended not to see Lieutenant Fraser elbowing Felicity Wheeler, reminding her - as the youngest officer present - that it was her duty to call the toast to the king. The young midshipman's voice wobbled alarmingly as she spoke; Susan kept her face impassive as she saw the mingled horror and pity crossing George Fitzwilliam's face. There were captains who would have made the young girl repeat the toast again and again until she could offer it in a steady voice.

Not me, she told herself. *But what were they thinking at the Academy?*

"Go through her file with a fine-toothed comb," she ordered, as the dinner finally came to an end. "Find out what - if any - concerns were noted by her tutors."

"Aye, Captain," Mason said.

Susan nodded as she called for port, then rose, signifying that the formal side of the dinner was now over. It was a grave breach of etiquette to leave before the dinner was formally finished, although neither she nor any other commanding officer worthy of the name would have objected in a genuine emergency. The vindictive part of her mind was tempted to stay for a great deal longer, just to force the midshipmen to stay in the compartment with her, but she dismissed the thought as unworthy of her. Instead, she paused long enough to exchange a few words with Prince Henry, then left the compartment. Her departure signified that the other guests could leave at will.

And Paul will make sure they are entertained, she thought, crossly. She hated the thought of her crew having problems, although she knew their problems paled in comparison to the ones she'd faced with Captain Blake. *I just wish I could do something.*

She strode into her cabin, took a mug of tea from the dispenser and sat down at her desk, calling up the middy files one by one. Both Simon Potter and Paula Spurgeon had files that suggested that what *wasn't* said was more interesting than what *was* said, although there was tantalisingly little detail she could use to start unlocking the mystery. Paula, judging by what *was* said, had managed to get her fingers burned rather badly. The confidential notes attached to her file made it clear that one more screw-up and she'd be looking at a permanent assignment to some lonely asteroid colony, if she wasn't unceremoniously discharged from the navy. Susan wondered, absently, just why she hadn't *already* been discharged and flicked through the file until she found her answer. Paula Spurgeon's stats were good, *very* good. It was hard to imagine that she hadn't been on the fast track to promotion before she fell off the rails.

Silly girl, Susan thought. *And what about your friend, Mr. Potter?*

The file was not particularly illuminating. Potter's career had been standard, thoroughly standard; he'd left the Academy two years ago and posted to HMS *Firebrand* as a junior middy. There were no major comments on his file, but she couldn't help feeling - reading his efficiency reports - that something had been left out. His reports neither recommended him for immediate promotion, on the grounds he could walk on water, or counselled against it. It suggested, to her, that his superiors hadn't known what to make of him.

We'll just have to see what happens, Susan thought. *And then we can decide what to do.*

But she couldn't escape the feeling, as she closed the terminal and headed to her bunk, that by the time something happened it would be too late to escape the worst.

———

"I think I'm a little drunk," Doctor Song said. The midshipman standing beside her put out an arm to hold her steady as she swayed. "I think I drank a little too much."

"It certainly seems that way," Henry said. For someone who claimed not to drink, Doctor Song had definitely drunk enough to make her more than a little tipsy. "I think you'd better come with me, doctor."

The midshipman looked surprised. "I can walk her back to her cabin, Your Excellency," he said. "It's my duty as her dinner partner."

Henry was tempted, but he shook his head. Doctor Song was already drunk enough to make a whole series of foolish decisions - and he doubted a young man could be trusted not to take advantage of them. Henry knew just what sort of arsehole he'd been at twenty - or however old the midshipman was - and his behaviour hadn't always been the best. Part of it had been the certain knowledge that the media would see to it that everything he did would be looked at in the worst possible way, but the rest of it - if he had been forced to be honest - had been youthful hormones mixed with alcohol.

"I'll take her," he said. He frowned in disapproval as Doctor Song kissed the midshipman on the cheek. "Dismissed, Midshipman."

Technically, he had no authority to dismiss anyone, but the midshipman merely bowed and retreated back to his fellows. Henry watched him go - there was something a little *too* smooth about the young man for his peace of mind - and then took Doctor Song's arm, helping her to walk through the hatch. She giggled and swayed against him as he led her down the corridor, his body sending pointed signals reminding him that he wasn't exactly an old man *just* yet. He reminded himself, savagely, that he was a married man. And even if he hadn't been, taking advantage of a drunk woman was beneath him.

"It was a hell of a party," Doctor Song pronounced, as they finally reached her cabin. "What do we do now?"

"You go to bed," Henry said, firmly. There would be a sober-up pill in the medicine cabinet, unless he missed his guess, but she'd probably be better sleeping it off naturally. "I think you had *far* too much to drink."

Doctor Song winked at him. "Are you going to undress me and put me to bed?"

"No," Henry said. Perhaps he *should* give her the pill after all. Only the memories of spending far too long throwing up everything he'd eaten after drinking himself silly convinced him otherwise. "You're going to stay in your cabin and sleep it off."

He closed the hatch, then keyed his wristcom. It wouldn't be hard to ask one of the research staff to keep an eye on her, even though she was technically their superior. She'd be dreadfully embarrassed in the morning, but at least she'd be alive. And she hadn't spent the night dancing naked on a table. The memory of the party his comrades had thrown, after they'd graduated as starfighter pilots, still made him smile. They'd assumed that they wouldn't survive the war...

...And far too many of them had been right.

The thought sobered him, although he hadn't really drunk enough to feel more than a pleasant buzz. He'd thought of himself as immortal, as a young man, but he'd come far too close to death before the war had come to an end. And now, as an older man with children of his own, he was going back to war. His life could come to an end in the twinkling of an eye.

And the brunt will be borne by the young, once again, he thought, as he headed back to his cabin. *And how many of the officers we dined with will survive?*

CHAPTER
THIRTEEN

George had often, far too often, felt a strange sinking feeling as a teenager when she'd been called to the headmistress's office. She'd known she was in trouble, she'd often known *why* she was in trouble, but it hadn't quite felt *real* until she'd been standing in front of the headmistress's desk, listening to her describing George's latest atrocity against all that was good and decent. Whatever else could be said about Mrs. Blackthorn, a sour-faced old prune if ever there was one, she was *good* at making an illicit midnight feast sound like a crime worthy of good old-fashioned hanging.

And now, looking at the efficiency report, she had the same sinking feeling.

Clayton Henderson was lazy. It was the only word she could think of to describe him, after looking at his reports. The ship had been away from Earth for a week, yet he'd been late to his duty stations five times and some of his maintenance work had been delayed. And even though she'd assigned punishment duty, he'd skimped on that too. The toilets hadn't been cleaned anything like as often as she would have preferred.

She rubbed her forehead, miserably. The XO should have noticed by now. Hell, she was surprised that some of the department heads hadn't already brought the matter to his attention, given how badly it impinged on them. They'd certainly not hesitated to chew *George* out over it, point-ing out that - as his immediate superior - it was her job to make sure that Henderson reached his duty assignments on time. And if Felicity hadn't been double-checking his maintenance work, George would have had her concerns about that too.

Fuck, she thought. Maybe she *could* just ask to be beached...but that would be nothing more than surrender. She had no doubt that Potter would pile all the shit duties on her, just to make it clear that he - not she - ruled the roost. And yet, with the way things were going, she doubted she could stave off disaster indefinitely. *Once the XO takes a good hard look at our stats, I'm fucked.*

She glanced at her terminal, checking the duty assignments. Henderson should have been back by now, but it was quite possible - if he'd been late again - that he'd been kept back, just like a naughty schoolboy. George pursed her lips at the thought, irritated. Henderson was twenty-two years old and had four years at the Academy under his belt. Any laziness should have been driven out of him by the end of his first year. God knew the tutors hadn't gone easy on a senior admiral's niece. George had worked off so many demerits in her first year that she'd half-feared she would be permanently trapped on punishment duty.

They wanted to knock the arrogance out of me, she recalled. The tutors had made it clear that an aristocratic name was no protection against the cold equations. *And yet I had no arrogance.*

The hatch opened. She looked up, just in time to see Henderson stride into the cabin and head straight for his bunk. Felicity followed him, looking as tired as George felt. She hadn't had an easy time of it, after the captain's dinner. Potter had hammered the correct way to offer a toast into her head and George, to her shame, had just let it happen. It hadn't seemed worth fighting over, not at the time. But now...

She stood. "With me," she snapped. She fixed Henderson with her stare as Felicity started, then wisely hurried to her bunk. "Now!"

"But I need to..."

"With me," George snarled. She gave him a look that cut off whatever pathetic excuse he'd meant to offer. "*Now!*"

She turned and led the way out of the hatch, stepping into the wardroom. Potter was sitting there, reading a datapad; she ordered him out of the compartment, hoping he'd have the sense to leave Middy Country entirely. God knew he'd spent entirely too much time mooning after the pretty researcher, although at least it *did* keep him out of her hair.

"Sit," she ordered, as she closed and locked the hatch. "What the hell are you thinking?"

Henderson looked up at her, indolently. "About what?"

George pulled the datapad from her belt and threw it onto the table. "You have been late for duty at least five times since we left Earth," she said. Her voice rose until she was almost shouting. "And it has been reported. What the hell are you thinking?"

"I do my duty," Henderson said.

"You are not…you are not a writer, someone who can pick his job up or put it down whenever he wishes," George snapped. She wondered, with a savagery that surprised her, just how much trouble she could get into if she slammed his head into the metal table. "You are *expected* to arrive at your duty station on time and do your fucking job! You do *not* get any fucking kudos for doing your job when it suits you! You do it when I tell you to do it!"

She closed her eyes for a long moment, fighting to keep her voice calm. "How many times are we going to have this discussion?"

Henderson opened his mouth, but George spoke over him. "Let me tell you," she snarled, clenching her fists in rage. She didn't even try to hide her anger. "We're not - because the next fucking time you screw up like this, word will get to the XO. And you know what that will do to you?"

She gripped the table to keep herself from lashing out at him. "I know what you're thinking," she insisted. She allowed her voice to become mocking. "You're thinking that the dumb bitch who lucked her way into becoming First Middy won't *dare* to take the matter to the XO. You're thinking that tattling on you will ruin her career. And you know what - you might be *right*! It *could* cost me my career."

Her eyes met Henderson's, daring him to speak. "I'll go to the XO anyway," she added. She wanted him - needed him - to believe her. "I can't win, not now. There's no way to come out of this without looking very bad, so I'll do the right damned thing and report you. Because there's nothing else I can do."

Henderson started. "But…"

"But nothing," George said. If she had to scream at him, she'd scream at him. "I don't understand why you're so fucking lazy. And I don't understand how you managed to get through the Academy while being so lazy. And I don't care what bullshit excuses you have to justify your failings! All I care about is whipping this damned department into shape!"

She fought hard to control her temper. "If you are late for your next duty station, I will go straight to the XO," she said. "And yes, it may cost me my position. I don't fucking care any longer. You're going to blow my career out of the water anyway."

Her voice hardened. "And after we have both lost our careers," she added, "I'm going to make sure that you never have a career again."

Henderson's eyes went wide. "But..."

"I have connections," George hissed. She felt dirty for even saying it, as if she'd crossed a line she knew she shouldn't even *approach*, but there was no choice. "You've looked up my record, haven't you? Or were you too lazy to even do that?"

She went on before he could muster a response. "I could get you fired and blacklisted right across the Human Sphere," she added. "You won't even be able to get a job flipping vat-grown algae burgers in a McDonald-Wimpy grease pit! Your prospective employers will take one look at your record and tell you to fuck off. And don't you *dare* think I wouldn't do it! You'll end your days on a work gang for non-payment of debts because you *certainly* won't be able to claim government support!"

Henderson swallowed. "I..."

"Shut up," George said. She allowed her voice to turn deadly cold. "There won't be any second chances, not now, not ever. Fuck up one final time and you'll be fucked up for good, understand? Now get the fuck out of my sight!"

She sat back on the chair as Henderson stumbled to his feet and hurried out of the compartment, his face ashen. George stared down at her hands, wondering if she'd *definitely* crossed a line. She'd never threatened *Fraser* with her powerful relatives, even when he was bullying her savagely. But then, she'd never threatened his career. A First Middy couldn't really get in trouble for being over-zealous. And it would have been hard to blame him for being furious if she hadn't handled her duties properly.

Damn it, she thought.

There was no escaping it. She *had* crossed a line. She'd made it clear, to Henderson, that she could and she would use influence and power that had nothing to do with her rank and position on the battleship. And now that she'd drawn that sword, using it again and again would be inhumanly tempting. She wondered how easy it would be to threaten Potter, to cow him so badly he never made another snide remark. It would be easy to turn into a spoilt brat...

...And it would be the end of her.

Uncle James would not be amused, she thought, as she heard someone approaching the open hatch. *And he'd see to it that I never commanded anyone, ever again.*

"George," Potter said. For once, his voice sounded normal. George eyed him suspiciously anyway. "I hear that you gave Henderson a right bollocking."

"No more than he deserved," George said, tartly. She wondered idly how he knew. The compartment was supposed to be soundproofed... maybe he'd just put two and two together and come up with four. She *had* kicked him out of the wardroom, after all. "What do you want?"

"To help," Potter said.

George scowled at him. "I thought you were too busy chasing your girlfriend," she said, nastily. She had no idea if Potter's relationship with the researcher was anything more than talk - if all the barracks room banter she'd heard had been true, no one would have had time for any actual work - but she found it hard to care. "Do you have any time to help?"

"I always have time for a pretty girl," Potter said. He winked, broadly enough to make her want to hit him. "And it's clear to me that you *do* need help."

"Fuck off," George said. She was so *tired*. "I don't need *your* help."

"Yes, you do," Potter said. "Let me take charge of Clayton, eh? I can make sure he gets to his assignments on time."

Or make sure he doesn't, because I will still get the blame, George thought. *It isn't as if I can authorise him to do anything.*

She forced herself to think, despite the tiredness pervading her entire body. Potter wasn't making the offer out of the goodness of his heart - she rather doubted he *had* any goodness in his heart. He wanted to embarrass her or to break her - and all he would have to do was nothing. And Henderson would be...resistant...to the suggestion he should obey a fellow midshipman, certainly one who wasn't First Middy. She wouldn't put it past him to openly defy Potter...

...And, just incidentally, ensure that George's career ended up in the crapper.

She picked up the datapad and checked the timetable. Perhaps, if she altered her own schedule a little, she could wake up with Henderson and frog-march him to his duty station before running to her own. But it would rapidly become impossible to balance both his assignments and hers, not when the ship was so shorthanded. It would be *her* who arrived at her station late, her who faced the XO when more complaints were filed.

"I can do it," Potter said. "You have my word."

"No, thank you," George said, sharply. "I've already had a nasty word with him."

Potter smirked. "And how effective was it the *last* time you had a word with him."

"Fuck off," George ordered.

She rose, picking up the datapad and returning it to her belt. The hell of it was that Potter had given her an idea. She could ask *Paula* to keep an eye on Henderson - her duty schedule wasn't quite aligned with Henderson's, but it was close enough to allow her to supervise him and make sure he made it to his duty station on time. And Paula, her career already at risk, would have an *excellent* reason to make sure she did as she was told. She'd go down with George and Henderson if all hell broke loose.

Potter looked as if he wanted to say something else, but clearly thought better of it. George was relieved. The urge to punch him was overwhelmingly powerful, even though she knew it would start a fight or get her in very hot water. She honestly didn't know what was stopping her, beyond sheer tiredness.

I'll have to talk Fraser into more lessons, she thought. Hand-to-hand combat was *good* for burning off stress. *And then I will have to find time to actually take them.*

She followed Potter out of the wardroom and then into the bunk-room. Henderson was nowhere to be seen - she wasn't sure if that was a good thing or not. His next duty assignment was in six hours and he really should be getting some sleep before he went on duty. But if she'd scared him so badly...

He could have problems adjusting to the new schedule, she thought, crossly. The Academy operated on a very regular schedule, but a warship couldn't afford the luxury. *But he could have told me about them and we could have worked out a solution.*

She stripped down, stepped into the shower compartment for a brief wash and then climbed into her bunk and set the alarm without bothering to get dressed. Potter hadn't even bothered with the shower before getting into *his* bunk, although she supposed it didn't matter. He had *seven* hours before his next duty assignment, the lucky bastard. Six hours of sleep, then one hour to shower and snatch something to eat...absolute heaven. She pulled the cover over the bunk, throwing the tiny space into darkness, then closed her eyes.

Happiness consists of getting enough sleep, she reminded herself, as she drifted off into a pleasant haze. Her tutors had told her that, time and time again. *And none of us are really getting enough...*

She jerked awake, five and a half hours later. *Something* had disturbed her, even though she wasn't sure what. It felt like she was standing watch at the Academy, half-asleep before hearing someone - or something - inching towards her. And yet...she tensed, wishing suddenly that she had a weapon. Henderson would have to be out of his mind to actually *attack* her, particularly without a formal challenge, but she'd threatened him with complete disgrace...

"Shower, then get to your damned duty station," a tired voice said. It took George a moment to recognise Potter, if only because the voice was almost unrecognisable. "You're on thin ice as it is!"

"But I need to *sleep*," Henderson whined. "I do..."

"Go now," Potter said, sharply. "Or are you a *complete* idiot?"

George didn't relax, even when she heard Henderson making his way into the shower and slamming the hatch closed. Was Potter trying to help? Or was he humiliating her by showing that *he* could boss Henderson around? She still wasn't sure just what had woken her from a sound sleep. Four years at the Academy had taught her how to sleep through a bunk-mate playing heavy metal and two more chatting loudly without stirring from her slumber. Had Potter woken her deliberately, against all etiquette? Or was she just being paranoid? She had no way to know.

Damn it, she thought. She reached for her wristcom and checked the time. Technically, she had another hour before she had to get up and eat before going back on duty, but she knew she wouldn't be able to get back to sleep. *Damn it to hell.*

She waited until Henderson had left the compartment - he was cutting it fine, although he *should* be able to make it to the tactical department in time - and then slid out of her bunk, dropping down neatly to the deck. Potter had gone back to sleep and was snoring loudly; beneath him, Felicity was sleeping quietly, without the sound effects. There was no sign of Paula, but - if George remembered correctly - she didn't get off duty for another hour.

On impulse, she glanced into Henderson's bunk as she strode to the lockers. His bedding was a mess, even though they'd been taught to make their beds every morning at the Academy before going to the mess hall for breakfast. She sighed, wishing she'd thought to make an issue of that when they'd arrived. Fraser had been keen that standards were maintained and he'd made sure the other midshipmen kept the beds neat and tidy. She'd just have to take it up with them later.

She dressed quickly, then headed for the hatch. A quick bite to eat and a coffee or two…then she could go back on duty. And who knew? Maybe she'd scared Henderson straight. If he didn't give her any more trouble, maybe she could explain his early problems as him trying to get used to a starship and irregular timetables. It might just work…

Sure, she told herself. *And maybe the horse will learn to sing.*

CHAPTER
FOURTEEN

"Tactical simulation online, Captain," Mason said. "I have the conn."

"You have the conn," Susan acknowledged, as she settled into the secondary bridge's command chair. "Alert me if anything changes."

She looked at Jean Granger. "Link us into the fleet-wide tactical simulation," she ordered, curtly. "And authorise the flag to activate the simulation at their discretion."

"Aye, Captain," the tactical officer said. "Simulation active...now."

George sucked in her breath as red icons flashed into existence on the display. Seventeen alien starships; three battleships, two carriers and twelve smaller vessels, flanked by an impressive swarm of starfighters. Intelligence had asserted, after analysing the first engagements extensively, that the newcomer starfighter technology was no match for humanity's, but they made up for that with aggressive tactics and a terrifying willingness to take losses. And their carriers seemed to carry two extra squadrons of starfighters...

They may feel that carriers are best employed hanging back from the wall of battle, she thought, as orders began to come in from the flag. Admiral Harper saw no reason to avoid battle, steering his squadron directly towards the enemy ships. *And we'll have to punch through their battleline to get to their carriers.*

"The carriers are launching their starfighters," Granger said. "The flag is ordering them to cover the task force."

Susan nodded. It was a fairly conventional posture, but with humanity's pilots badly outnumbered it was the best thing they could do. She might have considered ordering her starfighters to attack the alien carriers, if she'd been in command, yet the enemy would probably have doubled-back to cover their carriers while leaving their battleships to engage the human battleships. Keeping their starfighters off the battleships might seem a worthwhile use of their time.

"Stand by point defence," she ordered. "Prepare to engage."

She sucked in her breath as the alien ships belched missiles, each one moving an order of magnitude faster than any observed alien threat. The tactical analysts believed in posing threats that outdid *real* threats, on the grounds that anyone who could handle the simulations could certainly handle real life, but she'd always found it more than a little annoying. Their assumptions about alien capabilities might be badly off.

And no one has duplicated the range enhancers they use on their bomb-pumped lasers, she thought, grimly. *Who knows what else they have in their bag of tricks?*

"Order the kinetic point defence to engage," she ordered.

"Aye, Captain," Granger said.

Susan leaned forward as the buckshot cannons began to spit their tiny projectiles towards the enemy missiles. The enemy might think they had a range advantage, but they were in for a nasty surprise - unless, of course, they'd anticipated the countermeasure. Their sensors probably wouldn't pick up the buckshot - it was completely inert - but even the slightest evasive manoeuvre would be more than enough to save their missiles from destruction.

She smiled, coldly, as several of the red icons blinked out of existence, the remainder burning time and energy as they took evasive action. New targeting solutions popped up on the display as the tactical computers struggled to pick off the remaining missiles, but Susan doubted the umpires would allow the computers *too* many successes. Randomising the missile trajectories alone would make it harder to score a direct hit, although it wasn't as if the ship was in any real danger of running out of buckshot. A couple of hours spent mining an asteroid would more than suffice to replenish the expended projectiles.

"Enemy missiles entering attack range," Jean Granger reported. "They're targeting us..."

"All hands, brace for impact," Susan snapped. "I say again, all hands brace for impact."

Red lights flared up on the display as the warheads detonated, each one sending a stabbing ray of death towards their targets. *Vanguard* took four direct hits, the armour deflecting two of them and isolating the effects of the third. But the fourth struck a turret and knocked it out, the crew scrambling to escape before the entire section had to be sealed off. Susan scowled, grimly. The tactical planners had practically copied the damage her ship had taken during the first *real* engagement!"

"Turret Three is out of action," the engineer reported. "Damage control teams are on their way."

"Enemy ships entering engagement range," Reed added.

"Signal from the flag," Parkinson said. "All ships are to open fire."

"Open fire," Susan ordered. "And go to rapid fire as soon as the range closes."

She cursed under her breath as the three battleships spat death towards their targets, knowing all too well that most of the missiles would be completely wasted. The enemy point defence was good, very good; human missiles had to get closer before they could engage the enemy, giving the bastards more time to knock the missiles out of space. And the umpires were definitely on their side. Only a tenth of the missiles survived long enough to detonate; only a handful of the detonated missiles actually inflicted any real damage. The enemy were still coming.

"Switch to plasma cannons," she ordered, as the range closed still further. "Tactical, mark your man, then open fire."

The alien ships opened fire at the same moment, rolling over and over as they spat plasma fire towards the human ships. Susan noted, absently, that a dozen starfighters had simply vanished in the flurry, wiped out in passing as the capital ships fought to hammer each other into scrap. And yet, both sides had armoured their ships as much as possible. The damage they could inflict was very limited.

"Set missiles to blunderbuss pattern, on my authority and fire on my mark," she ordered, grimly. She keyed a command into her console, overriding the safeguards. "Fire."

"Aye, Captain," Granger said. "Missiles away…"

Susan allowed herself a savage moment of triumph as the missiles struck deep into the enemy's vitals, sending the entire battleship rolling away, streams of plasma and atmosphere pouring from her wounded hull. Granger didn't let up, unleashing a spread of nuclear missiles as the enemy ship fought to survive, the warheads slipping through the defences and detonating *inside* the enemy hull. The aliens built their ships to last, Susan had to admit, but it was too late. A chain of explosions blew the alien ship into debris.

"Signal from the flag," Parkinson said. "The Admiral wants us to assist *New York*."

"Acknowledge," Susan ordered. "Helm, move us into firing position."

She felt her smile grow wider as the three human battleships systematically pounded the alien ships into scrap. The aliens didn't run, even though they were outnumbered and outgunned; they held the line even as their damage started to mount up savagely. And then one of the alien battleships lurched forward, aiming directly at *Indianapolis*. Susan opened her mouth to shout a useless warning, but it was already far too late. The two battleships collided and vanished in an eye-tearing explosion.

"*Indianapolis* is gone," Granger reported. "I'm not picking up any lifepods."

Susan nodded, harshly. The Americans hadn't had *time* to get to the lifepods, even if they'd had time to realise their danger. And the remaining alien battleship was making its way towards *New York*. She barked a command and *Vanguard* rolled in space, bringing its turrets to bear on the alien ship. It was torn to ribbons before it could ram *New York*.

"The alien carriers are retreating," Granger said.

Of course they are, Susan thought. *They know they can't stop us now.*

She mentally tallied up the results, cursing under her breath. The good guys had lost a battleship and seen two more heavily damaged. *Vanguard* would need at least a week of repair work before she was ready to go back into action - and there was no way they could replace the lost turret without a shipyard. She glanced at *New York's* stats and frowned, again. The Americans hadn't lost a turret, but they'd definitely need to replace some of their armour before they went back into battle. And five smaller ships and thirty-seven starfighters had been lost. She'd been so fixated on the main engagement that she hadn't even *noticed*.

"Signal from the flag," Parkinson reported. "The exercise is terminated."

"Acknowledged," Susan said. She resisted, barely, the urge to rub her forehead. "Send copies of our records to the flag, then report to the mess for tea and coffee."

She watched the consoles go dark - the secondary bridge would have to be reconnected to the ship's control network, once the emergency crew had retaken their posts - then rose and headed to the hatch. Admiral Harper had made it clear that there wouldn't be any more formal gatherings before they reached Unity - the task force needed to progress as fast as it could - but he'd want to discuss the engagement in great detail. And then the analysts would tell them just what they'd done wrong.

And show us how they slanted the dice against us, she thought, darkly. *If they're wrong about alien capabilities, we might be in for a very nasty surprise.*

Her steward had left a pot of coffee on her desk, waiting for her. She poured herself a cup, then tapped the terminal, linking into the squadron command datanet. Admiral Harper was already calling for a conference, something she approved of. They'd have a chance to go over their mistakes before they forgot what they'd been thinking at the time. Hindsight was always clearer than foresight, but it wasn't an advantage anyone actually had during a battle.

"Susan," Admiral Harper said, as his holographic image appeared in front of her. "I'm afraid Captain Trodden will be buying the beer."

Susan snorted in amusement, although she knew it wasn't really funny. Actually *ramming* another starship was rare, particularly when the other ship's crew were alert. It had only happened once in actual combat, as far as she knew, when *Ark Royal* had rammed the very first Tadpole superdreadnaught and destroyed both ships. But losing a simulated battleship would be quite enough to get Captain Trodden in hot water. She was mildly surprised that Admiral Harper hadn't summoned Trodden to *New York* for the sole purpose of tearing him a new arsehole.

But the Yanks wouldn't want to wash their dirty underwear in front of us, she thought, as the other holograms blinked into existence. *Any post-engagement screaming fits will be held in the strictest privacy.*

"Thank you all for coming," Harper said. "As you can see, that was an...*interesting*...engagement."

"It could have been worse," Jeanette pointed out. "We *did* win."

"Technically," Keith Glass said. "We lost a battleship and had the other two heavily damaged. If we were deep in enemy space...well, I wouldn't care to have to fight my way back out again."

Susan nodded in agreement. "And the enemy carriers escaped," she added. "They could harass us from a safe distance, if they wished."

"Then we sneak around and engage them from the rear," Yegorovich proclaimed. The Russian seemed pleased with himself. A quick look at the stats told Susan that his pilots had done *very* well. "Losing a single battleship is hardly a disaster."

"Five thousand officers and men were killed - would have been killed, if it were *real*," Trodden said, crossly. "And we would have lost a third of our mobile firepower."

"It would have been worse if Susan hadn't thought to use missiles at an insanely close range," Glass pointed out. "We need to use that tactic in combat."

"They'll use it too," Captain Stewart warned.

"They have the technology," Glass said. "I'm sure they'll have thought of it."

Harper looked at her. "Susan?"

"It is a risk," Susan said. "But one we have to take."

She smiled as she studied the records. The boffins *had* come up with a single-shot bomb-pumped x-ray laser cannon, but the navy had rejected the concept on the grounds it was too dangerous. A single accident would have inflicted horrendous damage on the ship - and even without the accident, the firing system would have to be discarded immediately anyway. It wouldn't be hard to toss the radioactive chamber into a nearby star - fission power had been making a comeback since disposing of the waste had become remarkably easy - but it was still a cumbersome weapon.

"The analysts are already studying the engagement," Harper said, changing the subject as he looked around. "But do any of you have any issues we need to consider?"

"Our starfighters were largely wasted," Yegorovich said, flatly. "While we did kill over forty enemy starfighters, their contribution to the battle was minimal. They could have been considerably more usefully employed by a more aggressive commander."

Susan frowned and Glass looked angry, but Harper's image showed no visible reaction.

"They could have been sent against the alien carriers," he said, calmly. "But the aliens would merely have recalled their own starfighters..."

"We would still have a chance to take out their carriers before they could evade retribution," Yegorovich said. "A single warhead inside their launch tubes would be more than enough to make them think again."

He leaned forward, threateningly. "I understand the impulse to protect our capital ships," he added, "but these are not the days when carriers were so thin-skinned that a single plasma bolt could do very real damage. The task force could and did look after itself while the starfighters fought their own battle. Sending them against the enemy carriers would give them a chance to make a valid contribution."

And bring more glory to you, Susan thought.

But the hell of it, she had to admit, was that Yegorovich had a point. Unless the enemy's industrial and manpower base was *far* inferior to humanity's, replacing starfighters and their pilots wouldn't take very long at all. The Royal Navy had built up a reserve of starfighters over the past decade anyway, anticipating another conflict that would cost the starfighter pilots heavily. There was no reason to believe that the new enemies wouldn't have done the same, particularly if they'd been preparing for war for years.

But it would take far longer to replace a carrier, she thought. *And losing our entire starfighter complement in exchange for their carriers might well work out in our favour.*

She sighed, cursing their ignorance. There was no way to know if taking out two enemy carriers would degrade the enemy's order of battle by ten percent, one percent or point one percent. They had no fleet list; they didn't even have any hard data on the enemy's economic capability and what it *should* be capable of producing. But if the enemy had thousands of battleships, the war was within shouting distance of being lost anyway. *Humanity* didn't have thousands of battleships.

"We will certainly consider altering their priorities," Harper said, dragging her mind back to the meeting. "But we are mounting a long-term campaign, not an all-or-nothing engagement."

He glanced around the compartment, then went on. "Overall, we worked together better than I had expected, for a first engagement," he added. "We *do* need to work on our point defence datanet - several ships fell out of the network as the engagement heated up - but overall we have a solid base for our operations. The only real concern is a knife-range engagement that will give the enemy a chance to ram us."

"But a long-range engagement is likely to be nothing more than spitting at one another," Jeanette objected. "Even if we launch missiles on ballistic trajectories, they'll have plenty of time to evade or return fire."

"We'd be spitting into the wind," Captain Stewart agreed.

"We *do* have four squadrons of torpedo-bombers," Yegorovich pointed out. "A long-range engagement isn't going to be a complete disaster."

"Except that it will cost us badly," Harper said.

"Starfighters are expendable," Yegorovich snapped.

"We have no way to replace our losses," Harper said. His face darkened noticeably. "And even if we did, I would not spend any lives casually."

He cleared his throat. "Tomorrow, we will run another series of exercises - and we will *continue* exercising until we reach the border," he added. "I want all of you to concentrate on your internal exercises too. There is no way we will *not* take damage and I want your crews ready to react to it.

"But on the whole, we did fairly well," he added. "Dismissed."

His image popped out of existence, followed by the others. Susan sat back at her desk, then glanced at her terminal. The first set of reports were already waiting in her inbox, noting that *Vanguard's* damage-control teams had been badly hampered by the crowded corridors. No one had actually been injured, thankfully, but that wasn't going to last. Someone could be run over by a worker gurney and lose a leg, if they weren't careful.

Or worse, she thought. She'd heard quite a few horror stories about reporters who'd been seriously injured on warships, simply by not paying attention to safety regulations. It was hard to care about reporters - she'd heard too many horror stories from Prince Henry - but her crew were a different matter. *A crewman could end up dead - or we could fail to seal off a compartment in time. And that would cause all sorts of problems.*

She skimmed through the remainder of the reports, then rose. She'd discuss the entire engagement with the XO and see if they could find a way to cope with the excess personnel, even if that meant bunking the soldiers in Middy Country. It would be against tradition, but it would get at least *some* of them out of the way. And it might help solve some of the other problems too.

"Mr. XO," she said, keying her wristcom. "Please join me in my cabin when your duty shift ends."

"Aye, Captain," Mason said. "I'll see you there in thirty minutes."

CHAPTER
FIFTEEN

"You're not concentrating," Fraser said. She jabbed a messy punch at him, which he avoided with ease. "And you're more focused on your anger than on beating me."

George clenched her teeth, knowing he was trying to get on her nerves, and lunged forward, hoping to catch him by surprise. Fraser caught her arm and sent her toppling to the padded mat, wrenching her arm behind her and pinning it to the small of her back. George struggled helplessly, but he held her down effortlessly while he counted down from ten. She couldn't even get her other arm out and flail at him aimlessly. He'd won.

"I think I win," Fraser said, when he reached zero. "And you are…"

"He *thinks* he won," a new voice said. "He's got her trapped and helpless and yet he isn't *sure* he's won?"

George twisted her head. Two marines were standing by the side of the mat, looking down at them. She felt her face redden as Fraser let go of her, allowing her to roll over and sit upright. Her arm hurt - she was all too aware that he could have snapped it easily - but otherwise she wasn't sore. Somehow, that only made losing worse. The marines smiled at her, then nodded to Fraser. They seemed more *respectful* than Henderson or Potter.

"George, this is Corporal Christopher Byron and Private Frederick Stott," Fraser said. "Both fighters of great distinction…"

"And I had the pleasure of breaking his nose last week," Byron said. He was a short, muscular man; Stott, standing next to him, was tall and lanky.

But they wouldn't have qualified as marines if they hadn't been immensely competitive. "The Major told us he was the bee's knees."

"The Major hates my guts," Fraser said, mischievously. George, who knew it was a flat-out lie, rolled her eyes. "And he sent you to teach me a lesson."

"I did," Byron said. "Don't try to wrestle with someone who was *born* wrestling in the mud."

Fraser nodded, then rose and helped George to her feet. "I'd stay, but I need to have a long chat with George," he said. "But I'll see you here tomorrow?"

"It's a date," Stott said. He had a gruff accent, one George couldn't place. "I'll alert the doctor."

"Come on," Fraser said, nodding to George. "Shower, then we can chat."

George nodded. If there was one advantage to using the exercise compartments in Marine Country, it was access to their showers - and the marines had no water rations. She could luxuriate in the water for over ten minutes, washing the sweat from her body...heaven. But she had a droll feeling that the Major would have complained if she spent *too* long in the showers. She washed quickly, dried herself and then pulled her tunic back on. Beside her, Fraser did the same.

"So," he said, once they'd left Marine Country and walked to his cabin. "What's bothering you?"

George eyed him. "Is it so obvious, sir?"

"You've been looking tense all week," Fraser said. "And you let your temper drive you forward in the ring."

He met her eyes. "What's wrong?"

"I think I'm losing control of Middy Country," George said, reluctantly. Fraser could be a font of helpful advice, but he had a duty to report matters to the XO if he felt they were too far out of hand. "And I may have screwed up quite badly."

"You haven't been beached for a year, so you haven't screwed up *that* badly," Fraser pointed out, dryly. He poured two cups of tea and pressed one into her hand. "What happened?"

George sighed. "Let's see...Henderson has been late for his duty assignments five times, perhaps more," she said. "Potter is planning a coup, to all intents and purposes; Felicity is such a freaking doormat that she does whatever she's told…"

She shook her head. "Paula is the only one who is even *remotely* reliable and even she is…cold," she added. "I just have the impression she doesn't…she doesn't have any feelings for me."

Fraser lifted his eyebrows. "You *want* her to have feelings for you?"

George flushed. "Not like that, sir," she said. "She just…she just doesn't seem to care one way or the other."

"I see," Fraser said. He peered down at the table for a long moment as she sipped her tea. "I have a question. How do you *know* that being late isn't Henderson's only problem?"

"I…I don't, sir," George said. "If he's having problems adapting to shipboard life…"

"That's not what I meant," Fraser said. "You've got him doing maintenance work, right? Do you actually know he's doing it?"

George felt a shiver running down her spine. "His work is double-checked…"

Her voice tailed off. "By Felicity," she said. "I haven't checked his work myself."

Fraser gave her a sharp look. "Perhaps you should," he said. "I used to check *your* work."

"I know," George said. "I…how would *you* cope with Potter?"

"Beat the shit out of him," Fraser said, frankly. "But I suppose you can't do that, can you?"

"I might lose," George said.

"*Not* standing up to him won't make things any better," Fraser said. "And if he becomes First Middy, Henderson will become *his* problem."

George had to smile. "I don't want to lose the position, sir," she said. "And…"

Fraser reached out and tapped her shoulder, meaningfully. "You would hardly be the first midshipman to lose the position," he pointed out. "If a new middy with two years seniority were to join us, George, you'd be kicked down the ladder."

"I know," George said. "That would be a honourable way out, wouldn't it?"

"Yeah," Fraser said. "But until that happens...you need to decide just how far you're prepared to go to keep the position."

George sighed. She'd challenged Fraser, at least in part, because she'd thought she had nothing to lose. If she won, he'd leave her in peace; if she lost, things couldn't get any worse. But now...if she won, Potter would *still* worm away at her position, while if she lost she'd practically *give* him the post on a platter. He had her whichever way she turned...

...And nothing he'd done was against regulations.

"Thanks," she said. She finished her tea, silently grateful that she had another couple of hours before she needed to report for duty. She'd planned to catch a nap, but she suspected her time would be better spent checking Henderson's work. "Do you think there's something wrong with him?"

Fraser looked up. "Potter? There are always some manipulative little shits who want power and aren't fussy about how they get it," he said. "They know the rules backwards and forwards and won't hesitate to twist them out of shape to get what they want. And the ones with nerve, as well as intelligence, are always the most dangerous. Potter seems to be one of the worst."

"I meant Henderson," George said. She didn't like to think of Potter as being *brave*, although she had to admit he had both courage and cunning. "Do you think there's something medically wrong with him?"

Fraser caught her arm as she rose. "A person could have a medical problem and be a damn fine person for all that," he said. "But if that person is unsuited for military life, then he has to be discharged as quickly as possible, sentiment be damned. You must *not* let any problems he might have be used as an excuse."

He sighed. "And any problems would have been caught at the Academy," he added. "I think he just has a case of laziness - and the only cure for *that* is an aggressive First Middy kicking his arse every time he shows it."

"Thanks, sir," George said, dryly.

She downloaded a copy of Henderson's work reports, then made her way to the Jefferies Tubes and crawled into the passageways. She'd always loved making her way through the crawlspaces, pretending - in the privacy of her own mind - that she was sneaking around, unseen and unheard by the crew. She made her way down the ladder until she reached his workspace, then started to check his work against the manifest. It wasn't uncommon for a glitch in reporting to appear - even though work was supposed to be double-checked, just in case - but it *was* odd for a problem to appear on the very first component she checked. The serial number on the component and the serial number on the manifest didn't match.

Her eyes narrowed as she checked the next component, then the next. The pattern was strikingly clear - Henderson hadn't just skipped one or two components, he'd skipped them all. She knew that the components had a longer lifespan than regulations admitted - the Royal Navy's gear was always massively over-engineered - but it didn't matter. Regulations insisted - nay, *demanded* - that all such components be replaced after a week of active service and placed into storage, at least until they could be inspected by the engineering crews.

I'm dead, she thought, as she sat back on her haunches. *My career is over.*

She clenched her fists as bitter despair welled up inside her. Henderson might *just* have gotten away with being late, but this…he wouldn't get away with something that might have endangered the entire ship. Regulations were clear - and he'd ignored them. And *she*, as his superior, was going to land in hot water too. She had been meant to be keeping an eye on him and she'd shirked her duty. But she just hadn't had the time…

"Bastard," she swore. She picked up the datapad and checked the next two components, hoping against hope that she'd made a mistake. But she hadn't. The records said one thing - and they'd been countersigned by Felicity - but her eyes said another. "Filthy fucking bastard son of a…"

She took one last look at the second, then rose and made her way towards the nearest hatch, checking a handful of other components along the way. Henderson had to be out of his mind…was he on drugs? It was *just* possible that he'd smuggled something nasty onto the ship, although she had no idea when he'd found the time to take it. But it didn't matter. His career was about to fall straight into the crapper and hers was going to join it. She made her way out of the tubes and headed straight down to Middy Country. Henderson was on duty, but Felicity was in her bunk. Thankfully, none of the other midshipmen were around.

"Come with me," George snarled, as she opened the hatch and tore back the curtain. Felicity started awake, shocked. George felt a pang of guilt - opening the curtain was a severe breach of etiquette - but there was no choice. "Now!"

She was tempted not to give Felicity a chance to get dressed - she was sleeping in her underwear - but she allowed the younger girl to grab a nightgown before half-dragging her into the wardroom. Felicity looked completely confused and disorientated, rubbing her forehead as if she had a pounding headache. George wouldn't have blamed her if she had, not when she'd only managed to catch an hour of sleep before being unceremoniously yanked out of her bunk. There were *regulations* against what she'd done.

Not that it matters now, she thought, bitterly. *The XO will chew me up and spit me out, then the Captain will dishonourably discharge whatever is left.*

"I checked your work with Henderson," George said, without preamble. "You didn't check it at all, did you?"

Felicity looked surprised. "He said it would be fine..."

"Oh," George said. The urge to just slap the silly girl was almost overwhelming. "And by what *authority* did he *say* it would be fine?"

"His," Felicity said. "He's heir to a duchy..."

George stared at her in disbelief. Henderson the heir to a duchy? It was utterly impossible, completely beyond belief. She would have met him - or at least *heard* of him - long ago if he was a duke's firstborn son. Hell, he would probably have been considered a prospective husband for her...he *was* in the right general age bracket, after all. But he didn't have either the manners or the arrogance of an aristocratic trust fund brat.

"There isn't a Henderson Family," she pointed out. Dear God... hadn't Felicity thought to *check*? "I would know him, if he was a true aristocrat..."

"He said he was using a false name," Felicity said, pleadingly. "He said..."

"He was lying," George told her, flatly. She'd heard of young men claiming to be scions of the aristocracy, but this was the first time she'd ever *met* one. A faker would be easy to spot, just because of the gaps in his knowledge. "Believe me, if he was trying to pose as a commoner, he wouldn't have exposed himself to you."

She rubbed her eyes. "I found a dozen components where the serial numbers don't add up," she said, tartly. "That was in the section you double-checked yesterday - according to the paperwork. Did you actually do more than glance at it?"

"I did my own section," Felicity said.

George sighed. "And I assume he didn't bother to check yours?"

She clenched her fists as the younger girl began to cry. She was going to *kill* Henderson. It wasn't as if she could get in worse trouble…well, she supposed she could, but it hardly seemed to matter. What had he promised Felicity? A match with a ducal son? It would be very tempting to a young girl with so little to recommend her…

…And it would have come crashing down in ruins, sooner rather than later.

"Stop crying," she ordered, sharply. She'd never had any patience for girls who blubbered, rather than taking their lumps and getting on with life. No wonder she'd done her best to avoid finishing school like the plague. "How did you ever get through the Academy?"

"He told me if I did well, he'd marry me," Felicity said. Tears were dripping from her eyes, staining her uniform. "We were going to be together forever…"

"He's a liar and a user and quite possibly an idiot," George said. Perhaps Henderson *was* taking drugs. The discrepancies in the serial numbers *would* have been discovered, sooner or later. "And whatever he told you…I wouldn't put any faith in it at all."

She sat back and rubbed her eyes. There was no way she could hide this, even if she *wanted* to. Henderson had gone far beyond anything she could handle alone. No, she had to take it to the XO and…and then prepare for her return to Earth. If she was lucky, or her uncle intervened, perhaps she'd be allowed to resign quietly. And if she wasn't, she'd probably wind up dishonourably discharged for gross negligence.

Reaching for her datapad, she checked the timetable. "I want you to stay here," she said, slowly. Potter was the next midshipman due back and *he* wouldn't be on his way for at least another hour. She should search

Henderson's bunk and locker...no, better to leave that for the marines. The XO wouldn't want her to take the risk of contaminating evidence. "Do *not* leave this compartment until you are summoned."

Felicity looked up at her. "What's going to happen to me?"

"I have no idea," George said.

She shrugged. There was no way to avoid the simple fact that Felicity had been compliant in *all* of Henderson's games, including covering up his misdeeds. She doubted Felicity could expect anything better than a dishonourable discharge, if she wasn't booted straight into Colchester. The thought made George feel cold. They might wind up sharing a cell if the navy threw the book at them.

"Stay here," she repeated. "And *don't* even *think* about trying to warn him."

She considered confiscating Felicity's wristcom, just in case, but dismissed the thought. The younger girl had had enough of a scare, George thought. And besides, there wouldn't be much time for Henderson to do anything...hell, what *could* he do? Steal a shuttlecraft and escape...escape to where? There was literally nowhere to go.

Unless he wants to damage the ship, she thought. *But he couldn't leave his duty station without attracting attention.*

She took a long breath as she stepped through the hatch and peered towards the bunkroom. It wasn't hers any longer - or it wouldn't be, once the XO got through with her. Bitter resignation tinged her thoughts as she keyed her wristcom, using the XO's priority code. She could get in trouble for misusing it, but she doubted the XO would care, not once he heard what had been going on. He'd be too busy sorting out the mess.

"Yes, Midshipwoman?"

George sighed. "Mr. XO, I need to see you," she said, tiredly. "It's important."

There was a long pause, just long enough to make her worry. "Report to my office," the XO said, finally. She wondered, absently, if he was on the bridge. But the XO could put another officer in command if necessary. "I'll be there in two minutes."

"Yes, sir," George said. "I'll be there momentarily."

Taking one last look at the bunkroom, she turned and walked towards the hatch. No matter what she did, no matter what she said, she doubted she would see it again.

At least Henderson will get what's coming to him, she thought, tiredly. Given his crimes, it was quite likely he'd be sent straight to jail - or thrown out an airlock. *And Potter will get a chance to be First Middy after all.*

CHAPTER
SIXTEEN

"Let me see if I have this straight," the XO said. He sat behind his desk, studying George with unblinking eyes. "Midshipman Clayton Henderson has been falsifying entries in the ship's records, along with a multitude of other crimes?"

"Yes, sir," George said. She stood, ramrod straight; her hands clasped behind her back to keep them from shaking. "He was skipping on basic maintenance..."

The XO held up a hand. "And you only realised it today?"

"Yes, sir," George said. A dozen excuses bubbled to the surface of her mind, but she refused to use any of them. There was no avoiding the fact that she hadn't checked his work, relying on Felicity to do the task. "I take full responsibility."

"I see," the XO said. "And Midshipwoman Wheeler?"

"She was apparently tricked and seduced into helping him, sir," George said. She had no idea how far Felicity had gone with Henderson - relationships between bunkmates were frowned upon - but she would have been surprised if they hadn't found a chance to sleep together after being assigned to *Vanguard*. "I don't know what she was thinking."

The XO studied her for a long moment, then keyed a switch on his desk. George heard the hatch hiss open behind her and someone step into the compartment, but resisted the urge to turn and look. The XO's eyes never left her...she wondered, absently, just what he was thinking. She'd lost control of Middy Country and, almost certainly, lost her career too.

And Henderson will be going down with me, she thought. *There is that, at least.*

"You will be escorted to the brig," the XO said, curtly. "You will remain there until the captain has had a chance to consider your case. You *will* have a chance to defend yourself" - George bit down the urge to point out that she had *no* defence - "but until then you may consider yourself relieved of duty."

He looked past her. "Take her away."

George turned. A marine - Frederick Stott, she realised - was standing behind her, looking alarmingly competent in his shipboard uniform. She winced as he took her upper arm and led her towards the hatch, his grip light but very firm. She supposed she should be grateful he wasn't bringing out the handcuffs, she told herself; she didn't think she would cope very well with being frogmarched through the ship in cuffs. And the thought of Potter's reaction...

Forget Potter, she thought, as Stott walked her through the hatch. *He isn't your problem any longer.*

The corridors were almost deserted, she was relieved to discover, as Stott walked her down to the brig. Only a handful of crewmen saw her and it was possible, just possible, to believe that they hadn't realised she was in trouble. The thought sustained her, even as she realised it wasn't remotely accurate. Apart from the captain, there wasn't a single person on the ship who would be escorted by marines, *unless* they were in trouble.

"I have to search you," Stott said, as they entered the brig. "Are you carrying anything dangerous?"

"No," George said, bitterly.

She rested her hands on her head and forced herself to relax as he frisked her, quickly and efficiently. She'd hoped he'd leave her the datapad, but he took it - along with the wristcom - and dropped it into a locker. She hadn't been carrying anything else, save for a ration bar she'd scooped up before hurrying to meet Fraser. That too was dumped in the box and stowed away.

"You'll find the brig very comfortable," Stott said. He opened a hatch, revealing a compartment no larger than the middy bunkroom. "And don't hesitate to bang on the hatch if you need anything."

George gave him a sidelong look as he pushed her into the brig and closed the hatch. It was bare: a bunk, an old-fashioned toilet stool and nothing else, not even a book. She was going to be very bored, she knew, as she sat down on the bunk. But boredom would seem better than the inevitable end result of Captain's Mast...

And my career is over, she thought. *Maybe I should have killed Henderson after all.*

———

"What a fucking mess," Susan said. "I don't suppose there's any chance that Fitzwilliam made a mistake?"

"No, Captain," Alan Finch said. The Chief Engineer looked quietly furious. "I had the sections Henderson worked on rechecked, twice. No less than fifty-seven components had the wrong serial numbers, even though they should have been changed at least once in the last week. It didn't give us any real problems, thanks to over-engineering the components, but we might have been in real trouble if we had to channel excess power through that section."

"HMS *Warspite* lost power during her maiden voyage, Captain," the XO put in. "There was an arsehole on the ship who was stealing the replacement components and selling them onwards."

Susan nodded, sourly. "Do we have any explanation for his behaviour?"

"I searched his locker *thoroughly*," Major Christopher Andreas said. "He had five tablets of Happy Powder hidden in his dress uniform. The doctor thinks he was actually limiting his intake, even though it was having a bad effect on him."

"I see," Susan said. "Does that explain his behaviour?"

"It might," Andres said. "When he was high, he would have been preternaturally convincing and charismatic; when he was coming off the drug, he would have been lethargic and prone to bouts of depression and suchlike. There's a reason Happy Powder is on the banned list."

"And he smuggled it onboard my ship," Susan snapped. "How did he *get* it onboard?"

"We don't search middy knapsacks," Mason said. The XO pressed his fingertips together as he sat back in his chair. "As long as he was very careful, he should have been able to escape detection."

"He *did* escape detection," Andres pointed out. "We wouldn't know about the problem if Fitzwilliam hadn't checked his work."

"Which she should have done earlier," Finch snapped. "She's partly to blame for this, Captain."

"She had four new middies to supervise," the XO said, playing devil's advocate. "How many other First Middies do you know who have to supervise more than two newcomers?"

"That's beside the point," Finch said. "Henderson's stupidity risked the entire ship! She should have brought the concerns to you earlier."

"She would have risked her career," the XO said. "I'm not denying she acted badly, Mr. Finch, but she was placed in one hell of a mess."

Susan sighed, inwardly. She wasn't blind to the irony. Midshipwoman Fitzwilliam had been in the same situation as *she'd* been, when she'd realised just how dangerous it would be to leave Captain Blake in command. Report the matter to superior authority, knowing that it might cost her everything, or do nothing and hope for the best. At least Fitzwilliam hadn't plotted a mutiny. There was *that* in her favour, at least.

She slapped the table, hard. "Right," she said. "We need to act decisively.

"Midshipman Clayton Henderson is to remain in the brig, under medical supervision," she said, firmly. "He is *not* to be allowed to take any more of his pills. When we get back home, he can explain himself to a Court Martial Board. Under the circumstances, I don't think they'll hesitate before throwing the book at him. He can spend the rest of his life in Colchester."

"You could execute him," Andres pointed out. "There *is* precedent."

Susan shook her head. She *was* tempted, but there was no need. Henderson was hardly a threat, not any longer; he certainly hadn't *deliberately* set out to harm the ship. He'd spend the rest of his life - or at least a decade or two - in the harshest prison in Britain, then probably get kicked out of the country. There was certainly no way he'd ever be allowed back in space.

"No," she said. Henderson might beg for a bullet in the brain, when he realised what was coming his way, but she saw no reason to oblige him. Besides, executing him would just give her enemies more ammunition. "Let him live. He won't enjoy it."

She took a breath. "Midshipwoman Felicity Wheeler is to remain in the brig until we return to Earth, at which point she will be permanently beached," she continued. "She should have learned her lesson, but we cannot overlook her conduct. If there is no place for her in the navy, in the judgement of the personnel department, she can resign quietly if she wishes."

And that is as far as I am prepared to go for her, she added, in the privacy of her own thoughts. She'd met her fair share of men claiming to be the fifth son of some obscure aristocrat - or heir to power, position and fortune - because they found her skin colour exotic, but she'd never let any of them seduce her. Her father had taught her to beware of anything that looked too good to be true. *She'll have a chance to make a new life for herself.*

"There won't be any place for her," Finch predicted. "Not after her conduct..."

"Perhaps," Susan said. "We shall see."

She paused, looking from face to face. "I assume that Midshipman Potter and Midshipwoman Spurgeon have no role in this farce?"

"Apparently not, Captain," Andres said. "Mr. Potter was quite helpful in discussing Miss Fitzwilliam's failings - and Mr. Henderson's moral lapses - but there doesn't seem to be any reason to suspect him - or Spurgeon - of any role in the affair."

Susan frowned. She hadn't missed the hint of disgust in his voice.

"Midshipwoman Fitzwilliam is to be retroactively beached all the way back to day one," she said, keeping her voice icy cold. It was a harsh punishment, but milder - far milder - than Fitzwilliam had any right to expect. "In addition, she is to be transferred to the shuttle crews until it pleases me to return her to regular midshipman duties. Her record will be amended to note that she didn't bring this to our attention at first - and, when she had no choice, she did so in a manner befitting her position."

She looked from face to face. "If any of you have any objections, say so now," she added. "I will note them in my log."

"I cannot approve," Finch stated, bluntly. "The ship comes first, always."

"Duly noted," Susan said. "Anyone else?"

There was a long pause. No one spoke.

"Good," Susan said, finally. "Now, before I speak to Midshipwoman Fitzwilliam, are there any other issues we should address?"

Mason nodded. "Under the circumstances, Captain, Midshipman Potter would normally become First Middy," he said. "He has two years on Midshipwoman Spurgeon. However, I have a feeling that the young man played a significant role in the problems affecting Middy Country. I suggest, therefore, that we ask Lieutenant Fraser to serve as First Middy - and place a number of soldiers to fill the empty slots in Middy Country."

Susan felt her eyes narrow. "Is it that bad?"

"I think so, Captain," Mason said. "Midshipman Potter gives me bad vibes."

"See to it," Susan ordered. She raised her voice, slightly. "Any other matters of concern?"

"We will be quite short on manpower, Captain," Granger warned. "We'll only have two midshipmen on full-time duties."

"We'll endure," Mason said.

"If worst comes to worst, we'll put Fitzwilliam back in the slot," Susan said. "But for the moment" - she nodded at Mason - "we'll just have to endure."

She sighed, then glanced at her wristcom. "Major Andres, have Midshipwoman Fitzwilliam brought to my office in two hours," she added. "Everyone else, dismissed."

"You were quite light on her," Mason said, once everyone else had left the compartment. "It might be used against you, later."

"I know," Susan said. "But what else can I do?"

She watched him leave the compartment, then sat back at her desk. It was easy to say, with the benefit of hindsight, that Midshipwoman Fitzwilliam should have said or done something earlier. That, Susan was sure, was the line any Board of Inquiry would take. And yet, she understood just how many problems the poor girl had faced. It was hard to blame her for not coming forward before the whole situation had blown up in her face…

And now she has to be punished as an example to everyone else, Susan thought. She had grounds - if she wished to use them - to have all three of the midshipmen escorted to the nearest airlock and thrown out. Certainly, a strict interpretation of the regs would have allowed for it, although she suspected that any post-voyage board of inquiry would have taken a dim view of the whole affair. *And even though she's getting off lightly, she won't feel that way.*

She sighed, then reached for her terminal. She'd log the records of the meeting - including Finch's objection - and then write a detailed account of the affair for Henderson's court martial, while her memories were still fresh. Taking drugs was bad enough - she'd have to make sure that the doctor screened every last crewman before they reached Unity, just in case Henderson wasn't the only addict - but signing false statements into the files? *That* was far worse.

And he's brought a promising young officer down too, she added, in the privacy of her own mind. *And there's nothing I can do to mitigate it either.*

———

George had been grounded more than once, as a child, and she'd been sent to Coventry as a schoolgirl, but being in the brig was far - far - worse. There was nothing to do: no books to read, no movies to watch…nothing to do, but worry about the future. She lay on the bunk and counted to herself, wishing she'd been allowed to keep the wristcom. At least she would have known just how long she'd spent in the tiny compartment.

The hatch hissed open, sharply. "On your feet," a voice growled. It was a marine, but not one she recognised. "The Captain wants to see you."

George winced, but swung her legs over the side of the bunk and stood anyway. The marine searched her again, thoroughly - she had no idea how he thought she'd sneaked something into the brig - and then took her by the arm, leading her out of the compartment and up towards Officer Country. There were more crewmen in the corridors this time, she noted, wishing he wasn't gripping her upper arm so tightly. Did he think she'd try to get away?

Her heart was pounding loudly by the time they stopped outside the captain's hatch. The marine tapped a panel, opening the hatch, then motioned for her to walk inside. George hesitated - she knew she looked a mess - and then did as she was told. It was unlikely, she kept telling herself, that she could get in worse trouble. The captain could have her summarily stripped of rank and kicked off the ship, if she wished. And it was quite possible that she deserved it.

"Midshipman Fitzwilliam, reporting," she said, standing to attention.

The Captain studied her for a long cold moment. George stayed ramrod straight, silently bidding farewell to her career. The XO handled normal disciplinary matters...if the captain was involved, it was *serious*.

"I have considered your case in great detail," Captain Onarina said. Her voice was icy, but there was a hint of...*something* that gave George hope. "On one hand, you are culpable for not taking the problem to superior authority before it blew up in your face. Your decision, while understandable, ensured that the situation grew considerably out of control."

George nodded, slowly.

"You have a choice," the Captain added. "You may submit yourself to NJP, from me, or you may remain in the brig until we return to Earth and a court martial is organised. Choose."

"I choose NJP," George said.

She didn't have to think about it. The Captain might understand her position, but a court martial board definitely wouldn't. She'd heard too much about them from her uncle and some of her other relatives. And *they* would be hoping to nail her uncle as well as herself.

"Very well," Captain Onarina said. "You are retroactively beached; you'll start again from scratch. You will also be transferred to the shuttle crews until I see fit to order otherwise. Do you understand me?"

George winced. Losing all of her seniority was bad enough, but being trapped in the shuttlebay was worse...

...But at least she wasn't being executed. Or even imprisoned until the ship returned home.

"I understand, Captain," she said. "And thank you."

The Captain met her eyes. "There are moments," she said, "when you have to decide if you should put your career - and your reputation - ahead of the good of the ship. And the answer is always *no*; you should *never* put either ahead of the ship. You were lucky, Midshipwoman; luckier, I think, than you realise."

George swallowed, hard. "I understand, Captain."

"I'd be surprised if you did, at least completely," the Captain said. "Report to Lieutenant Fraser in Middy Country now, if you please; report to Major Andres tomorrow at 0900. I believe he has some work for you. Dismissed."

George snapped out a salute, then turned and walked out of the office. Her legs sagged almost as soon as the hatch closed, despite the hulking presence of the marine. She had been stripped of seniority, she had been shunted out of command track...

...And it looked as though Fraser had returned to the wardroom. He was going to *love* her.

It could be worse, she told herself. Captain Onarina had been right. She *had* been lucky, very lucky. *You could be waiting in the brig for a court martial.*

CHAPTER
SEVENTEEN

"We have four days to go before we reach Unity," Henry said. "Are you sure this will work?"

"It *should* work," Doctor Song said. She tapped the computer console thoughtfully. "I'm sure they will *hear* the message."

Henry scowled. "But will they reply?"

He looked down at the altered First Contact package and sighed. For something that had had some of the finest minds in the Human Sphere working on it, the First Contact package had been largely useless. The Tadpoles hadn't bothered to respond to signals, while the Vesy had been taught English and Russian by the Russians who'd discovered them. And the newcomers, whoever they were, hadn't replied either. There was no way to know if they were even *hearing* the signals.

"They can't be *that* alien," Doctor Song said. "They can build starships. What sort of mentality can do that and still be completely alien?"

Henry shrugged. "There are humans who do insane and irrational things just for shits and giggles," he said, tiredly. "And they are *human*. The Tadpoles can still surprise and horrify us after ten years of contact."

"We have an updated communications package," Doctor Song said, firmly. "They should be capable of receiving it and equally capable of understanding and replying. Given a few days, we should be able to build up a shared language. Discussing philosophy may take longer, of course."

"Of course," Henry agreed. The Tadpoles hadn't been able to make sense of humanity's religions - and humans had been equally perplexed by *their* religions. If, of course, they *were* religions. The xenospecialists weren't sure how accurate the translations actually were, if they were accurate at all. "As long as we can discuss peace, I'm sure the captain will be happy."

He nodded to the doctor, then turned and strode out of the compartment. The mood had darkened on the battleship as she proceeded inexorably towards the war front, her crews running double shifts as they watched for signs of alien contact. Henry had heard, during one of his frequent dinners with the captain, that the crew had been running training exercises, working desperately to prepare for the next encounter. And yet, it was hard to be *sure* what they would face. The latest update - gleaned from a Tadpole freighter heading in the opposite direction - insisted that Unity had not been attacked, but the update was still two weeks out of date.

And we don't even know if they can talk to us, he thought. *They may not be capable of talking to us.*

It seemed absurd, all the xenospecialists agreed. They were facing two races, not one. Henry doubted the aliens could agree on dinner, let alone put together a combined operation, without a shared language. Even if one of the alien races was the master and the other the slave, the masters would still need to tell the slaves what they wanted them to do. There was just too much room for misunderstandings.

He rubbed his forehead as he entered his cabin and made his way over to the desk. The research teams had mined human history extensively, then turned their attention to studying science-fiction and fantasy from the pre-space era. There had been alien races that were spider-like, monstrous bugs utterly beyond human comprehension…and races that had found radio waves nothing but pure torture. They'd opened fire on the assumption that the other side had fired first - and, technically, they'd been correct. But as neat as the idea was, Henry found it hard to believe. There was no shortage of radio noise in space.

We may not know anything until we actually capture a live alien, he thought. *And then we may have to work hard to get answers out of him.*

He sat down at the desk and checked the reports from his staff. They were ready for the alien, when - if - the marines managed to capture one.

Or so they thought. Aliens were not human, after all. The first prisoners captured during the First Interstellar War had nearly been killed through sheer ignorance, despite some of the brightest minds humanity had produced studying them. It was galling to realise that the Tadpoles had handled human prisoners - including Henry himself - better than humanity had handled their prisoners, but they'd had longer to prepare. And plenty of data about humanity in its natural habitat.

Four days, he told himself, as he closed the terminal. *And then we can begin.*

He keyed a switch, bringing up the record function. "It's been three days since I recorded a message for you," he said. He'd started trying to record individual messages for each of his children separately, but he hadn't had the time to keep it up. "We are still on the way, I'm afraid. Very little has happened since we passed that Tadpole ship…"

There were officers, Henry knew, who dreaded the day that human ingenuity finally cracked the secret of transmitting FTL messages. Whitehall - and JHQ - would be looking over their shoulders all the time, micromanaging operations and turning the officers into little more than puppets. And he could see their point. But he would have sold his soul for a way to send messages back home instantly, even if he couldn't hold a real-time conversation with his wife and daughters. He'd promised them, when they were born, that they wouldn't have to endure the twisted household he recalled from his childhood. Their father would treat them as *children*, not prize pigs on display.

"I hope to see you all soon," he concluded, although he knew it wasn't going to happen. Even if he took ship back to Earth at once, he wouldn't get there for at least two months. "And I love you all very much."

He turned off the recording, then sent the message into the storage node. It would wait there until a starship returned to Earth, whereupon it would be uploaded into the military network and passed on to its destination. The censors would probably insist on having a look at it - the damnable bastards - but he'd said nothing they could find objectionable. It was just a simple recording from a father to his children.

And when I get home, he promised himself, *I'll take them right back to Tadpole Prime.*

But, deep inside, he knew it was a promise he might not be able to keep.

———

It wasn't the first time George had worked on the shuttles - midshipmen were expected to learn how to fly and maintain the craft along with their other duties - yet it felt different when it was a punishment. The Senior Chief didn't treat her any differently, but his crewmen eyed her when they thought she wasn't looking, as if her disgrace would rub off. George did her work without complaint, returned to Middy Country to sleep in her bunk and then went back to work. She was honestly unsure if she should be relieved or not, even though she knew the entire affair would look very bad in her personal file.

"Hey," Fraser called, as she stepped into Middy Country. "Feeling better?"

George shrugged, expressively. Putting a lieutenant into Middy Country was a clear statement that higher authority felt that the middies couldn't handle their own problems, even through both Henderson and Felicity were in the brig. But it did have its advantages. She'd overheard Fraser's discussion with Potter that, miraculously, had turned the younger man into a decent officer. She hadn't known it was possible to deliver a dressing down in such an icy tone. And there hadn't been any problems since then.

"A little, sir," she said. Maintaining the shuttlecraft wasn't *bad*, but it was boring. The varied duties of a midshipwoman on command track were far more interesting. "How are you?"

"I've been better," Fraser said. He motioned for her to follow him through the hatch. "You want to come shoot off a few rounds?"

George would have honestly preferred to climb into her bunk and go to sleep, but she had the feeling that it wasn't an invitation she could refuse. Fraser hadn't spoken *much* to her, since he'd taken the topmost bunk in the wardroom, yet she would have been surprised if part of him wasn't hopping mad. He'd worked hard to get promoted *out* of Middy Country. She had half-expected him to pile all the shit duties on her as punishment for getting him tossed *back* into Middy Country. But he hadn't done anything of the sort.

She followed him through the corridors, fighting down a yawn. Potter wasn't talking to her, but Paula had let slip that both of the remaining midshipmen were being overworked. George understood, all too well. Everything Henderson had touched before his arrest had to be checked and rechecked, while the ship had been thoroughly searched for more drug tablets and any other surprises. The marines had found several stills, she'd heard, and a small collection of pornography, but no more drugs. George didn't know if she should be relieved or suspicious that something had been missed. *Vanguard* was easily large enough to conceal a few hundred tablets from all, but a very determined search.

"I hope you remember how to shoot," Fraser said, as they entered the shooting range. "It's been too long."

George nodded as she requested a pistol from the range safety officer, then checked it carefully. She wasn't sure what would happen to *her* if she was caught with the pink bullet - a marine tradition to teach new recruits how to keep their weapons safe - but she was sure Fraser would find a way to make her life miserable. She'd missed shooting and training with him, more than she cared to admit. Fraser was a harsh son of a bitch - she'd spent far too long hating and fearing him - but he *was* a good teacher.

"I think I remember the basics," she said, wryly. "Are we going to have another competition?"

Fraser rolled his eyes. "Not unless you've somehow managed to get better without touching a loaded weapon for the past month," he said, sardonically. "Unless you have a particularly unpleasant forfeit in mind, I suppose."

George coloured. She'd challenged Fraser to a shooting match, four weeks after he'd started to show her how to build on her skills. He'd wiped the deck with her and he'd made it look easy. In hindsight, betting toilet cleaning duties for the next week had been a dreadful mistake. She wasn't a bad shot, thanks to his supervision, but she was nowhere near his match.

"Not really," she said. She paused as a thought occurred to her. "But I *could* bet a chocolate bar on it, if you want."

"It would feel like a steal," Fraser said. "But if you want, I shall reluctantly accept."

He led the way into the range, then tapped a switch on the bulkhead. A number of holographic targets flickered to life in the semi-darkness, moving backwards and forwards like living people. Someone - probably one of the marines - had painted the targets to resemble the new aliens, fox-like teeth bared as they faced the humans. George stepped forward at his nod, then slotted the magazine into her pistol and opened fire. Her hit counter started to mount up as she ran through the first set of bullets, reloaded and opened fire again.

"Not bad," Fraser said, when she had finished. "Can I have a go?"

George stepped aside as Fraser reset the range, then opened fire. He was still quicker than her, firing off bullets in a steady stream and then reloading the pistol in one smooth motion that still left her breathless. She'd tried to load her pistol just as quickly, but it had always ended with her dropping something or accidentally jamming the weapon. Fraser hadn't been amused.

"I think I win," Fraser said, finally. "I hit forty-seven aliens to your twenty-two."

"We haven't finished," George objected. She glanced at him. "How accurate are these simulations, anyway?"

Fraser shrugged. "They're not," he said. "You should try the marine suite if you want *realism*. They've been letting crewmen run through their tactical simulations for a couple of pounds a head."

George glanced at him. "Isn't that against regs?"

"Depends how you look at it," Fraser said. "Major Andres appears to believe that it's good for the spacers to see how the groundpounders do their work."

He shrugged. "And it's a *very* good simulation."

"You've used it," George stated.

"It's fun," Fraser said. He put his pistol down on the table, then started to flick through the range options. "But there are all sorts of little surprises. You know the crap people pull in VR games? You can't do that in real life."

George smirked. "Really?"

"Oh, yes," Fraser said. "Try to hide behind glass when someone is firing a machine gun at you? Certain death. Throw grenades around at random? You'd better hope your comrades are smart enough to take cover. And ammunition? You actually *run out* of ammunition if you fire your weapon like a maniac, if your sergeant doesn't strangle you first."

"I never would have known that," George said, dryly.

"Good thing I told you," Fraser said. He nodded towards the range. A new set of holographic images appeared, aliens intermixed with human prisoners. "Just in case you didn't guess, George, there is *no* excuse for shooting the humans."

"I guessed that," George said, irked. She reloaded her weapon, then took aim as Fraser moved to stand next to her. "When do we start?"

Fraser tapped a switch. "Now."

George bit her lip as the aliens advanced, snapping and snarling. Whoever had designed the simulation was a right bastard. The alien captives were children - the oldest couldn't be more than twelve - begging and pleading to be saved. But the aliens were using them as human shields, lifting them up effortlessly to cover their bodies as they moved forward. She found it hard to choose her targets; she heard, time and time again, the dull raspberry that told her she'd hit a hostage. By the time the simulation came to an end, she felt tired, frustrated and quietly furious.

"You killed five hostages," Fraser said. "And you missed several of the aliens."

"Oh," George said. Only five? She'd thought it had been more. But it hardly mattered. If the situation had been real, she would have been responsible for five deaths...five *human* deaths. "How well did you do?"

"I killed one hostage," Fraser said.

George sighed. "How accurate is this?"

Fraser looked at her. "It's hard to say," he admitted. "Navy-issue pistols" - he nodded down at the one in his hand as he clicked on the safety, then removed the magazine - "are designed to pack a punch, but no one has any real data on alien strength or endurance. Hitting them with a single bullet might kill them or it might just piss them off."

"I see," George said. Fraser had made her research bullet wounds, back before they'd returned to Earth for the first time. Soldiers could take

147

terrifying punishment in the field, but - thanks to modern medicine - make a full recovery and return to the front line. "But a bullet in the head will still work?"

"I hope so," Fraser said. "That's where they keep their brains."

He turned and led her back out of the range, where they cleaned the weapons before handing them back to the officer. "We can get some coffee in the mess," he added, firmly. "Are you coming?"

"Yes, sir," George said.

"I hope the shuttlebay isn't boring you too much," Fraser said, as they walked through the long corridor. "How are you coping with it?"

"It could be worse," George said, reluctantly. She'd promised herself she wouldn't moan or whine over the cards fate had dealt her. Things could have been a *great* deal worse. "I actually enjoy flying the shuttles."

"You'll get your chance to do more than a little flying," Fraser said. "*Rumour* has it that we're going to be offloading the troops on Unity as quickly as possible."

"Unless the enemy get there first, sir," George said. "That's the plan, isn't it?"

"Yeah," Fraser said. "You'll be helping to fly them down to the surface."

He shrugged. "Shame there's no hope of any leave on Unity."

George was inclined to agree. "Is there anything there?"

"Not as far as I know," Fraser said. "There might be some bars, if we're lucky, but there won't be any big shore leave complexes."

"I wouldn't get any leave anyway," George said, dryly. "Maybe we should just dump Henderson and Felicity on Unity."

"They wouldn't want Henderson," Fraser said. "And while another breeder would be quite welcome, I am sure, I don't think they'd be too keen on Wheeler either."

George shrugged. She'd read everything she could find on Unity in the ship's database, but there had been surprisingly little. Unity *might* be the first true joint colony, yet it was clear that the human and Tadpole settlers had very little to do with one another. But then, they didn't really impinge. There was very little for them to fight over, not on the surface. Deep space was another matter.

"The captain made the call," she said. She looked up at him. "Was she right?"

Fraser made a show of glancing up and down the corridor before he answered. "I imagine she believed that the matter was best passed up the chain to her superiors," he said. "Sure, she *could* have executed both of them - and you - but she would be challenged for it afterwards. And there's no pressing need to rush to judgment."

He looked back at her, evenly. "But if she hadn't made the call she did," he added, "where would *you* be?"

"In shit," George said. "Thank you."

Fraser smirked. "You're welcome."

CHAPTER
EIGHTEEN

"Signal from the flag, Captain," Parkinson reported. "*Pinafore* and *Jones* are preparing to probe the tramline."

Susan nodded, feeling the tension on the bridge rising sharply. There were no settlements - human or otherwise - in the Yamane System, ensuring that the new enemies had had plenty of time to set up an ambush without fear of discovery. If, of course, they knew the squadron was on the way. But the star system was completely empty, as far as their sensor officers could tell.

And that means nothing, she thought, grimly. *An entire enemy fleet could be hiding a few million kilometres from us and we wouldn't have a clue.*

"Acknowledged," she said. "Helm, hold us here."

"Aye, Captain," Reed said.

Susan braced herself as the two green icons crawled towards the tramline and vanished. The task force had been in stealth for the last two weeks, altering course randomly to throw off any cloaked shadows, but there was no way to be *entirely* sure that they were alone. It was possible that Admiral Harper was being paranoid, as some of his detractors had alleged in the daily command meetings, yet the newcomers *had* managed to surprise a much larger joint fleet and kick its ass. If there *was* an alien starship watching them, that ship might *just* have managed to rustle up a welcoming committee on the far side of the tramline.

And that only happens in bad movies, she thought. *A couple of minor course changes would make interception impossible.*

Sure, her own thoughts answered her. *But it only has to work once.*

She pushed the thought aside as one of the green icons blinked back into existence, hanging on the tramline. Signals flickered between *Jones* and *New York* for a long moment, exchanging coded messages to ensure that the ship was intact and still under friendly command. Susan found it hard to imagine a force capable of boarding and subduing an alien crew - let alone flying the ship expertly - but she had to admit it was better to take precautions. Some of the *really* wild scenarios dreamed up over the last ten years had made nightmarish reading.

"Signal from the flag, Captain," Parkinson said. "We are to proceed through the tramline, condition-two."

"Good," Susan said. Condition-two meant that they'd arrived first, against the odds; there was no sign of an enemy presence within the system. It was still possible that there was a watching fleet, cloaked or merely stealthed, but at least there was a chance of being able to take up a defensive position before the enemy arrived. "Tactical?"

"All weapons and defences online, Captain," Jean Granger said. "We can move to condition-one within seconds."

Susan nodded. "Helm, take us through the tramline."

"Aye, Captain," Reed said.

Vanguard seemed to quiver with anticipation as she slid forward, flanked by the American battleships. The tactical display blanked out as the starship jumped through the tramline, then came back to life as she downloaded a tactical update from HMS *Pinafore*. There were a couple of interplanetary freighters making their way between the planet and the asteroid belt, but no sign of any other major interplanetary activity. Susan was surprised there was even so *much* activity, given how little economic value there was in it. The planet might have been intended to be an economic hub, but without major investment - and a handful of other colonies along the chain - it wasn't going to be anything more than a relatively small colony.

"Local space is clear, Captain," Charlotte reported. "The flag is deploying sensor drones to extend our reach."

"Keep a close eye on them," Susan ordered. She looked at Unity itself, hanging in the tactical display. The planetary government, such as it was, wouldn't have any idea the task force had arrived, not yet. Admiral Harper would have sent a message, as soon as *New York* moved through the tramline, but it would nearly seven hours before any reply could arrive. "Set course for Unity."

"Aye, Captain," Reed said. "Course laid in."

Susan leaned back in her chair as the task force began to move away from the tramline, heading directly towards Unity. The main tactical display was constantly updating, but apart from a small cloudscoop orbiting the nearest gas giant there was very little else within the system. There didn't even seem to be a stream of radio chatter from Unity itself. Susan couldn't help feeling, as she waited for something to happen, that even Terra Nova had more activity, although that proved nothing. Terra Nova had had truly staggering levels of investment since it had been discovered, despite all the political turmoil. Unity…had not.

"Signal from the flag," Parkinson said. "Admiral Harper intends to proceed with Unity-Five."

"Send back our acknowledgements," Susan ordered. She hadn't expected to have a chance to put Unity-Five into operation, but it looked as though they'd gotten lucky. Given a few days to set up the supplies they'd brought, they could turn Unity into more than just a speed-bump for the aliens. "And keep us on our current course."

"Aye, Captain," Reed said.

Susan exchanged a look with Mason. They'd expected to find the aliens dug into the system, perhaps even probing the systems further towards human space. But instead, Unity appeared to be completely untouched. It was possible, she supposed, that the aliens had decided that invading Unity wasn't worth the effort, but no military force worth its salt would have left *any* form of interplanetary communication intact. The freighters should have been blown out of space, along with the cloudscoop and the orbital satellite network. Leaving them intact made no sense.

Which is worrying, she thought. *If they're not attacking Unity, where are they going?*

She pulled up a starchart and considered it, thinking hard. There was no way to know just how much the aliens actually *knew* about the tramline geography, but if they'd captured a database - and she'd always assumed they had - they would know how Unity would offer them the chance to attack Tadpole Prime from two separate directions. Hell, if they duplicated the advanced stardrive, they'd be able to attack from *three*. But it was just possible that the aliens had also reasoned that they'd picked off more than they could chew...

But if that was the case, she asked herself, *would they not at least try to talk to us?*

She raised her voice. "Mr. Reed," she said. "ETA at Unity?"

"Twelve hours, Captain," Reed said.

Susan frowned, then rose. "Mr. Mason, you have the bridge," she said. There was literally nothing she could do, but wait. "Inform me the *moment* anything changes."

"Aye, Captain," Mason said. "I have the bridge."

––––––––

Henry had expected enemy missiles to come slashing in out of nowhere, hammering the task force before it had a chance to either evade or return fire, but the long crawl between the tramline and Unity had been utterly uneventful. A handful of messages had arrived from the planetary governor - a man Henry recalled as being somewhat out of favour in his native France - yet none of them had been particularly significant. Henry would have wondered, in all honesty, if the man even knew there was a war on, if Governor Labara's first message hadn't been a demand for immediate transport back to the Human Sphere. It didn't strike him as a good sign.

He forced himself to relax as the shuttle launched from the battleship and headed down towards the blue-green world below. Unity, like most Earth-like planets, was over seventy percent water, although it hadn't occurred to anyone - yet - that the Tadpoles had a claim to more of the planet's surface than their human counterparts. There would probably be problems, Henry conceded, as the planet slowly developed its industry, but for the moment there was hardly any contact between the two races. Unity was a united planet in name only.

But I suppose that's for the best, he thought, dryly. *Terra Nova taught us that humans of different races and creeds* can *get along, as long as there are a few dozen light years between them.*

He shook his head as the shuttle slipped smoothly into the planetary atmosphere and continued its descent, following the coastline towards Unity City. The settlement had clearly expanded over the last seven years - orbital imagery showed more buildings than he recalled - but calling it a city was stretching the point a little too far. Even assuming that every building held a family, he would have been surprised if more than a couple of thousand people lived in the city itself. Most of the population lived in tiny settlements, slowly turning the planet into a breadbasket to support future expansion.

Which probably means they won't be too keen to see us, he reminded himself. *And they may not know what's going on.*

He glanced at his orders - from JHQ and Admiral Harper - as the shuttle dropped towards the spaceport. The troops were to be landed to take up defensive positions, no matter what the settlers thought about it. Henry would have been surprised if Governor Labara had said a word against the plan, but the remainder of the planet's population was a different story. It was easy to imagine them objecting or, worse, resorting to force. The last thing they needed was a civil war as well as everything else.

The shuttle came to a hover over the spaceport, then slowly lowered itself to the ground. It didn't look as though the spaceport had been expanded, in the years since Henry had last visited, but he wasn't particularly surprised. There was just no pressing *need* to expand the facility when there was so little traffic. The shuttle landed with a dull thump; the hatch snapped open a second later, allowing him to smell the warm air. Like many other new colonies, it was a strange mixture of the familiar and the new. He couldn't help thinking that it smelled sweet.

"Your Excellency," George Fitzwilliam said. "Should I remain here?"

"Please," Henry said. "I don't think we'll run into any actual *trouble.*"

He stepped out of the shuttle and closed the hatch, idly wondering what had happened to the reception committee. He'd done his best to avoid formal ceremonies, particularly after he'd removed himself from the line of succession, but Governor Labara wasn't the type to avoid a chance to show off. Henry was surprised there wasn't a collection of ceremonial guards waiting for him, if indeed there *were* any guards. Unity was hardly populated enough to raise and support a regiment of soldiers.

Most of their security comes from the militia, he thought, as he saw a car entering the spaceport. *It isn't as if they need much.*

He smiled at the thought, then sobered as the car drove towards him and parked next to the shuttle. The driver would have been sacked on Earth for careless driving - if he wasn't outright arrested - but the rules seemed to be different on Unity. There was so little traffic passing through the spaceport that he wouldn't be surprised to discover that local children played football on the landing pads, regardless of the rules. Hell, he wasn't sure there *were* rules. He straightened to attention as the driver opened the door and stepped out, then saluted smartly.

"Governor Labara is waiting for you, Your Highness," the driver said. "Please will you come with me?"

Shoddy, Henry thought. Standards had definitely slipped. But then, he'd never been particularly impressed with Governor Labara. *He cared more for the title than doing his damn job.*

He climbed into the car and watched, grimly, as the driver drove away from the spaceport and down the road towards the city. The road should have been maintained, but it was clear, just to the naked eye, that Governor Labara's men had been skimping on their work. He could see the undergrowth advancing menacingly towards the road, threatening to start damaging the surface; the car bumped several times as it ran over potholes and other impediments. The city itself didn't look much better. A number of buildings were prefabricated - they looked good enough, he supposed - but the others, built of wood, looked surprisingly run down. And he was starting to wonder, as the car parked outside Government House, if his estimate of how many people lived in the city had been a little too high.

And if they're not here, he thought, *where are they going?*

He bit down on his anger, hard, as the driver opened the door. Governor Labara needed to go, the sooner the better. A faint, but unpleasant smell hung in the air as he followed the driver into Government House, silently noting the dank corridors, empty desks and barren offices. It felt as if he were walking into the lair of a dangerous animal, not the home of a government official. He had to clasp his hands behind his back to keep from going for his gun.

"Your Highness," Governor Labara said, as he was shown into the governor's office. He was fatter than Henry remembered, fat in a way that reminded Henry of a relative who'd binge-eaten to cope with life in the Royal Family. "I...welcome to Unity."

Henry met his eyes. "What the hell happened?"

Governor Labara looked, just for a second, as if he were too tired and worn to be angry. "No investment," he said, simply. "People stopped listening to me."

"What?" Henry pulled a chair from the side of the room and sat down, dismissing the driver with a wave of his hand. "Who stopped listening to you?"

"Everyone," Governor Labara said, darkly. "We are alone out here, Your Highness."

Henry bit down, hard, on the response that came to mind. "What happened?"

Governor Labara shrugged, impassively. "My authority was always very limited," he said, tartly. "I had no way to turn my decisions into law. There was no outside investment, no source of funds...most of the population either went to the farms or stayed in the city, doing nothing. My writ doesn't run outside the city itself..."

He looked up. "You brought troops, right? You can impose order?"

"I thought you wanted to be evacuated," Henry said. "Is that true?"

"There's nothing for me back home," Governor Labara said.

Henry nodded. No one was *that* interested in Unity, but it was rare - almost unknown - for a colony world to fail. Governor Labara would be lucky if he was merely pensioned off, after the Great Powers started asking pointed questions. Losing control of Unity - it was clear that the population had simply begun to ignore him - wouldn't reflect well on anyone. God knew he'd have to open discussions with the other factions...

At least they didn't have a civil war, he thought. *They didn't have the numbers or firepower to have a civil war.*

"Fine," Henry said, finally. There was no time to worry about assigning blame. "You and your staff - and everyone else who wants to go - will be lifted to orbit and shipped home. Your duties will be surrendered to the military officer on the spot. After the war...we'll find a way to sort out the mess."

He'd expected an argument, but Governor Labara merely nodded. The man was broken, Henry realised; broken beyond repair. Unity... wasn't entirely a failure, not if there was a thriving settlement, but it was clear that Governor Labara *had* failed. And yet, with so few tools at his disposal, what was he supposed to do? It wasn't as if he could call for help from the Great Powers. Unity enjoyed a particular immunity to gunboat diplomacy.

"You'll go back to Earth," he added. "Unless you want to retire here, I suppose."

Governor Labara shook his head, sharply. "I've had enough of this place, Your Highness."

"I don't blame you," Henry said. And it was quite likely that Unity had had enough of Governor Labara too. "But for the moment...I need to talk to the other settlers and see what we can work out."

"Good luck," Governor Labara said, rather harshly. His voice was bitter. "They never listened to me."

Henry sighed. It hadn't been an uncommon problem, in the three or four years after the First Interstellar War. A colony would lose contact with Earth and feel betrayed, eventually learning how to survive without support from its founders. And then, when contact was re-established, refuse to rejoin the rest of the human race. He couldn't blame the settlers for feeling betrayed - they'd been promised investment that had never materialised - but it wasn't his problem, not right now. He needed to lay the ground for landing the troops.

"I'll see what I can do," Henry said. He had force on his side, but the last thing he wanted - or needed - was a prolonged insurgency against the settlers. Anyone who survived and thrived on a world like Unity would be tough, hardy and a crack shot. "If nothing else, we have a great deal to offer."

"They won't trust you," Governor Labara pointed out. "And why should they?"

"Because there's a war on," Henry said, harshly. "Or didn't you *tell* them there was a war on?"

"They didn't believe me," Governor Labara said. There was something almost plaintive in his voice. Henry would have felt sorry for him, if he hadn't suspected that the Governor had played a major role in his own misfortunes. "They thought I was just trying to assert authority."

"They'll know there's a fleet in orbit," Henry said, finally. "And if that doesn't bring them to the negotiating table, we can decide what to do next."

Governor Labara leaned forward. "And if you can't?"

"I wish I knew," Henry said. "That won't be my decision."

CHAPTER
NINETEEN

"There should be no question of our response," Yegorovich said. The Russian's holographic image seemed to pulse with his indignation. "We should immediately declare martial law over Unity and crush these rebels with maximum force."

"They're not rebels," Prince Henry said.

"They are refusing orders from the government," Yegorovich snapped. "What would *you* call them?"

Susan resisted the urge to roll her eyes like a schoolgirl. The discussion had barely begun when it had been hijacked by Yegorovich, who seemed to take the political situation on Unity as a personal affront. She had no idea why - it wasn't as if Russia had contributed much towards the planet's settlement - but his demand for a harsh response to the situation on the ground was making it hard to focus on anything else.

"I have spoken to five of their leaders in the last day," Prince Henry said. "It is my belief that they have merely asserted a *de facto* independence from Governor Labara. There is nothing to be gained by contesting this, certainly not during the middle of a war."

"Rebels," Yegorovich thundered. He looked from face to face, clearly seeking support from his peers. "They should be punished."

"We have ten thousand troops, half of which are trained to operate the planetary defence systems," General Steve Kershaw said. The American Marine looked tired and frustrated, but his voice was calm. "We do not have the manpower to suppress an enemy who knows the terrain better than we do - and trying will make it impossible to actually set up the defences to resist attack! If we can find a diplomatic solution, we should."

"There is none," Yegorovich insisted. "We do not negotiate with rebels, traitors and terrorists!"

They're not terrorists, Susan thought.

Admiral Harper raised a hand. "Prince Henry?"

Prince Henry looked irked. "As I said, I have spoken to their leaders," he said. His voice was calm, but Susan could hear his annoyance. "They are willing to assist us in defending the planet, but not to discuss any political settlement until after the war. Governor Labara, it seems, was not a very good governor. Most of his edicts were…useless. This is a very common problem, to be fair, but made worse by the confused political situation surrounding the planet."

He took a moment to gather his thoughts. "They don't trust us," he warned. "And they have no *reason* to trust us. Our best step, I think, is to agree to their terms and prepare to defend the planet against a far more serious threat."

"This is a dangerous precedent," Yegorovich groused. "Was this how you treated the colonists on Cromwell?"

"There is nothing to be gained by harsh repression," Prince Henry said. "*There is a war on!*"

"True," Harper agreed. "General Kershaw, begin the landing operation. I want the ground-based defences in position as quickly as possible."

"Yes, sir," Kershaw said.

Susan frowned, inwardly, as Harper started discussing the task force's deployment orders and assigning missions to the smaller ships. She had no idea why Yegorovich was so steamed about the colonists, unless he feared that Russian colonists would be inspired to break their ties with Earth too. Or maybe he just saw them as traitors to humanity. Unity had had prospects, once upon a time. Whatever it had now, it wasn't quite the same.

"We'll also evacuate the planet's population," Harper added. "Prince Henry, how many actually want to *leave*?"

"Surprisingly few," Prince Henry said. "Almost all of the government workers have elected to leave, along with a handful of colonists, but the vast majority wish to remain in place. I've asked the evacuees to pack a single bag each, then head to the spaceport for pickup. I anticipate *some* protest."

"There will *definitely* be some protest," Kershaw said, bluntly. "You'll probably find at least one bastard who thinks he can take everything he owns with him."

"Order the marines to confiscate anything beyond a single bag," Harper said. "And if anyone causes trouble, they can be put in irons for the return journey."

"Yes, sir," Kershaw said.

Susan nodded. She'd been at school during the Bombardment, but her father had been recalled to the colours and ordered to assist with evacuating vast numbers of people from flood-stuck regions of Britain. His stories had been terrifying, both of people who had risked life and limb to save their fellows…and people who had taken advantage of the situation to loot abandoned houses or rape refugees at will. Some people, he'd said, had been too selfish to *think* about what they were doing. Trying to cart away their possessions wasted valuable space that could have been used for other refugees.

Harper cleared his throat. "We appear to have gotten into place ahead of the aliens," he added, bluntly. "Does anyone have any concerns?"

"We should be sweeping the next few systems," Captain Stewart said. "If the enemy intends to send an attack force towards us, we *should* be able to get a sniff of their presence."

"Their stealth systems are good," Harper pointed out. "But you're right - we should keep a wary eye on our approaches."

"There's another concern," Jeanette said. The Frenchwoman looked grim. "What if the enemy isn't planning to attack?"

Susan scowled. Intelligence had been sure that the enemy *did* intend to attack, but it was a supposition built on a web of tissue-thin evidence. It made sense, but it rested on a series of assumptions that might - that *might* - not be accurate. Politically, defending Unity made sense; strategically, it depended on what the aliens knew - and what they chose to do with that knowledge. It was quite possible that they had no way to know that Unity existed.

"The logic is sound," Yegorovich said. "Even if they don't care about the planet, they have good reason to want to secure the system."

"We have orders to secure the system ourselves," Harper said. "If no attack materialises, we can rethink our approach."

"And perhaps push upwards towards enemy-held space," Susan said.

"Quite," Yegorovich agreed. "It is sheer folly to *wait* to be attacked."

"Our orders stand," Harper said. "Now, concerning deployments of our picket ships…"

———

George let out a sigh of relief as she landed the shuttle neatly in the centre of the spaceport, then sighed as she saw the line of waiting refugees lurking behind the armed and armoured marines. They looked…wasted, she decided; they looked as if they couldn't wait to get off the planet, even though they would have to spend the next two months in a cramped transport until they reached Earth or Terra Nova. She keyed the console, opening the hatch, then leaned back in her chair to catch her breath as the soldiers disembarked, their sergeant shouting commands as they jogged towards the spaceport.

At least it isn't Tadpole Prime, she thought, numbly. *Landing there is an absolute nightmare.*

She poured herself a mug of coffee and drank it, slowly, as the marines organised the refugees. Unity was a breeze, as far as flying was concerned, but she had started to hate the spaceport with a passion. It was just too small for the dozens of shuttles making their way to and from the task force, while the surface wasn't quite solid and security was a joke. The marines had set up barriers, trying to get the refugees to line up to be processed before they were flown to orbit, but she was still nervous about accidentally landing on a dog - or a child.

"Line up," one of the marines bellowed. "Keep your bags on your chests until you're in the seats, then place them under the seat in front of you."

George gritted her teeth as the refugees swarmed onboard, pushing and shoving even though it was pointless. There was no way she could get them into orbit any quicker, no matter how loudly they demanded that the shuttle leave immediately. Hell, she had no idea why they were hurrying. There was no reason to believe that an attack was about to take place...

She rose as the last of the refugees sat down - the marines closed and secured the hatch - and checked their belts one by one, feeling rather like an air hostess. It wasn't a job she'd ever wanted, not after flying marines and soldiers down to the surface. The vast majority of the refugees were quiet, but there were a handful of screaming children that threatened to deafen her. She'd never wanted children and now she remembered why. Too much experience babysitting teenage children during her time at school.

"I need to send a message to the governor," a middle-aged man said. "Young lady, I..."

"Remain seated, sir," George ordered, flatly. She had no idea what had happened to the Governor, but there was no way she could send a message to him. "You can contact the Governor once you're on the transport."

She rubbed her forehead as she returned to her seat, then began the pre-flight checks while requesting a launch slot from the makeshift ATC. Unity didn't have *anything* that passed for an ATC, something that didn't really surprise her when there were only a handful of aircraft on the planet. The marines had had to set up their own, linking their sensors into the orbital network and the task force starships high overhead. It was almost frightening to be without the safety net. God help the colonists, she thought, if they needed an air ambulance or even an emergency shuttle ride to the city. It wasn't going to come.

Colonists are hardy types, she reminded herself, firmly. *And they knew the job was dangerous when they took it.*

"We are cleared for takeoff," she said, as the authorisation flashed onto her display. "Do *not* remove your seatbelts without permission."

"And don't flirt with the stewardesses either," one of the marines added. "And shitting your pants should be kept entirely to yourself."

George gave him a nasty look, then rested her hands on the controls, taking the shuttle into the air. The flight was smooth, surprisingly so, but she heard the sound of someone throwing up behind her anyway. She cursed under her breath - she was going to have to clear up the mess - and then concentrated on the flight. She'd smelled worse, during her career, but she would have bet good money that some of the other colonists were going to throw up too.

Maybe not that hardy, she thought, darkly. The shuttle passed through the upper atmosphere and set course for the transport. *Why did they even come here anyway?*

She overheard some grumbling behind her, but the marines managed to keep it from becoming anything more as she took the shuttle towards the giant transport as fast as possible. Hundreds of shuttles were buzzing around the airlocks, each one carrying thirty or forty colonists; she docked as soon as she could, then allowed herself a moment of relief as the refugees were urged through the hatch and into the larger ship. They were in for a nasty surprise, she thought, if they expected private cabins and showers. They'd be lucky if they had blankets to cover themselves once they were herded into the hold.

They'll want to go back down, she told herself, as she disconnected from the transport and set course for *Vanguard*. *But it's far too late.*

"The bastard vomited over the chair," one of the marines said. "You want me to clean it up?"

George was tempted, but she shook her head. She was the shuttle pilot. It was her responsibility. She'd clean it up as soon as she got back to *Vanguard*, before being ordered to take another flight down to the surface or - more likely - being told to take a nap. Regs limited just how long a pilot could spend on active duty and she was very definitely pushing the limits. But as long as there were refugees down on the surface, the operational tempo would have to be maintained.

"We're due to dock in two minutes," she said. "I'll deal with it then."

A platoon of marines was waiting outside the hatch when she docked, led by Corporal Christopher Byron. He winked cheerfully at her, as she went to clean up the mess, then spoke quietly to the marines who were already on the shuttle. George couldn't hear what he said, but they saluted him the moment he finished and hurried through the hatch.

"You'll be taking us down to the surface," Byron said. "Your orders should have already arrived."

George nodded and walked back to the pilot's seat, dropping the filthy cloth in the recycler as she passed. There would be time to wash the rest of the shuttle later, once she returned to the ship. The Senior Chief wouldn't be pleased at the smell, but there was nothing she could do about it. Her orders were waiting for her, as Byron had said; drop the platoon at the spaceport, then take a final load of refugees to the transport.

"Take your seats," she ordered, as she checked the ever-updating orbital map. "We leave in two minutes."

"Understood," Byron said.

———

"Local space is getting crowded, Captain," Charlotte observed. "There's a *lot* of sensor clutter out there."

Susan nodded, ruefully. Unity's orbital space had been nearly deserted when the task force arrived, but it was a very different story now. Hundreds of shuttles were making their way to and from the planet, dozens of automated orbital weapons platforms were being placed in orbit and several squadrons of starfighters were flying constant CSP formations around the planet. If the aliens had glanced at Unity from a distance and decided the planet was uninhabited - which struck her as unlikely - they certainly wouldn't make that mistake now.

"Make sure you catalogue it all," she ordered, firmly. It was hard enough watching for cloaked starships *without* hundreds of pieces of space junk that could confuse sensors and send operators scurrying in search of starships that weren't there. "We can at least *try* to avoid problems."

But better safe than sorry, her own thoughts warned her. *If we miss something, we'll have cause to regret it.*

She settled back into her chair, watching as the display constantly updated itself. There were so many shuttles moving through local space that it was a miracle there hadn't been an accident, particularly when the ATC was a makeshift piece of crap. She would have preferred to run everything from orbit, but the groundpounders had insisted on operating the system themselves. It made sense, she supposed. And yet, if the task force had to leave, the groundpounders would have to go quiet. A single betraying radio emission would attract a KEW.

"We got the latest report from the freighters, Captain," Parkinson said. "They saw nothing, apparently."

Susan nodded. She'd wondered why the two freighters had remained in the system and now she had her answer. Their long-term contracts kept them there, even though there was no hope of earning enough money to buy out their ships. The crews were demoralised - she'd heard that several of them had attempted to offer their services to Admiral Harper - and their commanders the dregs of the merchant marine.

Bloody bureaucrats, she thought. She just couldn't understand their logic. *Was it really so important that we had a space-based presence orbiting Unity?*

She pushed the thought aside as she checked the latest series of readiness reports. There had been a definite improvement over the last few days, although that might have had something to do with the soldiers being moved down to the surface. But she knew what would happen if they kept running endless exercises. Her crew would eventually lose their edge...

"Captain," Charlotte said. "I've got something odd on the passive sensor network."

Susan felt a flicker of alarm as she rose. "Show me," she ordered, striding over to the sensor console. There was a faint haze on the main display, suggesting trouble. Alerts were already flashing through the network. "What is...?"

Red icons flickered into existence on the display. "Incoming missiles," Jean Granger snapped. "I say again, incoming missiles!"

"Red alert," Susan snapped, whirling back towards her chair. She tapped her wristcom as she moved, opening a priority channel. "Set condition-one throughout the ship! This is no drill; I say again, this is no drill!"

She sat down as more red icons appeared. "Stand by all point defence," she ordered. This was *definitely* no drill. Thankfully, they'd been ready for *something*. They hadn't been caught with their pants around their ankles. "And lock us into the task force command net!"

"Aye, Captain," Granger said. Her fingers darted over her console. "Point defence armed, ready to fire; kinetic buckshot armed, ready to fire!"

And here we go, Susan thought.

———

George swore as the display filled with red icons, seconds before alerts started popping up in front of her. The alien timing had been diabolical. They'd opened their offensive just as she was entering the planet's atmosphere, forcing her to decide between plunging down to the surface - and risking being trapped - or trying to make her way back to the ship, knowing she might be blown out of space by a passing starfighter at any moment. And then a missile detonated far too close to her...

"Hang on," she snapped. She wasn't sure how the enemy had managed to slip so many missiles so close to the task force, but it hardly mattered at the moment. "We're going down!"

A second warhead detonated near the shuttle, sending a wave of electromagnetic disruption through space. More red lights flared up in front of her as a number of systems failed, one by one. George fought for control as the shuttle started to plummet...

...And fell towards the planet, far below.

CHAPTER
TWENTY

"Enemy vessels coming out of cloak, Captain," Charlotte reported. "I'm picking up thirty-seven ships, including five battleships."

Susan cursed under her breath. The aliens had them outgunned, *without* the planned network of orbital and ground-based defensive platforms. Their timing had been perfect, suggesting that they'd been watching Unity for some time…or treachery. She didn't *think* that any human would side with the aliens, but it was vaguely possible…

Worry about it later, she told herself. *We are at war.*

"Deploy additional sensor drones," she ordered. The aliens had made it far too close to the planet - and had even launched missiles on ballistic trajectories - without being detected. It said worrying things about their capabilities. "Prepare to move us out of orbit."

She glanced at the fleet command display and cursed under her breath. The aliens had *definitely* caught the squadron with their pants down, threatening to trap them against the planet if they didn't move swiftly. But Admiral Harper had yet to assume command, even though the fleet command network had gone active the moment the enemy had opened fire. Was he in bed? Should she assume command herself?

"Signal from the flag," Parkinson reported. "The task force is to assume beta-seven formation; I say again, beta-seven formation."

Shit, Susan thought. Beta-seven gave Harper the widest possible range of options, but it also forced him to set course away from the planet. If they'd had time to deploy *all* of the orbital defences, the aliens would have had a hard time securing the high orbitals…she shook her head, dismissing the thought. There was no point in crying over spilt milk. *Unity is already on its own.*

"Take us to our position within the formation," she ordered. "And stand by to repel attack."

The enemy ships opened fire, launching two- or three-stage missiles towards the human ships. Susan wasn't sure why they bothered - the point defence computers had plenty of time to track the missiles and determine the appropriate countermeasures - but she had to admit it made their point. And besides, they might have improved their bomb-pumped laser warheads again.

Or they might not have realised that we've improved our point defence, she told herself, as a solid wall of red icons closed in on the task force. *They may assume that they will be thrashing us from beyond our effective point defence range.*

"Picking up a new trajectory from the flag," Parkinson reported. "Starfighters are being deployed now."

"The enemy doesn't appear to have deployed starfighters of his own," Granger added. "I don't think any of their starships are actually *carriers*."

Susan shrugged. The enemy had presumably analysed the first engagements as intensely as JHQ, back on Earth. They had to *know* that their starfighters were inferior; they had to assume that they'd be wiped out in large numbers if they were matched against a human force. Or they might not have had any carriers on hand when they deployed their fleet. If they'd caught a sniff of the task force making its way towards Unity, they might just have decided to launch a spoiling attack with whatever they had on hand.

She sucked in her breath as the Russian and French starfighters lurched forward, half the fighters targeting the missiles before they entered attack range while the remainder headed towards the enemy ships, hoping to launch attack runs against their drives. She suspected the starfighters were about to take heavy losses - the enemy point defence was just as good as humanity's - but there was no choice. The enemy had a very definite firepower advantage.

"Enemy missiles entering point defence range," Granger reported. "Buckshot weapons engaging…now."

Susan leaned forward, watching the display as enemy missiles began to vanish. The buckshot projectiles weren't very large, but at the speeds the missiles were travelling a small marble would be more than enough to vaporise them. They started to perform evasive manoeuvres as the warhead command network realised that they were under attack, yet it wasn't enough to save dozens more. Only a handful of missiles reached attack range and detonated.

Vanguard shuddered as laser beams stabbed into her hull, but the armour absorbed the blow without even blinking. Susan allowed herself a tight smile - the time they'd spent modifying the hull plating hadn't been wasted - and then cursed under her breath as the enemy launched another barrage of missiles. This time, they seemed to be constantly altering their positions...unless they'd made a real drive breakthrough, part of her mind noted, they were going to be reducing their own range quite sharply. But the range was constantly shortening anyway.

"The first wave of starfighters is returning to the carriers," Granger said, quietly. "The CSP is providing cover."

Susan nodded. The Russian pilots had killed two enemy cruisers - and the French had given an enemy battleship one hell of a beating - but they'd paid heavily for their success. A third of the starfighters had been blown out of space, while two more were drifting towards the planet's atmosphere, their pilots either knocked out or dead. They wouldn't survive re-entry, Susan knew. Starfighters simply weren't designed to enter a planet's atmosphere under their own power. The last attempt to build a workable aerospace fighter had resulted in a design that couldn't hold its own against craft built for one of the two environments.

She said a silent prayer for the pilots - the carriers would presumably dispatch SAR shuttles, if the aliens didn't blow them out of space - and then turned back to the main display as the enemy ships entered missile range. Orders flickered up from the flag, ordering all three battleships to open fire; she snapped orders herself, then watched as a barrage of missiles roared towards the alien ships. It was useless, she suspected - the aliens were already moving their smaller ships forward to boost their point defence - but at least it would warn them to keep their distance.

"Enemy missiles entering attack range," Granger warned. "Detonating..."

Vanguard lurched, badly, as an x-ray laser stabbed into her hull. Susan cursed - deliberately or not, the aliens had struck an already-damaged section of the hull - then tapped her console, detailing damage control teams to do what they could. Reports from the analysis sections, already blinking up in front of her, suggested that the aliens were trying to take out the turrets in hopes of crippling the ship before they entered energy weapons range. They'd been taught respect for *Vanguard's* main guns during the last engagement, she knew. She would have been surprised if the enemy *hadn't* tried to cripple her before it was too late.

"Signal from the flag," Parkinson reported. "The task force is to move to gamma-four; I say again, gamma-four."

Susan exchanged glances with Mason. If Harper had decided to move to gamma-four, it meant that he intended to go on a raiding mission rather than either try to retake the Unity System or harry the enemy from a safe distance. It was the aggressive posture she wanted, although with so many enemy ships nearby it had more than its fair share of dangers. And it would make it easier for the forces on the ground to scatter before the enemy secured the high orbitals and started to drop KEWs.

The farmers are well-prepared to go to ground, she thought, grimly. Even knowing what they were looking for, the orbital analysts hadn't been able to pick out more than ten percent of the smaller homesteads. The bigger ones had been obvious - they'd have to be evacuated before the aliens arrived - but the smaller ones were well-hidden. *But if the aliens land a few hundred thousand troops, they're in deep shit.*

"Hold us in position," she ordered. The enemy ships were moving closer, their capital ships advancing while their lighter ships were reducing speed. She thought she detected an odd reluctance in their movements, although she had no way to be sure. It was certainly the smart thing to do. Main guns capable of thrashing a battleship wouldn't have any problems blowing a smaller ship out of space. "Are the carriers taking up their positions?"

"Aye, Captain," Granger said. "Enemy ships will be in energy weapons range in less than ten minutes."

Susan waited, feeling sweat running down her back. The tactical situation had suddenly become very simple. *Vanguard* - and the other two battleships - had to hold the line long enough for the carriers to put some distance between themselves and the enemy ships. But the enemy, by contrast, would try to take advantage of the manoeuvre to pound *Vanguard* and her sisters to scrap before they could escape themselves. *And* they had enough ships to chase the human ship as well as lay siege to the planet.

Mason caught her attention. "Captain, Midshipwoman Fitzwilliam's shuttle went down," he said, quietly. "She was transporting marines to the surface."

"Duly noted," Susan said, grimly. There was nothing to be done, not when the task force was already thrusting away from the planet. "If she made it down…"

She glanced at the display, hoping for insight, but space around the planet had become a blur of electronic fuzz. The aliens had devised their own versions of disrupter warheads and deployed them in vast numbers, despite the risk of jamming their own systems. She had to admit that it had paid off for them. Most military technology was hardened against EMP and other forms of electronic disruption, but there were too many exceptions. Active and passive sensors were easy to disrupt, if one was prepared to pay the price.

She might have made it down, she told herself. It was a bitter thought. She'd seen something of herself in George Fitzwilliam. And besides, the First Space Lord would not be pleased to learn that his niece had been killed on active duty. *And if she didn't, we will probably never find the body.*

The seconds ticked away as the two fleets converged. She couldn't help noticing that the aliens were keeping their smaller ships to the front, even though there was no way their point defence could stop *Vanguard's* main guns. It made no sense, unless they expected her to pull another blunderbuss stunt. But even then, it was unlikely they could save their ships from a very nasty blow. They'd have to be at practically point-blank range…

And they would never survive so close to our guns, Susan thought, vindictively. *Even our secondary armament would make mincemeat of them.*

"Raise the flag," she ordered. The range was steadily closing. "Admiral, I suggest that we target the smaller ships in our first barrage. Stripping them away from the enemy fleet will make it easier to break contact."

There was a long pause. "Tactical fleet orders are being updated, Captain," Granger said. "I think he heard you."

"Confirmed," Parkinson said. "We are ordered to open fire as soon as the enemy ships enter range."

"Then lock weapons on target," Susan ordered. The flag was already designating targets, making sure that two battleships didn't waste their opening barrage by targeting the same ship. "And prepare to fire."

She felt an odd flicker of discontent as the range closed, bringing the enemy ships within energy weapons range for the first time. *Vanguard* was *her* ship, but Admiral Harper would be the one giving the order to open fire - and she wouldn't even be repeating it to her tactical crew. But there was no choice. The fleet had to make its first shots count...

"Firing," Granger said.

Vanguard rolled in space, the turrets blazing out deadly pulses of plasma towards the enemy ships. Susan had the satisfaction of watching a cruiser explode under *Vanguard's* fire, two more destroyers staggering out of formation as they fought for survival, a second or two before the enemy returned fire. Red icons flashed up in front of her, warning that the enemy battleships had targeted *Vanguard's* drives. Thankfully, the armour seemed to be handling it.

For the moment, she thought. *But we're both firing at extreme range.*

Absurdly, the enemy seemed caught by surprise. Their remaining smaller ships were rapidly wiped out, save for one that managed a dizzying series of evasive patterns that eventually ended with the ship taking shelter behind a battleship. They didn't even seem inclined to adjust their own fire to target *humanity's* support ships! All five enemy battleships were concentrating their fire on the human battleships.

"Damage control teams report that enemy fire is weakening the armour in sections seven through nine," Flinch said, over the intercom. "There are limits to what we can do during a battle."

"Understood," Susan said.

Her ship shuddered, time and time again, under the constant bombardment. The enemy battleships didn't seem discomforted by the loss of their escorts; instead, they just kept pounding the bigger human ships. Susan silently tallied the damage as point defence weapons and sensor blisters were blown off the hull, each one reducing her ship's fighting power by a percentage point. They could be replaced - and they would be replaced - but it could only be done after the battle was over.

"Signal from the flag," Parkinson said. "Admiral Harper wants to launch missiles, blunderbuss pattern."

"See to it," Susan said. They'd tried the tactic time and time again in simulations, but too much depended on the assumptions fed into the computers. The tactic might work - or it might damage the human ship instead of the enemy target. "Fire at will."

She sucked in her breath as the missiles were launched. The enemy seemed to realise the danger, but it was too late; the warheads detonated one by one, sending deadly laser beams digging into their target's hull. She watched, feeling a wave of cold vindictiveness, as one of the enemy battleships rolled out of formation, spewing atmosphere. There was no chance to get a nuke through one of the gashes in her hull, but she had the feeling it didn't matter. The ship was so badly damaged that it might be cheaper to scrap her and build a new one instead of trying to make repairs.

Unless they have some reason to think repair work is quicker, she thought. *We still don't know anything about their industrial base.*

The four enemy battleships kept firing, wiping out a spread of missiles before they could detonate and tear into another enemy ship. Susan was surprised they didn't retaliate in kind, but the more she looked at the display, the more she suspected they *couldn't*. Two or three-stage missiles were *huge*, each one eating up three or four times the magazine space of a standard missile. They might well have shot their bolt during the early stages of the engagement, which might be why they were pressing so hard against the battleships. A long-range missile duel might well be impossible.

For them, she thought. *And it would be a waste of missiles for us too.*

A dull rumbling echoed through the ship as a second alien battleship started to pound at her hull. Susan gritted her teeth as damage reports continued to mount up. The armour was strong, but the hammering was steadily wearing it down. She needed time to make repairs, time she knew she wasn't going to get. The battle had turned into a battering match and she had a sneaking suspicion the aliens were going to win. A line of starfighters flashed past her to make another attack run on the alien ships, but the aliens picked off four of them before the remainder had a chance to salvo their torpedoes into their hulls. The only upside was that one of the torpedoes had destroyed an alien turret beyond immediate repair.

We need to adjust our tactics, she thought. *Battering matches cost us dearly even when we win.*

"Signal from the flag," Parkinson said. "We're to pick up speed to catch up with the carriers."

"Make it so," Susan ordered.

She winced as she heard an atonal thrumming echoing through the ship as the drives fought to crank out more power. The alien battleships were smaller than *Vanguard*, suggesting that they enjoyed a sharper acceleration curve. But would they choose to continue the engagement? There was no way to know if the alien reinforcements were closer than hers, although she would be surprised if they *weren't*. A long running battle might leave the alien fleet battered into uselessness, even if they won.

Green icons flashed past *Vanguard* on the display, the remaining starfighters heading back to their carriers. There were replacement fighters in the transports, she knew, but getting them manned and ready to deploy would take time they didn't have. The Russians, thankfully, had cross-trained hundreds of their personnel...she'd wondered at that, back during a dinner on *Admiral Kuznetsov*, but she had to admit it might just pay off for them. God knew that starfighters might be the difference between surviving the next few hours or dying hundreds of light years from Earth.

"They're sticking with us," Granger reported. "Their acceleration curves are quite impressive."

Brute force, Susan thought. The analysts weren't *certain*, but it seemed logical. They *actually crammed more drives into their hulls rather than seeking to improve their technology.*

"Continue firing," Susan ordered. The enemy tactics didn't quite make sense, unless they believed they would come out ahead if they traded five battleships for three. They might, if they had an entire armada of battleships on the other side of the tramline. "And hold us on our current course."

"Aye, Captain," Granger said.

"And watch for ramming attempts," Susan added. If the enemy were *that* determined not to let them go, an attempt to ram one of the battleships was all too likely. "Even a failed attempt to ram us could cause problems."

And that, she added silently, *is the understatement of the decade.*

CHAPTER
TWENTY-ONE

There was no time for panic.

George felt it yowling at the back of her mind as she fought for control, knowing that tumbling helplessly into the planet's atmosphere would mean certain death. The shuttle was spinning so rapidly that the gee-forces were tearing at her, despite the compensators; she prayed, desperately, that they wouldn't overload and fail completely. It would kill everyone on the shuttle so quickly that they wouldn't have any time to realise what had hit them before it was too late.

Alert after alert blinked up in front of her, screaming warnings. She ignored as many of them as she dared, knowing that the shuttle had been designed to fly with half of its systems out and a third of the remainder badly compromised. But she'd never had to fly in such desperate circumstances...the ATC was gone, but a glance at the near-orbit display was enough to tell her that enemy missiles were roaring towards the orbiting satellites and blowing them out of existence, one by one. There was no hope of rescue before it was too late. She couldn't even pull them out of the planet's gravity well.

"Hold on," she shouted, as she managed - somehow - to straighten out their flight. The hand of God Almighty slapped the shuttle as she crashed into the upper atmosphere, almost starting them tumbling again. *Something* flashed past them, but she barely had a second to register its presence - let alone figure out what it was - before it was gone. "We're going down."

The marines, thankfully, weren't panicking. They knew, probably better than she did, just how slim the odds of survival actually were. But they remained calm, even as the shuttle started to spin again. George felt a dampness between her legs as the shuttle twisted - just for a second, the hull shook so badly that part of her thought they'd already crashed - and did her best to ignore it. She'd worry about it later, if they survived.

Turbulence slammed at them as they descended, gusts of wind hammering at the shuttle in a manner she hadn't seen anywhere but Tadpole Prime. And she hadn't tried to fly there…she told herself, frantically, that the shocks weren't going to be deadly, even though she had a nasty feeling that the shuttle was on the verge of disintegrating. She wasn't flying a damn assault shuttle, or one of the craft that had been reengineered for Tadpole Prime. She'd certainly never expected to have to make an emergency landing from low orbit.

The gravity field flickered and faded for long seconds, then collapsed altogether. George scowled, then forgot about it as she struggled to locate a place to put the shuttle down. Half the drives - and the antigravity nodes - were out, rendering the craft barely a stage or two above a flying brick. She was mildly surprised, at the back of her mind, that the craft had held together after such a beating. The shuttle wasn't *designed* for combat operations or forced landings. Really, there wasn't much of a difference between it and a civilian design.

She allowed herself a sigh of relief as the flight straightened out, although she had no idea how long it would last. They couldn't stay in the air anyway, not when the enemy would be moving rapidly to invest and secure the high orbitals. A starship would have no trouble picking them off from orbit, no matter how desperately she tried to evade. She'd watched some of the recordings of military operations, during the later days of the Age of Unrest. A rogue nation simply *couldn't* fly aircraft when orbital weapons platforms armed with lasers and particle beams were ready to blow them out of the air. Hell, the Tadpoles hadn't been interested in occupying human cities on worlds they'd captured, but they'd definitely shot down air traffic and anything else that looked as though it might pose a threat.

The ATC was still silent. She hesitated, then gambled and sent a pulse message to one of the stealthed satellites orbiting the planet, requesting an update. There was no response. She briefly considered taking the risk again, then shook her head. The satellite would have replied, if it had been *able* to reply. Given how much firepower had been unleashed in the early seconds of the battle, it was quite possible that the aliens had swatted the satellite without ever noticing.

She glanced at the map, thinking hard. The shuttle didn't *need* the satellites to gauge its position, at least within a few thousand metres, but without a direct link to the ATC it was hard to be sure what was waiting for them on the ground. Unity wasn't Earth. Seven years of colonisation wouldn't have opened up more than a tiny percentage of the planetary surface for settlement. It was quite possible that they'd crash hundreds of miles from anyone who could help them, even though she'd spent the last few days shipping troops and equipment down to the surface. Ideally, she knew she wanted to put the shuttle down near Unity City...

But that will be their first target, she thought. *They'd have to be blind to miss the settlement.*

The shuttle rocked, violently, as another drive node failed. George cursed, savagely; they couldn't stay in the air much longer, no matter what she did. She lowered their altitude as much as she could, doing her best to ignore the increasing cacophony of alarms. If she made it back home, she promised herself that she'd send the designers a very sharp note. There was nothing she could *do* about the damage, certainly not when they were on the verge of falling out of the sky. The alarms were a distraction at the worst possible moment...

And then another drive node failed.

"Hang on," George shouted. The shuttle yawed, threatening to roll over and slam into the ground. Normally, the automatic systems would have compensated for the loss of the node, but they seemed to have gone offline too. "Brace for impact..."

She yanked the shuttle back around, fighting to come down as gently as possible, a moment before the ground came up and hit them. There was a moment of blackness - it took her a second to realise that she'd been stunned for a moment - and then the shuttle seemed to come apart at the seams. They tumbled, crashing forward, until they finally came to a stop. She sagged, silently relieved that they were alive. Under the circumstances, they'd been incredibly lucky,

Strong hands caught at her, undoing her strap and pulling her away from her chair. "Come on," a voice snapped. She was so dazed that it took her a moment to recognise Stott. "We can't stay here."

She couldn't move. Her entire body seemed limp. Stott lifted her up, despite the cramped conditions, and threw her over his shoulder. Someone was shouting outside, George registered; she wondered, dimly, what had happened to them. Her mind seemed to be spinning in and out of awareness, as if she was concussed. Had she hit her head at some point? She couldn't recall…

Something *jabbed* the side of her thigh. She jerked awake, feeling oddly cold. A pair of hands were roaming over her body; she tensed, then realised that the medic was checking for wounds. Her eyes opened - she hadn't even been aware they were closed - and saw a young man bending over her, holding a portable sensor in one hand. He held the sensor against her forehead, then looked relieved.

"You're unwounded," he said, softly. "How do you feel?"

"…Odd," George managed. Her mouth felt like she'd been drinking heavily, the night before. "What did you give me?"

"A very basic booster," the medic said. He held out a hand and helped her to her feet. "I would have preferred to give you something stronger, but the boss overrode it."

George nodded, slowly. The shuttle was some distance away, lying on the ground. She didn't need to be an expert to know that the craft was beyond repair. The hull was cracked in a dozen places and smoke was rising from the drive section. And, beyond it, hundreds of trees were lying on the ground. Any halfway competent orbital observer would have no difficulty locating the crash site, even if the shuttle hadn't been clearly visible from orbit.

"George," Byron said. The marine corporal looked relieved. "Can you walk?"

"I think so," George said. Her legs still felt wobbly, but nothing was actually broken. "Was…was anyone hurt?"

"A couple of the lads got banged up, but everyone's intact," Byron reassured her. "You did very well, really."

George looked back at the shuttle and smiled, despite her growing tiredness. Her instructors had told her, more than once, that any landing she could walk away from was a good landing, although the cadets had suspected that deliberately crashing the shuttles was a good way to get kicked out of the Academy. But then, when disaster struck, there was no longer any time to worry about anything, beyond landing as safely as possible. She'd got them down alive - she'd got them *all* down alive - and that was all that mattered.

"Thanks," she said.

"We can't stay here," Byron warned. "We're keeping radio silence, but I would be astonished if the aliens haven't secured the high orbitals. The next step will be a landing in force."

He glanced past her. George turned; Stott was kneeling near a tree, sorting through a collection of supplies. "Are we ready?"

"We've got everything useful, sir," Stott said. George was surprised at his formality. But then, they *were* on deployment. "There are a few more things we could take from the shuttle, but we don't know how much time we have."

There was a flash in the sky. George looked up and winced. Pieces of debris were falling from high orbit, the remains of the orbital defence grid burning up in the atmosphere. The sky was blue - it was late afternoon, if she recalled correctly - but she didn't need to *see* the alien ships to know they were there. And a single transmission would be more than enough to draw a KEW down on their heads.

"Get ready to march," Byron ordered. "We'll put some distance between ourselves and the shuttle, then decide where to go."

He glanced at George. "Stay with Stott and Kelly," he added, nodding to the medic. "If you have problems keeping up, tell them."

"And we won't hesitate to put a foot up your arse," Stott added. "We have to keep moving."

George nodded - she knew he wasn't joking - then watched as the marines hastily grabbed their weapons and started to move out. She'd never had any illusions about Byron and Stott - Fraser had made it clear that they were both very dangerous men, even if they *were* friendly - but she'd never realised what it was like to be surrounded by marines. They moved through the jungle as if they were born to it, weapons constantly at the ready. She followed Kelly, wishing she'd thought to exercise more on the ship. There was no way she was anything like as fit as the marines.

She glanced up, sharply, as she heard a low roar passing overhead. A shuttle was visible in the sky for a few seconds before vanishing in the distance. She tried to calculate its course, but gave up within seconds. She'd *tried* to put them down close to Unity City…yet she wasn't remotely sure where they'd landed.

"That wasn't a human shuttle," she gasped.

"Save your breath," Stott advised. He didn't even have the decency to seem winded, even though it felt as though they'd walked for miles. Hacking their way through the jungle was a slow process. "You're going to need it."

George nodded, keeping her mouth firmly shut. She'd have to go back to Hanover Towers, if she ever made it back to Earth, and apologise to her Sports Mistress. George and her peers had *detested* the woman - she'd always been happy to add extra laps or punish students she'd thought weren't pulling their weight - but without her steady pressure she knew she would have collapsed long ago. Even the Academy hadn't pushed her so hard. But compared to what the marines did, during their basic training, it had been nothing.

They're landing in force, she thought, as more shuttles echoed through the air. The falling debris was slowly tapering off, as if orbital space was now clear. Unity just hadn't had the network of satellites and defensive platforms orbiting Earth. *And they're heading right towards Unity City.*

Byron called a break, what felt like hours after they began the march. George sagged to her knees, taking the canteen of water Kelly passed her and drinking greedily. It hit her, a moment too late, that they might be on strict water rations…but none of the marines seemed to care. Their survival kits would include something to purify the water, she thought. The kits in the shuttles - the ones she'd had to check and recheck over the last month - certainly did. She just hoped there was nothing dangerous in the local water. Drinking brackish water, she recalled from half-remembered survival training, could be lethal.

"They landed over thirty shuttles, sir," a marine she didn't recognise said. "If they're the same size as ours, they landed over five hundred troops."

"It will be more," Stott predicted. "There's no way we would have seen them all."

"Five hundred troops," Kelly mused. "Hardly enough to secure an entire planet."

"They could have cleared the way using KEWs," the first marine pointed out.

"We haven't heard any," George managed.

"That means nothing," Byron said. He didn't seem annoyed at her question. "Sound does funny things, sometimes."

He pulled a map out of his knapsack and studied it thoughtfully. George wondered, absently, if he had a way to establish their location. It was possible to get a rough idea of one's position by watching the stars, but the stars over Unity were different - very different - to the ones over Earth. And the GPS system was down, of course. The aliens would hardly have left *that* alone when they'd blown everything else out of orbit.

"We keep making our way northwards, we'll eventually cross the Tangerine River," he mused. George wondered how he knew they were heading north, then saw the compass in his hand. "When we reach the river, we head down towards Unity City. Unless I completely misread the map, there should be a number of small settlements between the crossing point and the city."

Stott elbowed George. "There's nothing more dangerous than an officer with a map," he whispered. "We'll be going in circles if we're not careful."

"I haven't been promoted to lieutenant yet," Byron said, curtly. "And you can take point when we resume our march."

"Yes, sir," Stott said. He didn't seem particularly abashed. "How long should it take us to reach the river?"

"As the crow flies, less than a day," Byron said. "In practice…it could be a bit longer."

He glanced upwards, sharply, as another shuttle flew overhead. It wasn't heading for Unity City, George realised slowly; it was heading back the way they'd come. Byron bit down a curse and motioned for the marines to rise to their feet. George groaned, feeling her body aching as Kelly helped her up. She was going to be aching badly in the morning, if she actually managed to get any sleep. Her body felt as if she'd been going toe-to-toe with Fraser for hours.

Stott clambered up a tree for several moments, then dropped down neatly, looking grim. "It looks as if they're circling the crash site," he said. "If they check the shuttle, they won't find any bodies."

"They *will* find the booby traps," Byron said. "But they'll know we're on the loose."

George swallowed, hard, as the marines began to move out. Crash-landing was bad enough, but having to march through the jungle - and being hunted by the aliens - was far worse. She didn't even know if she had the endurance to survive the next few days, let alone keep up with the marines. Byron wouldn't abandon her, she was sure, but she'd just slow them down.

She glanced at Kelly, wishing she knew him better. "If they chase us," she said, "what do we do?"

"We'll have to try to break contact," Kelly said. "It depends on just what they do."

"Keep walking," Byron ordered. "If we're lucky, they won't be able to pick up…"

An explosion blasted up in the distance, cutting off his words. It took George a moment to realise that the shuttle had just exploded, after one of the booby traps had been triggered. The marines had rigged the shuttle to blow, hoping to kill as many of the aliens as possible…she shuddered, bitterly. She'd dealt out death when she'd been in control of *Vanguard's* main guns, but this was different. *This* was up close and personal.

"Now they're mad," Stott commented.

"Shut up and keep walking," Byron ordered, sharply. George could hear a hint of tension in his voice. The marines were trained to evade enemy hunters, but the enemy already had a rough idea where they were - and George would slow them down. "Jack, take the rear. If they're coming after us, we'll have to fight."

George scowled as she checked the pistol at her belt. Fraser had hammered shooting skills into her head, but she knew she was no expert. And the thought of shooting a person - even an alien - felt wrong...

Get used to it, she told herself. She could hear more shuttles in the distance. *You might have to fight soon.*

CHAPTER
TWENTY-TWO

"Enemy ships are altering position," Granger reported. "I think they're attempting to bring their main weapons to bear on *New York*."

"Discourage them," Susan ordered. Four battleships against *one* was a losing prospect in anyone's book. Did the aliens *know* that *New York* was the flagship? Or had they merely gotten lucky? "Launch a salvo of missiles, blunderbuss pattern."

The aliens snapped back with remarkable speed. She watched, grimly, as all nine of the missiles were picked off before they had a chance to detonate. A couple of tacticians had proposed ways to detonate the missiles *inside* the battleship, but Finch had flatly refused to even *consider* the possibility. It was bad enough, he'd argued, to detonate the warheads so close to the hull. Crippling their own ship would be a complete disaster, even if they'd had an overwhelming advantage over the aliens.

And we don't, Susan thought.

The range was growing open, despite the aliens fighting desperately to pick up speed. She had the feeling that their higher command was uncertain, torn between chasing down the task force and returning to Unity. There was an indecisiveness about their tactics that reminded her of some of the more complex multinational exercises she'd seen, when American and Chinese commanders had been unwilling to either commit themselves or back off. And there were *two* alien races facing humanity.

They might have different ideas about how to proceed, she thought. *If we could figure out how to talk to them, we might be able to drive a wedge between them.*

"Captain," Parkinson said. "We picked up a recorded transmission from Unity City, forwarded to us by one of the stealthed recon platforms. The enemy is landing in force."

Susan nodded, unsurprised. "And the groundpounders?"

"Withdrawing as planned," Parkinson said. "There's no update on any of our missing personnel."

"Understood," Susan said. Midshipman Fitzwilliam wasn't the only missing person, but she had a solid idea of where the others had been when the battle had begun. The shuttle pilots on the ground would have to abandon the spaceport - and their shuttles - and attach themselves to the groundpounders until the high orbitals could be liberated. "Forward the message to the flag, then wait."

"Aye, Captain," Parkinson said.

Susan quietly evaluated the situation. The task force was picking up speed, but the aliens were still snapping at their heels. She couldn't help wondering if they were being herded into a trap, even though she knew that a plan that *depended* on the opposing force make a specific move was doomed to failure. Admiral Harper had picked their exit vector largely at random. Even if the aliens *did* have an FTL communications system - and hundreds of physicists were still in deep denial - they'd have to be incredibly lucky to get a blocking force in place before it was too late.

Unless they're lurking on the other side of the tramline, she told herself. *But if they had to guess which way we'd go, they'd say we'd go to Tramline Three.*

She scowled. Second-guessing was all too easy, even though she knew better than to wool-gather in the middle of a battle. Logically, Tramline Three offered a chance to slip back towards human space or cut across to link up with the Tadpoles. It was the best option, if the fleet intended to avoid battle. But Admiral Harper had determined that they would head to Tramline Two, deliberately seeking a chance to inflict damage on the enemy.

And we're not even on a vector for Tramline Two yet, she thought. *The Admiral wants to break contact before we cloak and alter course.*

"Signal from the flag," Parkinson ordered. "All ships are to prepare for Breakaway-Five."

Susan sucked in her breath. The enemy was snapping at their heels too closely for *any* of the Breakaway plans, although she couldn't see any alternative. There was no point in deploying drones when it would be immediately obvious which of the sensor contacts were fake - the drones, whatever else could be said about them, didn't carry any weapons. And the *real* ships couldn't stop firing without giving the enemy a free shot at their hulls.

"It's too close," she snapped. "Communications, raise Admiral Harper."

"Aye, Captain," Parkinson said.

———

"They just opened fire," Doctor Song said. She sounded stunned. "They just opened fire."

"There *is* a war on," Henry said. Whatever the aliens had been thinking, back at the Battle of UXS-469, there was *definitely* a war on now. There was nothing to gain and a great deal to lose by revealing their presence without opening fire. "And why should they give up the advantage of surprise?"

"We should be trying to communicate with them," Doctor Song said. "Can't you send them the First Contact Package?"

Henry shook his head. "There's a battle underway, Doctor," he said. "Susan - Captain Onarina - would not authorise the message, even if there was a hope in hell of the aliens actually listening and responding."

"Then send the message yourself," Doctor Song insisted.

"It wouldn't work," Henry said. Captain Onarina would be furious if he hijacked her communications system, even if it were possible. He liked to think - he wanted to believe - that the aliens *could* be made to see reason, but he had the nasty feeling that the only way to get them to listen was to give them a bloody nose. "All we can do is wait and watch."

He saw the terror in her eyes and felt a glimmer of sympathy. He'd faced the prospect of a sudden violent death during the last war, but Doctor Song had never been on a warship until he'd invited her to accompany him. There was literally nothing she could do to affect the situation in any way, not when there was no time to deploy the communications package she'd worked so hard to build. All she could do was watch, wait and pray that *Vanguard* wasn't blown out of space.

"Thanks," she said, sourly.

"You'll be able to claim hazard pay, when you get home," Henry offered. "And you'll have one hell of a story to tell."

"It isn't worth it," Doctor Song said. Another low rumble ran through the ship. "Is it?"

"It depends," Henry said. "But if it wasn't you, it would be someone else."

———

"There's no way we can break contact, not now," Susan said. Admiral Harper's holographic face hung in front of her. "They're just too close to us."

"We can hide the carriers," Admiral Harper said. "It's the battleships that are the real problem."

Susan nodded in grim agreement. The last time a combined fleet had found itself in such a mess, a pair of Tadpole warships had sacrificed themselves to save the rest of the fleet. But now…even if she reduced speed and challenged the enemy ships directly, she wouldn't be able to win time for the remainder of the task force. They were caught between the devil and the deep blue sea.

With the certain knowledge that the enemy will be able to call for reinforcements, she thought, grimly. *The long stern chase can have only one ending.*

"Order the starfighters to hammer their drive sections," Susan said. "If we slow their ships, the remainder should pause long enough to break contact."

"And if we give them something else to think about," Admiral Harper said. "I'm re-tasking the set-four drones now."

Susan nodded. She would have sold her soul for an FTL communicator of her own. As it was, it would take nearly five minutes for Admiral Harper's message to reach its destination, five *more* minutes for the drones to reply and then…at least another five minutes before they knew if the plan had worked or not. And if it didn't, they would have to think of something else.

"I'm redeploying the starfighters too," Admiral Harper added. "If we're lucky, they can slow the enemy down too."

His image vanished. Susan sat back in her chair, concentrating on projecting an appearance of calm. The aliens had inflicted a great deal of damage, but none of it was crippling - not yet. Given time, it could be repaired. But if the aliens kept hammering away at her hull, sooner or later they'd do *real* damage. She'd already had to reorientate the ship to keep them from firing directly into a gash in the hull.

"The starfighters are launching," Granger reported. "They're heading straight for the alien ships."

Susan nodded, curtly. There was nowhere else for them to go. And the aliens, of course, would know it.

"Concentrate on hammering their point defence," she ordered. "Give the starfighters as much cover as you can."

"Aye, Captain," Granger said.

The seconds ticked away, ominously. She allowed herself a moment of relief - and hope - when one of the alien ships rolled out of formation, her drives clearly badly damaged, but the remainder just kept coming. Admiral Harper might reduce speed himself, matching three human battleships against the alien vessels, yet as the seconds ticked away and no order came, she realised the Admiral didn't consider it worth the match. And he might well be right.

"Most of the starfighters survived," Mason said, quietly. "Hammering their point defence did *something*."

Susan nodded.

"New contacts," Charlotte snapped. "Drone group four has gone active! I say again, drone group four has gone active!"

And let's hope the enemy believes what they see, Susan thought. So far from the enemy formation, there was little hope of them realising that they were looking at sensor illusions...unless their sensors were far better than she'd been led to believe. If they fell for the trick, they'd think that two *new* battleships were heading straight to the planet. *And then they will have to choose between continuing to chase us and saving the forces they've landed on the surface.*

She watched, waiting to see what would happen. If she'd faced a human commander, she would have expected - given his hesitant behaviour - him to break off, once presented with a suitable excuse. Such a mealy-mouthed CO could hardly be expected to gamble everything on the possibility of such a force being nothing more than an illusion. But the aliens were *alien*. They might just decide to keep chasing the task force anyway...

Or they might decide to call our bluff, Susan thought. *And if that happens, we may have some problems.*

"Captain," Charlotte said. "The alien ships are altering course."

Susan nodded in relief. The aliens were turning, slowly setting their course back towards Unity. They had no choice, she knew; if the sensor illusions had been real, they had to be headed off before they could reach the planet. She'd wondered if the American-made drones would present an overwhelming force, but that would have either convinced the aliens to keep going or break off completely. And then they might have started to ask too many questions...

"Signal from the flag," Parkinson reported. "We're to proceed along our present course, but be ready to slip into cloak as soon as possible. Once we're in cloak, we are to proceed to the RV point and cross Tramline Two."

"See to it," Susan ordered.

She wondered, grimly, just how long it would take for the aliens to realise they'd been tricked. If the task force was *very* lucky, the aliens might never realise it; the drones would deactivate their drives, then vanish somewhere in the inky darkness of space. But the longer the aliens had to actually *think* about it, the greater the chance they'd realise that they'd been conned. Two more human battleships, without escorts...they might start adding two and two together and getting the wrong answers.

And then they'll be more inclined to disbelieve their own sensors, she thought, coldly. *And that will work out in our favour, in the future.*

"Signal from the flag," Parkinson said, grimly. New orders flickered into place on the display. "We're to cloak in five minutes. Drones are deployed to mislead the enemy."

Susan nodded. At close range, there was no hope of fooling the enemy, but as the distance between the two forces grew larger it would be easier to make the switch without being caught at it. The drones would leave the aliens with the very definite impression, by the time they finally deactivated themselves, that the human ships were heading directly for Tramline Three. By the time the aliens finally realised their mistake, the task force would be through Tramline Two and heading for its rendezvous with the transports.

"Cloak us on command," she ordered. She keyed her console. "Mr. Finch, damage report?"

"Several pieces of hull plating need to be replaced, Captain," Finch said, "but overall we were remarkably lucky. Replacing the destroyed sensors and point defence will take about a week, though."

"And we need to do it," Susan said. She watched the timer slowly ticking down to zero, silently assessing the repair work they'd need to do. "What about the drives?"

"Some damage to Drive Three, but nothing we can't compensate for," Finch informed her, shortly. He sounded confident, which was a relief. If he'd been worried, she would have worried too. "I'd like to take it offline to do some repair work, but it can wait for a few hours if necessary."

"We'll see what we find on the far side of Tramline Two," Susan said. The alien ships were still falling back - the drones would already have begun to evade the alien ships, although time-delay meant they wouldn't see it on the display yet - but they would definitely have reinforcements on their way. "If we have a chance to shut the drive down, we'll do it."

"Aye, Captain," Finch said.

The timer reached zero. "Taking us into cloak, now," Granger reported. The lights dimmed, on cue. "The drones have gone active."

"They're not quite perfect," Charlotte noted. She sounded oddly amused. "Some of their power emissions are badly out of phase. They're certainly not adjusting themselves to match our current signature."

"As long as they fool the aliens," Granger said, crossly. Susan had the very strong impression she simply didn't like Charlotte very much. They rarely spent any time together, when they weren't sharing duty on the bridge. "At their distance, it's unlikely they can get a solid read on our power emissions."

"That will do," Susan said, tartly. She wanted a shower and several hours of sleep, but she knew she wasn't going to get either of them. "Helm, take us towards the RV point and through the tramline. Sensors, watch closely for any prowling alien ships. Tactical, be ready to *engage* any picket before it has a chance to sound the alert."

"Aye, Captain," Reed said.

Susan sat back in her chair as the battleship altered course, watching as the drones evaded the enemy battleships. The aliens would realise that they'd been decoyed, of course, but would they deduce that the battleships weren't *real*? There was no way to know. Logically, if there *had* been five battleships, they would have been concentrated together...but it was quite possible that the alien attack had gotten lucky. Admiral Harper might even have sent two ships away without realising he was about to be attacked...

There's no way to know, she told herself, sternly. *Concentrate on what you do know and leave the rest to Harper.*

She watched, grimly, as the reports from the damage-control teams continued to flicker up in front of her. The damage wasn't as extensive as she'd feared, but as the teams continued their survey it became clear that they had a great deal of work in front of them. Finch had already put together a basic repair schedule, yet too much depended on what they found on the far side of the tramline. Pausing long enough to shut down Drive Three and carry out repairs would only be possible if there wasn't a bad-tempered alien fleet on the far side.

And that's the quickest way to get reinforcements into the system, she thought. *They'll know it too.*

"The drones have shut down," Charlotte reported. It would have happened ten minutes ago, the reports only just reaching the battleship. "I don't think the aliens have a hope in hell of finding them."

Susan nodded. The American drones were only three times the size of the average missile, barely even a grain of sand on an interstellar scale. There was no way the aliens would locate them unless they got very lucky. And if they did, the self-destruct system would vaporise the drone before the aliens could begin to unlock its secrets. It would be annoying - she'd heard that the drones each cost five times as much as an assault shuttle - but there would be no choice. The drones were one of humanity's few advantages and they could not be compromised.

She braced herself as the tramline came closer. There was no way to exchange notes with Admiral Harper, not when she only had a vague idea of *New York's* position. A radio signal would betray their position to any prowling alien starships...she wondered, absently, if the boffins had detected anything before the sensors had been blasted from *Vanguard's* hull. A clue, anything to unlock the alien secret...

...If there *was* a secret.

There *had* to be a secret, she told herself. The aliens had done too much for her to believe that they were misinterpreting the data. She would have accepted one stroke of luck, one moment when everything just fell into place perfectly, but not dozens. No, the aliens had a way to coordinate their operations on an interplanetary, perhaps an interstellar scale. And it had to be duplicated before it turned into a war-winning advantage.

"Take us through the tramline," she ordered, quietly. "And be *ready*."

"Aye, Captain," Reed said. "Jumping...now."

CHAPTER
TWENTY-THREE

"They're definitely in pursuit," Stott said, quietly. "At least a platoon, maybe two."

George shivered. The marines had kept moving, but they'd heard enough to suggest that the aliens were giving chase - and that they could move much faster than the marines, even without her slowing them down. She had no idea why the aliens hadn't sent aircraft or assault shuttles to look for the survivors of the crash - or even why they were bothering, given their distance from Unity City - but it hardly mattered. The aliens were coming for them...

The marines kept making their way through the jungle, scattering booby traps and other surprises as they moved. George couldn't help feeling that they were leaving a trail of breadcrumbs that would lead the aliens right to them, but the aliens seemed to have their trail anyway. One of the marines had muttered something about stealth drones watching from so high overhead that there wasn't a hope in hell of picking them out with the naked eye. She'd heard enough about drones used to secure forward bases in the Middle East and Africa to know that they might not be able to break contact, if the aliens already had a solid lock. But it felt as if the aliens were only giving chase on the ground.

"This might be closer to their natural environment," Kelly speculated. George was sweating like a pig - even a couple of the marines looked winded - and she honestly wasn't sure how long she could keep going. Her uniform was torn and stained, practically beyond repair. She would have torn it off if she'd had time. "Unknown #2 might like the jungle."

George shuddered at the thought. The temperature was steadily rising; mist was rolling in from the distance, visibility dropping sharply. There were just too many trees pressing in around them, denying the marines a look at their enemy. And yet she could *feel* their presence in her bones, a grim awareness that kept her going when her entire body just wanted to collapse in the muddy ground. The marines, judging by their edgy glances and tight grips on their weapons, felt the same way too.

"Stow that chatter," Byron ordered, sharply. "Keep moving."

Kelly nodded - George was surprised he didn't salute - and kept walking. She was aware of him glancing at her every few minutes, silently gauging her ability to keep moving. It made her wonder what the marines would do, if she couldn't keep up with them any longer. Allow her to head off in a different direction, surrender to the aliens - or kill her themselves? She didn't want to consider the possibility, but it had to be faced.

The bastards will have taken plenty of captives in Unity City, she thought, crossly. *And I'm not important enough to deny to the enemy.*

She felt her legs start to hurt as she forced herself to keep moving, silently cursing the exercise facilities on *Vanguard*. If she made it back alive, she'd make sure she walked or ran at least a couple of kilometres each day. Her daily routine, enforced by regulations, was probably nothing compared to what the marines did before breakfast. She'd thought of herself as fit - she certainly wasn't the butterball some of her older cousins were - but she couldn't even *begin* to match the marines. And she was starting to think that her weakness would be dragging them down.

"You should leave me," she panted. She had no idea how Byron would react, but she would have been surprised if the thought hadn't already crossed his mind. "I'm just slowing you down."

"We don't leave anyone behind," Byron snapped. "Keep walking."

"They're still catching up with us," Stott noted. He slowed long enough to emplace another booby trap, talking all the while. "We should give them more of a bloody nose."

"We might have to," Byron said. "But if they have a solid lock on us, they'll call down fire from orbit."

George suspected it was a moot point. If the aliens caught up with them, they'd be trapped anyway. She had no idea *just* how many aliens were following them, but they had to be confident that they could overwhelm the marines. And that suggested at least a couple of platoons…

Unless they're not expecting us to fight, she thought, darkly. *Or they just want to shadow us without opening fire.*

She scowled, despite her growing tiredness. Ground-based combat had never been one of her specialities, but she *had* shot grouse and pheasant on her father's estates. Sending out a team of beaters to drive the birds into the gunsights was a standard procedure. The aliens could have one noisy force behind them, keeping the humans running forward, while emplacing a secondary force *ahead* of them. They might find themselves trapped before they realised they'd been caught. And then…

The marines won't surrender, she thought. Prince Henry might have been able to open communications with his captors, but she doubted *she'd* be that lucky. She dropped her hand to her pistol, wishing she had more than a couple of spare clips. But it still felt reassuringly solid in her hand. *And I won't surrender either.*

"George," Byron said, shortly. The marines had slowed, turning to peer back the way they'd come. "I want a word with you."

George was reluctant to stop - she had the feeling she wouldn't be able to get moving again, once she stopped walking - but she knew she had no choice. A chill ran down her spine, despite the oppressive heat, as she saw his face. He looked to have made a very unpleasant decision.

"Yes, sir," she managed. Her chest *hurt*. She wanted to throw up, but there was nothing in her stomach. Her breath came in gasps as she fought to keep from dry-retching. "What can I do for you?"

"We need bait," Byron said. "If they see you, they might just think you're alone."

George looked up, taking the time to study their surroundings. There was room for the marines to take up firing positions, directly ahead of her. If the aliens thought they'd caught up with the escaped pilots - or at least one of them - they might just come forward too quick to be careful. They'd impale themselves on the human guns. But if their CO decided to call down a KEW strike, after the engagement…

She shook her head. The only other option was eventually being captured or killed. She had no idea how the aliens were tracking them, but they definitely *were*. Giving them a bloody nose, as Stott had argued, was the only way they could even *hope* to break contact.

"Understood," she said, between gasps. "What do you want me to do?"

Byron explained, hastily, then motioned for her to stay where she was as he led the rest of the marines into the trees. George sagged to the muddy ground, feeling a conflicting series of emotions as she pulled the bottle from her belt and emptied the water down her throat. Her legs ached so much that she doubted she could walk again, at least without a hot bath and at least seven hours of sleep. But she knew she wasn't going to get either of them.

The marines had vanished, completely. She glanced at the trees, but saw no sign of their presence. Had they abandoned her? She didn't want to consider the possibility - Fraser had been at pains to assure her that the Royal Marines were honourable warriors - but she had to admit that she was a liability. She couldn't keep up with them, she couldn't outshoot them...what good was she, apart from being the bait? It wasn't as if they needed her for anything.

She reached for her pistol as she heard...*something* in the distance, approaching rapidly along the path they'd hacked through the jungle. It sounded like a hunting dog, breathing loudly as it found its target...she wondered, suddenly, if the aliens had trained dog-like creatures to track the human survivors. And then her breath caught in her throat as seven aliens stepped into the clearing. She froze as they levelled their guns at her, unable to take her eyes off them. She'd seen holographic images of the aliens - and the other two races humanity had contacted - but seeing them in person was very different. They looked almost...*surreal*.

Five of the aliens looked like humanoid foxes, but with fur that shaded from brown to a soft golden colour that made her want to run her fingers through the hairs. Their eyes flickered from side to side; they moved forward in jerky motions, as if they jumped forward and then froze on command. They wore nothing, save for a thin outfit that barely covered their genitals - if indeed they *were* their genitals. And, as the wind shifted, she smelt a strange unpleasant musk radiating from the alien bodies.

Behind them, the other two aliens were very different. They looked like humanoid cows, crossed with toads. Their leathery skin looked tough enough to qualify as armour in its own right; they moved slowly and deliberately, their every motion suggesting a ponderous inevitability. George wondered if they were in charge - they were certainly hiding behind the foxes - but she had no way to be sure. They might just be charged with bringing up the rear while the foxes led the way.

One of the foxes jumped forward, his gun aimed squarely at George's head. "Up. Now."

George did as she was told, moving as slowly as she dared. The longer they kept their eyes on her, the longer the marines would have to choose their targets. She wondered, absently, just how the aliens had known a little English, then told herself not to be stupid. English was the default language throughout the Human Sphere, certainly in interplanetary space. Even the simplest of children's educational programs included the basics. She kept her hands in sight, wondering just what was keeping the marines. Had they really abandoned her?

A shot rang out. George threw herself to the ground as three of the aliens toppled, the remainder taking up firing position and raking the trees with gunfire. One of the foxes moved forward so fast that it was a blur, almost reaching the marines before a stream of bullets practically tore him apart. His body crashed down to the mud, followed by another of the fox-like aliens. And then the gunfire came to a sudden end. Silence fell, broken only by grunts and gasps. One of the aliens was still alive...

"Corporal," a marine said. "I..."

George barely had a second to register the alien's movement, just before his claws slashed up and tore the marine's throat out. Stott jumped forward and landed on the alien, pounding the creature with his fists; Byron snapped orders, two more marines followed, one of them carrying a roll of duct tape. The alien fought like a mad thing, despite the beating, but the marines managed to tie its hands and feet together. It didn't stop fighting until there was no way left to resist.

"Well done," Byron said. He helped her to her feet, then patted her on the back. "I couldn't have done it better myself."

George nodded tersely, then stumbled over to stare down at the alien. It glared back at her, hatred - or something she assumed was hatred - clearly visible in its eyes. The stench was overwhelming, a scent that made her want to turn on her heels and run. Did the aliens use scent as a defensive measure? Or did they use it as a form of communication? She had no way to know.

"Interesting," Kelly mused. He was poking at one of the dead bodies, examining it thoughtfully. "The claws are completely retractable. This one didn't have a chance to flick them out before it died."

"Good," Byron said. He took a long look at the dead marine, then winced noticeably. "Get King bagged up. We'll carry his body with us."

He glanced at George. "Take a quick look at their equipment, but don't take anything," he added. "See what you make of it."

George had a feeling that he wanted her to remain occupied, but she didn't fault him. The aliens could easily have killed her, if they'd wished. She took a look at the remaining fox-like aliens, then moved to the other aliens. They were carrying several different pieces of oddly-shaped equipment, but - apart from the weapons - she couldn't even begin to guess what they were. One of them *might* be a radio - they *had* to have some way to remain in touch with their superiors - yet she didn't dare experiment. A single radio transmission would bring the rest of the invasion force down on their heads.

"Take samples of the alien blood," Byron ordered. "And then we'll take our leave."

Stott elbowed George as he passed. "Good work," he said. "We'll be sure to use you as bait in future."

"If I get back into orbit," George said, "I'm damned if I'm going back to the planet again."

She fell into step beside Kelly as the marines resumed their march, two of them carrying the bound alien as if he were an ox being prepared for the fire. The alien glared at every human in sight, but otherwise seemed surprisingly passive. George couldn't help wondering just how many other surprises the aliens had - and if the alien was merely biding its time, planning to escape as soon as it could. She glanced upwards, expecting to see a flight of shuttles heading back towards the ambush zone, but heard nothing. The aliens didn't seem to have noticed.

Oddly, she felt reinvigorated as they kept moving northwards. A handful of shuttles flew overhead, an hour or so after the ambush, but none of them seemed inclined to land anywhere nearby. She wondered, despite herself, just what the aliens *wanted* with Unity. If invasion and settlement was their goal, surely they would have bombarded the city from orbit along with every farm they could see. Unless they wanted slaves...unlike any other known race, the newcomers *were* a genuine multi-species polity. They might think that humans could be enslaved too.

They speak some of our language, she thought. *Were they preparing to rule?*

Byron kept them moving, with only a handful of breaks, until the sun finally began to set in the sky. George watched, grimly, as the marines gave the alien a drink of water and some food, careful to keep the alien pinned down as it was fed. The alien didn't show any sign of resistance, although it kept a sharp eye on its captors. George couldn't escape the feeling that it was just biding its time.

She looked at Kelly as a nasty thought occurred to her. "Can it eat our food?"

"The boffins think they shouldn't have any trouble with our food," Kelly said. He sounded oddly amused, although she had no idea why. "They certainly wouldn't be interested in our worlds if the biochemistry was poisonous to them."

"And we have nothing else to feed them," Byron said. The corporal strode over to squat down next to her, his face grim and worn. "If we poison the bastard, we poison the bastard...but at least we won't be deliberately starving it to death."

George nodded, slowly. The alien seemed to be eating and drinking avidly, even though the ration bars the marines carried tasted rather like cardboard. Perhaps they'd stumbled across something the alien would find tasty...or perhaps it was just too hungry to care. She silently went through everything she'd been told about establishing a common language, then leaned forward. If the alien knew some English, she could try to teach it some more.

She kept her voice low. If the alien hearing was far better than she'd assumed, even a normal speaking voice would sound like someone shouting in its ear. "Can you understand me?"

The alien twitched, but said nothing. George studied it for a long moment, unable to determine if it couldn't understand her or if it were merely playing dumb. The aliens might not teach their soldiers everything, not when there was a possibility of falling into enemy hands. And yet, there was *something* there…

"You're asking a question," Byron said. "Try making it an order."

George glanced at him, then looked back at the alien. "Tell me if you understand me."

"Yes," the alien grunted.

She sucked in her breath, trying to think. What did she *say* to the alien? And what would it tell her in return? Would it say *anything*, beyond name, rank and serial number? Did the aliens even *have* names, ranks and serial numbers? And why did it follow orders instead of answering questions?

Byron leaned forward. "Tell us your name."

The alien made a wheezing sound that reminded George of a tired dog. There was no way she could pronounce it for herself, assuming the alien was actually answering the question. It didn't seem inclined to offer explanations, or additional detail…she'd gone through a very basic Conduct After Capture course, but that had merely tried to prepare her for life as a POW. Had the alien gone through something similar? It certainly seemed reluctant to volunteer information.

She sighed. "Why did you attack us?"

The alien made no reply. She realised her mistake and tried again.

"Tell us why you attacked us," she said.

"You challenged us," the alien said. "We accepted the challenge."

George glanced at Byron. "We challenged them?"

"I don't know," Byron said. "I don't see how."

He rose. "Catch some sleep," he ordered. "We need to start moving when the sun comes up."

"Yes, sir," George said.

CHAPTER
TWENTY-FOUR

Susan had been expecting anything from a major enemy fleet lying in ambush to their reinforcements making their way towards Unity, but TPS-463 appeared to be deserted. A dull red sun, a handful of asteroids... there was little to attract attention from either the Tadpoles or the new aliens. She allowed herself a moment of relief, then started detailing her crew to begin repair work as the task force slipped away from the tramline. The aliens wouldn't have a hope in hell of tracking them unless they got very lucky.

"The repair crews are getting to work, Captain," Mason said. "Mr. Finch wants to take Drive Three offline for a few hours."

"If we don't encounter any enemy ships before we reached the RV point, he can take the drive offline," Susan said. She hoped - prayed - that the drive could remain active if they *did* encounter an alien fleet. *Vanguard* could keep going on three drives, if necessary, but her acceleration curves would drop sharply. "Is there any word from the sensor drones?"

"No, Captain," Mason said. He nodded towards the display. "If there's a colony here, it's thoroughly black."

Susan nodded. Black colonies - asteroids settled in secret - weren't uncommon in human space, but the Tadpoles didn't seem to have that problem. Tadpoles who found themselves in the wrong faction merely left to join a different faction, something that most humans would find hard to comprehend. But then, their politics were very different from anything a human would recognise. They practically enjoyed a post-scarcity society, deep below the waves.

"Keep a sharp eye out for trouble," she ordered. The aliens would realise they'd been tricked, sooner or later. She just wasn't sure what they'd do about it, once they did. Did they have enough ships to sweep *both* of the tramlines? Or cover Unity against the inevitable counterattack? "They'll be coming after us, sooner or later."

"Aye, Captain," Mason said.

Susan sat back in her command chair, feeling tiredness dragging at her bones. She'd been due to hand the bridge over to her XO just before the attack had begun; now, she felt as if she'd been awake for days, drunk on fatigue poisons. She needed rest - they *all* needed rest - but she couldn't leave the bridge until she knew they were reasonably safe. The enemy might be after them at any moment.

She kept a sharp eye on the long-range sensor display, even though she *knew* it was completely useless. The task force was running passive sensors only, watching carefully for a single betraying sensor emission…but if the aliens didn't radiate anything, there wasn't a hope in hell of detecting *their* ships. They'd have just as many problems tracking the human ships, Susan hoped, yet the repair work was going to throw up all kinds of sensor noise and transmissions that would lead the aliens right to them. She'd just have to pray that they had time to complete the most important repairs before the shit hit the fan.

"Signal from the flag," Parkinson said. "Admiral Harper requests the pleasure of your company in a holoconference."

"Understood," Susan said. She couldn't help feeling annoyed. She'd be right next to the bridge, but still…"Inform him that I will join the conference in five minutes."

She rose and glanced at Mason. "Mr. Mason, you have the conn."

"Aye, Captain," Mason said. "I have the conn."

Susan took one last look at the display, then strode into her office. The holoconference would take a few moments to organise, more than long enough to splash water on her face and order her steward to bring her a mug of very strong coffee. She checked the terminal automatically - it was astonishing just how many non-urgent reports could pile up in her inbox during a battle - and then walked into the head. The cold water made her feel better, but she knew it wouldn't last. She'd just have to hope the conference didn't take too long.

There was a chime at the door. She barked a command to open it, then blinked as Prince Henry stepped into the compartment. The prince looked tired, unsurprisingly; he'd been forced to watch, helplessly, as *Vanguard* and the remainder of the task force fought a desperate battle for survival. *He* would have had no duties to distract him from the possibility of a sudden violent death, if a missile detonated inside *Vanguard's* hull or the enemy merely battered her into scrap.

"Your Excellency," she said. "Admiral Harper requested your presence too?"

"Yes, Captain," Henry said. He sounded tired too. "And I have matters to raise with you myself."

Susan nodded, irritated. She liked Henry, but she was really too tired to discuss anything beyond the basics. Right now, her priority was repairing her ship and getting ready for the next engagement. Either the enemy would come storming after them or Admiral Harper would start raiding enemy shipping, as he'd planned. Whatever concerns Henry had to raise, she doubted they were any more important.

"Take a seat," she ordered, stiffly. The holoconference was about to begin. "I'll have the projector include you in the conference."

The hatch opened, revealing a steward carrying a steaming pot of coffee, two mugs and a large plate of biscuits. Susan smiled, despite herself, as the steward put the tray down on the table and retreated; the gallery staff must have known, somehow, that Prince Henry had joined her. But then, they *did* keep very good tabs on her visitors. She poured them both a mug of coffee, then munched on a chocolate digestive biscuit as the holographic images started to flicker into existence. It was amusing to note just how many of the commanding officers were drinking coffee themselves.

They can't feel any better than I do, Susan thought. *Whatever the final tally, there's no hiding the fact that we retreated from Unity.*

"I won't keep you long," Admiral Harper said. His image was expressionless, suggesting - to her tired mind - that his local processor was doing a little editing. She would have been surprised if he was the only one. Even in the military, holographic communications offered all sorts of options for creative editing. "Overall, despite the need to retreat, we handled the battle well."

"We lost," Yegorovich growled.

"We inflicted considerable damage on their forces," Glass pointed out. "Tonnage wise, we won the engagement."

"Bah," Yegorovich said. "We have no idea how badly we hurt their overall numbers."

"True," Susan agreed. "But we can take some comfort in the individual superiority of our numbers."

"It isn't enough," Yegorovich said. "We have a significant advantage in starfighters, but they cost us dearly. I'm currently readying the reserve squadrons..."

"I have faith in your ability to make them fit in," Harper said, quickly. "As you can see, a number of interesting patterns have appeared in the data."

"The aliens stayed with us until the balance of power appeared to shift decisively against them," Glass added. It was probably her tiredness speaking, but Susan couldn't help thinking, just for a moment, that he was remarkably handsome. "They gave chase and hung on like a gaggle of limpets, yet they were quick to back away when it seemed they could not win."

"They were oddly indecisive," Susan put in. "If they'd thrust forward harder, they might well have won the battle."

"My analysts suspect that the alien tactical doctrine calls for seizing the initiative and pushing forward as long as there is a hope, even a very slight hope, of victory," Harper said. "This fits with their activities in earlier battles, as some of you will recall. They didn't abandon their push from UXS-469 into Tadpole space until they ran into something so hard they couldn't hope to actually win."

"Which means they're a very aggressive race," Prince Henry pointed out.

"So are many humans," Captain Fletcher said. "There's no such thing as a true pacifist."

"Because they get wiped out," Captain Garret said. "Weakness invites attack."

Harper shrugged. "This is interesting," he said, "because it raises the possibility that the alien behaviours may actually be predictable. As long as there is a *chance* of victory, the aliens will strive to win. They won't try to break off, even at cost, as long as that chance exists."

"My analysts concur," Prince Henry said. He smiled, rather humourlessly. "The civilians are still in deep denial, but the general thrust appears to be the same."

"Which is why they chased us," Susan mused. "And yet, they didn't try to press their advantage as aggressively as we might have expected."

"There may have been two different mindsets involved," Glass offered. "If we really *are* fighting two different races, rather than one..."

"That's been settled," Prince Henry said.

Glass nodded. "Yes, but which of them is in charge? Is one race very definitely the master - or do they have a truly mixed society? And did one race see its culture destroyed by the other?"

"Ah," Yegorovich said. "Cultural imperialism."

Susan frowned. "For all we know," she said, "they have very different - and segregated - cultures and they merely cooperate. Biologically...how *can* they integrate?"

"They couldn't," Fletcher said.

"Exactly," Susan said. "They will always be separate at a very basic level."

She sighed at the thought. Her mere existence was living proof that black and white humans could produce children, but the whole idea of interspecies pregnancy was the stuff of bad science-fiction and worse erotic romance. There was no way a human mother could be impregnated with alien sperm - or vice versa. No matter how determinedly the aliens worked towards building a single culture, they would always be defeated by biological reality. They could *never* be one race.

"There would be advantages," Yegorovich mused. He sounded oddly amused. "They wouldn't be fighting over women, I suspect, and they probably agree not to talk about each other's quirks."

"That's our arrangement with the Tadpoles," Henry said. "Some of their culture disgusts us...but we ignore it, as long as they keep it to themselves."

"This is a very interesting discussion for another day," Harper said firmly, "but we are moving away from the topic at hand."

He paused, glancing from face to face. "My staff and I have been putting together a plan to return to Unity at the earliest possible moment," he added, "but before then I intend to poke through both of the other two tramlines within the system. If we find a suitable target, we will - of course - attack. The aliens will *have* to be rushing forces to Unity as quickly as possible. Hitting them in transit will force them to be more careful..."

"Unless they merely want to take the world from us," Yegorovich sneered. "Has anyone noticed the timing?"

He went on before anyone could say a word. "They didn't attack the planet before we arrived, even though they certainly should have had a big head start on us," he added. "And they didn't attack the planet after we were dug in, ready for them. No, they attacked at the worst possible moment - for us. Someone told them we were coming."

Susan scowled. She'd had the same thought.

"Of all the paranoid theories," Jeanette snapped. "Is there anyone stupid enough to think they can make a deal with aliens, of all people, and get away with it?"

"People used to make deals with Nazis, Communists and Radical Islamists," Yegorovich pointed out. "And yes, those deals tended to explode in their faces, but they still made the deals."

"Your country made a deal with the Nazis," Garret said. "And then you were caught with your pants down."

"*Exactly*," Yegorovich said. "Did someone on the task force tell the aliens we were coming?"

"There's a simpler explanation," Glass said. "We believe the aliens have some form of FTL communications. If they had a spy ship hidden somewhere within Sol, Captain, they wouldn't find it too hard to warn their superiors that the task force was on the way."

"If they can do that," Yegorovich said, "they might well win the war."

Susan considered it, despite her tiredness. If the aliens *had* been watching Earth, they might well have seen the task force depart. Hell, the alien spy might have been *following* the task force, shadowing it until there was no mistaking its destination. A chill ran down her spine as she considered the implications. It was a revolutionary shift in the balance of power, if Glass was right. The alien high command wouldn't need to wait weeks or months for news to come back from the front. They'd know - instantly - what had happened and what needed to be done.

And they'd be able to dispatch reinforcements at once, she thought. *They might not even have considered invading Unity and opening up the chain until we started to move reinforcements to the planet.*

Her imagination filled in the details. The alien high command, trying hard to bring its forces to bear against the Tadpoles, suddenly learning that an allied fleet was on its way to Unity...and moving forces to block their way. Hell, there was no reason to take the risk of placing a scout ship in Sol itself...the enemy ship could be easily hidden within any of the systems the task force had crossed during the voyage. If *she'd* had such a system, *she* wouldn't have hesitated to picket every system between Earth and her target. The aliens might just have had real-time data on the task force's progress, giving them plenty of time to mount a response.

"The situation is not hopeless," Harper said, sharply. "And I do not believe that *anyone* would betray us to the aliens."

Yegorovich snorted, but didn't continue the argument.

Harper looked at Henry. "Did your experts pick up anything... unusual?"

"Nothing," Henry said. "We didn't have time to seed space with hundreds of passive listening platforms, as we planned, but battle and post-battle analysis, so far, hasn't turned up any clues about how their FTL communicators actually *work*."

"They may not have been using them," Glass mused. "There was only one major enemy force."

"That's true, Captain," Henry said. "For the moment, I'm afraid the boffins are still stumped."

"They'll be looking into it back home," Yegorovich said.

"We won't know about it," Henry reminded him. "Even if they crack the secret, they won't tell us."

"Probably not," Harper agreed. "All we can do is hope that the *next* battle offers us more data."

He cleared his throat. "Overall, we did well," he said. "And we did give them a bloody nose."

"Yes," Yegorovich said. "But they gave us a beating too."

"We will repair our ships," Harper said. "And then we will go on the offensive."

Susan sighed, inwardly, as Harper closed the conference, the holographic images popping out of existence one by one. It was hard to feel optimistic when tiredness was dragging her down, hard to think clearly when her brain just wanted sleep. There were drugs she could take, she knew, but they tended to come with bad side effects. She rubbed her eyes as the last image vanished, then blinked in surprise as she recalled that Prince Henry was still in the compartment. She'd honestly forgotten.

"Your Excellency," she said. "What can I do for you?"

"Some of the experts were wondering why we made no attempt to transmit the First Contact Package," Henry said. He spoke with the air of a man asking a question to which he already knew the answer. "They'd like a comment from you."

"They caught us with our pants down," Susan reminded him, dryly. If nothing else, it had been a sharp lesson in just how good the aliens *were* at sneaking around. "And we had no time to do anything, but fight and run."

She met his eyes. "Just how deeply *are* they in denial?"

"They're academics," Henry said, without heat. "They don't really understand the way the human mind works, certainly outside their little bubble. There's no way that they can really grasp, at an instinctive level, that aliens aren't just humans in funny outfits and dumb prosthetics glued to their foreheads."

He shrugged. "Most of the ones who were with me on Tadpole Prime know better, of course," he added. "But they have a habit of believing that the newcomers are just like the Tadpoles, rather than a whole new culture - *two* whole new cultures - in their own right."

Susan nodded in agreement. A specialist on Ancient Rome was hardly a specialist on Imperial Japan - and both of those powers were *human*. Someone who had spent the last ten years studying the Tadpoles might not be able to escape his preconceptions, when asked to look at a whole new race. But the academics who had no experience with non-human life might be even worse.

"I'll keep an eye on them," Henry added. "I don't think they'll do anything stupid, but you never know."

"We'll see about transmitting the package when we return to Unity," Susan said. She doubted it would be possible, but there was no harm in trying. The aliens might just respond, after a battle they had to find profoundly unsatisfying. "Until then...good luck."

Henry nodded, then drained his mug. "Get some sleep," he advised. He gave her a tired smile as he rose and headed for the hatch. "We're going to be here for a while, aren't we?"

Susan nodded. She watched him leave, then eyed the washroom longingly for a long moment before lying down on the sofa and forcing herself to relax. A few hours of rest wouldn't kill her, her treacherous mind insisted...Mason had everything in hand. She could snatch some time to herself before returning to the bridge. And then...

She closed her eyes. A moment later, she was sound asleep.

CHAPTER
TWENTY-FIVE

"Captain," Charlotte said. "I just picked up a flash from Platform #45. We have five enemy ships entering the system from Tramline Two."

Susan looked up. The repairs had taken nearly ten days, but *Vanguard* was as close to combat-ready as she'd ever be, without a proper shipyard. Her crew was *very* well trained, after the last series of battles. Replacing a point defence weapon or a sensor blister was the work of an hour or two. *New York* had taken heavier punishment - she had a nasty feeling that the aliens *had* realised that she was the flagship - but the Americans were confident that she'd be ready to return to battle in two more days.

"Interesting," she mused. If they'd been human ships, she would have assumed that they knew nothing about the situation ahead of them, but that assumption might not hold true for the aliens. "Can you give me a breakdown?"

"Two carriers, two cruisers and one starship that might just be a frigate," Charlotte said, carefully. Her fingers danced across the console, teasing data from the records. "The platform didn't get a clear look at her."

Two carriers, Susan mused. *We could take two carriers.*

"Raise the flag," she ordered. Admiral Harper would have to make the final call, but she couldn't see why he would refuse her permission to engage. "And then plot an intercept course."

She considered possible options as she waited for Admiral Harper to reply. The alien starfighters were flying CSPs around their carriers, which meant that sneaking up on them was almost certainly impossible.

And, even though the carriers massed nearly twice as much as *Vanguard*, their acceleration curves would almost certainly be sharper. If the aliens detected *Vanguard* sneaking up on them, they'd reverse course while dispatching their starfighters to harry the battleship…

Doing unto us as we did unto them, she thought, as Admiral Harper's face popped into existence in front of her. *And that would definitely be annoying.*

"Captain," Admiral Harper said. "You believe we should engage?"

"Yes, sir," Susan said. "Two carriers - insufficient escorts. We won't get a better shot at them."

"True," Admiral Harper agreed. "Do you have a plan?"

"Loan me the two carriers and I will," Susan said. It would mean giving the honour of victory to the carriers and their pilots, but she didn't mind. Depriving the aliens of two carriers was more important than outscoring the Russians or the French. "If we can't sneak up on them, we might at least give them a nasty fright."

"Of course, Captain," Harper said. "They will scream for help, of course."

Susan nodded. She'd already considered the possibility. "With all due respect, Admiral, we still won't get a better shot at them," she said. "And they may well have figured out that we didn't jump down the other tramline by now too."

"Point," Harper agreed. "I'll assign the carriers to you. And good luck."

"Thank you, sir," Susan said.

Harper's face vanished from the display. Susan took a moment to tap her console, organising her thoughts before sending the planned engagement vectors to the two carriers. It would require some fancy timing, but if they messed it up they could fall back and the enemy would never know that the carriers had been there. She half-expected the carrier commanders to object to her assignments yet, to her surprise, they made no objection. But then, she *was* offering them a clear shot at the enemy ships.

"Take us out," she ordered, finally. "Make sure the cloak doesn't slip or the whole exercise will be worse than useless."

She leaned back in her command chair as *Vanguard* came to life, her drives slowly propelling her away from the RV point. There was no way to be *entirely* sure of where the aliens were, not yet, but as long as they had no reason to take evasive action they'd remain on a least-time course to Unity. Their damned FTL communications system gave them too many advantages, she reflected sourly. She'd sell her soul for a system that allowed her to manipulate her forces in real-time.

The REMFs would love it, she thought, darkly. *They'd be able to tell us what to do from a safe distance.*

She wondered, absently, if the aliens had the same problem. She'd read the reports from the researchers - more speculation than hard facts - only to decide that there was just too little for anyone to go on. And yet, the more she thought about it, the more she *knew* they were missing something important. A master couldn't give orders, surely, without slaves who understood his language? Slavery simply didn't work very well in an age of high technology, although there were parts of Earth where it had been making a comeback for years. A slave in an advanced factory had too many options for making his masters miserable. Or had the aliens somehow solved that problem?

If they can talk to one race, they can talk to more, she told herself. *And yet, they didn't even try to open communications with us.*

"Captain," Charlotte said, an hour later. "I'm picking up the alien carriers on passive sensors, within the projected cone."

"*Very* within the projected cone," Susan said. She would have been impressed if it hadn't been clear that the aliens had maintained a least-time course to the tramline. If nothing else, it added weight to the theory that the aliens had put the invasion force they'd sent to Unity together in a hurry. "Are they maintaining an active sensor watch?"

"No, Captain," Charlotte said. "But they *are* maintaining a constant CSP."

"Good," Susan said.

She wished, once again, for an FTL communications system of her own. If all had gone according to plan, *Napoleon* and *Admiral Kuznetsov* had taken up position on the other side of the alien ships, ready to play their role in the operation. But she wouldn't *know* they'd taken up position until she lured the alien starfighters out of position, giving them a clear shot at the carriers. She didn't think that either of the commanders would screw up deliberately, but mistakes happened in wartime. Whoever had convinced the politicians that the military machine was perfectly efficient had clearly been a masterful spin doctor.

And then the bastards started expecting miracles, she thought, coldly. *They didn't have a realistic idea of what we could do.*

She pushed the thought aside. "Mr. Reed," she said, calmly. "Stand by to execute Spoof on my order."

"Aye, Captain," Reed said. "Spoof protocols engaged and ready."

Susan glanced at the timer. If she waited, if she gave the carriers more time…she ran the risk of losing her own position. And that would introduce too many random variables into the operation. She'd hoped, if nothing else, that the operation would test the theory that the aliens were thoroughly aggressive, as long as there was a chance of victory. But if they missed their window…"

"Activate spoof," she ordered. "Now."

Vanguard quivered as Reed flushed power through her drives. From the outside, it should look like a major power fluctuation in the cloaking device, accidentally betraying her position to the enemy. Susan imagined, just for a second, that the enemy carriers literally flinched before she started to bark orders. If their attempt to sneak up on the aliens had failed so spectacularly, their best option was to try to catch the carriers before they could take evasive action.

The long seconds ticked away, then…

"Enemy carriers are launching fighters," Charlotte reported.

"Stand by point defence," Susan ordered, coolly. There were a *lot* of starfighters. She made a mental note that intelligence's estimate of just how many starfighters the aliens could fit into their carriers was badly inaccurate, then turned her attention to the display. "Prepare to reverse course."

"Aye, Captain," Reed said.

Susan smiled, grimly. So far, so good. The aliens had launched their starfighters, as she'd expected; now, she had to give them a shot at a victory. And then…they'd only kept twenty or so starfighters for their own defence. It didn't seem to have occurred to them that they were being lured out of place.

"Reverse course," she ordered.

"Aye, Captain," Reed said. "Operation Run Rabbit Run is now underway."

Susan shot a quelling look at the back of his head, then watched as the wall of alien starfighters closed in rapidly. They presumably felt that a clear shot at a battleship was worth the risk, particularly after the hammering their battleships had taken at Unity. She wondered, absently, just how quickly the aliens could repair their ships, then decided it wasn't an immediate concern. All that mattered was surviving the next few minutes.

"Engage as soon as they enter weapons range," she ordered, grimly.

"Aye, Captain," Granger said.

The aliens fell on *Vanguard* like wolves on the flock. Their starfighters might have been inferior, Susan noted, but they knew how to fly them. *Vanguard* could pump out thousands of plasma bolts every second, yet only a handful of alien starfighters died before entering attack range and returning fire. The only upside, as far as she could tell, was that the aliens didn't seem to have devised a torpedo-mounted bomb-pumped laser. If *that* happened, the entire concept of interstellar war would be flipped over, once again.

Battleships will become unviable, she thought. *And even armoured carriers would become chancy.*

"Minor damage to the hull," Finch reported. "But they're blowing holes in our point defence again."

Susan nodded, unsurprised. Weakening *Vanguard's* point defence would be their first priority, certainly when they had to believe there was no way the battleship could escape wave after wave of tiny attackers. And the damage *was* mounting up. But if the timing was right...

"Captain, the carriers have launched their fighters," Charlotte reported. "They'll be engaging the enemy carriers in four minutes."

Susan allowed herself a smile as the alien starfighters wheeled around. There was no indecision, not this time. The aliens would know that their carriers were suddenly naked and helpless as the human starfighters raced towards their targets. And if they lost the carriers, they would be doomed. There would be no hope of escaping before they ran out of life support and suffocated somewhere in deep space.

"Raise the carriers," she ordered, grimly. "Warn them to be ready for suicide attacks."

She felt her smile grow wider as the alien starfighters raced away from *Vanguard*, too late to have a hope of saving their carriers. They'd been lured out of place and now they'd have to pay for it. If they'd been human, she would have urged the carriers to accept surrender, but there was no way to communicate with the alien pilots. The alien carriers spat wave after wave of point defence towards the human craft, yet there was no way it could save them. A single warhead detonating inside their launch tubes would be disastrous.

"Carrier One is under heavy attack," Charlotte reported. "She's..."

Her voice broke off. "Scratch one flattop," she said. "I say again, scratch one flattop."

Susan nodded. The alien pilots were overloading their drives, but it still wasn't enough. She watched, vindictively, as the second carrier staggered to one side, then lost power completely as a chain of explosions wrecked her innards. Somehow, miraculously, her hull survived, but Susan would have been astonished if any of her crew had. Even if they *had*, there was no way they'd last long enough for help to arrive.

"Scratch a second flattop," Charlotte repeated. Moments later, the escorts were picked off too. "The enemy ship is nothing but a ruined hulk."

"Take us to her location," Susan ordered. The enemy starfighters were screaming past the ruins of their ship, angling directly towards the human carriers. "Inform Prince Henry that he is to ready his technical analysis crews."

She glanced at the sensor records as the Russian starfighters turned to face the oncoming storm while the French starfighters returned to the carrier, ready to defend them. The aliens had never been particularly careful, but now they seemed completely heedless of their own safety as they fell on the human carriers. Susan watched, knowing she could do nothing, as they roared towards their targets, firing savagely. Four starfighters slammed into *Napoleon* before the last of the alien craft were wiped out. Susan could only hope that the damage had not been that severe.

"Signal from *Napoleon*," Parkinson said. "She's lost one of her launch tubes, but is otherwise undamaged."

"Acknowledge," Susan ordered. Losing a launch tube was irritating - and it would slow down deployment until they reached a proper shipyard - but it was better than losing the entire ship. "Can we pull anything from the alien hulk?"

"Unknown," Granger said. "Her innards were pretty badly fried."

Susan glanced at Mason. If the alien warship designers thought along the same lines as their human counterparts, it was unlikely that anything sensitive would have survived. They'd captured alien debris before and learned next to nothing from it. But she had to admit that it was just possible that *something* had survived.

"Order the techs to do a basic survey," she said, quietly. "If they find anything, we can commit resources to pulling it out."

"Aye, Captain," Mason said.

Susan leaned back, thinking hard. The hell of it was that the alien reinforcements would probably already be on their way. If their FTL communications really did allow them to send messages from system to system... she cursed under her breath, angrily. She would like to *know*, for sure, just what the aliens could actually do. A system that wasn't particularly useful, outside interplanetary distances, would still be a game-changer, as far as the tactical situation was concerned.

They may assume that there's no hope of salvaging the situation, she thought. *But we've definitely told them where we went, after Unity.*

"Communications, record a message for the flag," she ordered. She waited for Parkinson's nod before continuing. "Admiral Harper, the operation was concluded successfully. We will attempt to determine if we can recover anything from the wreckage, but I doubt it will be possible. However, I recommend that we move immediately through Tramline Two, as planned."

She paused. "Attach our sensor records, then send the message," she added. "And inform me the moment he replies."

"Deploying shuttles," Mason said. "They're taking a look-see now."

Susan nodded, tightly. It would be at least an hour before Admiral Harper got back to her, assuming he made his mind up at once. She rather suspected he would have been planning to vacate the system at once, anyway, but his ship would be limping along until her repairs were completed.

But there was no choice. If the aliens reacted quickly, they'd have an excellent chance to catch the task force scattered over the next system.

But not if we're already moving, she thought. *They'll have to make some excellent guesses about which way we'll go.*

She worked her way through it as the seconds ticked away. Moving through Tramline Two ran the risk - or offered the opportunity - of running into whatever other reinforcements the aliens were sending to Unity. They'd be alerted by now - she dared not assume that the FTL communications system didn't work on an interstellar scale - but they'd still have no idea where the human ships were until it was too late. But moving through Tramline Three offered a least-time course back to Unity.

They'll know it, she told herself. *But they won't be able to be sure which way we'll go.*

If the researchers were correct - and it certainly looked as though they had a good handle on the alien mentality - the aliens would be *furious*. They'd want to hunt the task force down as fast as possible, but where would they send their ships? The sheer inability to decide would drive them mad, particularly given the likely consequences of guessing wrong. They'd know when the task force showed itself, she assumed, but before then...

"The techs just sent in a basic report," Mason reported. "They believe that the interior of the ship is completely gutted. There's little hope of recovering anything."

Susan nodded, unsurprised. "Recall them," she ordered. She briefly considered completing the job, but decided it was pointless. The aliens could do what they liked with the drifting hulk. "And then set course for the RV point."

"Aye, Captain," Mason said.

"Message from the flag, Captain," Parkinson reported. "Code green-blue-seven."

"Belay that order, Mr. Reed," Susan ordered. "Set course for Point Haven instead."

"Aye, Captain," Reed said.

"We're moving on," Mason said, quietly. "Moving further away from Unity."

"We can double back," Susan said. She had no idea how strong the aliens were in the sector - there were few colonies between Unity and alien space - but she rather suspected they were still scrambling to get reinforcements into the region. "And they'll be kept guessing."

Or so we hope, she thought.

"The techs have returned," Mason informed her.

"Helm, take us to Point Haven," Susan ordered. She glanced at Granger. "Tactical, cloak us as soon as we begin to move."

"Aye, Captain," Granger said.

She leaned back in her chair as the battleship started to move, linking up with the two carriers as they made their way towards Point Haven. The aliens couldn't have a lock on them, not now; they'd have to guess at the task force's destination, with only a 50/50 chance of being right. And even if they *were* right, they'd still have to scrape up the forces to hunt the task force down and destroy it. Would they take the risk of leaving Unity uncovered? Or would they decide that securing the planet wasn't worth the effort?

We may not be making that much of an impact, she thought. *But every ship we draw away from the war front may make a very big difference.*

CHAPTER
TWENTY-SIX

The alien peered at her through dark unreadable eyes.

George returned the alien's stare, careful to keep a distance from its chained form. The carefully-prepared cells - not that they were *called* cells - on *Vanguard* were nothing more than a distant memory. Keeping the alien in a cellar, chained firmly to the concrete wall, would probably look very bad, when they returned to Earth, but there hadn't been any real choice. The locals had flatly refused to try to find somewhere more suitable to keep a prisoner.

Which isn't too surprising, George thought, as she worked to formulate her next set of questions. *Our captive's friends tore apart their world.*

"Tell me how many of you there are," she said.

The alien - the marines had dubbed him Woof - gazed at her uncomprehendingly. George wasn't sure if he didn't understand or if he was playing dumb, although she'd heard enough spoken words from the alien to suspect that he'd only been taught a very limited set of human words. He reminded her more of a British tourist off to see the continent than someone who was genuinely interested in talking to the locals on their own terms. But she would have been surprised if the alien leadership *had* wanted them to speak human languages. They might have been seduced away from their cause.

"Tell me how many are there in your unit," she tried again.

"Twelve," the alien rasped.

George frowned. They'd killed six aliens and captured one. If Woof was telling the truth - if the alien even understood the question - there should have been five more aliens chasing the marines. What had happened to them? She rather doubted the booby traps had caught more than one or two of them, not when the marines hadn't had the time to make them really unpleasant. Hell, the reports from the scouts suggested that the aliens were experienced soldiers, surprisingly good at picking out the traps from the surrounding landscape.

"Tell me how many landed on the planet," she said.

The alien looked as if he wanted to answer, but said nothing. George scowled as she heard someone opening the door behind her, although she didn't take her eyes off the alien. Woof had shown a surprising reluctance to escape, but she knew just how fast the aliens could move. If Woof had managed to work a claw out of the chains, she would be merely the first to die.

"Corporal wants you up there," Private Waters said. He jerked a finger upwards as he moved into sight. "Your friend is staying down here for the moment."

"Understood," George said.

She rose, nodded curtly to Woof and headed to the door. There were two armed guards outside, with strict orders to open fire if the alien broke out. Byron had warned George, twice, that the guards wouldn't hesitate to shoot, even if Woof was using her body as a human shield. They didn't dare take the risk of letting the alien out of the farmhouse. Given the speed the aliens could move, they wouldn't have a hope of catching up before it was too late.

The interior of the farmhouse itself looked half-abandoned. George had heard, from the resistance fighters, that the original owners had headed further away from the city, even though they were a good forty kilometres from the spaceport. But then, an aircraft could cover the distance in minutes, reaching its destination before anyone could prepare for its arrival. And the invaders were certainly ruthless enough to kick down the doors and come in shooting, if they had some reason to suspect trouble. She walked up the stairs and into the living room, where Byron and an officer she didn't recognise were bent over a hand-drawn map. It looked like the spaceport and the city, sketched by a child.

"George," Byron said. "Did you get anything useful from the prisoner?"

"No, sir," George said.

She scowled in frustration. She'd seen some of the preparations Prince Henry had made, massing a remarkable collection of brainpower and technological support in preparation for a sustained assault on the alien language. But she didn't have any support, not even a standard laptop terminal. Byron had flatly refused to allow any of the marines - or her - to carry anything that might radiate a betraying radio signal. Unlocking the alien language was well beyond her capabilities.

Byron nodded. "Do you get the impression he's holding out on us?"

"I don't think so," George said, after a moment. "He behaves himself very well, I think. But his language is very limited. I don't think he was taught enough English for a proper conversation."

She sighed. She'd been forced to take French lessons at school and she'd been left with the impression that French was a very rude language. But that was just her perceptions talking, her understanding of one language impeding her ability to comprehend another. How much worse must it be, she asked herself, if the second language wasn't even *human*? The aliens might look humanoid, but they were clearly inhuman. Their way of looking at the world might be very different from hers.

"That wouldn't be too surprising," Byron said. He frowned as he looked back at the map. "I don't think there's any evidence that they're actually interested in interrogating civilians."

George peered at the map herself. "What *are* they doing with civilians?"

"Everyone they caught, they tossed into a camp," the officer she didn't recognise said. He had a strong American accent, strong enough to make her blink. "The fools who stayed in Unity City had nowhere to hide."

"Oh," George said. "How are they being treated?"

"Well enough, as far as we can tell," the officer said. "But they're very definitely prisoners."

"The aliens have been sending out patrols over the last two days," Byron added. His finger traced a pattern on the map. "They've been moving further and further away from Unity City."

"Trying to provoke contact with us," the officer mused. He looked at George. "What else can you tell us about our prisoner?"

George took a moment to gather her thoughts. "He doesn't seem to have any problems eating our food and drinking water," she said. "As far as we can tell, he appears to be completely healthy. His…bodily wastes… have been taken away and buried. We've tried to wash his fur, but he didn't seem to appreciate it. The musk…isn't exactly pleasant. It's actually made a number of his watchers jumpy."

Byron frowned. "It doesn't affect you?"

"I tell myself that the sensations aren't real," George said.

She leaned forward as she spoke. "Mentally, he appears to be completely passive," she added. "He obeys orders, when he understands them. I've discovered that he appears to react better to orders that are issued slowly, giving him time to comprehend them. In some ways, it's like talking to a particularly dim-witted child."

"But English is very definitely not his first language," Byron pointed out. "Being a captive can't be very good for his mental health either."

"Yes, sir," George said.

She met his eyes. "I've tried to measure his intelligence through a number of counting games, like the ones I was taught in school," she added. "He's definitely capable of adding two and two together…"

"I'm sure that will rock the scientific community," the officer said, dryly.

George ignored him. "Numerically, he's very good," she said. "I managed to teach him the signs for multiplication and division, as well as a few other concepts. He's far from stupid. But we don't have a way to break the language barrier, either by teaching him more of our words or by learning to speak his language. At least, not yet. We're just not set up for it here."

Byron nodded. "Can you get anything useful from him?"

"Very little," George admitted. "He insists, repeatedly, that we challenged them, not the other way around. Past that…we just don't have enough words in common to discuss political concepts or the enemy leadership structure. He simply won't be drawn on dozens of topics."

She shrugged. "It's a little hard to interrogate someone when they can't understand your questions."

"A common problem," Byron said, dryly. He gave her a tight smile. "I think I'm starting to understand how the aliens *think*."

He tapped the map. "They hammered a few of our installations from orbit, but they otherwise held their fire - they didn't liberally spread KEWs around. That's what *we* would do, if we had to invade a planet - blow up anything that looked remotely threatening. But they landed and engaged our forces on the ground."

"And they chased us through the jungle," George reminded us.

"Yeah," Byron said.

"I'm honestly wondering if they just like challenges," he added, after a moment. "They might just have attacked the Contact Fleet under the assumption that we might feel the same way too."

George shook her head. "They'd have to be mad."

"Or alien," Byron said. "Dominance rituals are not uncommon for us, even though we tend to think of them differently. Why shouldn't the aliens be the same?"

Like Potter trying to undermine me, George thought. She wondered, suddenly, what had become of the ship. There hadn't been any time to draw a last update from *Vanguard* before she'd crashed on Unity. *And me, trying to keep him firmly in his place.*

"If that were true," she mused, "they'd run the risk of encountering a race that saw the attack as an unforgivable insult. And that race would chase them all the way back to their homeworld and lay waste to it."

"It's a possibility," Byron agreed. "We're not innocent when it comes to botched First Contacts either."

George nodded. First Contact with the Tadpoles had led to war…and First Contact with the Vesy had screwed their society up beyond repair. And First Contact with Woof's people - the Foxes and the Cows - had sparked off a *second* war. But the idea of a race that attacked newcomers on sight, as a test of strength, was absurd.

But we haze newcomers too, she thought. Perhaps, in hindsight, it had been a mistake to decide not to hold initiation rites on *Vanguard*. She'd had the feeling they'd do more harm than good, but it might have taught Henderson a lesson before he lost everything. *Perhaps the aliens are more like us than we care to admit.*

"Yes, sir," she said. "What are we going to do now?"

"Wait," the officer said. "Right now, we don't have a hope in hell if we launch a frontal assault on the aliens. They *still* hold the high orbitals, after all, and their reluctance to launch KEWs may no longer hold true if it looks like we're winning. Wait…and harry their forces as they move further and further away from the city."

Byron looked at her. "A team of intelligence specialists are on their way," he added. "Once they arrive we'll be heading towards the city ourselves. You included."

"Unless you want to stay," the officer said. "Can you make yourself useful here?"

George shrugged. She wasn't a xenospecialist - she didn't even have the basics. She couldn't get any further with Woof without a great deal of help, but anyone with the experience and ability to help her wouldn't *need* her. All she could really do in the farmhouse was make the tea. But she could shoot and she could make herself useful to the marines…

"I'd prefer to come with you," she said to Byron. "Is that all right?"

"It should be," Byron said. "Gather your crap. We'll be leaving in the next hour or so."

"Yes, sir," George said.

She wondered, as she returned to the room she shared with two of the marines, if she should go back to the cellar and say goodbye to the alien, then dismissed the thought. The alien was unlikely to have any feelings about it, while the intelligence staff would probably be annoyed at the thought of her saying *anything* to the alien. She hoped they could draw *something* from Woof, but she had a feeling it would be futile without a great deal of computer support. The alien language included quite a few words and tones that normal human hearing couldn't detect, let alone understand.

Talking to the Tadpoles is even worse, she thought. *At least these aliens don't need voders to shape human words.*

She picked up her knapsack and checked her gear, making sure she was carrying food, water, a small medical kit and ammunition. Stott had spent an hour going through the pack with her, pointing out all the little inefficiencies and how many things she could do without, at least for the next few days. If she had to grab her bag and run, he'd said, the less she had to carry the better. She finished checking the knife she'd borrowed from one of the marines, then rose, pulled the bag over her shoulder and glanced into the mirror. Her uniform was long gone, replaced by an outfit that made her look like a poor farmer. She just hoped the aliens weren't in the habit of opening fire when they saw a human.

No, they're in the habit of arresting everyone they can find, she thought, grimly. *And if they catch me, they'll put me in the pen too.*

She rubbed her forehead, then hurried back down the stairs. A pair of grim-faced officers had arrived and were speaking quietly to Byron, their air of self-importance more than enough to confirm them as intelligence specialists. George's uncle had told her, in some detail, that intelligence officers were rarely more than half as smart as they thought they were - and that they had a tendency to believe that their theories were correct, merely because they were the ones who'd come up with them. Line officers, he'd insisted, should always take an intelligence officer's word with a grain of salt.

"It's not that they're bad people," he'd said, afterwards. "It's that they're so smart they often put their theories before the facts, instead of keeping an open mind and being prepared to change their theories, based on the facts."

"Ah, George," Byron said. He gave her a dark smile as the intelligence officers hurried towards the cellar. "Don your coat. You'll need it."

"Of course," Stott teased. "She's pulled."

"I'll be pulling the trigger in a moment," George warned. The marines seemed to like poking at her, although there was little real malice in it. They were testing her, just as midshipmen were tested...and the aliens tested each other, if their theories were correct. "Is it a mere five hundred kilometre walk this afternoon?"

"Oh, no," Byron said. "I thought we'd march south to Unity City."

George frowned; Stott stepped in. "But Unity City's *north*, sir."

"Of course," Byron said. "We're going to march all the way around the globe and take them by surprise."

He chuckled, then opened the door. George had wondered if it was wise to be moving about in the daytime, but as she peered out she saw dark clouds and heard the rumble of thunder in the distance. The rain started to patter down as they made their way out of the farmhouse, then grew worse and worse as they slipped beneath the jungle canopy. Visibility fell to almost nothing within seconds, leaving her feeling as though they'd walk right into an ambush without a hope in hell of seeing it. But there was no sign of anyone as they walked onwards.

She cursed under her breath as water started to leak through her coat, drenching the clothes underneath. The marines didn't seem any better outfitted than herself, but they kept moving without complaint. George forced herself to keep moving, thinking of hours spent with Peter Barton and moments of quiet comradeship with Fraser in the hopes of distracting herself from her waterlogged clothes. If she ever made it back to Earth, she promised herself, she'd convince Barton to join her somewhere hot and exotic...where there was no risk of being shot by alien monsters. And if he didn't want to join her, she could easily find someone else...

The hours ticked away, thunder and lightning crashing high overhead. George just kept walking, feeling her tension slowly draining away. Her body felt...content, despite the wind and the rain. It was almost a disappointment when they slowed to a halt, waiting on the edge of the jungle. She wiped water off her face and waited with the marines until a local appeared, carrying a gun in one hand and a lantern in the other. He exchanged a few words with Byron, then led them towards a hidden farmhouse. It was worked into the trees so perfectly that it was surprisingly hard to see. George would have found it charming, she freely admitted, if she hadn't been drenched to the bone.

"Get undressed," the local ordered, as soon as they were inside. The air smelt oddly familiar, although she couldn't place the scent. "Once you're dry, there are some new clothes and food in the next room."

"Do as he says," Byron ordered, sharply.

George nodded, tearing off her sodden clothes and carefully placing them in a basket by the door. Thankfully, the local had thought to provide towels as well; she dried herself hastily, then walked through to the next room. The marines followed, looking as tired and subdued as she'd ever seen them. It was clear that they had been pushed to the limit too.

"Eat up," the local urged. The food looked like stew; it tasted, she discovered, rather like a rabbit curry she'd eaten once, back at school. "There are sleeping pallets overhead."

"Good idea," Byron added. "We'll be going on the offensive tomorrow."

George shivered, despite the heat. All of a sudden, she felt very cold.

CHAPTER
TWENTY-SEVEN

"The system appears clear, Captain," Charlotte reported.

Susan nodded. The task force had moved through Tramline Two as soon as they'd linked up again at Point Haven, but the new system - known only by a Tadpole catalogue number - appeared to be empty. There was no sign of any enemy presence. She reminded herself, again, that that might well be meaningless, but searching the entire system for a cloaked ship would be worse than looking for a needle in a haystack.

"Maintain a careful sensor watch," she ordered. "Alert me the moment anything enters the system."

"Aye, Captain," Charlotte said.

"Signal from the flag," Parkinson reported. "The task force is to proceed along a dog-leg course to the other tramline, then jump through."

"See to it," Susan ordered. Admiral Harper had little choice. If the aliens deduced which way the task force had gone, they'd know where they'd be *going*. "Keep us in cloak."

"Aye, Captain," Reed said.

Susan frowned as the battleship moved forward. Admiral Harper had added several hours to the transit time by moving off the least-time course, but she couldn't fault his decision. *New York* still needed repairs; hell, *Vanguard* and her crew needed time to rebuild the point defence and sensor blisters for the second time. It was a frustration, but it wasn't something she could do anything about. The damned components couldn't be armoured to match the main turrets without rendering them nearly useless.

"Mr. Mason, you have the conn," she said. "I'll be in my ready room."

She rose and walked through the hatch, then settled down on the sofa for a quick nap. It wasn't ideal, but she didn't want to move *too* far from the bridge if they encountered any patrolling enemy starships. She must have been more tired than she thought because she fell asleep almost at once and didn't wake until her alarm pinged, seven hours later. There had been no enemy contacts at all, she noted, as she splashed water on her face. The system appeared to be completely empty.

"Report," she ordered, keying her wristcom. "Status?"

"The task force will be crossing Tramline Two in ninety minutes," Reed said. He'd taken the conn after Mason and Granger had both retired to their cabins. "We didn't spot a single enemy vessel."

"Understood," Susan said. "I'll join you on the bridge in thirty minutes."

She checked her appearance in the mirror, then walked out of her ready room and started a long tour of her ship. *Vanguard* might have been battered, she discovered as she walked from compartment to compartment, but morale was still high. A share in the credit for smashing two enemy carriers had probably helped, even though there would be plenty of arguments - when they got home - over just who had done most of the work. Perhaps it was a relief, after all, that the ships hadn't been captured. An argument over who deserved the prize money would have been far worse.

And the Admiralty would pay through their nose for a captured alien ship, she thought. *Ark Royal* had captured an alien vessel, back during the *first* war, but no one else had managed to duplicate their feat. *Even a small fraction of the proceeds would go a very long way.*

She smiled at the thought as she walked through the engineering department. Mr. Finch was directing half of his crews to patch up the overworked components and making the other half run successive damage-control drills until they could do it in their sleep. Susan couldn't help wondering if he was overdoing it, but she pushed the thought aside.

There was little hope of limping back to a shipyard if the battleship took serious damage. If they couldn't repair it on their own, they were in deep shit.

We'd be screwed, she thought. *It would be the end of us.*

She returned to the bridge and took command, then checked the reports from the tactical analysts as the task force made its way towards the tramline. There was little new, unfortunately, but the analysts seemed to believe that there were several new ways to spoof the enemy sensors. It would be wonderful if they were correct, Susan thought, but she had her doubts. Enemy *stealth* systems were so advanced that it was hard to believe that their sensors weren't *equally* advanced. They'd certainly have tried to fool their own systems before testing their sensor masks on passing aliens.

"Signal from the flag," Parkinson said. "We are to pass through the tramline as planned."

"Understood," Susan said. "Take us through as soon as you can."

She braced herself as the display blanked, then flickered back to life. A G2 star, a handful of planets...including one right in the middle of the life-bearing zone. It would have made an excellent prospect for colonisation, she thought, if it hadn't been further from Earth than Unity. The Tadpoles had established a small colony in the waters, according to the database they'd shared with their human allies, yet it hadn't lasted. She couldn't help wondering why they hadn't maintained and expanded the colony, but the files offered no explanation...

"Enemy contacts," Charlotte snapped. "Seven starships; I say again, seven starships!"

Susan leaned forward. Seven enemy ships, perhaps more...orbiting the single life-bearing world. None of them seemed larger than a cruiser, save for one that was easily ten times the size of a battleship. She narrowed her eyes as she studied the power readings, then decided that it was probably an oversized freighter. If the aliens had figured out how to produce an actual *warship* over twenty kilometres long, the human race might be in some trouble.

But it would also be one hell of a target, she thought, amused. *Vanguard's* armour was staggeringly capable of absorbing damage, but there was no way to hide the simple fact that she handled like a pig in mud. *Bigger isn't always better.*

"They may have a colony," Parkinson mused. "I picked up flashes of radio traffic from the surface."

Prince Henry will be pleased, Susan thought. *We can try to make contact.*

She smiled, rather dryly, at the thought. The aliens weren't normally talkative - or at all - and they *certainly* wouldn't be talkative after the task force blew apart the starships in orbit. She wondered, briefly, about trying to open communications before they engaged the enemy ships, but she knew Admiral Harper would never agree. The smaller enemy ships couldn't hope to best the task force, yet if they realised what was bearing down on them they could easily outrun it.

"Signal from the flag," Parkinson said. "The task force is to alter course towards the alien settlement and secure the high orbitals."

"Acknowledge," Susan ordered. "Helm, take us towards our targets."

She leaned back in her chair as the seconds ticked away, wondering just how many sensor platforms the aliens would have seeded through the system. The war was barely a year old, depending on how one looked at it; the aliens couldn't really have found the time, she was sure, to scatter more than a few dozen around the system. And yet, if *she* was establishing a colony so close to enemy space, she would have made sure to secure the system as much as possible.

But they may not have known about Unity, she thought, tiredly. It had been so much *easier* during the last war, when everyone had been sure the Tadpoles had captured a number of databases from Heinlein. *We don't know how much they know, so we can't guess at what they might do.*

Charlotte sucked in her breath as alarms sounded. "Captain, we just got swept with an active sensor," she snapped. "They know we're here."

Susan cursed. "Drop the cloak, then accelerate," she ordered. The aliens would be unlikely to stick around, but they could *try.* If nothing else, they could make it impossible for the aliens to retrieve anything useful from the planet. "Time to target?"

"Nine minutes at current speed," Granger reported. "The carriers are launching starfighters now."

"Enemy ships moving out of orbit," Charlotte added. "They're heading into deep space."

Susan nodded as she saw the course projections. The aliens weren't heading for any of the tramlines, although that meant nothing. They might - they probably would - alter course as soon as they were out of sensor range or cloaked. And there was nothing she could do about it. The starfighters might inflict some damage, if the warships didn't hang around to defend the freighters, but it would be minimal.

Every little bit helps, she told herself. *And every freighter we blow up now is one that won't be threatening us again.*

"Launch probes towards the planet," she ordered. "And sweep space ourselves. I want to find any other sensor platforms within range."

"Aye, Captain," Charlotte said.

Susan watched, grimly, as the alien warships fought to keep the human starfighters off the freighters. There was nothing wrong with their formation, she noted, but they just didn't have the firepower to make a major difference. The giant freighter stumbled out of formation, then exploded as a trio of Russian fighters volley-fired torpedoes into her hull, pieces of debris flying in all directions. Susan glanced at the live feed from the analysis department and scowled. It looked, very much, as though the giant hulk had been empty when she'd been blown apart. The remaining enemy warships picked up speed as soon as the last of the freighters died, heading onwards into space while the human starfighters returned to their motherships. They had every prospect of making it out before it was too late.

"Cowards," Reed muttered.

"Practical," Susan corrected.

But she had to admit she found it odd too. She liked to think she would have fought and died in the defence of innocent civilians - she'd sworn an oath to die for her country, if necessary - but the aliens had *known* it would be futile. It said odd things about their mindset. On one hand, they fought savagely when there was a chance of victory, however slim; on the other, they pulled back at once as soon as victory became completely impossible. They hadn't even tried to damage the task force before retreating.

They don't think like us, she thought. *She* would have launched a few long-range missiles on ballistic trajectories, if only to keep the enemy from becoming too comfortable. *And they have different ideas about how to fight a war.*

"Check the probes," she ordered, as the battleship continued to move towards the planet. "I want every ground-based defence station noted and marked for destruction before we enter orbit."

"I'm not sure just what we're seeing," Charlotte said. "If they have any ground-based weapons, sir, I can't find them."

Susan glanced - again - at the reports from the analysts. The alien settlement had been easy to locate - it looked as though the aliens had landed nearly twenty thousand of their personnel in less than a year - but there didn't seem to be any recognisable defences. She puzzled over it for a long moment, then decided that the aliens might feel that mounting weapons on the planetary surface was unwise. They would draw fire, after all...

And it's impossible to keep a determined attacker back, she mused. *Not without orbital weapons platforms too.*

She contemplated options for a long moment, knowing that Admiral Harper would have to make the final call. Blasting the entire settlement from orbit would be easy, but regulations forbade mass slaughter without authorisation from JHQ. Admiral Smith had made it policy, back during the First Interstellar War, not to bombard alien populations, even with provocation. And he'd stuck to his guns even after the Bombardment of Earth.

And yet, we can't land either, she thought. *We dropped most of our marines on Unity.*

She checked the records, just to be sure. *Vanguard* had two platoons of marines - twenty men - and none of the other ships were in much better shape. Collectively, they had around two hundred marines. There was no way they could hope to secure the enemy population, not without massive use of KEWs. And that would just make it harder to work out a more permanent peace agreement.

Unless they want to be punched in the snout before they actually bother to talk to us, she thought. She'd met a few men like that, but she found it hard to believe that an entire race would have such an odd society. *But slaughtering aliens who cannot fight back is dishonourable.*

"Signal from the flag, Captain," Parkinson reported. "Admiral Harper is ordering us to take the L2 position, then wait."

Susan lifted her eyebrows. "*Wait?*"

"He also requests that you join a holoconference," Parkinson added. "He's calling the other commanders now."

A holoconference in the middle of a battle, Susan thought. She was surprised. Harper had never struck her as *indecisive*. But then, they *were* looking down on a helpless alien world instead of confronting a raiding fleet. *He may want cover for whatever he wants to do.*

She glanced at Mason. "You have the conn," she said. "I'll be in my ready room."

"Aye, Captain," Mason said. "I have the conn."

Susan nodded and rose, taking one last look at the tactical display before striding into her ready room. The holoconference was already underway, four of her fellow commanders striding around in holographic form. It was, technically, bad form to start a conference before everyone had linked into the network, but under the circumstances it was hard to blame Harper. All the theoretical questions about what they'd do with an alien population had suddenly become frighteningly real.

"Greetings," Harper said, when the last of the commanding officers had joined the discussion. "As you know, we have effectively taken an alien-settled world…"

"It belongs to the Tadpoles," Captain Stewart injected.

"If they still have a colony here, it's deep below the waves," Yegorovich growled. "I think we can safely say they're not important here."

"As I was saying," Harper snapped, "we have taken one of their worlds. We have to decide what to do about it."

"Blow the place into rubble," Yegorovich said, flatly. "That's an invasion force, not a settlement."

"That's a group of civilians," Susan snapped back. "Do we *want* to start setting precedents for mass slaughter?"

"They might well have killed everyone on Unity," Yegorovich stated, bluntly. "Do we want to set a precedent for *not* retaliating?"

"We don't *know* what's happening at Unity," Glass said. "For all we know, the aliens are keeping their distance from the human population."

"They need the land, same as us," Yegorovich reminded him. "They'll want to kick our settlers off the planet if they don't want to kill them."

Harper clapped his hands, once. "I will not condone mass slaughter," he said, firmly. "This world does not pose a threat to us. They are completely incapable of hitting our ships from the ground."

"Unless they have some strange superweapon," Yegorovich grumbled.

"Surely we would have seen evidence of it by now," Jeanette said. She looked doubtful. "With all due respect, Admiral, what do you expect us to do?"

"We can move on now," Harper said. "Or we can attempt to make contact with them."

"We could also kidnap a few dozen of the bastards from the surface," Yegorovich pointed out. "Wouldn't *that* be a good way to get samples for the researchers?"

Susan shuddered. The thought of being scooped up because a group of aliens wanted samples was chilling. From a cold-blooded point of view, Yegorovich was right; from the point of view of common humanity, he was very wrong. Besides, an alien farmer might not know anything of use.

"We can certainly *try* to open communications," she said, softly. "If nothing else, we have a chance to study one of their settlements from a distance."

"You appear to have forgotten that the enemy is hunting us," Yegorovich sneered. "We need to keep moving. Blow the planet up or leave it alone, Admiral. We don't have time to do anything else."

"There is enough time to *try* to open communications," Harper said. "And we would have ample warning of a new attack force entering the system…"

"We couldn't rely on that," Captain Garret said. "They have cloaking devices too, Admiral."

Harper nodded, slowly.

"We compromise," he said. "We remain here for an hour. The xeno-specialists can use that time to attempt to open contact. If they succeed… well and good. If they fail…well, we're no worse off than we are already. And then we head onwards to the next system."

"We could bait a trap for the aliens," Susan offered. "We do have a whole series of tactics we were planning to use."

"Which we were intending to deploy when we return to Unity," Yegorovich said. "Using them early will make them useless."

"They will also be useless if we don't *survive* to return to Unity," Susan snapped, sharply. Yegorovich was alarmingly good at getting under her skin. "If we have a chance to scatter or destroy another small alien force, Captain, we should take advantage of it."

Harper leaned forward. "We will do what we can to take advantage of whatever opportunities fate dumps in our path," he said. "But right now our priority is leading the enemy away from Unity so we can slip back and recover the world. If they can be tempted into trying to trap us here…"

Susan had her doubts - everything they'd learned about their new foes suggested they were remarkably pragmatic when they *knew* they'd lost - but she kept them to herself. Harper was right about one thing, at least. This *was* an opportunity to attempt to open communications with the aliens…

…And if they succeeded, the war might come to an end before more youngsters had to die.

CHAPTER
TWENTY-EIGHT

"They're not answering," Doctor Song said. "Your Excellency, *why* aren't they answering?"

Henry shrugged. He had no answer, save for the obvious. The communications techs had picked up enough alien transmissions to be fairly sure which frequencies they used. They certainly shouldn't have had any trouble picking up the signals, nor adapting their receivers and computers to *read* them. God knew their technology wasn't *that* different from humanity's. But neither *Vanguard* nor any of the other ships had picked up a reply.

Doctor Song lowered her voice as she nodded towards the communications specialists at the far end of the compartment. "Are they…are they sending the messages?"

It took Henry a couple of seconds to realise what she meant. "Yes," he said, flatly. Anyone who thought the military didn't want peace was an idiot. It was military personnel who did the fighting and dying, if peace came to an end. "They're sending the messages. The aliens are just not bothering to reply."

He understood her frustration, though. The techs had worked hard to put the contact package together, making it as simple as possible. Given a few weeks of open communications, the two races should have been able to establish a common understanding. But the aliens hadn't bothered to reply and all the careful procedures remained unused. There was certainly no hope of establishing a dialogue. It was frustrating as hell.

"We should go down to the surface," Doctor Song said. "If we tried to talk to them in person…"

"Out of the question," Henry said. He'd asked the captain, but she'd told him that the admiral had flatly vetoed any missions to the surface. Given the number of handheld weapons the aliens were carrying, clearly visible to the orbiting sensors, he had to agree that any attempt to land would be risky. "We have to rely on our radios."

"But they're not replying," Doctor Song snapped.

Henry shrugged. There *was* a great deal of data flowing into the ship - it would keep the analysts happy for months - but almost none of it was immediately useful. They knew next to nothing about the alien chain of command, their leadership structure or anything else that might help them work out who could answer their calls. The only really useful piece of information was some recordings of the alien language, giving the computers more to work on as they struggled to devise a translation program.

He didn't blame Doctor Song and her team for being frustrated. In all honesty, he didn't feel any better. He'd built his career around talking to seemingly-inscrutable aliens. But Admiral Harper was right. Quite apart from the risk of being killed or captured, the task force might have to leave the system in a hurry. Anyone down on the surface when the shit hit the fan might be left behind, trapped amidst the aliens. It was not to be borne.

"Keep studying their transmissions," he said, softly. "You might manage to crack their language."

Doctor Song looked doubtful, but did as she was told.

———

"The aliens didn't reply," Prince Henry said, twenty minutes before Admiral Harper's deadline. "There's no way to know if they heard our signals or not, Captain, but they certainly didn't reply."

"They *should* be able to hear our signals," Mason pointed out. "We're using their frequencies."

Susan held up a hand. "And there's no way to provoke an answer?"

"Not from what we have on hand," Prince Henry said. "Given time, we might learn enough from their transmissions to have a valid chance at sending them a message in their own language, but that may take some time."

"It always does," Susan mused. She sipped her coffee thoughtfully. "How long did it take to crack the Tadpole language?"

"It took us under a year, with their help, to establish a way to share information," Prince Henry said, bluntly. "Captain, it is *important* that you understand some of the problems we encountered along the way. In all honesty, there are...aspects...of the Tadpole language that we don't understand and may *never* understand. Their culture includes a number of assertions about the universe that we simply don't share."

He leaned forward. "To us, family is important. Knowing where you came from is important. We are intimately connected to our parents and siblings even if we hate the ground they walk on. To them, family is utterly unimportant. They don't have families, they don't have siblings; they only have faction-mates, which can be changed at the slightest provocation. The concepts of *treason* and even *loyalty* are largely alien to them."

Susan frowned. She was immensely loyal to her father, to the point where she'd been threatened with expulsion or jail several times for bloodying the nose of anyone who insulted him. And why *shouldn't* she be loyal? Her father had brought her up on his own, raised her to be a good and decent citizen...she was damned if she was abandoning him, now she was an adult. He'd certainly not abandoned her like so many fathers tried to abandon their children.

"You can imagine what this does to their society," Prince Henry added. "How much of our culture is based around family, around love and romance and finding your place? They don't have *any* of it."

"No romantic chick-flicks," Mason said.

"No *Romeo and Juliet* either," Prince Henry countered. "And no Trojan War."

"You make it sound like a bad thing," Susan groused. Her studies suggested that the *real* cause of the Trojan War had more to do with trade routes than a runaway wife, but the latter made a better story. "What do you know about our new enemies?"

Prince Henry smiled. "First, we still don't know which of the two races is actually in charge," he said. "They *do* seem to be intermingled on the ground, but we've observed members of both races giving orders to members of the other race. The cow-like aliens, by the way, *do* seem to have both male and female genders."

He shrugged. "Or at least that's how we've accounted for differences between them," he added, after a moment. "We may still be wrong."

Susan frowned. "They're truly intermingled?"

"It's starting to look that way," Prince Henry said. "As far as we can tell, most groupings include representatives from both races. Any group larger than three or four is almost certain, based on our observations, to include at least one representative from both races. I think we only ever saw one exception, a gaggle of ten fox-like aliens on the prowl."

"It makes no sense," Susan said.

"Perhaps it does," Mason said. "Britain had…problems…accepting and absorbing large numbers of immigrants, but America generally did a better job breaking down the old cultures and assimilating the newcomers. This could be the same problem on a bigger scale."

"They can't biologically integrate," Susan pointed out, again.

"They might not *want* to," Mason countered. "And that might work *better* for them."

Susan wondered, absently, if he had a point. The easiest way to get in trouble in a foreign country, according to her father, involved women. Social mores were different from place to place. A woman could wear a bikini in public in Britain and no one would bat an eyelid, but she'd be stoned to death in a Middle Eastern hellhole; a man could sleep with a woman in Britain and no one would care, but he could be tortured or killed if he did it somewhere rather less civilised. Contact between the different human societies might have been less unpleasant if they hadn't been able to interbreed…

And if interbreeding was impossible, she told herself sternly, *you would not exist.*

"We probably won't find out until we manage to convince them to talk to us," Prince Henry said. "But unless we find a way to force them to answer…"

Susan frowned. "Do you think we should reconsider snatching a couple of aliens from the surface?"

"I'd advise against it," Prince Henry said. "The Tadpoles might not care if a handful of their people get kidnapped, but our new friends might think differently."

"Probably," Susan agreed. The Vesy had practically lined up to *beg* to be allowed to join the training courses to improve their technological base, but they had good reason to want to learn. "Did you learn anything else?"

"Well, their family groups seem to include both races," Prince Henry said. "If it wasn't clear that they *were* two different races, I would have wondered if we were looking at a single race."

"Oh," Susan said. "And how does that work?"

"Unknown," Prince Henry said. "But their mating rites do seem to involve a struggle for dominance. It may be that two partners fight and the loser is the one who has to carry the children."

"Or the other way around," Susan mused. "Or they might *both* get pregnant."

"It's a possibility," Henry agreed. "But again, we may never find out until we ask them."

Mason cleared his throat. "Could one of them be a domesticated animal?"

Susan looked up, interested. There had been all sorts of plans to uplift animals to sentience, but most of them had been buried after the Age of Unrest. Perhaps they'd be dusted off again, now that humanity had encountered other intelligent races…she honestly wasn't sure how she should feel about that. Would intelligent dogs and cats be humanity's allies or deadly new threats?

Perhaps not the dogs, she thought. She'd had a dog as a little girl and there were days when she still missed the mongrel puppy terribly. *But the cats might wage war on us.*

"I don't think so," Henry said. He looked doubtful. "It is *possible*, I suppose, but genetic analysis of their DNA - their DNA-analogue, I should say - suggests they come from different worlds. They simply don't have anything in common. If they are advanced enough to take a sub-sentient creature and uplift it into intelligence…it says worrying things about their capabilities."

"Yeah," Mason agreed. "I watched the Draka movies too."

Susan shuddered. Anyone capable of reengineering a chimpanzee or a dolphin into something intelligent would be capable of crafting the most savage biological warfare weapon in living history. Hell, if something that unpleasant got loose, there wouldn't *be* any living history. Humanity had enough experience with the - thankfully limited - viruses that *had* been released to know that it was one particular genie that should remain firmly sealed away in the bottle. It might not be possible to put it back in, after it escaped.

A chill ran through her. They didn't have to craft a virus that would exterminate humanity, not if they were *that* advanced. She'd read reports - most of them classified - suggesting that various parties had designed viruses intended to make their victims more obedient or merely too stupid to know what was happening to them. And if there were two races intermingled on the planet's surface, was it possible that one of them had been warped and twisted to make it possible?

Or was she just being paranoid? She hoped so. God, she hoped so.

"The most likely theory is that one of them discovered the other and integrated it into their society," Prince Henry said. "And given how successful they seem to have been, it must have taken place thousands of years ago."

Susan nodded, pushing her dark thoughts out of her head. Her father would never have countenanced talk of going back to Jamaica - as if she'd ever *lived* there - and he would certainly not have tolerated her attempting to rediscover her roots, but her father had been an unusual man. She'd met a couple of Americans who'd talked about going back to Africa, even though it had been over four hundred years since their ancestors had left the dark continent. Given the nightmares sweeping over most of Africa, Susan had honestly wondered if they were out of their minds.

They just wanted somewhere to belong, she thought. *And they didn't realise they were right where they belonged.*

"Then there's no hope of driving a wedge between them," she said. "Unless we're misinterpreting the data."

"It's possible," Henry agreed. "But we won't know for sure until we actually get to ask them questions."

Susan sighed. It all came back to finding a way to communicate…

…And, if they *couldn't* communicate, hammering the aliens until they were no longer a threat.

"I'll keep working on the problem," Prince Henry said. "But all the data we're picking up suggests that we will need to thump the aliens before they actually listen to us."

"We'll get right on that," Mason said, dryly.

Prince Henry nodded as he finished his coffee. "I'll have a full report for you and the admiral after we leave the system," he said. "It just won't be as insightful as you might have hoped."

Susan nodded. She'd known people who would have bitched and moaned about having to operate under the strict protocols laid down by their superiors. Prince Henry, it seemed, merely got to work. But then, he *had* been a starfighter pilot. The breed was disrespectful and prone to bending the rules, but they still understood the importance of discipline. And they also understood the limits of what they could do with their craft.

"I'm sure it will make interesting reading," she said. "One other thing - do we know what they can eat, now? Both of them?"

"Our long-range analysis agrees that they can eat our crops," Prince Henry said. "I suspect we can probably eat theirs too, although we might not *like* it. Taste is merely a matter of biochemistry, after all."

He gave her an odd smile. "We already knew that, I believe, but it's nice to have confirmation."

Susan nodded. Her father hadn't cooked many foreign meals when she'd been a child, but she'd tasted quite a few during her time in boarding school. She wasn't sure if the headmistress was intent on exposing her students to other cultures or merely aiming for some variety, yet Susan had been surprised by how many of them she'd actually enjoyed. One of her classmates had even chatted about opening a dining hall herself, after she left…

"So we can feed them," Mason said. "Once we take a few prisoners, of course."

"Yep," Prince Henry said. He rose. "I'd better make sure the researchers aren't doing anything stupid."

"They *might* steal a shuttle," Mason said. "How many movies start with that exact same gag?"

Susan snorted as Prince Henry left the compartment. *He* could have flown a shuttle - Susan knew he'd spent a great deal of time in the simulators - but could any of the researchers naive enough to think that stealing a shuttle and trying to contact the aliens directly was a good idea actually fly? It definitely sounded like the plot of a bad movie. She'd be astonished if they even managed to land safely.

Assuming there aren't any MANPADs waiting for them, she thought, grimly. *They might not be able to touch the ships in orbit, but firing on shuttles is a different thing altogether.*

"We should be able to get a good movie out of it," Mason said, deadpan. "Or should we have the shuttles guarded anyway, just in case?"

"They wouldn't be able to leave the ship without the flight codes," Susan said. She shook her head. "Are we ready to move on?"

"Yes, Captain," Mason said. He looked at the images on the display for a long moment. "It beggars belief. How can they...have a friendly relationship with one race while attacking two more?"

"Maybe they just find us hideously ugly," Susan speculated, dryly. "It isn't as if humans haven't used such a silly excuse to start a war."

"Could be," Mason said. He made to rise. "I'll go back to the bridge, if you don't mind. You can have a rest."

"Thank you," Susan said, dryly. "How are things in middy country?"

Mason didn't look thrown by the sudden change in subject. "They have improved, I think," he said. "But Fraser reported that neither of the two remaining midshipmen seemed concerned about Midshipwoman Fitzwilliam."

Susan nodded, feeling a stab of sympathy for the unfortunate young woman. Midshipmen weren't required to *like* the First Middies - some of them could be bullies worse than anyone they might have encountered at school - but they *were* supposed to respect them. George Fitzwilliam hadn't just lost control of the wardroom, she'd poisoned it. Fraser would have to stay in charge, for the moment, but afterwards? The three remaining midshipmen - two, if George Fitzwilliam was dead - would have to be assigned elsewhere. And God alone knew who they'd get next.

"Keep their noses to the grindstone," she ordered, shortly. "And our two prisoners?"

"In the brig," Mason reminded her. "Very little has changed, I'm afraid."

Susan nodded. In the movies, something would happen to allow the two idiots to redeem themselves. A suicide mission, perhaps; something with a minuscule chance of survival. But in the real world, they'd be judged when they were taken back to Earth and then sentenced, without a hope of escaping their fates. And then...

The alarm rang. She keyed her wristcom, sharply.

"Report," she snapped.

"Captain, this is Granger," a voice said. "Long-range sensor platforms just picked up an enemy fleet, transiting Tramline One. The current course projection has them heading directly towards the planet."

"Understood," Susan said. She rose, nodding to Mason. "ETA?"

"Four hours, based on the last projection," Granger said.

"Bring the ship to condition two," Susan ordered. "I'll be on the bridge in a moment."

She looked at Mason. "If they came from Tramline One..."

"They might have been rerouted from Unity," Mason finished. "And if *that* happened, we might have a clear shot at the planet."

"We might," Susan agreed.

CHAPTER
TWENTY-NINE

At least I'm not the bait this time, George thought, as she clutched the rifle and waited, hidden by the side of the road. *There's nothing luring them towards us, but their own determination to secure the area.*

She felt sweat trickling down her back as she heard the sound of engines growing closer, echoing off the roadside. The aliens didn't seem to use vehicles and technology *that* different from the vehicles she knew, although the marines had warned her that they *did* seem to have brought more ground vehicles with the invasion force than she would have expected. And it was possible, too possible, that there were unblinking eyes overhead, watching the patrol as it made its way down the road. The aliens seemed reluctant to call in KEW strikes, particularly at what the marines called 'danger close' ranges, but they might change their policy at any moment.

"Here they come," a voice muttered.

George glanced at the resistance fighter - a girl who freely admitted she'd been a tearaway at school before her parents had accepted the offer of free passage to Unity - and then peered back along the road, just in time to see the first alien vehicle moving into view. It looked like an odd combination of a tractor and a truck, although she'd been warned that they were armoured and carried enough firepower to make any would-be insurgents very unhappy. The marines had warned her that many of their vehicles on Earth were armed and armoured too, suggesting the aliens found themselves fighting low-intensity wars on a regular basis. As far as George could recall, the Tadpoles had never tried to occupy human-ity's colonies directly; they'd only secured the high orbitals and left the colonists alone. It made her wonder what they'd intended to do with the human race, if they'd won the war.

She pushed the thought aside, her grip tightening on her rifle, as the aliens came closer. The resistance leader had told them, in bloodcurdling terms, precisely what would happen to anyone who opened fire ahead of time; she fought, desperately, to remain calm as the aliens swept towards the ambush point. There were more of them now, five truck-like vehicles and two outriders, both mounting heavy weapons that swept from side to side, searching for a target. They wouldn't be able to stand up to a tank, Byron had assured her, but George was all too aware that a few layers of foliage wouldn't be enough to stop a pistol shot, let alone something that was almost certainly a machine gun. If the aliens caught sight of them - or smelled humans on the air - they'd open fire as they tried to fight their way out of the trap.

There was a *click*. George had barely a second to brace herself before the IED exploded, right underneath the lead vehicle. The blast picked it up and flipped it over, crashing head over heels until it slammed into a tree and came to a halt, burning brightly. Two resistance fighters launched antitank missiles at the same instant, aimed at both of the outriders. The aliens managed to fire off a burst of machine gun rounds before they were destroyed, but they went wide. George let out a breath she hadn't realised she'd been holding, then hefted her rifle as the aliens swarmed out of the remaining trucks. A dozen fell to the ground as a wave of gunfire rang out, but others took cover and fired back, their bullets whipping through the foliage as they searched for targets. George kept her head down as she heard rounds cracking over her head, firing rapidly as she searched for targets. They seemed to have the remaining aliens pinned down, but they couldn't get to them either.

She smiled, coldly, as she heard the CRUMP-CRUMP-CRUMP of the mortars. Moments later, a handful of shells landed right on top of the alien position, blowing their cover into flaming debris. She saw an alien blasted away, his fur blazing with fire; she watched, dispassionately, as he slammed into the ground and lay still. The remaining aliens rose to their feet and charged, firing madly. She cringed, despite herself, as they ran straight into the human gunsights and were blasted down, one by one. They never stood a chance.

WHAM! The ground rang like a bell. She glanced back, just in time to see a pillar of smoke rising up from where the mortars had been sited. The aliens had apparently decided to stop pissing around and drop KEWs - after all, none of their people were anywhere near the mortars, as far as they knew. She hoped - prayed - that the mortar crews had managed to pack up their weapons and bug out before the hammer came down, but she had no way to know. They might well have been caught in the blast even if they had managed to dismantle the mortars and run for their lives.

The whistle blew. George picked herself up, took one last look at the burning remains of the alien convoy, then turned and fled into the jungle. She could hear the sound of helicopter blades chopping through the air, suggesting that the aliens were dispatching reinforcements as fast as they could. A whole string of attacks had been planned, using resistance fighters and a number of other stranded personnel. If they were lucky, she told herself, the aliens simply had too many threats to give priority to any of them.

She gritted her teeth as the sound of helicopters grew closer. The marines - and other regular forces - had a handful of MANPADS, but they were reluctant to deploy them unless there was no other choice. And they had few other weapons that would make an impact on their armoured hulls. She'd heard that one of the resistance fighters had brought a helicopter down with a rifle, but she knew enough about their armour to know that it was almost certainly nothing more than a rumour. Byron had pointed out that it would have had to be a *very* lucky shot, too lucky to count on anything like it happening twice. Stott had even suggested that the helicopter crew had had other problems and the resistance fighters had merely taken credit for an electrical fault. It had happened before, he'd said.

And if they have very good sensors, she thought numbly, *they might be able to see us through the foliage.*

A burst of gunfire rattled out in the distance. Someone - either through panic or the cold certainty that they'd been detected - had opened fire on the helicopters with an automatic weapon. George was torn between relief and horror as the helicopters turned away from her and then opened fire, lashing the ground with machine guns and small rockets. The sound provided cover as she scurried north after three of the other resistance fighters, even though she knew it meant that men were dying. Thankfully, the aliens didn't seem inclined to give chase on the ground.

I suppose they have too many other problems right now, she thought. *If even half of the attack plans came off, they'll think they're under attack everywhere.*

She relaxed, slightly, as they kept moving, slowly to a walk as it became increasingly clear that the aliens had lost the trail. George wasn't as sure of that as she liked to think - she had the nasty feeling that the aliens could sniff out humans - but they probably did have too many other problems. She doubted that any of the attacks had inflicted serious damage - there was no way the resistance could get at the orbiting starships - yet it *would* keep the aliens busy. If the cost of occupying Unity grew too high, the aliens might just pull out.

And if they decide to burn the planet to ash instead, she asked herself, *what then?*

Byron hadn't answered the question, when she'd asked, but one of the resistance leaders had pointed out that there many other choices. There was no way to know which side would win the war, nor what the terms of the eventual peace treaty - assuming there *was* a peace treaty - would be. Hurting the enemy badly was their only real hope of convincing them to leave Unity alone - or at least to share it with the other two sets of colonists. George had hoped that the Tadpoles would assist the humans, but apparently they'd withdrawn beneath the waves as soon as the high orbitals had been lost. It was hard to blame the Tadpoles - some of the human leaders had admitted they would have liked to do the same thing - yet it was a major problem. Their support might have been invaluable.

She pushed the thought aside as they finally stumbled into the resistance camp. It wasn't much, merely a handful of makeshift shelters buried deep within the forest, but it was as safe as anywhere else on the planet. George knew it wouldn't be safe - remotely safe - if the aliens located the camp and dropped a KEW on it, yet there was no point in bitching about it to anyone. The colonists who didn't want to fight - or leave - had headed further away from Unity, hiding far from the settlements until they knew who had won the war.

And I chose to stay and fight, George thought. *What was I thinking?*

She sat down and slumped against a tree, watching through tired eyes as the remaining fighters slowly filtered into the camp. She'd left with thirty others - a combination of resistance fighters and volunteers from the stranded naval parties - in the morning; now, only fifteen fighters had returned to the camp. The dead had been left behind, either blasted to dust by the KEW strike or gunned down by the aliens. She wondered what the aliens would do to the bodies and hoped, grimly, that they'd be civilised enough to merely bury or cremate them. There were all sorts of things one could do with a captured body, she knew from her studies. Entire towns and villages had been firebombed, during the Age of Unrest, for producing even one or two terrorists. The aliens might do the same.

"You look beat," a familiar voice said. "Wounded?"

George looked up. Kelly was squatting beside her, holding out a glass of water. "No," she said, taking the glass and sipping it gratefully. "Just tired."

"Makes you one of the lucky ones," Kelly assured her. "Any engagement you can walk away from is a good one."

"I've heard that before," George said. "We ran."

"He who fights and runs away, lives to run away another day," Kelly misquoted. "And standing and fighting, George, would have gotten all of you killed."

George finished the water and looked up. "How bad was it?"

"From what I've heard, a quarter of the fighters who went out were killed or wounded," Kelly said, grimly. "There's no way to know how bad it was at the other camps, of course."

George nodded. The days of instant communications on Unity were over, as least until the aliens were chased out of the high orbitals. Anyone stupid enough to turn on a radio transmitter would get a KEW dropped on his head, seconds later. And the ground-based telecommunications infrastructure of Earth simply didn't exist on Unity. The disparate camps were linked together by runners, men who might suffer accidents or get caught as they moved from camp to camp. She knew that General Kershaw was out there somewhere, controlling his detachment of American Marines, but she didn't know where. What she didn't know, Byron had pointed out, she couldn't tell.

Or be made to tell, she thought. *If they interrogated me, how long could I hold out?*

She shuddered at the thought. The prospect of capture had haunted her mind ever since they'd landed, although she doubted the aliens knew or cared about her. If she'd been at risk of falling into terrorist hands, she would have made preparations to kill herself, rather than take the risk. Snuff movies showing what happened to soldiers who fell into enemy hands were still common, despite dire retribution. The bastards would take their time with her, she knew. They'd think the First Space Lord's niece deserved special treatment…

"You're coping well," Kelly said. "Did you ever consider going into the groundpounders?"

George shook her head. A couple of her uncle's cronies had tried to talk her into it, but it hadn't really made much of an impression. Most of the *really* good regiments were still closed to women. There were no shortage of postings open within the Adjunct General's Corps - the men and women who handed everything at the rear - but it wouldn't have been the same. And besides, there would be no hope of command. The British Army had learned harsh lessons about promoting men without combat experience and that went double for women.

"I spent enough time at school to know I didn't want to go crawling through the mud for the rest of my life," she said, instead. "We had a complete…"

She broke off as she heard someone shouting in alarm. "Code Blue! Code Blue! Get up and move to the south, now!"

George rose automatically, grabbing and checking her rifle as she moved. Kelly unslung his from his shoulder and then grabbed her arm and led her towards the south. The other resistance fighters were moving too, glancing around in alarm. Kelly waved to one of the leaders - a burly man who had never introduced himself - and snapped out a question. The man glanced at him in surprise, then nodded.

"One of the spotters reported a major flight of enemy helicopters heading this way," he snapped, grimly. "They're aimed right at us."

"They found us," George said.

"It looks that way," the man agreed. "We have to be gone before they arrive."

"Tell everyone to sneak out, preferably east or west," Kelly said, sharply. "And warn them to expect trouble."

The man glared at him. "What do you mean?"

"They're not stupid," Kelly snapped. George tensed as she heard the sound of helicopters, again. If she ever got home, she rather doubted she'd ever be able to hear a helicopter again without flinching. "Coming right at the camp is stupid."

"That's what they're doing," the man snarled. "Or should we just stay here in the hopes they're bluffing?"

"They're making you look at one threat," Kelly said. "Ten gets you twenty that there's a much quieter force massing behind us, ready to scoop up as many of our people as they can..."

A burst of gunfire rattled out behind them. George jumped.

"Shit," the man said. "What do we do?"

"Break and scatter," Kelly said. "And I suggest you hurry."

He nodded to George, then led her towards the western side of the camp. The sound of shooting was growing louder; George realised, to her horror, that Kelly had actually understated the problem. While they'd been congratulating themselves on their success, the aliens had launched a column of their own into the jungle. Quite how they'd tracked the resistance fighters down was a mystery, but it hardly mattered. All that mattered was getting away as quickly as possible.

"Don't shoot unless you have no choice," Kelly muttered. The helicopters flew low overhead, their weapons yammering away at targets on the ground. "There's no hope of saving this camp now."

"Yes, sir," George muttered. "What happened...?"

"Save it," Kelly advised. "We just have to hope they didn't have time to throw up a proper cordon before they launched their attack."

George nodded and kept walking, keeping her head down as they inched westwards. The sound of gunfire faded, only to spark up again as the aliens overran clumps of resistance fighters and crushed them. She had no idea if the aliens were bothering to take prisoners or not, but she had the nasty feeling that they weren't even *trying*. They'd been stung badly by the raids and probably wanted a little payback.

Assuming they think like us, she thought, sourly. Woof *hadn't* thought like a human, if her first impressions had been accurate. *They might believe in peace through mass slaughter.*

She pushed the thought aside as Kelly led her onwards, ducking low as they heard footsteps crashing through the jungle. Humans or aliens? She had no way to know. Kelly relaxed, slightly, as they kept moving without stumbling over an alien patrol. Maybe they'd made it clear...

Sure, her own thoughts mocked. *And maybe they're watching you to see where you go.*

She caught Kelly's attention an hour later, when all they could hear was the jungle's normal background noise. "Where do we go now?"

"There's an RV point, some distance from here," Kelly said. "We'll go there and wait. The boss will send someone to check on us."

"Unless he's been caught or killed too," George pointed out.

"If no one shows up in a day or two, we'll have to think of something else," Kelly said. "But until then, going to the RV point is our best bet."

George looked at him, sharply. "What happens if they have a lock on us?"

"I don't think they do," Kelly said. "And just in case they're smelling us, we'll take a cut through the river. But if they can track us through the jungle, resistance is hopeless anyway."

"Oh," George said.

"Unless you want to head south and hide," Kelly added. "But where would you go?"

"I wouldn't know," George said, stiffly. She realised, too late, that she was being teased. "I don't want to run."

"Nor do I," Kelly agreed, dryly. He gave her a brilliant smile and then turned to lead her onwards. "And that's why we're heading to the RV point."

CHAPTER
THIRTY

"Report," Susan ordered.

She sat down in her command chair as soon as Granger vacated it, studying the reports from the stealthed platforms. The alien ships were *indeed* coming from Tramline One, just as she'd been told - did that mean they'd come from Unity? Or had the aliens merely rerouted yet another group of reinforcements dispatched to Unity? The damned FTL communications system threw all of her normal predictions up in the air.

"Two battleships, seven cruisers," Granger said. "Plus two starships that *might* be escort carriers, although they haven't launched starfighters. The build's right for freighters, but the acceleration curve suggests mil-grade drives."

Mason took his own console, his hands tapping away on the keys. "Do we know if they're the ships we fought at Unity?"

"I'm not sure," Granger admitted. "But my gut says no."

Susan glanced at her. "Can you explain why?"

"The aliens took a battering at Unity," Granger said, slowly. "These ships - the newcomers -don't appear to have taken any punishment. And that suggests that they're actually reinforcements, rather than the ships we've already seen."

"Which adds credence to the theory that the aliens are desperately trying to scrape up forces to secure this sector," Mason commented.

Susan scowled. It was a tempting thought. She wanted to believe it. And hell, it made a certain kind of sense. The aliens were throwing everything they had against the Tadpoles, trying to break through the network of heavily-guarded star systems surrounding Tadpole Prime. Discovering that there was *another* empire on the far side of Tadpole space had to have shocked the hell out of them, even if they *did* like a challenge. Defeating the Tadpoles before the human race could mobilise its forces would be their priority…

Which means that they need to keep us from rolling up this sector and then stabbing straight into their territory, she thought. *And they'll be trying desperately to reinforce their attack forces with everything they can scrape up.*

"Let us hope so," she said. "Communications, has there been any update from the flag?"

"Nothing, apart from the alert signal," Parkinson informed her.

Admiral Harper hasn't decided what to do, Susan thought. *And nor have I.*

She considered the problem as the task force slowly moved away from the planet, every sensor on alert for signs of cloaked starships sneaking up behind them. Two battleships, seven cruisers and two ships that *might* be escort carriers? The task force could take them, but how much of a task force would they have left? They might win the battle, only to fall easy prey to the *next* alien force.

We could try to break contact now, she thought. *But Harper won't want to leave without scratching their hulls.*

"Signal from the flag," Parkinson reported. "New trajectories are being uploaded now."

Susan nodded, curtly, as the display updated. Harper was playing it safe, just enough to annoy the aliens without overcommitting himself. The task force would have a chance to engage long-range fire - and starfighter attacks - with the aliens, without ever coming within energy weapons range. And if it were timed well, the aliens would lose *their* chance to take a shot at the human ships.

"Take us into position, then follow the Admiral's lead," she ordered, smoothly. "Stand by to move to condition one when we close on the enemy ships."

She took one last look at the enemy planet, feeling a flicker of sympathy for Prince Henry and his staff. They'd have to explain to the boffins why the task force was moving away from the planet, despite not having managed to establish a communications link. Perhaps they *would* have been better advised to kidnap a few aliens from the surface, even though it might have caused long-term problems. But then, kidnapping civilians was one thing that would guarantee a violent response on Earth. The Great Powers had learned that lesson the hard way.

At least they'll be alive to gripe about it, she thought. *They wouldn't be so safe if we allowed ourselves to be trapped against the planet.*

"Interesting formation," Mason mused, as he replayed the transmissions from the recon platforms. "They're not concerned about being attacked."

"Someone on the planet must have been updating them in real time," Susan said. She felt a flicker of envy, again. Despite the problems she knew it would bring in its wake, she *still* wanted an FTL communicator. "They *know* they're safe."

She contemplated the problem as the minutes ticked by, slowly becoming hours. Did the aliens have FTL sensors too? They'd seen no sign of them at any of the engagements, but did the analysts know what to look for? If the aliens had real-time data on the task force's movements on a tactical level, as well as a strategic level…it would make the way far more uncertain. The aliens might just have an unbeatable advantage.

"Communications," she mused. "Did you pick up *anything* from the planet?"

"Just normal radio waves and burst transmissions," Parkinson said. "I believe we recorded a number of aliens speaking in the clear. The analysts are working on them right now."

Susan scowled. A clue. That was all they needed. A clue. Anything could be studied, anything could be duplicated, if only they had a clue. But they had no way to know how the FTL communicator *worked*. No wonder, she admitted sourly, that so many politicians and analysts questions its mere existence. But she'd seen the aliens pull off too many tricks to believe otherwise. They *had* to have some way to send messages at FTL speeds.

"They could be telepathic, Captain," Mason commented. "One or both of those races could be telepathic, just like those aliens in Stellar Star…"

Susan bit down a groan. Quite why Stellar Star's fans didn't download a few million gigabytes of porn from the datanet was beyond her. The movies could be amusing, she admitted, but they were really nothing more than softcore porn. And as for the aliens...

"I don't think that's too likely," she said. "There's never been a proven case of telepathy, has there?"

"Not amongst humans, Captain," Mason said. "But the Tadpoles are supposed to have a profound understanding of each other's feelings."

"It isn't the same," Susan said. The thought of having her mind read was creepy, yet was it possible? Could an alien mentality make sense of human thoughts? "And besides, if they *could* read our minds, they'd know what we were planning before we did it."

She dismissed the thought and studied the display. The aliens were coming into sensor range, altering course to push their battleships forward while keeping the two unknown ships at the rear. It *did* look as though they were escort carriers, Susan noted. The Royal Navy had rigged out a number of freighters to carry fighters during the First Interstellar War and the aliens might have had the same idea. And escort carriers were far more vulnerable to a determined attack than a fleet carrier. But there was no way to be sure until they started launching fighters.

"Signal from the flag," Parkinson reported. "Starfighters will be launched in fifteen minutes, mark."

"Understood," Susan said.

The aliens weren't bothering with any fancy tricks, despite being heavily outgunned. They were merely steering towards the task force, weapons at the ready. Susan eyed the near-space display, wondering if they were being conned - an entire alien attack fleet could be sneaking up on them, hidden behind a cloaking field. The force in front of them could merely be the decoy. And yet, the more she studied the readings, the more it seemed that local space was clear.

They fight as long as they think there's a chance to win, she mused. *Do they think we took more damage than we did?*

She cursed the waiting under her breath as the minutes slipped away, the alien fleet maintaining its silent course. Prince Henry's staffers sent message after message, covering every frequency they knew the aliens used, trying to get the aliens to talk. But there was no reply. Perhaps they *were* telepathic after all...Susan considered the thought for a long moment, then dismissed it. Telepathic aliens would *know* the Contact Fleet had come in peace, wouldn't they? Unless their telepathy was limited to their own race.

And to think that everyone claims that telepathic communication would make us better people, she thought, sourly. *It doesn't seemed to have worked for the aliens.*

"The carriers are launching now," Granger reported. "Enemy fleet..."

She stopped, just for a second, as the display blazed with red icons. "Enemy fleet has opened fire," she reported. "I count over five *thousand* missiles."

Susan sucked in her breath sharply. The aliens hadn't converted the freighters into escort carriers, they'd converted them into arsenal ships! She'd seen the concept mentioned a few times, in some of the less reputable military journals, but she'd always considered them impractical. It simply wasn't possible to fire off enough missiles to make a difference...

That bit of military wisdom may fall today, she thought, grimly.

"Point defence to full alert," she snapped. "Link us into the datanet and prepare for impact."

"They've launched outside standard range," Mason commented, quietly.

Susan nodded, grimly. The aliens *wouldn't* have fired unless they knew they had a chance of hitting something, even if their targets had no point defence at all. No, they were two or three-stage missiles...she didn't know why the aliens were deploying so many missiles, but she had to admit that it seemed to pay off for them. They'd get a free shot at the task force's ships.

And with so many missiles, she thought, *they will score a hit.*

"The starfighters are advancing towards their targets," Granger reported. "They're being diverted onto the battleships."

"Smart thinking," Mason said.

"True," Susan agreed.

She studied the situation for a long moment, thinking hard. The aliens were moving the arsenal ships forward threateningly, but it had to be a bluff. Fitting a thousand missiles into their hulls - their workers had to have stripped out nearly everything else, save for the drives - would be quite hard enough. There was no way they could fire a second barrage. All they could do was try to soak up a few missiles that would otherwise be aimed at their battleships.

And we have to ignore them, she thought. *Unless...*

"Keep an eye on them," she ordered, coolly. "They may feel they can get away with ramming us."

"Aye, Captain," Charlotte said.

Susan gritted her teeth as the wall of missiles swept towards the task force. The alien ships were picking up speed, moving faster now they weren't carrying their load. Normally, they wouldn't have a hope of getting close to her ships, but with so many missiles - and the alien battleships - flying around, they might just get lucky. And even if they didn't, they'd distract her gunners at the worst possible moment.

Damn them, she thought. *There's no way this should have paid off for them.*

She watched, grimly, as the missiles began a careful series of evasive patterns, altering course slightly to throw off her gunners. Someone had *definitely* reported back, after the Battle of Unity. There was no way to deny it now. An alien analyst had noted what the humans had done and devised a very simple counter. And yet, how the hell had they managed to cram so many control links into a missile, even an oversized one? The time delay alone...

Except there isn't a time delay, she thought, grimly. *They have FTL communications.*

The alien missiles flew into her point defence envelope. Dozens vanished, but hundreds survived to press their offensive against the human ships. Susan clutched her command chair, unable to take her eyes off the display as USS *Beacon*, HMS *Bradshaw* and FS *Jean-Paul* died in fire. Beyond them, seven freighters were blown apart by the hail of missiles, none carrying anything like enough armour to survive the impact. Susan cursed under her breath, knowing what that would mean for their long-term plans. Losing the freighters was bad enough, but losing the supplies they carried was far worse.

"Incoming missiles," Granger snapped.

"All hands, brace for impact," Susan snapped. "I say again..."

Vanguard rocked, savagely. Susan swore as four of the displays flickered alarmingly - the outer network of sensor blisters must have been badly damaged - and then leaned forward as reports started to come in from the rest of the ship. They'd taken a beating - and one of their armour plates had practically been shattered - but they'd survived. And the deluge of missiles was over.

"Report," she ordered.

"Heavy damage to starboard armour plating," Mason said. He was bent over his console, reading the reports as they came into the bridge. "Damage-control teams are on their way, but the entire section may need to be sealed off. Some considerable internal damage too."

He looked up. "Captain, if that had happened to us last year, we'd be dead in space."

Susan nodded. "And the remainder of the squadron?"

"*New York* took another battering," Granger said, grimly. "*Edinburgh* and *Hamburg* took a pasting themselves. Captain Stewart appears to believe that he can repair his ship, but Captain Doorman is ordering his crew to abandon ship."

"Deploy shuttles to recover the lifepods," Susan ordered. "And the carriers?"

"No damage," Granger said. "They weren't included in the attack pattern."

She paused. "The enemy fleet is reversing course."

Susan gaped. The enemy didn't get to hammer her ships and then waltz away! But it looked as though that was *precisely* what the aliens had in mind. Did they feel they couldn't win a close-range engagement, despite the battering they'd already handed out? Or did they believe that they *hadn't* inflicted so much damage? Or were they sensitive to further losses...

Or maybe we're completely wrong about them, she thought, sourly.

"Request orders from the flag," she said. The task force *could* chase down the alien battleships, even though it was clear the starfighters hadn't inflicted any *real* damage on the alien ships. And killing the cruisers wouldn't be hard. But at what cost? "And then get me a full damage report from *Edinburgh*."

It could be the other race in command, this time, she thought, numbly. *Maybe they have a different approach to life.*

She scowled as she worked the problem over and over in her head. The old 'diversity is strength' mantra had gone out of fashion during the Troubles, when *diversity* had become a swearword, but she could see some value to it. If combining British and American ideals had produced some interesting concepts, who knew what would happen if one combined ideas from two different races? Humanity had learned a great deal from the Tadpoles - and, she suspected, the reverse was also true.

"Captain Stewart has forwarded his damage report," Parkinson said. "He has reiterated his determination to save his ship."

Susan didn't blame him, but the odds were *not* in *Edinburgh's* favour. The cruiser had been badly damaged - her hull had been broken in a dozen places - and she was probably heading for the scrapyard, even if she made it home. She knew just how Captain Stewart was feeling, but there wasn't any *time.* Even if *Edinburgh* sneaked away from the remainder of the task force, she'd still have to crawl through enemy-held space to reach the nearest safe harbour.

And the nearest safe harbour would actually be in Tadpole territory, she thought. *The newcomers might be doing their best to invade it.*

"Signal from the flag," Parkinson said. "The task force is to reverse course and head through Tramline Two."

Susan exchanged glances with Mason. Heading through Tramline Two meant continuing on the arc Harper had planned, back before the engagement. It gave them the chance to slip back to Unity, but it also ran the risk of encountering other alien forces. But there was no choice. The aliens might just miss the task force crossing an alien-grade tramline. They certainly wouldn't miss the task force heading back the way it had come. The battleships orbiting Unity would be ready and waiting for them.

"Acknowledge the order," Susan said. "And get me a direct link to Captain Stewart."

"Aye, Captain," Parkinson said.

Susan barely had a moment to compose herself when Captain Stewart's face appeared in front of her. His bridge looked battered, but he and his crew were alive. And Stewart himself looked determined, very determined.

"Captain," he said. "My crew and I intend to make our own way home."

"Don't be a fool," Susan snapped. She understood his feelings, she understood them all too well. "You'll be caught and killed on the way home."

"Not if we're careful," Stewart said. "Captain, we can do it."

Susan gritted her teeth. If Stewart was right, he'd set an epic that lived up to the trail blazed by Admiral Smith and *Ark Royal*. But if he was wrong, the Royal Navy would never know what had killed the cruiser. The enemy...or a technological failure, after the ship had been battered beyond endurance?

But, technically, she had no right to order him to abandon ship.

"Good luck," she said, finally. "And make sure you get back alive."

"Of course, Captain," Stewart said. He tossed her a jaunty salute. "And thank you."

His image vanished. Susan stared at where it had been for a long moment, then pushed her emotions to one side. There would be time to worry later, after they were away from the aliens and heading home.

"Set course to Tramline Two," she ordered, sharply. "And move us out with the rest of the task force."

"Aye, Captain," Reed said.

A light flashed on the display, then vanished. "That was *Hamburg*," Granger said. "They triggered the self-destruct once the ship was evacuated."

"Understood," Susan said. She closed her eyes for a long moment in silent salute. "Helm, get us out of here."

"Aye, Captain."

CHAPTER
THIRTY-ONE

"You are going to buy me a drink after this, aren't you?"

Stott grunted, but didn't stop searching George, first with his hands and then with a sensor rod she vaguely recognised from the Academy. George did her best to look professional, although it wasn't easy with her hands locked on her head and a marine pawing her. Stott wasn't molesting her - his touch was professional - but it still bothered her. The thought that she might be considered a potential traitor…

If they somehow got a bug on me, I might have led the aliens directly to the camp, she thought. *And Kelly and I could have led the aliens here too.*

"I'd offer to buy you a drink, but rumour on deck is that you're screwing a gunnery dude," Stott said. "I wouldn't want to muscle *him* out with my hyper-masculinity and general sexiness."

"I'm surprised you even know the *word* hyper-masculinity," George growled, feeling her cheeks redden. Fraser had been right. Someone *had* noticed…she was surprised the word hadn't reached her sooner. But then, what she did on her shore leave was no one's business, but her own. "Do you even know what it *means*?"

"Sure," Stott said. "It's the power of raw animal magnetism that draws chicks to me like flies to meat."

He struck a dramatic pose. "Do you not feel any desire for me?"

"I feel a strong desire to ram something down your throat," George said, crossly. "A grenade, perhaps, or my gun."

"I'd just bite it off," Stott assured her. He clapped her on the shoulder in a manner she assumed was meant to be reassuring. "But I wouldn't want to steal you from someone who actually *works* for a living. If you were dating a REMF from the outer darkness…why, I'd be trying to get into your panties like a shot."

"You'd look very nice in them," George said. "I can loan you a pair when we get back to the ship, if you like."

There was a harsh bark of laughter. They both looked up. Byron was standing nearby, his arms crossed. "She's got you there," he said. "And besides, wasn't it you who was caught banging the general's wife?"

"It wasn't *her* who complained," Stott protested. He sobered, suddenly. "She's clean, sir."

George scowled. "I told you I wasn't bugged."

"You wouldn't know," Byron said, grimly. "Bugs these days are so tiny they can't be seen with the naked eye. And if the damn thing has gone dormant, we wouldn't know about it until they reactivated it - and then it would be too late."

"Shit," George said. "But surely we have to keep going?"

Byron gave her a humourless smile. "That's what dozens of insurgent groups thought," he said. "They regrouped after we clobbered hell out of them - or let a few of the bastards break out of the camps - and then we came down on them like a ton of bricks."

He nodded for her to follow him as he led the way deeper into the camp. It was actually smaller than the last camp, although a couple of armoured vehicles had been placed near the fringes and heavily camouflaged. George was surprised to see them - she'd been told that all armoured vehicles had been destroyed during the invasion - but none the less pleased. The aliens would be in for a nasty surprise when - if - they tried to sneak up on the campsite.

"Fred seems to like you," Byron observed. He turned to smile at her. "But not in that way, I'm afraid. He's *accepted* you."

"Thanks," George said, doubtfully.

"It's a good thing," Byron assured her. "For us" - he waved a hand to indicate the camp - "it's never easy to know if we can count on the navy. There have been times when the navy has been utterly superb, performing wonderfully, and times when they've been too busy sipping their tea to do their jobs. We never know if the pilot flying us down to the surface is going to land in the teeth of enemy fire or going to panic the moment the first MANPAD is shot at the shuttle and misses by a mile."

"I thought you had your own pilots," George observed.

"We can't always depend on them being assigned to us," Byron said. He nodded towards the hidden tent. "And well…you *could* have curled up into a ball, upon crashing, and insisted on being carried all the way home. I've had intelligence specialists working with me who didn't really understand what they'd been asked to do until it was too late."

He opened the tent, then nodded to her. "But you're doing fine," he added. "Keep it up."

George said nothing as she followed him through the second flap. Fraser had pushed her hard, during her first deployment; Stott…had openly teased her. She honestly wasn't sure how to feel about it. But then, she told herself, at least she wasn't being praised for her body or her clothes. It was for something she'd done.

"Ah, George," Kelly said. He was leaning over a table, examining a mangled alien body through a microscope. "What do you make of this?"

George stared. "Are you a trained xenospecialist?"

"I'm the best on hand," Kelly said. "I did have to take a course in xeno-medicine, before a brief deployment to Vesy, but they're a very different race. Frankly, I think xenomedicine is going to be divided up into several different subsections before too long."

He nodded down at the body. "What do you make of cow-face here?"

"Nothing," George said. The Cow was lying on the table, its chest cut open to reveal a handful of organs. She couldn't tell if it was male or female. "I am *not* a doctor."

"I can tell," Kelly said.

He tapped the leathery skin. "I can *also* tell that these bastards are *tough*," he added. "They seem to be slow and lumbering, according to the reports, but they can take a *lot* of damage before they go down. Their skulls are heavy too - frankly, I wouldn't expect a headshot from a pistol to take one down. Realistically, they're strong and nasty and very tough. Try not to get into a punching match with one."

"I see," Byron said.

George leaned forward. "Do they have any weaknesses?"

"I think their vision and sense of smell are both worse than ours," Kelly said. "But I suspect we won't know for sure until we manage to talk to them. There's also a set of genitals right where you'd expect them, so a kick there *might* upset them."

Byron frowned. "*Might?*"

"I didn't have an intact corpse to dissect," Kelly admitted. "But...well, the one I examined didn't have anything like as many nerve endings leading to the penis as I might have imagined. It's possible they don't get anything like as much out of sex as we do - it's also possible that their penis might break off, the first time they have sex, and regularly impregnate the woman."

"Ouch," George said. She glanced at the two other bodies, stacked like cordwood at the rear of the tent. "Are any of them female?"

"Not as far as I can tell," Kelly said. "They all have recognisable male organs, but nothing resembling a vagina or a womb. It's *possible* that I'm making a mistake, though. I'm not an xenospecialist."

"So you keep saying," Byron said. "Do you have anything else to offer?"

"Just that none of the Cows allowed themselves to be captured," Kelly said. It sounded as though they'd had the same discussion earlier. "All five of the ones we tried to capture committed suicide when it looked as though they'd be taken prisoner."

George looked up. "How? Why?"

"The *how* is easy," Kelly said. He opened the alien's mouth and pointed to a broken tooth. "Unless I miss my guess, that tooth contained a very strong neurotoxin that caused instant death. I've done some preliminary research on the remains, but without a proper lab I can't tell you anything about it, beyond the fact it's *very* poisonous. And it isn't species-specific either. Don't let them poison you with it."

"Interesting," Byron said.

"They killed themselves rather than be taken captive," George mused. "What did they think we'd *do* to them?"

"I don't know," Kelly said. He shrugged. "The Foxes, if battered enough, become completely submissive. We've taken seven additional captives and they all appear to be cooperating on bended knee. We even gave them a chance to escape and none of them took it. But the Cows refuse to allow themselves to be taken prisoner."

George shuddered. "I don't want to think about the mentality of a race that does *that*."

"We do," Byron said. "Each of us is primed to commit suicide, if necessary."

"You have a poison tooth too?" George asked. "But..."

"The exact details are classified," Byron said, shortly. "But yes, we can end our lives if we believe there's no other choice."

He shrugged. "Aren't there poison jabs in spacesuits?"

George swallowed, hard. She knew they were there - the instructors at the Academy had explained their presence - but she didn't want to think about them. If she was lost somewhere in the vastness of interstellar space, if there was no hope of rescue...she could kill herself, quickly, cleanly and painlessly. Or so she'd been told. No one who had used the suicide jab - and a handful of spacers had, in the Royal Navy's long history - had come back to complain about the pain.

"Yeah," she said.

"We're not ordinary crewmen," Byron said, quietly. "We're not even squaddies. We're Royal Marines, the best fighters in the world. Even the SAS respects us. If we are captured...our captors will do what-ever it takes to get information out of us. Or worse. Suicide...there are times when suicide seems the best of a set of bad choices. And if that happens..."

George looked at him. "Would you do it?"

"I don't know," Byron said. He caught her shoulder and led her out of the tent. "None of us know, until the shit hits the fan. And then we find out."

Night was falling over the camp as they hurried towards the mess hall. A handful of soldiers - marines and others from the multinational force - were eating ration bars with forced enthusiasm and drinking water. They looked tired, George noted. They'd expected to have plenty of time to set up their defences on the ground, not get forced into hiding bare days after the task force had arrived. She wondered, suddenly, just what had happened to *Vanguard* and the rest of the task force. There had been no word since the task force had left orbit.

They could all be dead, she thought, suddenly.

She took the ration bar he offered her automatically, her mind elsewhere. *Vanguard* could be gone, her crew reduced to atoms scattered through space; Potter, Paula, Fraser, Peter Barton…they could all be dead. The thought hurt; she sagged to the ground, suddenly feeling very tired. If the task force was gone, what would happen to them? How long would it be before Unity was liberated? Would Unity be liberated at all?

"You can sleep, if you like," Byron told her. "There's a sleeping bag in the next tent for you."

George looked up at him. "What happens if the task force doesn't come back?"

"We keep fighting as long as we can," Byron said. He reached out and tapped her ration bar meaningfully. "Eat. Now."

She unwrapped the bar and took a bite, grimacing slightly at the cardboard taste. It seemed to be a rule of thumb that ration bars always had to taste of nothing - when they didn't taste faintly unpleasant - but she understood the logic behind it. The manufacturers could easily make the bars taste of milk and honey - or anything, really - yet that wouldn't encourage people to get off them. It wasn't *hard* to earn enough to put something tastier than government-issue ration bars on the table.

"Pity we don't have a cooking pot here," Byron said. He sat down next to her and munched his ration bar with every appearance of enthusiasm. George was surprised he was such a good actor, although she supposed he had to set an example for everyone else. "You know what I could do with a cooking pot?"

George shook her head.

"Pile in a dozen of these pieces of shit," Byron said. He waved the remains of the ration bar in the air, then swallowed it in a gulp. "Mash them together in water, then add Tabasco and a few other sauces. Boil it up, then eat. It doesn't taste half bad."

"I suppose it would taste better than these," George mused.

"Oh, of course," Byron said. "But then, anything would taste better than these."

He shrugged. "When we're in the field, we don't get a team of cooks producing roast beef and potatoes for us," he added. "We have to make do with field rations. And you won't believe the smell."

"It could be worse," one of the other soldiers offered. He sounded American. "I was there during the Great Mutiny at Manhattan FOB."

George frowned. A mutiny? "What happened?"

"Oh, we were outside the wire for two weeks," the soldier said. "The local assholes decided to take advantage of the bombardment by raiding a number of settlements under our protection. We spent those weeks cruising around and teaching the fuckers a lesson."

He paused for effect. "And then we drove back to the base and lined up in front of the chow hall," he added. "They'd really done Uncle Sam proud. It was like stepping into a burger bar from the last century. The burgers were huge, the freedom fries crispy…they'd even got straws you could share with your partner."

George stared at him. "On a military base?"

"It's Little America," the soldier said. "The better officers keep trying to put a stop to it, but it never lasts."

He smirked. "You have to imagine the scene," he added. "There's this bunch of REMFs sitting at the tables, wearing clean uniforms and combat boots…a couple even have a pair of women on their knees…and then we come marching in. Fourteen soldiers, wearing uniforms that haven't been washed in two weeks; dusty, grimy, smelly as fuck…

"The bastards panicked! They jumped up in shock! And this weak-chinned moron goes up to the LT and says we can't come in. There's an immediate rumble behind the LT because every last one of us is just gagging for something that doesn't taste like recycled goat droppings. And the LT, who was a bloody-minded son of a bitch, just picks the fobbit up, drops him in the trash can, marches up to the counter and orders about a hundred burgers and a couple of dozen rounds of freedom fries.

"You should have seen the looks on their faces," he added. "They couldn't have looked more shocked if a herd of man-eating tigers had walked into the diner. But some bastard must have called the MPs on us, because they marched in while we were stuffing our faces. And the LT tells them to take a long walk around the block until we've finished."

He laughed. "He was a character, I'll say."

George nodded. "What happened?"

"We finished our meal and left in good order," the soldier said. "LT gets his ass chewed a couple of times by the base commander, but his *actual* superior knows the score. And by the time we got back home, the whole story had turned into a stirring battle, a mutiny against particularly stupid REMFs."

"And they changed the rules after that," Byron said. "Didn't they?"

"Just a little," the soldier said. "But the way things were out there...the LT barely managed to avert a *real* mutiny. We were starved and pissed and we weren't going to take *no* for an answer."

"Ouch," George said.

Byron grinned. "It's a bad idea to get between the soldier and his food," he added. "A few years ago, there was a base commander who thought he should ration food. Some dickhead in procurement stopped chasing up whores long enough to calculate that everyone should have a certain level of food and no more. So the base commander started locking up the food supplies."

"And you started raiding them," George guessed.

"Correct," Byron said. "*Everyone* started raiding them."

He gave her a smile, then beckoned her to her feet. "Let's go," he said. "You'll be going back out tomorrow."

George followed him towards another hidden tent. The interior was dark, but she could hear faint sounds of snoring from the inside. She hesitated, then looked up at him.

"You said I was doing fine," she said. "Is that true?"

"I would not have been surprised if you'd requested to be sent well out of the danger zone," Byron said. "And I would not have blamed you. This is not what you trained for. But you stayed and you impressed us."

"I'm not as good as you," George protested.

Byron poked her in the chest, between her breasts. "You had a few paltry lessons in shooting and self-defence at the Academy," he said. "We spent six months getting the shit kicked out of us during Basic Training. Your experience of combat after the Academy is a handful of bouts, bouts which follow certain rules; my experience is over four years in various combat zones. You follow the navy's rules on exercise; we do press-ups and runs every morning before breakfast, just to keep in shape."

He snorted. "Believe me, if you were keeping up with us, I'd hate to think about what the Major would say."

"Thanks," George said. She had to smile. "But I do want to go back to the ship."

"So do I," Byron said.

He nodded towards the tent. "Now go get some sleep," he ordered. "You're going back out tomorrow."

CHAPTER
THIRTY-TWO

"They're definitely shadowing us, Captain," Charlotte said.

Susan nodded, studying the display. The alien ships had reversed course themselves after the human ships had broken contact, following the task force while maintaining a safe distance from human weapons. Shaking them was not going to be easy. They were almost certainly close enough to pick up on any bait-and-switch - perhaps even to track the task force if it retreated into cloak. She dared not make any assumptions about the capabilities of alien sensors.

"And they'll track us all the way to Tramline Two," she mused. In some ways, it was reassuring. It proved that the aliens didn't have any form of FTL *sensor* capability. "And they'll cross the tramline shortly after us."

She contemplated the virtues of an ambush for a long moment. Getting a clean shot at a starship that had just jumped through a tramline - with its sensors disrupted by the jump - was every tactician's dream. But the more she looked at it, the more she doubted they could pull it off. The aliens would be aware of the possibilities too - and take steps to avoid the danger.

And if we lurk near the tramline, we give up our chance to lose them, she thought. *That could make life difficult in the next system.*

"Signal from the flag," Parkinson reported. "The task force is to continue on course, best possible speed."

"Acknowledge," Susan said. She glanced at Mason. "Mr. XO, what are the damage reports?"

"The majority of the damage can be handled while under way," Mason reported. "But there are elements that can only be handled at a dead stop."

"Which we're not going to have a chance to do for a while," Susan said. She had no idea what the aliens had in mind, but if they saw the task force slow to carry out repairs they'd certainly launch an attack. They'd never have a better chance at weakening or destroying the remainder of the fleet. "Inform Mr. Finch that he is to perform as many repairs as possible."

"Aye, Captain," Mason said.

Susan pressed her lips together in disapproval as the task force continued along its course, the aliens shadowing them at a safe distance. She had to admire their timing, as awkward as it was. If the task force turned to confront them, they risked major losses; if the task force continued on course, their shadows could keep a lock on them while rustling up reinforcements from the nearest enemy formation. And it would be awkward, indeed, if the task force were to return to Unity as planned. An enemy force shadowing them would ensure that they were caught between two fires.

And we don't know where else the aliens might have reinforcements, she thought. *We might be being herded into a trap.*

She called up a starchart and studied the tramlines for a long moment. The aliens wouldn't have any difficulty charting them out, although they might not be able to access the alien-grade lines of gravimetric force. Unless that had changed...it had taken humanity nearly six months to duplicate the Tadpole Puller Drive, but the human boffins had had a working alien model to study. Had the aliens recovered a working drive from the remains of the Contact Fleet?

They shouldn't have been able to recover anything, Susan reminded herself. *But we will never know.*

"If we proceed through Tramline Two, we will arrive in TPS-272," she mused. The Tadpoles had taken a look at the system some time before First Contact, according to the records, but they'd never considered it particularly important. "And from there, we can proceed into TPS-271 through the alien-grade tramline. They wouldn't be able to follow us."

She keyed her terminal, opening a private link to Admiral Harper. "As you can see, sir," she said, "we do have options."

"Making a dash for that tramline might be a wise idea," Harper agreed. "But they *would* know where we were going, even if they couldn't follow us."

Susan agreed. TPS-271 had only two serviceable tramlines, one of which was alien-grade. If the task force took the other tramline as soon as they could, they'd still have to jump through three successive star systems before they returned to Unity. Even if the aliens *couldn't* follow the task force, they'd have ample time to reverse course to head to Unity themselves or summon reinforcements. The damned FTL communicator made matters far too complicated.

"And they might have a reasonable chance of getting there first," Susan mused. The haphazard distribution of the tramlines ensured that the aliens actually had a *shorter* trip back to Unity, even if they wasted time searching for the task force before realising they'd been tricked. "Particularly if we have to stop and make repairs."

"True," Harper agreed. "We'll make the transit into TPS-272 in any case. And then we can fart around a bit before attempting a breakaway operation."

"Understood," Susan said. "I'll see you on the far side of the tramline."

She closed the connection, then leaned back in her command chair as the task force neared the tramline, altering course sharply a bare ten minutes before they were due to jump. If there *was* an enemy fleet taking up ambush position on the far side of the tramline, their aim would be thrown off if the task force appeared somewhere unexpectedly...she hoped. The shadows could, she assumed, give real-time updates to a fleet lying in ambush...

But surely it would be better to set an ambush in this *system*, she thought. Admiral Harper had deployed a dozen sensor drones to sweep their path, but they knew - all too well - that the alien cloaking devices were very good. *They already have a force coming up behind us.*

Nothing showed on the sensor display, no barrage of missiles materialised out of nowhere as the fleet reached the tramline and jumped into the next system. Susan held herself steady, fighting the urge to cringe, as the sensor display went blank. If the aliens *were* waiting in ambush, they'd never have a better shot at *Vanguard* and they knew it. But, as the display started to fill with icons, it became clear that the enemy *weren't* waiting for them. The system was almost completely deserted.

"I'm picking up a mining and cloudscoop station orbiting the gas giant," Charlotte said. She glanced back at Susan. "There aren't any freighters or warships in the system as far as I can tell."

Susan frowned. Placing a refuelling station *here* might make sense to a bureaucrat, but anyone versed in *practical* matters would know better. It wasn't as if Unity and the handful of other Earth-comparable worlds in the sector didn't have their own gas giants. Just for a moment, she wondered if they'd run into a *third* unknown alien race before the power signatures flickered up in front of her. No, the Foxes and the Cows were definitely responsible for establishing the station.

"That makes no sense," Granger protested. "Putting a station here..."

"Their drives might be inefficient," Mason suggested. He didn't sound as though he believed his own words. "Or they may feel they need the redundancy."

"We can ask them, afterwards," Susan said. "Continue to sweep the system for surprises."

"Signal from the flag," Parkinson put in. "The task force is to adjust course to TPS-272-3 and prepare to destroy all enemy targets."

Mason scowled. "He's giving up a free shot at their hulls!"

"Stow that chatter," Susan said, sharply. Mason had a point - but she doubted the aliens would be foolish enough to transit the tramline on the exact same vector. Why would they *want* to give the task force a chance to hammer them with impunity? "Helm, set course for the gas giant."

"Aye, Captain," Reed said. "We will enter firing range in seven hours, thirty-two minutes."

"We could try to capture the cloudscoop, Captain," Granger suggested. "It would give us a look at their tech."

"If they're foolish enough not to blow it up before the marines arrive," Susan commented.

She scowled. It was definitely odd. *Humanity* had set up refuelling dumps in transfer systems during the early days of space exploration, but advances in drive technology had soon rendered them useless. Maybe the aliens were just being careful. A cloudscoop near an inhabited world would be a priority target for any raiding forces. Or maybe there was something in the system they were missing.

The display glimmered in front of her. She studied it carefully, but saw nothing. There *could* be an asteroid settlement - a whole *string* of asteroid settlements - yet as long as the settlers were careful there was no way they'd be detected. Her sensors were picking up enough asteroids to support millions of settlers…there were people, back on Earth, who believed that one day the entire human race would live in space. Susan wasn't *that* attached to a planet - they were big targets that couldn't run away - but she rather doubted it unless technology advanced considerably. Asteroid settlements were terrifyingly vulnerable.

A flurry of red icons blinked into life on the display. Susan leaned forward as the enemy fleet snapped into existence, close enough to continue tracking the task force without exposing its hulls to human weapons. She silently complimented the alien shipmasters - they'd carried out a very tricky manoeuvre without apparent problems - and then glanced at Mason. He didn't look pleased.

"Enemy fleet settling into pursuit course," Charlotte reported. "They're still maintaining a safe distance from us."

Susan rubbed her forehead. She was tired, too tired to remain in command. And yet, she didn't want to leave the bridge. Cold logic told her there would be plenty of warning before their shadows could open fire, if they decided to abandon the pursuit and attack, but she didn't really believe it. There could be a cloaked enemy fleet taking up an ambush position ahead of them.

"Mr. XO, you have the conn," she said. "Alert me the moment the enemy ships move onto attack vector."

"Aye, Captain," Mason said. "I have the conn."

Susan nodded, then rose and walked to the hatch. It hissed open, allowing her to step out into the corridor beyond. She wanted to sleep - she *knew* she should sleep - but instead she walked down the corridor, past the marine standing guard at the hatch to Officer Country and onwards to sickbay. A number of crewmen were lying on beds, others sitting on benches with wounds that weren't considered immediate problems. She waved them down when they made to stand, then hurried past them into the doctor's office. Doctor Adam Chung looked tired, as if he were about to fall asleep on his feet. Susan didn't blame him.

"Doctor," she said, quietly. "How bad is it?"

"Thirty-seven dead, five missing and presumed dead," Chung said. Susan had always liked him. Like her, he was a mixed-race child in a world that didn't always accept them. But now, he sounded as tired as he looked. "Their bodies have not yet been recovered."

And may never be found, Susan thought. If someone had been near the damaged hull plating, their body might have been vaporised - or sucked into space. And if that had happened, there wasn't a hope in hell of recovering the body. *They'll be drifting in space until the end of time.*

She took a seat and motioned for the doctor to sit too. "And the wounded?"

"Forty-seven wounded, Captain," Chung said. "Seven, perhaps eight of them will probably have to claim a medical discharge. We've done all we can for them - and we might have been able to do more, if we hadn't been overworked - but our best was insufficient. The remainder should be able to return to active duty within a couple of months, at most."

Susan shuddered. Triage was one of the realities of military life. A doctor had to choose which patients to treat first - and put a lightly-wounded patient, the one with a better chance of survival, ahead of a badly-wounded patient. She understood the logic - there was no point in wasting limited supplies on someone who was likely to die anyway - but it didn't sit well with her. And she hoped, deep inside, that it never would.

At least they're not going to die, she thought. *They will live...*

She shook her head, bitterly. Modern medicine was a wonderful thing. She'd broken her arm as a child and the doctors had fixed it within a day. There were vaccines against tooth decay, treatments that could freeze her reproductive cycle and delay menopause indefinitely...even medical procedures that could permanently change the colour of her skin! But it had its limits. If her crewmen couldn't be treated in time, they'd be doomed to spend the rest of their lives as cripples. And no matter how kindly they were treated, they'd never be independent again.

And some of dad's friends had real problems, Susan reminded herself. *And so did some of the people I knew after the flooding.*

"Try and do everything you can for them," she said. "Is there *anything* we can do?"

"I'm considering freezing them," Chung said, flatly. "But that procedure carries its own risks."

Susan nodded. A couple of primitive starships - starships only by courtesy, really - had been launched on interstellar colonisation missions before the first tramline had been discovered, their crews frozen in cryogenic suspension. They'd been recovered later - much later - when they'd reached their destination, but the procedure had killed nearly two-thirds of the would-be colonists. And many of the survivors had mental problems that had plagued them for the rest of their lives.

They claim to have improved the process since, she thought. *But it's very much a last resort.*

"Make sure you explain the risks to them," she ordered. "And if they are reluctant to undergo the procedure, don't force it on them."

"Of course, Captain," Chung said. He sounded a little offended at the implication he would have forced the procedure on anyone. "They will know the risks before we put them on ice."

"Good," Susan said. She rubbed her forehead, feeling a nasty headache building behind her eyes. "And I'm sorry."

"Don't worry about it," Chung said. "We all have problems."

He pointed a finger at her. "And I would suggest you slept," he added. "If you stay awake, you're not going to be any good to anyone."

"I keep being told that," Susan said. She rose. "Keep me informed, please."

She walked out of the office and moved from bed to bed, exchanging a handful of words with the crewmen who'd been wounded. A number had been sedated; others looked to be in good cheer, even as they contemplated the prospect of life as a cripple. Susan couldn't help being reminded of some of her father's friends, the men who'd fought and bled for a country that hadn't been sure if it wanted to accept them. They'd had the same hearty air of cheerfulness even as the world turned against them.

And they were all good people, she thought, as she glanced down at one of the sedated crewmen. Something had taken his legs, leaving his lower body a broken mess. He'd been incredibly lucky to survive long enough to reach sickbay - and now he would have to remain sedated until a new pair of legs could be grown for him. *They didn't deserve to suffer.*

She pushed the maudlin thought out of her mind as she left sickbay and returned to her Ready Room. One of the harsh truths of life in the military - one civilians should have learned too, after the Bombardment - was that life *wasn't* fair. War chewed people up and spat them out, civilians as well as soldiers. Part of the reason she'd gone into the navy, if she were forced to be honest with herself, was that there was less collateral damage in space. But in a universe where aliens might decide to solve the human problem with planet-wide bombardment, she wasn't sure if that really held true.

Her sofa looked tempting as she entered the compartment, but she checked the tactical display before lying down for a brief nap. There hadn't been any major change, save for the disappearance of the alien arsenal ships. The alien CO had probably sent them to be reloaded, knowing they were useless without their missiles. Susan cursed under her breath, then walked over to the sofa and lay down. If she was lucky, she'd be able to get a few hours of sleep before she had to go back to the bridge.

Sure, her conscience reminded her. *And what about all the wounded crewmen? And the ones who died under your command?*

Susan gritted her teeth, her body feeling almost too tired to sleep. She *cared* about her crew, cared about them in a way Captain Blake had never cared. But then, he'd been too busy trying to hide his own loss of nerve to show any empathy to the men and women under his command. It was hard to feel *any* sympathy for him. He'd known he wasn't suited to remain in the command chair, yet he'd stayed...

And nearly got the entire fleet destroyed, Susan thought.

She pushed the thought away, angrily. There was nothing she could do for the dead, let alone the wounded. They couldn't even hold a formal ceremony to remember the dead until after they completed the operation! And the wounded would have to cope...she knew, deep inside, that many of them would be carrying their scars, physical and mental, for the rest of their lives. Maybe some of them would be able to live a normal life...

They knew the job was dangerous when they took it, she told herself, savagely.

It didn't help.

CHAPTER
THIRTY-THREE

Susan didn't feel any better, six hours later, when she stepped back onto the bridge to discover that the situation hadn't changed. The task force was nearing the gas giant, the enemy fleet was still maintaining its distance and there was no sign of any other enemy starships in the system. She glanced at the reports from the long-range probes and frowned, not particularly reassured, when they continued to insist that the fleet was closing in on a cloudscoop and asteroid mining facility of indeterminate purpose.

There must be something else here, she thought. *But what?*

A series of messages from Admiral Harper popped up in front of her when she sat on the command chair. She flicked her way through them, silently cataloguing the ones of immediate use and filing the others away for later examination. Harper planned to execute a breakaway operation after inspecting and destroying the alien facility, then head directly for Tramline Two and onwards to Unity. The aliens would still have a chance to get there first - there was nothing they could do about that - but at least the task force would have an opportunity to make repairs.

She forced herself to wait as Mason and Granger returned to the bridge, looking disgustingly fresh after two or three hours of sleep. Susan reminded herself to keep an eye on the tactical officer - she'd had even less sleep than Susan herself - then motioned for Mason to take his console as the task force closed in on its target. She wondered, despite herself, just what the aliens were thinking. Logically, they *had* to know that their facility was doomed.

"Captain," Charlotte said. "I'm picking up multiple shuttles heading away from the cloudscoop."

Susan frowned. "An evacuation?"

"It looks like it," Charlotte said. "The shuttles are heading on a wide course that will keep them well away from us."

"Trained workers," Mason noted. "They have to be."

"Yes," Susan said.

She wondered, as the shuttles fled the alien facilities, if Yegorovich would demand the right to give chase. From a coldly logical point of view, slaughtering trained workers - workers the aliens would need years to replace - made perfect sense. It would deal a minor blow to the alien industrial base, at least until the aliens trained new manpower. But from an emotional point of view, slaughtering fleeing aliens - who might well be civilians - was a horrific act, one that might make it harder to convince the aliens to talk peace. She knew, all too well, that *humans* would not react kindly to such an act.

But we don't know if that's true of them, she thought. *And we don't know what they're really doing in this system.*

"Signal from the flag," Parkinson said. "*New York* intends to engage the alien facilities with mass drivers. The remainder of the task force is to stand ready to offer support."

Susan nodded. "Keep us on course," she ordered. If the shadowing aliens had ever intended to save their facilities, they'd had their chance. "And be ready for anything."

She watched, grimly, as *New York* opened fire, spewing out a stream of projectiles towards the alien facilities. A warship would have seen them coming and evaded, but the facilities probably had nothing more than station-keeping thrusters. She frowned as a handful of point defence units sprang to life, picking off a dozen projectiles, only to be smashed out of existence by the remainder. Moments later, there was nothing left of either facility, save for a handful of pieces of debris falling into the gas giant's atmosphere.

"Targets destroyed," Granger said. "I say again, targets destroyed."

Susan looked at the main display. "Any sign of new alien activity?"

"None," Granger said. "The system appears to be quiet."

Susan exchanged a glance with Mason, then shrugged. If there *was* something hidden in the system, they weren't going to find it. Ideally, a couple of stealthed pickets could remain and keep an eye out for alien activity, but the task force didn't have any ships to spare. She eyed the shuttles, still fleeing as fast as they could, then dismissed them. The alien shadows could pick them up, after the breakaway.

"Signal from the flag," Parkinson said. "All ships are to proceed to Point Break, then prepare for evasive manoeuvres."

"Acknowledge," Susan ordered. "Helm, do you have the updated course heading?"

"Aye, Captain," Reed said. "It isn't *very* challenging."

"As long as you don't leak," Mason pointed out. "One sniff of our presence and the entire exercise will be worse than useless."

"It wouldn't be *that* bad," Susan said. "Merely...annoying."

She waited, patiently, as the task force picked up speed, rushing away from the gas giant at a speed that would have been unimaginable, only a century ago. The aliens would have their chance to get to Unity first - there was no escaping that, unless they found a way to destroy the shadowing force before heading for Unity themselves. All they could do - all they could hope to do - was buy some extra time.

And it may be for nothing, anyway, she thought. *What if they did send additional forces to Unity?*

"Signal from the flag," Parkinson said. "The task force is to begin diversionary operations on their mark."

"See to it," Susan ordered. The enemy fleet still had a solid lock on their hulls, but that was about to be shaken. And yet, would it be shaken *enough*? "Are the drones deployed?"

"Aye, Captain," Granger said. "The drones are in place."

They'll tumble to this, sooner or later, Susan told herself. Human ECM seemed better than alien ECM, although there was no way to be *entirely* sure. *And they'll certainly try to duplicate our systems for themselves.*

"Signal from the flag," Parkinson said. "Diversionary operations are to begin in ten seconds."

"Do it," Susan said. She leant forward, bracing herself. "And stand ready to cloak."

"Running diversionary operations now," Granger said. "The drones are active; I say again, the drones are active."

"Take us into cloak," Susan ordered. She glanced at the fleet display to make sure that the laser communications links were in place. "Now."

The lights dimmed, briefly. "Cloak engaged, Captain," Granger said. "The drones have taken our place."

Susan nodded, slowly. If the alien sensors were no better than *humanity's* sensors, they wouldn't have seen anything beyond a burst of distortion. They should have missed the drones going active at the same time the task force cloaked...if everything went according to plan, the aliens would continue to chase the drones, unaware that their *real* targets had slipped away.

We could use this to surprise them, she thought. She'd had a few ideas along those lines, during the tactical brainstorming session. *But they might be watching for us.*

"Signal from the flag, Captain," Parkinson said. "The task force is to breakaway and head directly for Tramline Two."

"Helm, take us out," Susan ordered. "And be *very* careful."

She kept a wary eye on the display as the task force and the drones diverged. The aliens should - *should* - see the task force circling around, as if it intended to plunge back into Tramline One and return to the previous system. If they were fooled, everything should go according to plan...

And if they're not fooled, she thought, *they'll have an excellent chance to catch us with our pants around our ankles.*

The seconds ticked away, each second feeling like an hour. It wasn't a good position to hold, not when there was an alien fleet breathing down their necks. Laser communicators or not, the task force was too spread out to coordinate a proper defence if the aliens *weren't* fooled. If *she* had been in command of the alien fleet, Susan knew, she would have lunged forward, soaking up whatever losses she had to take to catch the battleships on the hop. It would have been far from ideal for both sides, but it would have given the aliens a chance to inflict terrible damage at a very minimal cost.

"The aliens appear to be shadowing the drones," Charlotte reported, finally. "As long as they keep their distance, they shouldn't realise that they *are* drones."

"Very good," Susan said. The longer the deception lasted, the greater the chance that they'd get away with it. "Helm, what's our ETA at Tramline Two?"

"Five hours," Reed reported.

We could move faster, Susan thought. *But that would be far too revealing.*

She forced herself to wait, grimly, as the seconds became minutes and the minutes became hours. The aliens seemed to be fooled, all right; they were shadowing the drones, as if they hadn't noticed any substitution at all. And yet, she had the odd sense that someone was being conned. The aliens might *just* have put a fleet in TPS-271. But then, that would have required either a vast number of starships - in which case the war was already within shouting distance of being lost - or precognition. And precognition would probably be enough to win the war, too.

Despite herself, the thought made her smile. *They're telepathic and they can see the future?*

Mason looked at her. "Captain?"

"Continue on our current course," Susan ordered. They'd have a chance to slow down and make repairs in TPS-271, unless the aliens *had* outguessed them. "And keep a sharp eye on the drones."

The hours passed steadily, with no sign that the aliens had seen through the trick. Susan just hoped that that was accurate, knowing - all too well - that the aliens wouldn't have any trouble guessing where the fleet was going. If they hadn't known about the alien-grade tramlines before the Battle of UXS-469, they sure as hell did now.

We knew they existed, Susan reminded herself. *But we needed help to access them.*

"Signal from the flag," Parkinson said. "We're to proceed through the tramline as planned."

Susan bit her lip, tasting blood. Harper was right to want to get through the tramline as quickly as possible - the longer they remained in the system, the greater the chance of something accidentally giving the trick away - but she couldn't help feeling that the aliens would have a surprise up their sleeves. TPS-271 was an obvious destination, after all. It would give the task force its best chance at making repairs before it had to go back to the war.

But they can't be everywhere, she thought. *Everything we've seen suggests that they are scrambling desperately to scrape up reinforcements for this sector.*

Her own thoughts mocked her. *Or is that just what you want to believe?*

"Stand by all weapons," she ordered, as the task force approached the tramline. She'd hoped that Harper would send a smaller ship through first, but the Admiral had decided that the entire fleet should make transit as soon as possible. "And prepare to repel attack."

She took one last look at the live feed from the drones - now outdated by several hours - and braced herself for the jump. The displays went blank...just for a second, she thought something had gone horrifically wrong...and then cleared, displaying a bright G2 star. The system had been earmarked for development, she recalled from the files, but the Tadpoles hadn't gotten around to settling it before the new war began. If it hadn't been so far from Earth, she had a feeling that a few human consortiums would have bid for settlement rights too.

As long as they didn't have to share the outer system, she thought. Unity had been a fine idea, but it was clearly appallingly bad in practice. *Our legal system and theirs are just not compatible.*

"The system appears to be deserted, Captain," Charlotte reported. "There's no sign of any orbital or planetary activity."

"And all the usual caveats apply," Mason commented.

"It looks that way," Susan said. "Contact Mr. Finch. Ask him for an estimate - a honest estimate - of how long we will need to complete repairs."

"Aye, Captain," Mason said.

Susan nodded, studying the display as more and more pieces of information flowed into the system. TPS-271 had seven planets: one Earth-compatible, four rocky and two gas giants, as well as a sizable asteroid field. It would *definitely* make a good home for a colony, if the legal issues and questions of ownership could be sorted out. And there were plenty of groups on Earth who would regard the distance from the homeworld as a blessing, rather than a curse. She was just surprised they hadn't tried to settle Unity.

We needed a fixed government to negotiate with the Tadpole settlers, she reminded herself, dryly. Once the war was over, that was a problem that was going to need to be solved. *The groups that wanted their own world didn't want a government imposed on them.*

"Captain," Mason said. "Mr. Finch reports that it will take at least nine hours - he would prefer twelve - to carry out the most important repairs. The remainder can be handled once we're back underway."

"Signal the flag," Susan said. "Inform Admiral Harper of the situation and request permission to hold position long enough to carry out repairs."

"Aye, Captain," Parkinson said.

Susan glanced down at her console as more and more reports flooded the system. The engineers were good, but they *were* prone to overestimate how long it would take to accomplish a particular task. She would have been more impressed if it hadn't made it harder to make plans, although it was better to be safe than sorry. Losing a fusion core midway to Unity would be very embarrassing, even if it wasn't disastrous.

"Signal from the flag," Parkinson said. "The task force will hold position here for fifteen hours, then head straight for Unity."

He's cutting it fine, Susan thought, grimly. *If the aliens tumble to our game now, they'll race to Unity at once. We'll have barely a couple of hours to smash the first force before all hell breaks loose.*

She glanced at the fleet display and swore under her breath. *New York* had taken a beating too; *Indianapolis,* thankfully, had only taken minor damage. But with two damaged battleships, Admiral Harper clearly thought it would be better to make repairs before going back to the front. And she had to admit he had a point.

"Hold us here," she ordered. "Mr. XO, inform Mr. Finch that he has clearance to begin repairs as soon as possible."

"Aye, Captain," Mason said.

Susan sat back in her chair and opened the tactical folder, then reviewed all of the details of the last two engagements as her crew went to work. The alien tactics made sense, she thought, but there was something about them that bothered her. They could have pushed their advantage against the task force…yet that would have meant soaking up more casualties. Were they showing a sensitivity to losses, suggesting that her original theory was correct…or was she merely engaging in wishful thinking? There was no way to know.

She read through the tactical reports with a growing dissatisfaction. The analysts believed that the arsenal ships couldn't be reloaded at speed, although Susan knew that couldn't be taken for granted. Besides, two-stage missiles were over three times the size of conventional missiles and three-stage missiles would be even worse. The aliens had expended a vast number of warheads to score a handful of hits on the task force… she wondered, idly, just what their financial officers made of it. She knew *exactly* what human politicians would say if the navy requested permission to build so many wasteful missiles.

You plan to fire off five thousand missiles, she imagined the Leader of the Opposition saying, *and you only expect to score five hits?*

The thought made her smile. Missiles were cheaper these days - mass production brought the price down - but they weren't *that* cheap. Everyone *knew* that battleships and big guns were the wave of the future, conveniently ignoring the days when light carriers and starfighters had been considered the latest innovation in war. If there was one truth about humanity - and about every other known intelligent race - it was that they had no shortage of ingenuity when it came to devising new ways to kill one another. No doubt something would replace *Vanguard* in time.

Until then, she thought, rising, *I have a job to do.*

She toured her ship, supervising the repairs, and then caught a long nap before finally returning to the bridge. The crew's morale seemed to be good, despite the battering *Vanguard* had taken. They knew they'd taken a pounding - and that some of their comrades hadn't survived - but they also knew they'd given the enemy the slip. Susan just hoped, as she returned to her command chair, that they were right. The drones wouldn't last forever…

And then they'll know they've wasted their time, she thought. *What will they do then?*

"Signal from the flag," Parkinson said. "The task force is ready to move out."

"Take us into position, then set course," Susan ordered. "And keep the cloak in place."

She ran through it in her head, one final time. Seven days transit time between TPS-271 and Unity. And then...

"Mr. XO, you have the conn," she said, once *Vanguard* was underway. "I'll be in my Ready Room."

"Aye, Captain," Mason said.

Susan smiled as she rose and left the bridge. There was no way to avoid the fact that they were going to be outgunned, certainly if the alien reinforcements beat them to Unity, but she'd had an idea. And if they were lucky, it might just be enough to give the aliens a very nasty surprise.

And if we're right, she thought, *we might just win back the entire sector in one fell swoop.*

CHAPTER

THIRTY-FOUR

The settlement was a burned-out ruin.

Well, not *quite*, George acknowledged. Night was falling rapidly, but she could still see more than she wanted to see. A couple of buildings were still standing: a brick house and a large barn that the aliens had apparently decided would make an excellent barracks for their troops. But the remainder of the settlement, a village that wouldn't have been out of place on her family's estate, had been burned to the ground. A handful of bodies, lying by the side of the road, stood in mute testament to what the aliens had done to the residents who hadn't managed to flee. George had heard, as the small party had made their way towards the village, that the aliens had rounded up all of the settlers and shot them out of hand.

She felt horror - and disgust - welling in her gut as she stared at the bodies. Four of them were clearly men, perhaps the men who'd taken a series of shots at an alien convoy as it tried to make its way along a nearby road. But the other five were women and children, the youngest barely a babe in arms. What had *he* - or *she* - done to deserve to die? The body was so badly damaged that it was impossible to tell if it had been male or female. She imagined the aliens laughing as they watched the humans die - as terrorists had done during the war - and felt a cold relentless hatred. Even the Tadpoles, who had bombarded Earth, had never made it so personal.

"Remain calm," Stott whispered. "There will be a chance to get at them later."

George nodded, packing her emotions and locking them away inside her mind as she studied the alien positions. They didn't seem to be very alert, she noted; there was a handful of aliens on guard duty, but the remainder were inside the barracks, doing whatever aliens did between looting and burning human settlements. Perhaps they were just catching up on their sleep, she thought, darkly. It was what humans would have done.

"They're not that alert," she muttered. "Should we move?"

"Not yet," Stott said. "Watch them carefully."

The night grew darker as the alien guards maintained their steady patrol. George peered at them through her NVGs, realising that the boffins who'd dissected the first alien bodies had been right. The aliens *could* see in the dark like cats, unless they'd had their eyes modified or ocular implants inserted into their sockets. She felt sick at the concept, but she had to admit it might be a useful idea. There was something to be said for not needing a light - or heavy equipment - to move around under cover of darkness.

She looked up, silently counting the stars in the sky. A handful would be alien starships, she knew, although the insurgents didn't have many binoculars capable of picking them out. It wasn't as if anyone had anticipated needing a ground-based observatory on Unity - hell, there *wasn't* such a thing anywhere on *Earth*. Why would astronomers bother with a ground-based structure when building a radio telescope on the far side of the moon was a simple matter of logistics?

Or putting one in deep space, well away from Earth, she reminded herself. *There's no interference out there.*

The night was silent, save for a handful of nocturnal birds flying around in the shadows as they hunted for prey. George had heard that the aliens had shot a few of them, probably hoping to supplement their rations with a little meat. The resistance had been doing the same, although they'd been moving away from areas where plants and animals from Earth had been taking root. Unity's far smaller biosphere had fewer edible creatures. She cocked her head to one side, listening carefully, but heard nothing moving through the night. The aliens seemed to be completely off-guard.

But they might be the bait, she told herself, sternly. She hadn't forgotten the alien force that had attacked her first camp - or the reports of several other camps being located and destroyed after the first wave of attacks. *They might be trying to lure us into complacency.*

Stott touched her upper arm. She jumped.

"The resistance will fire the first shot," he reminded her. "If they get in and out without trouble, we'll make our escape shortly afterwards. Do not fire unless fired upon."

George nodded, curtly. Byron had gone through procedures repeatedly, time and time again, before allowing her to escort Stott. She wasn't blind to the trust he'd placed in her - or the possible consequences if she screwed up. Stott, she suspected, would have preferred to have been escorted by another marine - or a resistance fighter - although he'd said nothing. She doubted his newfound respect for her went *that* far.

But they need to conserve their marines, she thought, grimly. *Sending me out to fight - and die - makes sense.*

"I'm ready," she muttered.

Stott glanced at his watch, then keyed a switch. Moments later, George's goggles went white - just for a second - as a makeshift rocket flashed out of the surrounding jungle and slammed into the barn, smashing down the door and exploding inside. The structure burst into flames, an almighty fireball that blasted upwards; she saw, very briefly, an alien shape wrapped in fire before it collapsed back into the shadows. A hail of shots followed, dropping the guards before they could react. George watched them fall and felt nothing, but cold vindictive fury.

Let them die, she thought, savagely.

Silence fell, save only for the collapsing barn. The resistance fighters would be already bugging out, if they were still following the plan; they'd be halfway home before the aliens managed to mount a response. If, of course, the aliens *did* mount a response. They had to know, she assumed, that there would be a chance to catch the resistance on the hop, but they also knew that time wasn't on their side. It was quite possible, as Byron had pointed out repeatedly, that they would merely drop a few KEWs on the scene and declare it a draw...

And then she heard the sound of helicopters.

"Here they come," Stott breathed. "Do *nothing*."

George bit down her irritation as the helicopters flashed overhead, their machine guns chattering loudly as they poured a hail of fire into the jungle. Someone must have been watching from high overhead, George noted; they were taking care to strafe the spot where the resistance fighters had been, even though they were long gone. She hoped, grimly, that the aliens didn't decide to start shooting at random - or, for that matter, unleashing salvos of their antipersonnel rockets. But they held their fire.

"Interesting," Stott mused.

One of the helicopters came to a halt over the village, a handful of alien troopers rappelling down to the ground as the other helicopters swept around the settlement, guns searching constantly for targets. George pressed herself into the ground as one flew right overhead - she fancied that she could feel the beating of its rotor blades as it passed - and then looked up, again, to see the Foxes searching the village. She couldn't help noticing that they seemed surprisingly unconcerned about the bodies, human and alien alike. There was no attempt to pick up and bag the bodies for burial or whatever the aliens *did* with their remains.

Perhaps they feel the bodies aren't important, she thought. A thought struck her and she frowned. *Or perhaps they're just leaving them until they've finished sweeping the remains of the village.*

The aliens moved in odd jerky patterns. One moment, they were standing still; the next, they'd be moving so quickly that she could barely see them run. They were hard to see, even against the burning barn. She blinked hard, forcing herself to watch as the aliens converged on one another, just long enough to exchange a few words before sprinting away again. And then one of the helicopters ducked low, dropping ropes towards the ground. The aliens grabbed hold and were lifted up, back into the dark sky.

And then they were gone.

George blinked. "What the fuck?"

Stott chucked, rudely. "Come on," he said. "We don't want to be anywhere near if they drop a KEW on the settlement."

He picked up his bag, then turned and led the way into the darkness, following a path George knew she would have had difficulty following even in broad daylight. Branches lashed out at her as she hurried after him, slipping and sliding in the mud. The marines insisted she should be grateful for the rain - it obscured their trails nicely - but she found it a nightmare. She was half-convinced she'd slip and break her neck as she walked behind him.

"Their logistics must be beginning to bite," Stott commented, half an hour later. They probably wouldn't be *safe*, if the aliens decided to blast the entire area, but so far they hadn't bothered to do anything. "Did you notice they didn't use any rockets?"

"They did use machine guns," George pointed out. "Why...?"

"The resistance lured a couple of helicopters into a trap," Stott said. "I imagine the aliens leant from that experience."

George nodded. "You mentioned their logistics?"

Stott laughed, even as he walked faster, forcing her to hurry after him. "You think your logistics are bad? Ours are worse. Everything we need to bring to the party has to be transported from Earth - or one of the forward bases, if we're lucky. A factory ship can produce some items, true, but not everything. A single MANPAD needs to be shipped all the way from Earth to wherever we want to use it.

"I imagine the aliens have the same problem," he added. "There's fuck-all industry here, so everything they need has to be brought with them. Quite a pain in the ass if the insurgency stays active longer than they expected."

"I see," George said. She'd assisted *Vanguard's* officers with logistics, but she'd never had to handle it herself. Stocking Middy Country was easy compared to deploying a marine unit and making sure it had all necessary supplies. "So they might just run out of bullets?"

Stott shrugged. "Depends on what they brought with them," he said. "Bullets are easy, with the right tools - other things are not. Now, keep walking. I want to be back at the camp before the sun rises."

George nodded and followed him, trying to think about something - anything - other than the distance she had to walk to reach camp. If the aliens really *were* having logistics problems, what did that mean? That the resistance could simply walk in and retake their world once the aliens ran out of bullets? Or that the aliens might just withdraw to a single defensible point and call down KEWs on anything that looked threatening? She didn't want to think about what that might mean for the prisoners, if the shit hit the fan. The aliens didn't seem to be actively torturing or abusing them - not like the Vesy, if some of the darker reports were accurate - but that might change. She was all-too-aware of the human bodies she'd left behind at the destroyed settlement.

"Bah," Stott muttered, as dawn began to break. "You'll be doing more push-ups later, young lady."

"Yes, sir," George said, stiffly. "But we're nearly there."

Stott surprised her by laughing. "Try saying that to a sergeant," he said. "But make sure you do it from a safe distance."

He said nothing else as they reached the edge of the camp and passed through the outer defence lines. Byron had made sure to have all the approaches picketed, although he'd admitted that trying to put up a fight - when the aliens arrived - would be nothing more than suicide. George had been surprised when he'd told her the evacuation plan, but she had to admit it made sense. There was no point in a number of marines and resistance fighters getting themselves killed for nothing.

"Get something to eat and drink, then join us in the tent," Stott ordered, once they were through the lines. "The boss will want to speak to you."

George nodded and hurried towards the mess. The food hadn't improved, not entirely to her surprise. There was nothing stopping the marines from hunting, but Byron was paranoid about cooking the food, even a safe distance from the camp. No one had argued. After the aliens had uncovered and destroyed a number of camps, none of the inhabitants felt like taking risks.

Apart from the ones we have to take, George thought. *Like going out and watching as the aliens take a pasting.*

She stepped into the tent and took a pair of ration bars from the box, opening one and stuffing the other in her pocket for later. The mess seemed almost deserted - coming to think of it, the entire camp seemed under-manned. She frowned as she chewed the ration bar, then carefully placed the wrapper in the rubbish bag before heading for the flap. Stott had told her, during one of their training sessions, that all rubbish had to be bagged up and transported well away from the camp. A skilled intelligence special-ist could learn a great deal about the unit merely be studying its waste.

"George," Byron said, as she walked into the command tent. "What do you make of it?"

"They were reluctant to give chase," George said. "And they conserved their ammunition as much as possible."

She paused. "And they also showed a lack of respect for their own bodies."

"That fits with their previous behaviour," Kelly put in. "They don't seem to care about leaving their dead behind."

Byron looked disturbed. "Don't they know how much damage some-one could do with a single alien body?"

"I suspect it's tradition," Kelly said. "We evolved a tradition of trying to recover the bodies of our fallen long before anything unpleasant could be done with them."

"Maybe," Byron said. He glanced at George. "I've received word from General Kershaw. A message was forwarded to him through the network of stealthed relay satellites."

George looked up, sharply. "They're here?"

"The task force has apparently returned to the system," Byron said. "We're moving out tomorrow."

"To get into position," George said. She stopped as she realised the implications. "If they see you coming…"

"It's a risk we have to take," Byron said. "The aliens have a large gar-rison on the surface, George. If we can pin them down, we might just be able to prevent them from doing something drastic."

George blinked. "I thought you would have wanted to destroy the garrison."

"If the aliens stay in orbit, they'll just smash us flat," Byron pointed out. "And if the task force retakes the high orbitals, the aliens can either surrender or get smashed flat themselves."

"Without risking everything," George said.

Byron nodded. "I'd prefer for you to head south to one of the refugee camps," he said. "But if you want to join the resistance fighters as they prepare to reinforce us, you may do so."

George swallowed, hard. She hadn't *liked* her first experiences of combat. Part of her would have been delighted to withdraw to the refugee camp and wait to see what happened. But the rest of her knew she'd never forgive herself if she retreated. She'd signed up to risk her life for her country.

"I'd prefer to join you," she said, honestly. "But if the resistance will have me, I'll be there."

"They'll be glad to have anyone who can fire a gun," Byron said. "You don't have the training to fight beside us, not here."

"I know," George admitted. "When do we leave?"

"In two hours," Byron said. "The operation is apparently due to kick off this evening."

"So go get packed," Stott put in. "And make damn sure you have plenty of ammunition. It's meant to be used."

George nodded, shortly. It wasn't as if she had anything to pack, apart from the ammunition and a handful of ration bars. She only had one set of clothes, after all; she was all too aware that she was dirty, smelly and not fit for human company. Her sister would probably fall over in a faint if she laid eyes on George. She might wonder, in all honesty, if George was even *human*.

Not that she would enjoy being here either, George thought, as she walked to the supply dump. *She would hate it.*

The thought made her smile. Anne, her sister; Anne, who had long blonde hair that took the maids nearly half an hour to prepare; Anne, who wore gowns from a bygone age whenever she thought she could get away with it; Anne, who had never been told *no* since she'd been a little girl; Annie, who had never done anything more taxing than lifting a fan to coyly hide her eyes…the thought of Annie crawling through the mud was absurd. George had to fight down a giggle as she imagined Anne making her way through the jungle, her dress tattered and torn before she'd even walked a mile…

She sobered, sharply, as the full implications struck her. This time, they wouldn't be picking on isolated patrols and alien encampments; this time, they'd be going after the garrison itself…and if they lost, if the task force lost, they'd die. She'd never see her sister again.

I'm sorry, Anne, she thought, morbidly. She'd written the standard letter before *Vanguard* had departed Earth - and another before they'd first
entered the Unity System - but she knew it wouldn't be enough. *I'd like to
see you, one more time.*

She took a long moment to calm herself, then walked into the supply
dump. If she got home, she would have time to talk to her sister again…

…But for the moment, she had to prepare for war.

CHAPTER
THIRTY-FIVE

"Two battleships in orbit, one carrier and five destroyers holding position at the L2 point," Charlotte said, studying the records from HMS *Pinafore*. "There's no sign of their other battleships."

"They may have been banged up worse than we thought," Mason said. "Has the flag issued any updated orders?"

"No, sir," Parkinson said. "They may be still evaluating the sensor records."

Susan nodded. HMS *Pinafore* had slipped close enough for passive sensor scans, but going active would have betrayed her location to a watchful alien scout. The aliens might not have had the time - or the equipment - to set up a network of recon platforms, yet they would be watching for any trace of the task force. They *had* to know that the task force had escaped its shadows and headed back along a course that would bring it to Unity.

"We can take them, Captain," Mason said. "We've got more starfighters as well as the big guns."

"It looks that way," Susan agreed. She was mildly surprised that Admiral Harper hadn't already given the order to attack. The aliens *might* have additional starships of their own waiting in cloak, but the task force would have plenty of time to break off if the balance of power suddenly swung against them. "Tactical, your analysis?"

"The ships appear to be at readiness, Captain," Granger said. "I'd say they were at condition-two, if they were human."

"Noted," Susan said. She doubted that Admiral Harper would want to sneak up on them, not when the aliens were likely to see the task force coming. Besides, the plan for a joint assault on the ground as well as in space demanded that the aliens were lured away from the planet. "Continue to monitor their position."

"Aye, Captain," Granger said.

"Signal from the flag, Captain," Parkinson said. "The task force is to advance, formation delta; I say again, formation delta."

So we're giving up all hope of surprise, Susan thought. Formation Delta was nothing more than a direct challenge, advancing in full array without even the slightest attempt to hide. It should appeal to the aliens, if the xenospecialists were right. *But if we're outgunned, we should have a chance to break free before it's too late.*

"Helm, take us out," Susan ordered. "Tactical, prepare to drop the cloak on cue."

"Aye, Captain," Reed said. "Estimated time to contact, two hours and forty minutes."

Susan settled back in her chair as the task force slowly crawled away from the tramline, picking up speed as the cloaking devices were switched off. The aliens wouldn't have any problems seeing them, despite the time delay. They were practically broadcasting their location to the entire system. Her instructors at the Academy would probably have exploded with rage, she thought, if anyone had tried that tactic in the simulator tank, but it might just work against the aliens. If they really liked a challenge, the task force was offering them one they should find irresistible.

"They'll see us in less than thirty minutes, Captain," Granger said. "Unless they do have a ship watching the tramline."

Susan shrugged. For once, the presence of a cloaked spy ship wasn't a concern. They *wanted* the aliens to see them. But if there were other cloaked ships in the system...she shook her head. The task force was surrounded by a dozen sensor probes, watching carefully for anything that might indicate the presence of a cloaked ship - or fleet. If they picked up a hint of trouble, they had plenty of time to break off. Or so she kept telling herself.

"Hold us on course," she ordered. It would be nearly an hour before they knew what the aliens were doing, although as the task force converged on the planet the time delay would fall to zero. "And keep a *sharp* eye on the sensors."

She kept her own eyes on the sensor display as more and more data flowed in from the remote probes. The aliens, it seemed, hadn't had the time to establish their own cloudscoop, let alone set up an asteroid mining station of their own. She wasn't too surprised - they had to know their grip on Unity wasn't strong - but it didn't look as if they'd bothered to survey the remainder of the system either. It made her wonder, grimly, just how many records they'd captured from the contact fleet.

But Unity is right on the edge of the war front, she mused. *If they're operating on a shoestring too, they're not going to want additional commitments.*

The thought made her smile. Unity wasn't a system of little importance - the tramlines running through the system offered the aliens a chance to attack the Tadpole flank or plunge into human space - but holding it was going to be costly. The aliens might have made a serious mistake, tactically speaking, by invading the planet. They'd feel compelled to hang onto the surface when leaving the colonists to their own devices might have seemed a better idea. It wasn't as if they couldn't have emplaced a handful of automated weapons platforms in orbit, keyed to fire on anything leaving the atmosphere. Anyone trapped at the bottom of the gravity well would have been powerless to affect the course of the war.

"They're adjusting position," Granger said, sharply. "I think they're preparing to leave orbit."

They will have left by now, Susan reminded herself. The time delay was still a significant factor. *And they'll be coming out for us.*

She watched, grimly, as the situation developed. A human enemy might have thought twice about setting out on an intercept course, particularly against a force that outnumbered him, but the aliens clearly didn't intend to run. Instead, they were heading directly for the human ships, their carrier moving up behind the battleships. Susan wondered, as she studied its acceleration curves, if she was looking at an alien version of *Ark Royal.* The carrier definitely seemed to be older and slower than the carriers they'd killed earlier. And if that was the case...

"Signal the flag," she ordered, quietly. "That carrier may be tougher than the others."

"Aye, Captain," Parkinson said.

Susan braced herself as the two alien battleships came closer, their carrier already launching fighters in attack formation. Admiral Harper barked orders over the datanet, commanding the human carriers to launch their own fighters. The French starfighters formed a CSP, protecting the task force, while the Russians plunged forward, intent on crippling the enemy ships. Susan watched, grimly, as enemy point defence fire began to take a toll. It looked, very much, as though the enemy had taken the time to analyse their earlier encounter and improve their targeting.

"The enemy point defence has improved by at least twenty percent, Captain," Granger reported, grimly. "And that carrier is definitely armed to the teeth."

"Looks like it," Susan agreed. The alien carrier was spitting out pulse after pulse of point defence fire, despite its fighters trying desperately to damage or destroy a number of human ships. It certainly seemed to be heavily armoured, perhaps more heavily armoured than a *Theodore Smith*-class carrier. The Russians simply weren't making much of an impact on her hull. "Mark her down for targeting if she comes into range."

She glanced at the tactical display as the alien ships converged on the task force. The alien battleships had moved apart, clearly intending to pass *between* the human battleships while pounding at their hulls. It wasn't a tactic *Susan* would have cared to use, but it *would* give them a chance to inflict a staggering amount of damage in a relatively short space of time... at least until they were destroyed. Each of their ships would be exposed to the fire of at least two human battleships.

"Enemy vessels will enter missile range in five minutes, energy weapons range in ten," Granger reported. "Captain?"

"Hold the missiles until they are closer," Susan ordered. "They'll just be picked off if we open fire at this range."

The last of the seconds ticked away as the Russian starfighters wheeled about and fled back to their carrier, their numbers depleted by a third. Susan frowned as the tactical datanet tallied the damage, realising that the aliens hadn't lost more than a handful of their point defence weapons. Enough to be annoying, true, but hardly enough to be fatal.

And their main guns were as heavily armoured as *Vanguard's* own turrets. The starfighters hadn't managed to inflict more than scratches on their paint.

We're going to need to devise new torpedoes, Susan thought, grimly. *Something that makes the starfighters more than gadflies to battleships.*

"Enemy ships entering energy range," Granger reported. "They're locked onto us."

"Open fire," Susan ordered.

Vanguard unleashed a spray of plasma fire, flashing through space and slamming into the nearest alien battleship. The aliens opened fire at the same moment, their fire crashing into *Vanguard's* hull. Susan glanced at the status display and allowed herself a moment of relief as their hasty repairs remained intact. The battleship might be in danger of losing most of its point defence and external sensor blisters, but the main body of her hull would survive.

"The enemy ship is taking damage, but not enough," Granger reported. "Their hull appears to be as strong as ours."

"Concentrate fire on their turrets," Susan ordered. She barely noticed a starfighter - human or alien, she wasn't sure - fly into one of the streams of fire and vanish. The pilot would have died before realising his mistake. "See if you can shut down their weapons."

"Aye, Captain," Granger said.

Susan gripped her command chair as the entire ship started to shudder under the relentless bombardment, parts of the hull finally starting to give way under the strain. Mason barked commands, directing the damage control teams to some compartments and ordering others evacuated; Susan watched, grimly, as the alien ships grew closer. The entire battle had turned into a battering match and, although she was sure the humans would win the battle, the task force was going to be battered into uselessness.

"The enemy carrier is launching missiles," Granger reported. "They're aimed at *New York.*"

They must think the battleship's point defence is gone, Susan thought. The aliens might well be right. *New York's* point defence systems weren't any tougher than *Vanguard's.* And if they do...

She leaned forward. "Launch missiles, blunderbuss pattern," she snapped. "And ramp up the ECM as much as possible."

"Aye, Captain," Granger said. "Missiles launched...*now.*"

Susan watched, bracing herself, as the aliens reacted - too late. Five of nine missiles were vaporised before they could do more than separate themselves from *Vanguard*, but the remaining four missiles detonated within seconds, blasting streams of deadly energy into the alien battleship. Susan watched, feeling a grim exultation, as the alien ship rolled over, desperately trying to shield the damaged portion of its hull even as she kept firing. But it wasn't enough to save them from a pounding as *New York* fired directly into her exposed hull, slamming pulse after pulse of plasma fire deep into the ship.

"The enemy battleship is losing power," Granger reported. She frowned. "Captain, the other battleship is moving up in support."

"Concentrate fire on the second ship," Susan ordered. The aliens were pushing forward, ramping up their drives well past the maximum safe levels...she swore, inwardly, as she realised what they had in mind. "Communications, alert *New York*. They're going to ram!"

It was too late. All three battleships were now pounding on the alien ship, but it kept moving forward with a stately inevitability that chilled Susan to the bone. *New York* had barely begun its evasive manoeuvre when the alien battleship slammed directly into her hull, overloading her drives and weapons at the same moment. Susan watched, in growing horror, as a chain of explosions tore both ships apart, sending chunks of debris spinning off in all directions. She'd watched footage of the final flight of *Ark Royal*, over a decade ago, but this was worse. Far worse...

"*New York* is gone," Granger said, hoarsely. "Captain..."

"I know," Susan snapped. There hadn't been time for *New York* to launch lifepods. It was possible, vaguely possible, that there were survivors, but if Admiral Harper had survived he was completely out of contact. "Inform the datanet that I have assumed command, then order *Indianapolis* to continue firing on the alien battleship."

She watched, grimly, as the alien ship tried desperately to evade their fire, but her main drives were gone. A human ship would be trying to surrender, she thought; the aliens, it seemed, were determined to keep firing even as their ship was torn apart. The remainder of their ships moved closer, one attempting to ram *Vanguard* only to be vaporised by a salvo from her main guns. And then the alien ship lost power completely and went dead.

"Cease fire," Susan ordered, sharply. "I say again…"

The alien ship exploded. Susan wondered, for a long moment, if one of the last shots had hit something vital, then decided that it was more likely that the aliens had triggered the self-destruct, rather than risk something important falling into human hands. Human ships were designed to purge and destroy their databanks before surrendering - if only to render the ship useless - but the battleship had taken immensely heavy damage. The aliens might have believed, not unreasonably, that they couldn't guarantee that their ship's secrets would be safely destroyed.

And even a look at their ship would tell us a great deal about them, she thought, as the debris field expanded rapidly. *But they didn't even launch lifepods*!

"The enemy carrier is reversing course," Granger reported. "She's recovering her starfighters."

"Pursuit course," Susan snapped. She was damned if she was letting the carrier slip away, after losing *New York* and Admiral Harper. The task force had taken one hell of a battering, but it had won the day. "And signal the planet. Inform them that the skies are clear."

"Aye, Captain," Parkinson said.

He paused. "Captain Yegorovich is requesting permission to launch his own starfighters in pursuit."

Susan hesitated. There was no reason to think that *Vanguard* and *Indianapolis* couldn't smash the enemy carrier between them. She might need Yegorovich's starfighters for the next engagement, if the enemy reinforcements arrived before hers. Yegorovich wanted glory, yet he and his pilots had done more than their fair share during the campaign.

"Denied," she said, finally. "The starfighters are to return to their carriers and prepare for antishipping strikes."

She glanced at Unity on the display, then returned her attention to the enemy carrier. If all had gone according to plan, the marines - and the other groundpounders - would be attacking the enemy garrison now, forcing it to keep its head down. Once the enemy carrier was gone, the task force would return to Unity and reclaim the high orbitals. If the enemy refused to surrender afterwards - even when they had been clearly beaten - she'd pound them into scrap from orbit. The marines had made it clear that the aliens didn't seem to have landed anything that could target her ships.

"Captain Yegorovich doesn't sound pleased," Parkinson said. "But he has accepted your orders."

Susan nodded, curtly. Yegorovich hadn't liked her when they'd first met - and he probably still didn't like her - but at least he was professional enough to follow orders. She gave him credit for that, at least, as she watched the enemy carrier come slowly into range. It launched its starfighters again, as the battleships closed in, but it was already too late. There was no way they could hope to escape.

"Broadcast a demand for surrender," Susan ordered. The marine report had noted that the aliens had definitely learned *some* English. "Inform them that we will treat them well, if they surrender."

There was no response, save for the alien starfighters screaming closer, firing missiles as they closed in on their targets. Susan cursed, wondering just why the aliens were so reluctant to admit defeat. Didn't they *know* they were doomed? A carrier, no matter how armoured, couldn't stand up to a single battleship at knife-range, let alone two. There were just too many fragile places in her hull.

"Open fire," she ordered, quietly.

The alien carrier opened fire itself, spitting defiance towards her tormentors as she writhed under their fire. Susan watched, grimly, as pieces of hull plating were blown off, plasma fire smashing through her recovery decks and obliterating her innards. A chain of explosions ran through her hull, eventually destroying the entire ship in a final savage explosion. The starfighters desperately tried to ram the human ships, but it was pointless. Susan allowed herself a moment of relief as the last of the starfighters vanished, then glanced at the main display. The battle was over.

"Dispatch additional damage control teams to critical areas," she ordered. "And then prepare to alter course…"

"Captain," Charlotte said. "Long-range sensors are picking up two *more* alien battleships on an intercept course!"

Susan swore. No wonder the carrier had tried to fight rather than surrender. She'd known that reinforcements were on the way. The battle wasn't over after all. And that meant…

"Alert the task force," she ordered, grimly. Two battleships against two battleships…it would have been a fair fight, if her battleships weren't already badly damaged. But getting out of the system before the aliens intercepted them might well be impossible. "Prepare to engage."

"Aye, Captain," Parkinson said.

Mason shot her a worried look. "Captain, we're in no state for a fight."

"I know," Susan said. The damage reports were still rolling in, yet it was already clear that her ship was going to need at least two months in a shipyard before she was ready for anything. "But can we get away from them?"

She smiled, suddenly. "And besides," she added, "I've just had an idea."

CHAPTER
THIRTY-SIX

George had always liked the dark.

It wasn't something she could explain to anyone else, although she'd tried more than once when her mother had caught her out of bed in the middle of the night. There was just *something* about how the world looked different in the dark, something about how the most familiar things could become strange and eerie in the darkness. Sneaking through the estate in the dark had been an adventure, creeping around the school after Lights Out - and trying to slip into the male dorms - had merely added extra spice. But now, grimly aware that the aliens would be rushing to relieve their garrison, she thought she understood why so many others were scared of the dark. *Anything* could be out there, lurking in the shadows.

She crouched low by the roadside, peering southwards. The aliens had taken over the spaceport for their garrison, landing enough troops and supplies to set up a near-impregnable command base. She rather doubted they were satisfied, given the *amount* of supplies they'd had to land in a very short space of time, but it would suffice - for the moment. And yet, the groundpounders - including her friends - were sneaking up to engage the enemy, unless something had gone badly wrong.

And once the garrison comes under attack, the enemy outposts will send everything they have to break the siege, she thought, grimly. *And we have to stop them.*

She glanced at her watch, feeling the butterflies in her stomach growing stronger. This wasn't an insurgent hit-and-run raid, this was a deliberate attempt to hold the line and force the aliens to *bleed*. She looked up at the stars, wondering just how many of them were alien starships and automated weapons platforms. If the aliens genuinely thought they were losing, they were likely to call hell down on the planet. Blowing up the entire settlement and calling it a draw might just suit their mindset.

Depends which one of them is in charge, she reminded herself. Cows committed suicide when captured, it seemed; Foxes went submissive. *A Fox might concede defeat and surrender.*

"Ten minutes," a voice said, quietly. The man beside her looked nervous, although the darkness made it hard to be sure. "They'll be ready, won't they?"

"They're the best of the best," George assured him. "If they can get into position to attack the garrison, they can do it."

She took another look along the darkened road, trying to pick out the emplaced heavy weapons and MANPAD teams. But she saw nothing. She hoped the aliens wouldn't see anything either, at least until it was far too late. And yet, she knew all too well that the aliens might just blast their way through the resistance barricade in their mad rush to reach the spaceport. They weren't likely to engage a tiny force when their garrison was under threat.

"I hope you're right," the fighter said. "We're gambling everything on this operation."

George nodded. The resistance had plenty of pistols and rifles, but they were *very* short on heavy weapons. No one had seen any need to supply the planet with anything heavier than a handful of automatic weapons. She suspected, cynically, that the policy was more intended to deter the colonists from rebelling than anything else, but it hardly mattered now. All that mattered was that they were gambling the handful of heavy weapons they *did* have on a single operation. If it failed, the resistance would be reduced to nothing more than a nuisance, at least until more supplies could be shipped to the planet.

And they won't be, George thought. *There will always be somewhere more important than Unity.*

She looked north, just in time to see the illumination round explode over the spaceport, casting an eerie pearly white light over the scene.

Byron had argued for attacking in darkness, but he'd been overruled by the American General, who'd pointed out that darkness actually favoured the Foxes more than the humans. Moments later, she heard gunfire echoing from the north, followed by flashes and flares as mortars strove to drop rounds into the heart of the enemy position. A bright light rose off the ground - a helicopter, she assumed - only to be swatted down by a MANPAD. Another made it higher before it too was blown out of the air.

"It looks different from back here," the fighter muttered.

George shook her head. It was easy to pretend that it was just another Bonfire Night, but she knew that her friends were fighting and dying to keep the enemy pinned down. She couldn't see it as anything other than a bloody battle. God alone knew how many groundpounders had survived - no one had told her - but almost all of them had been assigned to the attack.

"Hey," someone called. "We have incoming!"

George turned, just in time to see the shape of five alien vehicles racing along the road. They were completely unlit, but there was just enough light for her to see them as they drew closer and closer. She had to admit they'd done well to get out of the patrol base and race for the garrison, even though it was likely to cause her problems. But then, she might be looking at an alien quick reaction force. The remainder of the outpost's defenders might be readying themselves for departure even as the QRA was nearing its destination.

She lifted her rifle and took aim, then ducked as the first IED exploded under the lead vehicle, flipping it up and tossing it into the jungle. The second vehicle ground to a halt, aliens spilling out in combat formation; she opened fire with the remainder of the fighters, hosing down the aliens with grim determination. She kept firing, even as the remaining vehicles moved to cover the infantry, their machine guns blasting streams of fire into the jungle. She'd wondered if the aliens were having supply difficulties - and Byron had agreed with her that it was possible - but if they were there was no sign of it as they fired endless streams of bullets through the nearest trees.

There was a flash of light, then a stream of fire as the first antitank missile was fired, straight into the side of the nearest alien vehicle. It exploded a split-second later, sending the aliens scurrying for new cover as the resistance exploited the opening. The other alien vehicles pulled back, only to come under fire themselves. George watched, feeling an odd burst of pride mixed with fear, as the remaining vehicles were destroyed. The resistance had slowed the aliens down, if only for a few minutes. They'd be in no shape to help the garrison.

The aliens must have known they were in trouble, but they didn't seem inclined to fall back and escape into the darkness. Instead, they found more cover and continued to fire, sniping at the resistance with brief bursts of fire. They *could* see in the dark, George noticed, as the illumination round began to burn out. Their shooting was distressingly accurate for creatures that shouldn't have been able to pick out the resistance fighters from the surrounding jungle.

Someone tapped her shoulder as the alien fire intensified. "Pull back," a fighter snapped, when she turned to look at him. "Now!"

George nodded and glanced at the man who'd chatted to her earlier. He was dead, his body lying beside her. A bullet had struck the side of his head - his brains were leaking out onto the muddy ground - and she hadn't even noticed! She gagged, despite herself, then crawled backwards, not daring to rise. The alien shooting was actually intensifying, even though they *must* be running short of ammunition. They were certainly spending it freely.

She moved deeper into the jungle, feeling safer as the darkness enveloped her. The sound of shooting was growing louder, along with a hail of explosions that suggested that the aliens were trying to counterattack. Her ears ached - no matter how she tried, she couldn't determine just what was going on as she rose and ran to the next rally point. The sound of engines in the distance grew stronger as she reached her destination, warning her that more alien vehicles were on the way. They'd link up with the stranded infantry, she assumed, and then launch a thrust down the road.

Or they'll try to sneak through the jungle, she thought, grimly. *They'd take us in the rear if they had a chance.*

"Take a grenade," someone ordered. The resistance fighters had already started to set up a barricade, half of them digging a trench while the other half felled trees so they fell across the road. "And get ready to join the fight."

The noise grew louder as the first alien vehicle appeared, surrounded by a handful of alien soldiers. They were advancing forward at a remarkable speed, but clearly watching for traps instead of impaling themselves on the resistance's guns. George braced herself, hastily checking her ammunition. She cursed under her breath a moment later. She'd gone through nearly two-thirds of her supply without even noticing!

An explosion enveloped the first vehicle, sending its infantry escort scattering in all directions. George cursed as two more vehicles appeared, their machine guns opening fire and practically disintegrating the barricade. She clung to the earth as the ground shook around her, suddenly very aware that the trench was very fragile and provided very little protection. There were so many bullets flying overhead that she didn't dare lift her head and look out of the trench. Fear practically held her frozen as she cowered at the bottom - she could practically *smell* the aliens as they advanced on the trench. And then a helicopter, flying overhead, was blown out of the sky by a direct hit. Shocked out of her paralysis, George pulled herself up and peered over the side of the trench...

...And beheld a disaster.

The aliens had smashed the resistance position, leaving only a handful of fighters alive as more and more aliens marched onto the scene. She hadn't expected much from the barricade - it wasn't as if they'd had hours to get it in place - but it had been blasted aside with casual ease. And the aliens were marching forward, weapons at the ready. They'd find her...

George scrambled out of the trench, crawling as fast as she could towards the edge of the jungle. She felt stark naked, utterly exposed. There was no way she could count on the darkness to hide her, not when the aliens could see in the dark. It felt as if a pair of crosshairs had been drawn on her back, as if she could feel, deep inside, that someone was pointing a gun at her. She heard footsteps behind her, a pitter-patter that wasn't remotely human; she tried to turn and bring up her rifle, but it was casually snatched out of her hands before she could fire a shot and tossed into the distance. And then the alien slammed her face-down into the muddy ground, pushing her nose and mouth into the dirt. She struggled, but it was useless. The alien was far stronger than her.

She choked as she tried to breathe, then went limp. Woof had submitted when the marines had beaten him, hadn't he? Perhaps, if she submitted too, the aliens would spare her life...there was a long moment when she thought she'd failed, that she was about to die, then the alien hauled her upright and held her effortlessly in the air. Claws flickered out of his palm and sliced her clothes away, leaving her naked and helpless. She stared numbly at the creature, wondering just what was about to happen. All those Z-Grade movies about aliens coming to Earth to steal women couldn't be true, could they?

The alien dropped her to the ground and spun her around, resting one hand on her naked shoulder. She stayed very still, remembering the razor-sharp claws that could slice through her neck as easily as a hot knife through butter. The alien gave her a gentle push, marching her towards the remains of the ambush site. A handful of other human prisoners were kneeling on the ground, as naked as herself, their hands on their heads. Four aliens were guarding them, weapons at the ready. George couldn't help wondering if she was being marched to her execution. The aliens couldn't be *pleased* with everything that had happened since the attack had begun.

"Sit," the alien said.

It pushed her down at the same moment. George knelt, placing her hands on her head. The aliens marched around, exchanging comments in their barking tongue; she wished, suddenly, that she was better at reading their moods. She'd killed a couple of foxes on her father's estate - Anne had hated the whole idea, claiming it was cruelty to dumb animals - but she'd never bothered to learn how to read them. And even if she had, the aliens weren't actually *related* to Foxes. They merely looked similar.

She glanced northwards. The sound of firing was getting louder. Her captors didn't seem to know what to do - had they killed their commanding officer? Or did their CO not know what to do either? They didn't *know* what was lying in wait down the road. A whole string of ambushes - or an open road to the garrison. Charging down it blindly might just get them all killed.

They might just force us to walk in front of them, George thought, grimly. *And that would get us killed.*

She shuddered, helplessly. Human shields…two centuries of brutal combat since the dawn of the Age of Unrest had taught the military not to flinch when terrorists and insurgents used human shields. Western military forces had done what they could to save the poor unfortunates used as human shields, then hunt down the bastards who'd used them and hang them from the nearest lamppost. But the aliens couldn't be expected to know that, could they?

I can't do it, she thought, grimly. *Whatever they want me to do, I can't do it.*

She closed her eyes in pain. She'd gone through the Academy's version of the Conduct After Capture course, but no one had seriously expected her to be captured in the field. Maybe that had been a mistake - Prince Henry had been captured in the middle of a battle - yet ending up on Unity during the war had been utterly unexpected. She'd expected, when she'd considered it at all, that she would be taken into custody after a surrender. The rules were different then, at least for humans. God alone knew what the aliens considered them to be.

The barking grew louder as the aliens chattered away. She opened her eyes in time to see one of the aliens jabbing at another with his claws, starting a fight. The second alien lunged, claws extended; George watched, in growing horror, as they tore at one another, droplets of blood splashing everywhere. She fought the urge to rise and run for her life as the fighting grew more savage, a moment before the first alien caught the second in the chest with a clawed hand. The second alien slumped to the ground, dead. None of the other aliens seemed to care.

And to think I thought that battling Fraser was bad, George thought, stunned. Middies were expected to jostle for position, but killing someone - even seriously *hurting* someone - would be grounds for a court martial. *What sort of military allows its people to kill one another?*

The victor turned to its comrades and barked a long string of orders. George couldn't understand a word, but being hauled to her feet and pointed down the road was easy to understand. She braced herself to refuse if the aliens tried to force her north, even though she knew it would get her killed; the aliens, instead, ordered her south. Other aliens materialised out of the jungle as they moved, looking grim and despondent. Had they lost the fight? Or were they merely waiting for their space-based comrades to end the battle?

She glanced at the other prisoners, who looked as stunned as she felt. Everyone had *known* the aliens had stopped taking prisoners. Had the aliens accepted their submission? Or had they merely decided not to waste bullets shooting prisoners? George considered the idea, then dismissed it a second later. The aliens didn't need to *shoot* the prisoners to kill them. A single slash of their claws would be more than enough to finish the job.

Gritting her teeth, she looked upwards. It was growing darker, but she could see the first glimmers of daybreak in the distance. And the shooting was still going on...she imagined Byron and the marines punching through the defences, storming the spaceport, slaughtering the alien commanders...

It didn't matter, she realised dully. If the aliens were beaten in orbit, the navy could hammer their positions on the ground; if the aliens drove the task force away, *they* could hammer the imprudent humans from orbit. The battle on the ground *might* have put pressure on the aliens, as Byron had hoped, or it might have been completely immaterial. She had the nasty feeling, as she marched to an unknown fate, that it was the latter. Hundreds of lives - and countless pieces of irreplaceable equipment - had been lost. And it might have been for nothing.

The battle will be decided up there, she thought, tiredly. Perhaps she should have gone to one of the refugee camps after all. It would have made her feel like a coward, but how much use had she actually *been*? *And everything down here is just a side show.*

She sighed, bitterly, as she kept walking. There was nothing else she could do.

CHAPTER
THIRTY-SEVEN

Susan felt cold as the two enemy battleships advanced towards the human ships, surrounded by nine smaller ships and a light carrier. Or something she *assumed* was a light carrier, she reminded herself. After the arsenal ships, she'd be damned if she took anything that *looked* harmless lightly again.

"Confirm," she ordered. "Those are our former shadows?"

"Confirmed," Granger said. "They're definitely the same battleships - but they seem to have picked up a couple of other escorts somewhere along the way back here."

Susan nodded, grimly. There was no hope of avoiding engagement, not with both *Vanguard* and *Indianapolis* badly damaged. Their drives couldn't hope to ramp up enough power to escape the aliens, while she knew - all too well - that there were no reinforcements on the way. She *could* use drones to try to trick the aliens into believing that there *were* reinforcements entering the system, but she doubted they'd fall for the same trick twice. And that left her with no option, save for a long-range duel against an enemy she knew outgunned her.

"Alter course," she ordered quietly, as her idea came to life in her mind. "Bring us about - let them chase us."

"Aye, Captain," Reed said.

Susan briefly contemplated their options. The two battleships could fight a heroic rearguard operation while the remainder of the task force fled, but that would mean surrendering to the inevitable. And it wasn't in her nature to simply give up. Besides, if she carried out the engagement properly, the smaller ships could disengage even if the battleships were destroyed. The carriers wouldn't be able to stand up to the battleships, but they were fast enough to outrun them and their starfighters could dispose of anything fast enough to catch the fleeing ships.

"Signal to the task force," she ordered, slowly. "The carriers are to launch starfighters on attack vector as soon as the enemy reaches attack range. Their objective is to weaken the battleship point defence and sensor nodes as much as possible."

"Aye, Captain," Parkinson said.

Susan watched the display, wondering if any of the commanding officers would object. The reasoning that had put her as Harper's second no longer applied, not after all of the surviving commanders had had their taste of combat against the new aliens. And yet, they had to know that there was no time for a debate. As she watched, acknowledgements flowed in from all of the remaining ships. Even Yegorovich had accepted her command without a fight.

Probably because he'll never have a better chance to paint another alien battleship on his hull, she thought, cynically. *And because Russia's reputation won't survive a disaster if he causes it.*

She forced herself to wait, as calmly as she could, while the alien ships slowly converged with hers. The task force was moving away from the planet now, daring the aliens to follow them. Susan would have been surprised if they'd declined the challenge. Hammering the ground forces on Unity was important, but taking out two enemy battleships and two carriers would be far more *useful*. It took far too long to build a battleship, despite the best efforts of humanity's shipyards. *Vanguard* and *Indianapolis* simply couldn't be replaced very quickly.

And the aliens will know it too, she thought, numbly. *Their technology is on a par with ours.*

"Enemy ships will enter starfighter attack range in twelve minutes," Granger reported.

"The carriers are signalling that they're ready to launch the attack," Parkinson added.

"Good," Susan said. She looked at Mason. "I have some specific orders for you."

She ran her hand over the console, sending him the tactical diagram she'd worked out as the alien ships grew closer. It was chancy, she had to admit - and she wasn't sure the programming could be adapted in time - but it was their best chance of actually surviving the next few hours. Mason's eyes went wide, yet he took her diagram and began to work without question. He knew, as well as she did, that they couldn't survive another close-range engagement.

We're going to have to work on our missiles, Susan thought, sourly. *And we might have to start investing in long-range missiles after all.*

"I think this will work," Mason said. "But if they notice it ahead of time...we're sunk."

"Quite," Susan said. She sucked in a breath as the timer continued ticking down to zero. "If they like a challenge, we'll *give* them a challenge."

She watched him issuing orders, then turned to look at the main display. The aliens *had* to know they had the whip hand, even though she had far more starfighters than they could hope to deploy. They might take a beating - they *would* take a beating - but they'd destroy at least two battleships in exchange. And then...even if the carriers survived, they'd never be able to retake Unity without reinforcements.

Come on, you bastards, she thought, savagely. *Tempting target right here.*

"The enemy has entered starfighter attack range," Granger reported.

"Order the carriers to launch," Susan said. "And tell them I said good luck."

She gritted her teeth as the remaining fighters - Russian and French - flashed towards their targets, without holding anything in reserve. The alien carrier launched its own starfighters a moment later, choosing to keep them as a CSP rather than send them out to attack the human ships. Susan didn't blame him. His carrier only carried three squadrons, nowhere near enough to break through the wall of point defence protecting her ships. And besides, they might make a difference against the starfighters closing in on the battleships.

Not enough, she thought, as the two sets of starfighters began to exchange fire. *Nowhere* near *enough*.

The enemy had definitely improved their point defence, she noted, just like the last set of enemy ships. Had they been sharing notes over the FTL communicator? She clenched her jaw at the thought - the latest reports suggested that the analysts were *still* unaware of how the damned system worked - and then pushed the thought aside. There was quite a bit of debris drifting through the system, after all. Her techs would have a chance to examine the remains in hopes of finding something - anything - that might point them in the right direction.

"The enemy point defence has taken a beating," Granger reported. "A number of the pilots also attacked the enemy drives with torpedoes, but they're very heavily armoured. Damage appears to be minimal."

Pity no one ever managed to produce antimatter in large quantities, Susan thought. She'd heard a great deal about successive attempts to man-ufacture antimatter, but none of them had actually produced something that could be deployed. *Mounting anything larger than a nuke on a torpedo is out of the question.*

"Order the starfighters to continue the engagement," Susan said. "And start ramping up the ECM. I want them jumping at shadows."

"Aye, Captain," Granger said. She paused. "The enemy ships will be in missile range in five minutes."

"Understood," Susan said. It wasn't wholly accurate - they were well within two-stage missile range - but it would suffice. The enemy either didn't have any more long-range missiles or had chosen not to fire them. "Keep spoofing their sensors as much as possible."

"Aye, Captain," Granger said.

"Signal to the fleet," Susan added. "Decoy drones are to be deployed in" - she glanced at the timer - "seven minutes. They are to go active as soon as they are launched."

She paused. "And all ships are to immediately commence ECM pulses."

"Aye, Captain," Parkinson said.

Susan had no trouble hearing the puzzlement in his tone. The aliens had a hard lock on the task force. There was literally no point in deploying decoy drones, not when the aliens would have no trouble sorting the real ships from the decoys. Hell, deploying the drones might give the aliens unwanted insights into how the technology actually *worked*. She was mildly surprised that Captain Trodden hadn't called her to complain. The drones were American technology and, despite a series of international treaties, their secrets were closely guarded.

But the aliens will have problems with their sensors, she thought. *And that's the important point.*

"The alien ships are entering missile range," Granger reported. "They're opening fire."

Susan smiled, rather coldly. The aliens *had* to know they were wasting missiles, unless they'd come up with a surprise of their own. Humanity had quite a few missile warheads that were designed to make it harder for the enemy to isolate and destroy individual missiles, but none of them worked very well in the field. The boffins made all sorts of promises; very few of them, in her experience, were ever kept.

"Stand by point defence," she ordered, smoothly. "And fire as soon as they come into engagement range."

"Aye, Captain," Granger said.

She paused. "The starfighters are rearming," she added. "They're going to be out again in five minutes."

"Good," Susan said.

She gritted her teeth as the alien missiles entered her point defence envelope. A number were blown out of space, but two survived long enough to detonate and send bomb-pumped laser beams stabbing into her ship. *Vanguard* lurched as red lights flared up on the status display - she realised, grimly, that they weren't going to have to fake engine trouble after all - and then settled as the damage control teams went to work.

"They struck one of the gashes in the hull," Mason reported. "We have serious trouble…"

"Prepare to reduce speed on my command," Susan ordered. She glanced at the status display, hoping - praying - that the battleship would hold together long enough for her to carry out her plan. "Mr. XO, are the missiles programmed?"

"Yes, Captain," Mason said. "They're ready."

"Signal to the fleet," Susan ordered. There was no longer any time to delay. She'd just have to hope that the aliens were *determined* to kill her ships. "The decoy drones are to go active, then all ships save for *Vanguard* and *Indianapolis* are to accelerate. *Vanguard* and *Indianapolis* are to reduce speed on my command."

Captain Trodden is going to love this, she thought, as the acknowledgements came in from the remainder of the fleet. *Indianapolis didn't take anything like so much damage. They might even have been able to evade the enemy if I'd ordered them to leave.*

She pushed the thought aside. There was no longer any time for doubts. Either her plan worked or they all died quickly. She was damned if she was surrendering, even if she was *sure* she could keep anything classified out of enemy hands. God alone knew what the aliens would do to them, but she doubted it would be pleasant. The task force had probably hurt their pride quite badly...

"All ships have acknowledged," Parkinson said.

"Missiles ready for ballistic launch," Mason added.

"Launch the missiles," Susan ordered.

She looked at Parkinson. "Order *Indianapolis* to reduce speed in seventy seconds."

"Aye, Captain," Parkinson said.

Susan braced herself. The aliens were activating more and more sensors, despite the hundreds of blisters the starfighters had blown off their hulls, but they didn't seem to be taking the threat entirely seriously. And why not? They *knew* where the task force's ships were. The hail of electromagnetic distortion was nowhere near powerful enough to hide the ships, certainly not at such close range...

"Helm, reduce speed," she ordered.

Vanguard seemed to shiver as she slowed, allowing the aliens to catch up. They weren't entirely faking either, Susan noted; two of her drive rooms had gone offline, with a third hovering on the brink. *Indianapolis* reduced speed too, swinging her weapons around to flail desperately at the aliens. And the aliens, scenting victory, roared forward. She could just imagine their slavering expressions as they saw their prey, helpless before them.

They evolved from hunting animals, she thought. *They're predators, just like us.*

"Trigger the missiles," she ordered.

The aliens had no time to react before they impaled themselves on the bomb-pumped lasers, the deadly beams stabbing straight into their hulls at point-blank range. One of the battleships rolled over and exploded - she guessed that one of the beams must have struck something vital - while the other staggered to one side, spewing plasma and atmosphere from a dozen wounds. She barely managed to launch a salvo of missiles of her own before her main power failed completely.

"Order the starfighters to go after the other ships," Susan ordered, sharply. The alien escorts had been smart enough to stay out of weapons range, although there was no way they could outrun or fend off the starfighters. "Tactical, scan the remaining battleship."

"Aye, Captain," Granger said. "There's no obvious power sources left intact. It's possible that their hull depressurised completely."

Susan exchanged a long glance with Mason. The chance to take an alien ship intact...it was a dream come true. And yet, she doubted *all* of the ship's crew were dead. The Royal Navy's shipsuits provided *some* protection against the vacuum of space, if the worst happened and a ship lost atmospheric integrity. None of the survivors would be very *happy*, but they'd be alive.

And if there are survivors, and they trigger the self-destruct, she thought, *they'd take out a boarding party...if they wait.*

She keyed her console. "Major Andres, prepare a mission - volunteers only - to take possession of the alien ship," she ordered. "Ideally, any surviving crewmen are to be captured and transported back here, but bear in mind that one of them might be able to trigger the self-destruct."

"Aye, Captain," Major Andres said. There was a long pause. "My entire unit has volunteered."

Or been volunteered, Susan thought. *But they know the risks.*

"Deploy as soon as possible," she ordered. The remaining alien ships had been destroyed, the victorious starfighters returning to their motherships. "I'll assign *Pinafore* to remain alongside and provide assistance, if necessary."

"Aye, Captain," Major Andres said.

Susan closed the channel. It was a hell of a risk, but one she had to take. Only one non-human starship had been captured in all of humanity's history, yet that starship had provided the clues that had led humanity to victory in the First Interstellar War. Capturing a second ship, even one that had been badly damaged…it had to be attempted. She closed her eyes for a long moment, saying a silent prayer for Major Andres and his men, then watched as their shuttles were launched, heading straight towards the alien ship.

Godspeed, she thought.

"Helm, take us back to the planet," she ordered. "Communications, attempt to raise the forces on the ground."

"Aye, Captain," Reed said.

Susan waited, grimly, until a response finally arrived. "Captain, General Kershaw reports that the aliens have surrendered," Parkinson said. "They just threw down their arms."

"Tell him to secure the prisoners and await relief," Susan ordered, after a moment. She doubted she had many groundpounders left - all of the soldiers *Vanguard* had shipped to Unity had been dropped on the planet - but there were crewmen with weapons training if necessary. "Once we're in orbit, we'll provide whatever support he requires."

"Aye, Captain," Parkinson said.

Mason smiled. "We won," Captain," he said.

"Barely," Susan said. "*New York* is gone; *Vanguard* and *Indianapolis* are both heavily damaged…it could have been a great deal better."

"Yes, Captain," Mason said. "But no battle plan ever survives contact with the enemy."

"True," Susan agreed. She raised her voice. "Stand down from condition one, but continue to maintain a full sensor watch. We don't know how many other alien ships are racing to the system."

She leaned back in her command chair as *Vanguard* picked up speed, inching towards the planet. No, they *didn't* know how many more alien ships were on the way - if indeed there *were* any more alien ships on the way. She'd seen nothing to disprove her first theory, after all. Unity *was* rather far from the war front. And while the aliens might have been prepared to commit forces to secure a pathway into Tadpole space, were they actually ready to throw good money after bad?

I guess we're about to find out, she mused. *But until then, we should savour the victory.*

————

George sat in the makeshift camp and waited while the aliens argued, barking and hissing at one another like dogs that were on the verge of going for each other's throat. Even the arrival of a couple of Cows hadn't changed the situation, although it was quite interesting to watch how the two races reacted to one another. The Foxes seemed inclined to fight each other to settle the matter; the Cows seemed inclined to wait and see who came out on top. She wondered if they were deliberately pushing the Foxes into conflict, but there was no way to tell. Their language was completely beyond her understanding.

She glanced up, sharply, as one of the aliens strode towards her, holding a gun. A *human* gun, she realised in surprise: a weapon she didn't recognise. She braced herself, half-expecting to be shot, then recoiled in shock as the alien held the weapon out to her. Her mind raced - maybe it was a trap, yet she couldn't think of any reason why they would bother - as she took the weapon and held it. And then the alien - *all* of the aliens - prostrated themselves in front of her.

George felt her mouth drop open. "What?"

"I think they've surrendered," one of the captured fighters said. "The spacers must have won."

"So it seems," George said. She couldn't think of any other explanation. There was no logical reason for the aliens to surrender, unless they already knew they'd lost the battle high overhead. "What do I do now?"

"Take them back to the garrison," the fighter suggested. "What *else* can we do with them?"

CHAPTER
THIRTY-EIGHT

"What a fucking mess," Henry said.

The shuttle circled Unity City - or what had been Unity City - long enough to let him get a good look. A number of buildings had been smashed flat, while others had been converted into alien barracks or outposts. The streets had been torn up by armoured vehicles, leaving them looking like muddy pathways on the verge of sinking completely. And there were no civilians in sight. The remainder of the population had fled to the countryside.

"It can't be real," Doctor Song said. "Why...why would they *do* this?"

Henry shrugged. "They wanted security - and control," he guessed. Smashing Unity City was largely pointless, from a tactical point of view, but it *had* made it clear that the Foxes and the Cows were here to stay. "And besides, I assume they wanted the planet too."

He turned his gaze away from the porthole as the shuttle dropped towards the spaceport and landed neatly in front of the alien buildings. No aliens were in sight, he noted, as they stepped out of the hatch, merely dozens of soldiers from five different nations. The alien technology was being made ready for transhipment to orbit, but Henry rather doubted the analysts would learn anything new from it. Like humanity, the Foxes seemed to prefer to rely on simple technology as much as possible. If nothing else, it was much easier to repair.

"Your Highness," General Kershaw said, as they were shown into the nearest building. "It's good to see you again."

"And you, General," Henry said. General Kershaw looked tired, but happy. "What have you done with the prisoners?"

"We captured over four *thousand* aliens, mostly Foxes," General Kershaw said. "A number of Cows chose to commit suicide rather than be taken alive, but the remainder surrendered as well. So far, we don't have any idea why some surrendered and others didn't - they may just have different ideas on the subject."

He shrugged. "For the moment, we have them all under armed guard," he added. "There were…incidents…when the resistance fighters set out to capture surrendering aliens, so I've had my people take sole responsibility for guarding the camp."

Doctor Song leaned forward. "Incidents?"

"A number of prisoners were shot out of hand," General Kershaw said, bluntly. "The resistance fighters have no reason to love them, doctor."

"Keep the rest of them safe, for the moment," Henry said. "And don't let the resistance get close to them."

He rubbed his eyes, tiredly. In hindsight, he should have anticipated the problem. Unity would never be the same again, even if the war ended tomorrow and the planet *finally* received the investment it deserved. The colonists could hardly be blamed for wanting a little revenge. But it would make it harder to convince the aliens to surrender in the future.

"We won't, Your Highness," General Kershaw assured him. "But I'd suggest taking them off-world as soon as possible."

"That might not be easy," Henry said. The task force had assumed it would be taking custody of a handful of alien prisoners, not thousands. "We might have to move them somewhere else."

"Plenty of small islands on the planet," General Kershaw said.

He sighed. "I wish you and your team the very best of luck in untangling their language," he added. "So far, none of them have given us any trouble, but they speak very little English."

"It's a start," Doctor Song said. "Proper computer assistance and such-like will help us to decipher their speech."

Henry nodded. He had a private suspicion that the aliens who had committed suicide were all senior officers - and that the survivors would know little of tactical value - but interrogating the POWs would still teach Doctor Song and her team a great deal about the aliens. There were dozens of unanswered questions that could be *finally* answered, once the language barrier was broken. He couldn't wait to see how many of their preliminary conclusions were actually accurate.

"I'll escort you to the camps," General Kershaw said. He held up a hand. "I should warn you that we're operating under strict rules. If they take you hostage - or anything along those lines - we won't make any concessions."

And you'll shoot through us, if necessary, to stop them, Henry thought. *A prisoner riot would be disastrous.*

He shook his head as General Kershaw led him through the complex. Even if they did break out, the aliens had nowhere to go. Unity was *very* hostile territory for them, particularly after the groundpounders had captured or destroyed their weapons. He doubted a single alien would survive long enough outside the wire to be rescued, if the task force lost control of the high orbitals for a second time.

"Interesting design," he mused, as they passed through a pair of heavy doors. "It's clearly designed for more than one race."

"Yep," General Kershaw said. "We think both races would have found this comfortable."

Henry nodded as they walked through a final set of doors and out into the open air. He grimaced at the smell - a mixture of piss and shit and alien musk - as he gazed towards the wire. The POW camp was really nothing more than a large patch of ground, surrounded by two rows of barbed wire and patrolled by armed guards. Inside, hundreds of aliens sat on the muddy ground, looking around listlessly. He couldn't help thinking that they looked a very sorry lot.

"Shit," Doctor Song said, quietly.

"Quite," General Kershaw agreed.

Henry looked at him. "They gave you no trouble?"

"None," General Kershaw said. "And they didn't even give each *other* trouble, either."

Henry frowned, wondering what *that* meant. Well-trained human soldiers could remain calm and disciplined even in captivity, but poorly-trained and led soldiers could turn on their former officers. He'd read case studies from the Age of Unrest where officers had to be separated from their men - if the officers hadn't fled to avoid capture - just to keep them from being lynched. And yet, the aliens didn't seem to have turned on their own leaders...

"We'll figure it out," he said. Perhaps *no* officers had survived. "We'll figure everything out."

"Good luck, Your Highness," General Kershaw said.

———

"You're taking *Vanguard* home?"

"I'm afraid so," Susan said. She'd invited Captain Trodden and Captain Yegorovich - as the senior captains after her - to a private dinner, two days after Unity had been liberated. "She's simply too battered to endure another engagement."

"I wish I could disagree with you," Trodden said. "But she definitely needs a shipyard."

"You'll be taking the wounded home with you," Yegorovich mused. "Did *Edinburgh* make it back?"

"Not as yet," Susan said. She scowled at the thought. Maybe *Edinburgh* would make it back to Unity...or maybe she'd already been destroyed in transit. Or suffered a catastrophic drive failure somewhere in the depths of deep space. "I hope you'll see her here."

She looked up at the starchart, cursing under her breath. There had been no sign of a renewed enemy offensive, but she had no illusions about the task force's ability to continue the fight if a *third* enemy force showed up. The carriers could harry the enemy from a safe distance, yet the battleships couldn't hope to win an engagement against superior force.

"You'll have command," she said, addressing Yegorovich. "If the enemy shows up in force, beat a swift retreat. No heroics."

"The colonists will love that," Yegorovich said, darkly.

Susan shrugged. Most of the colonists had faded into the countryside, abandoning Unity City until the war was finally over. The remainder had requested passage on the task force back to Earth. Susan knew, all too well, that *Vanguard* couldn't accommodate them all, but she'd try to take as many as possible. The aliens might return to Unity at any moment.

"We need reinforcements," she said. "After that - we can think about heroics."

"True, Captain," Trodden agreed. He didn't show any resentment at being passed over for command, although he was technically junior to Yegorovich. But then, the next engagement would be a carrier battle. "You'd better make sure they send us reinforcements ASAP."

"I'll do my best," Susan said. A full task force - battleships and carriers - would be enough to stab back up the network of tramlines towards UXS-469 - and then into the alien star system that had been discovered by HMS *Magellan* and HMS *Livingston*. Hitting the aliens where they lived would force them to pull forces back from the front, giving the Tadpoles a breather. "But you know how reluctant some senior officers can be to take risks."

"Don't want their ships scratched," Trodden agreed.

"Ships are always scratched - or lost," Yegorovich said, disdainfully. He sniffed. "It's what they're lost *for* that counts."

Susan shrugged. She could see his point, but she also knew just how time-consuming it *was* to produce a battleship, even if the Admiralty could convince the Treasury to sign a blank check. Losing *Vanguard* would put a crimp in future operations, at least until more battleships were commissioned. And that would take far too long.

"It doesn't matter," she said, firmly. "All that matters is doing our duty."

"Of course, Captain," Trodden said.

"I'll be leaving two of the xenospecialists with you," Susan added. Prince Henry had requested permission to stay on Unity, but Susan had vetoed it. "They'll continue to study the alien POWs. I hear they're making progress in cracking their language already."

Yegorovich barked a harsh laugh. "The bastards have every reason to cooperate," he commented, nastily. "They have to tell us what they actually *need* to live."

Susan nodded. The xenospecialists *thought* they knew what the aliens needed - and the aliens certainly seemed to be having no problems eating human rations - but there was no way to be entirely sure.

And besides, having the ability to ask for better conditions would give the interrogators a chance to make connections with individual aliens. They might be shocked by their defeat, they might be submissive…but there was no reason to think that would last forever. Having a rapport between humans and aliens might make the difference between putting together a peace that both sides could endure and continuing the war to the bitter end.

"Of course," she said. "We'll be taking a number of aliens back home with us."

"The soldiers will love *that*," Trodden muttered, darkly.

"We have to learn to understand them," Susan said. "If nothing else, we have to know how to make them quit."

"Hit them hard," Yegorovich said. "They're a lot like Russians, you know."

Susan lifted her eyebrows. "How so?"

"My people are either masters or slaves," Yegorovich said. "And if you can convince one of us that you're the master, he'll think he's the slave."

"That says a lot about you," Trodden said. "And to think there was a time when your country was once called the freest in the world."

"A mistake," Yegorovich said. "A *foolish* mistake."

Susan sighed. "Be that as it may, we have other concerns," she said. "We'll be departing in two days. And then you'll be on your own."

"We'll be fine," Trodden said.

"And we'll make any alien who pokes his nose through the tramline very sorry," Yegorovich added. "Just get reinforcements out here as quickly as possible."

———

George felt drained as she stepped through the hatch to Middy Country, drained and tired and dirty as hell. There hadn't been any showers on the planet's surface; there had been no way to wash, save for a handful of wipes and odour-suppressors. Her uniform was probably a lost cause - coming to think of it, she had no idea where it had gone! Someone would probably make her write a report to account for its loss, she thought, rather morbidly. They'd been required to explain any missing supplies back at the Academy.

She walked into the wardroom and sighed. The soldiers were gone; Fraser, too, had packed up his possessions and left. The sight gave her a pang, even though she couldn't blame Fraser for extracting himself from Middy Country as soon as possible. He'd spent far too much time in the wardroom *before* his promotion. She undressed rapidly, dropping the muddy clothes in the basket for disposal and hurried into the shower. Thankfully, the XO had given her an extra water ration when he'd debriefed her, after she'd returned to the ship.

Stupid, she thought, as warm water cascaded down her body. She understood why there *was* a water ration, but it struck her as pointless elitism. *It isn't as if any of us have time to waste in the shower.*

She still smelt unpleasant as she turned off the water and dried herself thoroughly, then glanced at herself in the mirror. Her body was covered in bumps and bruises, but Kelly - when he'd examined her after the battle - had assured her that most of them would fade within the next few days. There was certainly no permanent damage, he'd added. He'd offered treatments, but she'd declined. There were too many people who'd been seriously wounded during the battle.

And too many others who won't come home at all, she reminded herself. *I was very lucky.*

A cool breeze struck her as she stepped out of the shower and opened her locker, retrieving her spare set of clothes. No one had declared her dead, much to her relief. The chocolate bars she'd saved from Anne's care package were still there, waiting to be eaten. She pulled her clothes on, then opened a bar of milk chocolate and munched on it gratefully. After four weeks of combat rations, it tasted heavenly.

The hatch opened. "Well, look who's come home," Potter said. Paula was right behind him, her face impassive. "Stellar Star herself!"

George blinked. "*What* did you call me?"

"Stellar Star," Potter said, again. "You captured an entire *army* of aliens wearing nothing but your birthday suit!"

George coloured. By now, *everyone* knew she'd walked her prisoners back to the garrison while stark naked. There just hadn't been anything to wear! The marines hadn't given her a hard time over it, but several of the others she'd met while she was assisting at the spaceport had teased her. She wasn't surprised, not really, that the story had already spread to orbit. It was too good not to be told.

"And you disregarded regulations," Potter added. "*Just* like Stellar Star."

"No doubt," George snarled. She would almost sooner have been accused of abusing her family connections. "She has the fucking script-writer on her side."

"And a uniform that's two sizes too small," Potter said.

"Shut up," George said, sharply.

"I don't think so," Potter said, as Paula pushed past him and headed for her locker. "I'm the First Middy now, George. And I will *not* tolerate any more shenanigans."

George gritted her teeth, fighting down the urge to either storm past him or hit him as hard as she could. She'd made mistakes - she was honest enough to admit that she'd made mistakes - and none of the excuses she might have offered were good enough to save her from the consequences. Everything she'd done on Unity would look good on her record, but would they look good *enough*?

"You'll do as I say from now on," Potter added. The amused arrogance in his voice made her see red. She had distant relatives who sounded *precisely* like that. "And…"

George felt her temper snap. Without thinking, she pulled back her fist and punched him in the nose, sending him crashing backwards to the floor. Potter stared at her in numb disbelief, clearly shocked. He hadn't thought she *could* fight, George realised. Hadn't he heard about her fight with Fraser? But then, she'd *lost* that fight. Potter might have assumed that Fraser had beaten obedience into her. She'd certainly never given him any trouble when he ran the wardroom.

I won some respect from Fraser, George thought. *And Potter never realised it.*

She stepped forward, ready to hit him again. "I think you've just lost the wardroom," she said, dryly. She quirked her eyebrows, invitingly. "Unless you want to go tell the XO that you got beaten up by one of your middies?"

Potter rubbed his nose. It was bleeding, blood dripping from his nostrils and staining his white uniform. George wondered, absently, if she'd broken it. *That* would be difficult to explain, particularly when the doctor put it back together. The doctor knew better than to ask awkward questions, but she might just raise the issue with the XO. Potter...would have to admit, to his superior, that he'd lost the wardroom.

And the XO will probably throw the lot of us out of the airlock, George thought. *He has to be running out of patience by now.*

"Fuck," Potter said. He glared at her, but made no move to get up. "Paula, the wardroom is yours."

"I think George should have it," Paula said. George glanced around. There was a faint smile playing over Paula's face. "Congratulations, George. You're First Middy - again."

"Thank you," George said, suspiciously. She couldn't avoid the feeling that she was being mocked. "And now *that's* settled, shall we at least *try* to get along?"

She helped Potter to his feet, keeping a sharp eye on him. "I'm going to sleep for the next seven hours," she added. Sleeping in the same cabin as Potter was a risk, but she was damned if she was showing fear. "And after that, we'll redo the duty roster."

"And start heading back to Earth," Paula said. The amusement hadn't vanished from her face. "I'm sure it will be an interesting trip."

George scowled. She knew, all too well, what she'd have to do when she reached Earth.

"Yeah," she said. "*Interesting.*"

CHAPTER
THIRTY-NINE

George rose to her feet - along with the rest of the spectators - as the court martial board filed back into the courtroom. Admiral Soskice led the way, followed by Admiral Flanders, Commodore Richmond, Commodore Ashworth and Captain Summers. She'd been nervous when she'd heard that Admiral Soskice had been assigned to head the panel - he was one of her uncle's political enemies - but he'd been professionalism itself during the two days she'd testified before the board. It hadn't really helped, not really. She'd left each session with a pounding headache and the certainty that she would soon be joining Midshipman Clayton Henderson and Midshipwoman Felicity Wheeler in front of the court. She was still surprised that she *hadn't* been arrested shortly after their return to Earth.

"Be seated," Admiral Soskice ordered.

There was a long shuffling as the spectators took their seats. George allowed herself a moment of relief that the media hadn't been invited, although she'd been warned by her advisor that enough of the proceedings had leaked out to spark an intensive media campaign for answers. The only good point, as far as she was concerned, was that her name hadn't been mentioned directly - at least, not yet. She had no idea what Potter had said, when he'd been called to testify, but she had no doubt he would have tried hard to throw her under the bus.

She peered down towards the accused, sitting at the front of the chamber. Henderson looked defiant, even though he *had* to know that the case against him was ironclad; Felicity looked scared, as if she couldn't quite

335

believe what had happened to her. George felt a flicker of sympathy, mixed with a flare of annoyance at the younger girl's stupidity. Air-headed bimbos were *never* interesting, certainly not when they had nothing resembling common sense. Felicity, granted opportunities that were denied to the vast majority of the British population, had seen fit to throw them away for a chimera. And to think it wouldn't have been hard to *check* Henderson's claims...

"The board did not require long to reach a verdict," Soskice said. His voice echoed in the chamber. "Midshipman Clayton Henderson is found guilty of all of the charges levelled against him, including smuggling proscribed substances onboard HMS *Vanguard*, gross dereliction of duty and attempting to cover up said dereliction of duty. His actions posed a serious threat to the battleship's operational health, all the more so as Henderson was aware that *Vanguard* was expected to encounter and engage the enemy.

"We do not feel that this was deliberate treason. There is no evidence that Henderson was in the pay of any foreign power or non-governmental organisation, nor is there any evidence that he saw himself as a lone wolf operator. However, his actions may well have been inadvertently treasonous as *Vanguard* was going to war."

George saw Henderson pale. A charge of treason - even inadvertent treason - would be enough to get him hung. And yet, what he'd done *was* treasonous. Making the mistake was bad enough, but trying to cover it up was worse. Far worse.

"We acknowledge that the graduating class at the Academy was pushed forward to meet the anticipated demands of the war," Soskice continued. "However, all cadets were taught the importance of maintaining starships, the importance of keeping *accurate* records and the dangers of any sort of mood-altering drug. Henderson was not, at any point, *forced* to take the drugs. Indeed, his addiction could have been cured if he'd approached the doctor - a private medical clinic would have sufficed for the purpose, if necessary. The claim that Henderson cannot be blamed for poor decision-making while under the influence does not hold water. Choosing to take the drug, in and of itself, was a very poor decision.

"Furthermore, the lies Henderson told - to his fellow cadets and later to his fellow midshipmen - undermined the integrity of the Royal Navy. We want - we *need* - to believe that our officers and men are honest fellows, men and women of the highest integrity. To lie - to lie in a manner most shameful - cannot fail to cast the reputation of the navy into doubt."

There was a long chilling pause.

"A plea for mercy on account of Henderson's youth was entered by the defence," Soskice said. "We do not find the plea convincing. Four years at the Academy should have taught Henderson the difference between right and wrong. However, as many people who have made significant mistakes have gone on to lead successful lives, we offer Midshipman Henderson a choice. He may spend the next ten years in Colchester Military Detention Centre, if he wishes, or be summarily exiled to a stage-one colony world as a Conscripted Immigrant. In both cases, he will have the chance to make a new life after he has served his time.

"If he doesn't give us an answer by the end of the day, it will be Colchester."

George winced, despite everything Henderson had done. Either way, his life as he knew it was over.

"The case of Midshipwoman Felicity Wheeler was more complex," Soskice said, after a long moment. "There is no question that she made a dangerous mistake by believing Midshipman Henderson's lies. He chose to seduce her - professionally if not sexually - and she chose to believe him. It would have made no difference if Henderson was truly the aristocrat he claimed to be. His actions were against military law and naval regulations and, by supporting him, Midshipwoman Wheeler broke the regulations herself.

"It is never easy to know when one should report a comrade, perhaps a friend, to higher authority," Soskice admitted. "We look poorly on *sneaks* even when the sneak is actually in the right. And once someone has made that first fatal decision, it's easy to make the next decision and the next. We acknowledge that Midshipwoman Wheeler was caught in a tissue of lies and deceptions that left her unsure which way to turn. But we cannot condone her actions."

George braced herself. Whatever was coming, she knew, wasn't going to be pleasant.

"Midshipwoman Wheeler is hereby dishonourably discharged from the Royal Navy," Soskice said. "She will be entitled to pay up until today, as she was more than willing to cooperate to untangle Henderson's web of lies, but nothing else. However, we are prepared to fund her emigration to a colony world, if she wishes it. Emigration may give her a chance to build a whole new life."

Felicity started to cry. George felt another stab of sympathy, even though she couldn't help feeling that Felicity had gotten off lightly. A dishonourable discharge would look very bad on her record, but she wouldn't be spending time in jail...*and* she had the skills to make something of her life, if she wished to try. And going to a whole new world would give her the chance to start afresh...

"This is an uncomfortable chapter in the navy's long history," Soskice concluded, as a pair of marines removed the prisoners. "But we feel that it can now be closed. The court is adjourned."

George sagged, slightly, as the spectators began to clear the room. If the court was now adjourned, did that mean that she was free and clear? Or did it mean that the board had decided that her services on Unity cancelled out her failings? Or...

She felt a tap on her shoulder and glanced up. Lieutenant Johnston was standing there.

"Midshipwoman," he said, as George hastily stood and saluted. "Admiral Fitzwilliam would like to see you in his office."

"Yes, sir," George said. She suppressed a groan with an effort. Her uncle could have waited, couldn't he? A meeting on the estate would have caused far less comment. But he *was* the First Space Lord, after all, and Britain was at war. He might not have *time* to visit the estate before she returned to duty. "I'll see him there at once."

She made her way through the network of corridors until she reached her uncle's office. The marines at the hatch waved her through without comment, something that suggested - very strongly - that her uncle had ordered them to let her through without any security checks. She wasn't sure if she should be relieved or outraged. Nelson Base was an orbital fortress, one of the most secure locations in the world, but there was a *lot* of traffic passing through. A spy might just manage to get through the checkpoints because everyone *knew* it was supposed to be impossible.

"Admiral," she said, as she stepped through the secondary hatch. "Midshipwoman Fitzwilliam, reporting as ordered."

Her uncle studied her for a long moment as the hatch rolled closed. "George," he said, shortly. "Stand at ease."

George relaxed, slightly. This was the man who'd put her on her first pony, the man who'd first inspired her to join the navy, but he was also her superior officer. She knew, all too well, that he wouldn't go lightly on her, just because she was his brother's daughter. He couldn't afford to show any *hint* of nepotism when the country was at war. The Old Boys Network was only tolerated as long as it produced results.

Or a complete absence of disasters, George thought. *We've had too many problems caused by inbred idiots promoted above their competence.*

"It was an interesting trial," her uncle said, after a moment. "It could have been much worse."

"Yes, sir," George said.

"You *did* fuck up," her uncle added. He pointed a long finger at her. "You do understand that, don't you?"

George nodded, slowly. There was no way to avoid it. She'd mismanaged all four of her middies, saving - perhaps - Paula. Henderson and Felicity had been put in front of a court martial, while Potter had sullenly tolerated her authority over the two months it had taken to crawl home. She wasn't responsible for their actions, but she *was* their superior officer. Her first taste of command had been a near disaster.

"Yes, sir," she said. She didn't bother with excuses. They'd never impressed her uncle - or her father - in the past, even when she'd been a little girl. "I made a whole string of mistakes."

"Yes," her uncle said. "The board *did* look at your conduct" - George stiffened - "and considered filing formal charges against you. However, it was decided that your willingness to bite the bullet and report the matter to Commander Mason, even at the cost of your own career, made up for certain lapses in judgement. It was *also* pointed out that you had a raw deal: four new midshipmen, two without any shipboard experience. You didn't have the time to handle everything."

George said nothing. She rather suspected her uncle had already made up his mind.

"There's also the matter of your conduct on Unity itself," her uncle added. "You saved a number of marines from certain death when your shuttle went down, then you fought beside the resistance and eventually captured a number of alien soldiers. There may be some slight...*questions*...about the exact circumstances of the latter, but both the marines and the xenospecialists have recommended you for commendations. You may not get them, but you will have that on your record."

"At least the media didn't get the full story," George muttered.

"Quite," her uncle said. "But don't count on that lasting."

George nodded. Most of the reporters assigned to the task force had been on *New York* when she'd been destroyed, but she had no doubt that some of the crew would talk to the media as soon as they went on leave, if they hadn't already. She was mildly surprised that she hadn't been forced to read a headline reading *NAKED ARISTOCRAT CAPTURES ALIEN STORMTROOPERS*. Aliens, nudity, aristocracy, violence...what more did the tabloids want? She just hoped there hadn't been a camera recording the scene.

She closed her eyes for a long moment, then looked up at her uncle. "What's going to happen to me?"

Her uncle shrugged. "Do you think I exert any influence over promotions boards?"

"You're the First Space Lord," George pointed out. "You must have *some* idea. A crawler on the board might already have decided to toady to you."

"I try to discourage toadies," her uncle said, crossly. "They rarely have anything useful to say."

He met her eyes. "You have two weeks of leave owing, barring accidents," he added, shortly. "Where do you intend to go?"

George frowned. "Anne wants me to visit the estate," she said. It wasn't something she *wanted* to do, but there was no point in refusing. "And then I was going to go on holiday somewhere."

"I suggest you be discreet," her uncle said. George coloured at the unsubtle implication that he knew about Peter Barton. "You don't need more scandal."

He tapped the datapad on the desk, meaningfully. "You can go back to *Vanguard*," he said, "or you can transfer to another ship. I'm not sure if you'll be able to stay as First Middy in any case - *Vanguard* will be receiving new midshipmen after the first set of repairs have been completed. Service on another ship, in any case, will probably help your future career. But there is another option.

"You did well on Unity. And the marines recommended you for one of the more secretive military units under our flag."

George's eyes narrowed. "And they want me for…for what?"

"You'll get the rest of the details once you join, if you do," her uncle said. "Suffice it to say that it involves both ground and space combat. And…well, the odds of getting through the training course are not good."

"And if I choose not to," George said, "what happens?"

"You go back to *Vanguard*," her uncle said. "No one outside a very select group will ever know that the offer was made."

"I didn't like it," George said. "I mean, I didn't like being on the ground."

Her uncle raised his eyebrows. "What happened to the girl who insisted on building her own treehouse and then sleeping in it, when she didn't go on muddy rambles through the estate?"

"I still enjoy the outside world," George said. She coloured at the memory. She'd ruined one of her best dresses on one of those rambles and her mother had *not* been pleased. "But I didn't enjoy the fighting on the ground."

"Not everyone does," her uncle said. "And there is no shame in declining, if you don't feel you are up to it."

"I'd sooner stay on the battleship," George said. She took a long breath. "Can I ask you something? Between you and me?"

Her uncle nodded, curtly.

"When you were an officer," she said. He lifted an eyebrow and she winced. "I meant, when you were a *younger* officer…were you ever tempted to abuse your social rank?"

"I did," her uncle said, flatly. There was a hint of bitter guilt in his voice. "I tried to take command of *Ark Royal*. It was just before the Battle of New Russia, you see. I thought the Old Lady would give me a chance to claim a carrier command, without having to fight for one of the slots on *Formidable* or *Illustrious*. Captain Smith managed to convince his superiors that I didn't know enough about *Ark Royal* to take command. And he was right."

"*Formidable* died at New Russia," George said, quietly.

"She did," her uncle confirmed. "You were born with rank and status, just as I was - but abusing that status is the quickest way to lose it. Either you get removed from command by your superiors or your juniors start resenting you."

He met her eyes. "Why do you ask?"

"I used it," George admitted. It wasn't something she wanted to talk about, but she felt as if she had no choice. "I wanted to put someone in his place. And I did. But it might well have been a mistake."

"It might have been," her uncle agreed. "What I did was *definitely* a mistake. And I had to face up to it when the crunch came."

George nodded, realising what he was trying to say. She had to take responsibility for herself. Using her social rank to put Henderson in his place…mistake or not, she had to take responsibility for it. And, whatever the consequences were, she had to deal with them.

Her uncle sighed. "You have a shuttle flight to London," he said. "You'll be officially on leave from the moment you land at Heathrow. If you want to take up the marine offer, contact them - I'll send you the communications code - within a week; if not, report back to the shipyard when your leave expires. And I suggest you try to stay away from the media."

"Yes, sir," George said. She had the nasty feeling they'd be staking out the estate and anywhere else she might care to go. "I wouldn't want to say a word to them."

"No one with any sense wants to talk to the media," her uncle said. He reached out and shook her hand. "And George, whatever you decide, know that your father and I are very proud of you. You lived up to the finest traditions of the family."

George swallowed, tasting bile. She couldn't help wondering just how much they *knew* about how badly she'd screwed up. Potter would have told the court martial board everything, wouldn't he? Or had he decided that it would be wiser to merely stick to the facts? No one could blame him for that, could they?

But I could have been convicted on the facts alone, she mused, as she saluted and turned towards the hatch. *He didn't even need to lie.*

CHAPTER
FORTY

"There's a more detailed report securely lodged in the datacore," Prince Henry said, as they sipped tea in the First Space Lord's office. "But I can give you the basics right now."

Susan nodded. She'd heard some of the research team's preliminary conclusions during the long flight home, but Prince Henry had been reluctant to discuss anything until they reached Earth and had a chance to compare notes with other xenospecialists. And she'd had too many other problems nursing a battered ship home to worry about it. But now she was curious.

"We think we have the basic story pinned down," Prince Henry continued. "The Foxes are *incredibly* competitive - we think the competitive impulse is deeply ingrained into their very being. They formed factions that warred with other factions, each of which had sub-factions that warred together to gain political control. Factions that lost would be absorbed into the victors, only to see the victors split up as new conflicts emerged. We think they were actually fighting Flower Wars - if you'll excuse the expression - for the longest time. War had actually become *ritual.*"

Susan leaned forward. "Flower Wars?"

"The Aztecs used to fight ritualised wars with their subject states," the First Space Lord said quietly. "They were really nothing more than an excuse to blood warriors and capture prisoners for sacrifice. Naturally, their subjects resented it hugely...which is why so many of them sided with the Spanish when they arrived."

"Yes, sir," Prince Henry said.

"What we think happened, eventually, was an interplanetary war that actually threatened their entire civilisation," he said. "We don't have many details and almost all of what we *do* have are nothing more than rumours, repeated amongst both Foxes and Cows. What *is* certain is that one faction managed to build an STL colony ship and flee to another star system. Much to their surprise, they discovered another alien race living there."

"The Cows," the First Space Lord said.

"Correct," Prince Henry said. "The Cows were apparently defenceless, so they got squashed rapidly. They couldn't integrate completely into the predominant social structure for biological reasons, so they ended up filling a different set of roles. Over the years, the two races merged as closely as possible. Their society makes extensive use of both races, to the point where it's a genuine union. They effectively share power and authority."

He shrugged. "The Foxes can't resist a challenge," he added. "It's how they sort out their pecking order. When the Contact Fleet arrived in UXS-469, they attacked; judging us weak, they continued the attacks. I don't know if they *realised* that they were facing two races, rather than one, but I doubt it would have mattered. The challenge was all that mattered to them."

Susan leaned forward. "Let me get this straight," she said. "They beat the crap out of us at UXS-469, so they expected us to roll over and surrender?"

"Basically," Prince Henry agreed. "And when we refused to surrender, they just continued the war. They're locked into it now."

The First Space Lord cleared his throat. "Can we talk to them?"

"Yes and no," Prince Henry said. "We can speak to them in their own language now, but I doubt we can convince them to surrender - or even come to terms - without battering them senseless. The good news is that if we convince them that they've lost, they will surrender; the bad news is that getting them to that point will not be easy."

"Of course not," Susan mused. "They need to *feel* defeated, right?"

"We believe so," Prince Henry said. "They know, very well, that losing a battle does not mean losing a war."

"And they have advantages," Susan said. "Their FTL communications device, for one."

"Yes, Captain," Prince Henry said. "I'm afraid we still haven't cracked that particular puzzle."

The First Space Lord tapped the table. "So we have no choice, but to continue the war," he said. "There's no hope of making peace."

"We reinforce Unity, sir, then attack upwards towards Alien-One," Susan said. "It will give us our best chance to convince them that they've lost."

"It should work, sir," Prince Henry agreed. "If nothing else, it might well cause splits amongst the two races."

Susan's eyes narrowed. "Why?"

"We have fewer Cows to study," Prince Henry said. "But we think, however, that they are less wedded to the concept of throwing bricks at wasp nests. There's a certain .. solidity about them that the Foxes seem to lack. It's possible that they might turn on the Foxes if they think the costs of continuing the war will be too high."

"But you don't *know*," the First Space Lord said.

"No, sir," Prince Henry said. "We're dealing with aliens - and realistically, our ability to predict what our fellow humans will do isn't *that* good. People tend to jump in unexpected directions. But if nothing else, going on the offensive - properly on the offensive - will give us the chance to put an end to the war before it's too late."

"I'll have to discuss it with others," the First Space Lord said.

He cleared his throat. "Captain Onarina, I would like to compliment you on your success during Operation Unity," he continued, his tone markedly more formal. "Your actions were in the finest traditions of the Royal Navy, particularly after you were forced to assume command of the entire squadron. I do not believe that any concerns have been raised about your conduct."

Susan nodded. "Thank you, sir."

"*Vanguard* will, of course, require time in the yards," the First Space Lord added. "I'd prefer it if you were to make yourself available to the analysts on Nelson Base. They are still crunching the data, but they could make use of your perspective."

"I understand, sir," Susan said. Mason was not going to be pleased, but she knew better than to think it was a *request*. "I'm due to attend the funeral ceremony at Arlington tomorrow for *New York* and her crew, visiting my father on the way, but after that I will be happy to transfer to Nelson Base."

"Admiral Harper's death was a shame," the First Space Lord said. "He deserved better."

"Yes, sir," Susan said. She had no doubt that her career would have gone straight into the crapper, if Harper had made a fuss about her assumption of command during the first catastrophic battle. "He was a good man."

And so were his crew, she thought, privately. *None of them deserved to die like that.*

"He was," the First Space Lord agreed. He gave her a tired smile. "Before you go, you should know that both Henderson and Wheeler requested to emigrate from Earth."

Susan nodded, slowly. She hadn't expected anything else, at least not from Henderson. The odds of surviving ten years in Colchester were low, particularly for someone accused of borderline treason. One of the inmates would stick a knife between his ribs if he wasn't kept in solitary confinement, yet the guards couldn't be relied upon to do what it took to protect him. They'd hate Henderson too. But Wheeler...

The girl had promise, she told herself, sharply. *But she chose to throw it away.*

It felt like a personal failure. She knew, deep inside, that it would *always* feel like a personal failure. She'd been Felicity Wheeler's commanding officer. There would never be a time when she didn't ask herself, deep inside, if there was something she could have done. But she knew, no matter how much she wished to deny it, that Felicity had dug her own grave. The navy had trained her, the navy had *trusted* her...

...And she'd let the navy down.

Vanguard would need new middies, she thought. Both Simon Potter and Paula Spurgeon had requested and received transfers off *Vanguard*, rather than staying on the battleship. Susan wasn't too sorry to see the back of Simon Potter - Mason's reports hadn't made him sound like a very good person - but Paula Spurgeon had been considered reliable. And if she'd stayed, despite…*irregularities* in her past, she might well have been First Middy. George Fitzwilliam simply didn't have the seniority any longer.

"Thank you, sir," she said, finally.

The First Space Lord nodded. "Dismissed, Captain," he said. "And, once again, well done."

Susan rose and took her leave.

————

The First Space Lord waited until Prince Henry had also left, then he keyed a specific code into his console. Moments later, one of the partitions slid back to reveal a hidden door, concealed behind a painting of *Ark Royal*. His predecessor had had a surprising sense of the dramatic, Admiral Sir James Montrose Fitzwilliam had always thought, but he had to admit that the secret passageways could be useful. There were some secrets that even his aides weren't privy to.

Paula Spurgeon stepped through the hatch, her long blonde hair tied back in a bun. She was still wearing her middy's uniform, James noted, but she'd been careful to remove her ship's name and anything else that might link her to *Vanguard*. Perhaps she was being paranoid, he thought, yet some secrets could only remain secret if only a handful of people knew them. If her identity became common knowledge, she wouldn't be anything like as effective.

"Commander," he said. "I trust you enjoyed your voyage?"

"It was interesting," Commander Paula Spurgeon, Royal Navy Intelligence, said. "I actually quite enjoyed some parts of it. Pretending to be young again…"

She smiled, rather thinly. "Your niece is learning," she added. "Maybe not as quickly as you would prefer, but she *is* learning."

"I'm glad to hear it," James said. "But she wasn't who I asked you to watch."

Paula nodded. "As per orders," she said, her tone markedly more formal, "I kept a close eye on Captain Onarina and her crew. There was no evidence that they were up to anything beyond the normal duties expected of a naval crew. I was unable to eavesdrop on some of their more private conversations, but there were no hints of conspiracy or any plan to either subvert Admiral Harper's command or mutiny against the crown. Captain Onarina comported herself as a commanding officer should."

"That's a relief," James said. He hadn't *wanted* to assign a watchdog to *Vanguard's* crew, but a number of his people had insisted. There was no escaping the fact that Captain Onarina *had* committed mutiny, even if it *was* in a good cause. "Do you feel it's worth continuing the surveillance?"

"I don't believe so," Paula said. "I would have expected her to exclude Granger and the other newcomers from her conferences, if there was a conspiracy underway. She did not, despite the fact that Granger was not her first choice for tactical officer. The ship endured problems, of course, but none of them can reasonably be blamed on her."

She shook her head. "In short, every instinct I have tells me that Captain Onarina may be willing to bend the rulebook a few times, but she isn't plotting another mutiny - or worse."

James nodded. "Did you come close to being detected?"

"Perhaps," Paula said. "Your niece did seem to think there was something odd about me, even though I did - eventually - give her the cover story. My decision to surrender the wardroom to her probably looked a little odd."

"It would have done," James agreed. No midshipman with dreams of wearing a lieutenant's uniform would ever meekly surrender the wardroom. "But she didn't ask too many questions?"

"None," Paula said. "Really, she was too busy riding herd on Potter. The boy is a complete spoiled arse."

"No doubt," James said.

He cleared his throat. "I'll expect your full report by the end of the week," he added. "Until then, dismissed."

Paula saluted, then left the room. James watched the hidden hatch slide back into place, then keyed his console. If there was nothing wrong with *Vanguard* and her crew, it was time to start planning for offensive operations of his own.

The hatch opened. Commodore John Naiser and Captain Juliet Watson-Stewart stepped into the compartment. James rose to his feet to greet them, accepting their salutes before shaking their hands. The man who had built *Vanguard* - and the woman who had revolutionised tramline theory - deserved more than a little respect.

"John," he said, as he motioned for them to sit. "How's the husband?"

"We're doing fine," Naiser said. "Philip is currently looking for a tutoring post, after we were called back to Earth."

"I may know someone in need of a tutor," James said, as his aide brought a tray of tea and biscuits. "I'll put in a good word for him, if you like.

He accepted a cup of tea, then waited for his aide to leave before continuing. "I assume you've read the reports from Unity and Tadpole-45?"

"Yes, sir," Naiser said. "They were very detailed."

"We may have a theory to account for their FTL communications," Juliet said. Her voice was very quiet, even though married life had given her more self-confidence. "We know that it's possible to vibrate the tramlines. They may have a way to cause them to resonate at a distance."

James frowned. "How is that even *possible*?"

"The tramlines do react to gravity wells," Juliet said. "And we know it is possible to generate a pseudo-gravity field. They may have a way to use one to send messages down a tramline."

"But we don't know how," Naiser said, quickly.

"Not yet," Juliet said. "We can and we will unlock the secret, Admiral."

"Glad to hear it," James said. "It so happens that we might have a way to give the aliens a good hard kick up the arse. If, of course, we can get political clearance to proceed. But it will require some new hardware from you.

"And if Prince Henry is right," he added, "one good hard kick up the arse is all we will need."

End of Book Two
HMS Vanguard will return in:
We Lead
Coming Soon

Coming Soon From Chris Kennedy!

THE DARK
STAR WAR

CHAPTER
ONE

Bridge, *Harvest of Flesh*, Sssellississ System, December 12, 2021

All eyes turned toward Calvin as he strode onto the bridge of the Ssselipsssiss ship. Although he'd been onboard for over a week, Terran time, it was the first time he'd been allowed on the bridge. Or pretty much anywhere else. Considering the lizard-like creatures had invited, no, demanded Calvin come with them, they really weren't making him feel very welcome. None of the Ssselipsssiss said a word; the only sound was a hiss from the lizard sitting in the central chair.

Calvin's only companion during the journey had been the Aesir Farhome, with infrequent visits from Ssselipsssiss Ambassador Gresss. The elf-like Farhome was only partly sane, on a good day; he was not the best traveling companion. After a week, Calvin was starting to doubt his own sanity.

Lieutenant Commander Shawn Hobbs, or 'Calvin' to his friends, still wasn't sure why he was even *on* the disgustingly-named battleship. Certainly, he was a hostage the Ssselipsssiss were using to make sure the crew of Calvin's ship, the Terran Space Ship (TSS) *Vella Gulf*, didn't bring a Mrowry invasion force with them when they returned. The lizards had already lost most of their territory in the current war, including their capital, and they were desperately clinging to their last few systems. A Mrowry invasion would have wiped them out.

Based on what Calvin had seen so far, though, it didn't look like the Ssselipsssiss would be able to hold their remaining systems without outside help. Given that they'd fired on the Terrans unprovoked the first time the two races met, Calvin wasn't sure that their annihilation was such a bad idea.

Unless their enemy was worse and, in this case, it looked like it was.

Based on the enemy's tactics, it appeared the Ssselipsssiss were fighting the same alien race, the Shaitans, that the Terrans were. If so, the Ssselipsssiss could almost be seen as Terra's friends. Well, probably not 'friends,' but maybe they could be considered allies…at least until their war with the Shaitans ended.

The Terrans and the Ssselipsssiss would probably have to redefine their relationship after the war, assuming they were both still around. That appeared unlikely, as no one had been able to stop the Shaitans' advance; so far, the best the Terrans had been able to achieve was a stalemate with them in the Aesir's home system.

The Shaitan race lived in another universe and only jumped into the Terran universe to fight. The ability to jump back to their own universe made them hard to fight, because the Shaitans could determine where and when to accept battle. The fact that they had weapons which distorted time also caused…issues.

"I think what Captain Skrelleth meant," Ambassador Gresss said, "was, 'Welcome to the bridge.'" At seven and a half feet tall, the ambassador was an impressive sight. Maroon in color, the bipedal lizard wore a red velvet robe with black trim, along with what looked like black stretch pants. The robe had a small golden patch on the left side that announced his ambassadorial rank, as well as a large amount of gold jewelry around his neck and wrists.

The ship's captain turned to glare at Calvin, his eyes glowing like the ends of two lit cigarettes. He hissed again and said, "What the captain really meant was, 'Your presence pollutes the sanctity of my vessel and is an affront to everything I feel is good and holy.'"

"Out of curiosity, Captain Skrelleth, how many times have you fought the enemy?" Calvin asked.

"I have fought them twice," the captain replied.

"I see," Calvin said. "And how many of their ships did you destroy in those encounters?"

"We haven't been able to destroy any of them," Captain Skrelleth admitted, "although we did get a couple of laser hits on one last time. We were close to destroying it, but then it disappeared."

Calvin nodded his head. "And during those two battles, how many ships did you lose?'

"We lost nine ships, including four battleships," the captain said.

"And your capital planet?"

"Yesss. It fell in the last battle. Its loss was unavoidable."

"So let me get this straight, captain. You've lost nine ships in two battles, your capital planet has been captured by the enemy and you have only succeeded in *hitting* an enemy ship twice. You didn't destroy two ships; you just scored two hits on a single enemy ship. Is that correct?"

Captain Skrelleth hissed. "Yesss, that is correct, but that is because they are able to vanish. We can't get them to fight us."

"You want the enemy to fight on your terms, when theirs are working so well?" Calvin asked. He turned to the ambassador. "I think I've found your problem."

"Careful, Terran," the captain warned, jumping from his seat. He was even larger than the ambassador, standing nearly eight feet high. He pointed a claw at Calvin, his tail twitching. "Another word about me, and I will be forced to kill you, despite what protection the ambassador offers you. Be *very* careful about what you say next."

Calvin turned back to the ship's commanding officer. "I do not mean to be disrespectful, but my point is, so far, your race is losing this war. Badly. Not only are you losing, you are being systematically eliminated as a race. At the moment, the only way you can stay alive is to run from them; every time you fight you lose."

"What do you expect?" Captain Skrelleth asked. "They can disappear at will and pop up and hit us with weapons we can't defend against. I suppose *you* can do better against them?"

"Absolutely," Calvin said. "I have fought them twice, and I have destroyed two of their ships. The second time, we boarded the ship and fought them hand-to-hand, prior to setting explosive charges which we detonated once we were clear. Can we do better? *We already have.*"

"*You* boarded one of their ships?" the CO asked. "I do not see how this is possible."

"Yes, I led a team that boarded one of their vessels. If we are fighting the same enemy, which I think we are, I have not only been aboard one of their ships, but I have fought them up close. I tell you this not to brag, but so you will see me as an asset to use in your fight against the Shaitans and, hopefully, treat me with a little more respect. I can help you, if you will let me."

Captain Skrelleth shook his head, retreated to his command chair and sat down. He turned his gaze to the view screen, which showed a chart of the system. After a few moments, the twitching of his tail slowed. When he spoke, his voice was calm and under control. "I do not like you, nor do I want you onboard my ship," he said; "however, if you have information on how to defeat the enemy, I am willing to listen."

"We could fight them better if my ship were here," Calvin said, "but there *are* some things I would recommend to help defend this system." He paused to look at the view screen. "Is that status correct?"

"Yesss, that is everything we have in the system, and where it currently is positioned."

Damn; the lizards were even worse off than he had thought. "Is there any reason why all your ships are around the planet?" Calvin asked.

"The enemy could appear anywhere, and we must protect the planet," Captain Skrelleth answered. "We only have three planets left; we cannot afford to lose this one."

"The enemy's forces can't appear anywhere," Calvin corrected; "they have to use the stargate to come into the system. If you position your ships around the stargate, and mine it with everything you've got, you will stand a better chance of keeping them out. If nothing else, at least you will get a chance to shoot at them before they can jump to their own universe."

"Do you *know* that to be truth, or are you just guessing?" the captain asked. "You are asking me to leave the planet undefended. We *cannot* lose it."

Calvin paused a few seconds, debating whether to tell his enemies everything he knew. Giving away your own capabilities to a culture that would rather eat you than talk to you was…complicated. He sighed. In for a penny; in for a pound.

"I know this to be true. I have been to their universe; they do not have stargates there."

Captain Skrelleth's eyes snapped around to glare at the ambassador. "The Terran has been to their universe? Why I was not made aware of this?"

Ambassador Gresss made a shooing motion with his hands. "I have told you several times that the Terran had information on the enemy and urged you to talk to him. We would be better prepared right now if you had listened to me."

"You talk too much," Captain Skrelleth replied. "You politicians always talk too much. How was I to know that this time you actually had something useful to say?"

"What's important is I *have* been to the other universe," Calvin said. "I know they don't have stargates, so they have to use the ones in our universe. When they come through, there will be a few moments while their systems stabilize when you can shoot them. System entry is your best, and probably your only, chance to defeat them. Once they get loose and can jump to their own universe they are very hard to bring to battle…as you have already found out."

The captain scratched a scar on his shoulder while he looked at the display. "Sometime, you will have to tell me how you were able to travel to the universe of the enemy," he said. "I would dearly like to fight there and have the wreckage of their ships fall onto *their* planets." He turned back to Calvin. "I take it we cannot do it without some sort of equipment that is only aboard your ship?"

"Unfortunately, that is true," Calvin admitted. "I wish we could jump this ship to their universe, but it isn't possible. We will have to fight them here."

"If that is the case, do you have any other suggestions for how to fight them?"

"You have to fight them at the stargate. Move every ship you have to the gate and put every mine you have in front of it, set to detonate automatically when a ship comes within range. You *have* to stop them there; if you don't, I don't think you can hold this universe against a massed assault."

"Perhaps you are more than just prey, after all," Captain Skrelleth said, his gaze returning to the status display. "I will do as you suggest, Terran, but you better not have lied to me. If I find out you have, I will kill you myself, before the enemy has a chance."

"It's in my own best interest for you to be victorious," said Calvin. "Here are some other things you can do..."

Visitor's Quarters, *Harvest of Flesh*, Sssellississ System, December 12, 2021

"So you finally met our host?" Esdren Farhome asked. The Aesir had the dark hair and pale blue skin typical of a Drow, the belowground-dwelling Aesir. Tall and thin, he also had the pointed ears typical of the elven race.

That was his normal appearance, anyway. Farhome was also an Eco Warrior, an elite soldier who could manipulate matter at the microscopic level using nanobots. His specialty was life, and he could use his nanobots to change a living being's size and shape, including his own.

Although Farhome's sanity was questionable most days, today seemed to be a good day. "Yeah, he's every bit the fun-loving Ssselipsssiss you would expect him to be," Calvin replied. "After he decided he wasn't going to kill me and eat me, he actually listened to some of my advice. They are going to move to the stargate and try to hold there."

"Well, you do have more experience fighting the Shaitans than any-one else," Farhome replied. He cocked his head and added, "On second thought, the Ssselipsssiss may have more experience *fighting* them, but you have more experience actually beating them."

"I'm happy Skrelleth listened to me," Calvin said, "but that doesn't mean we have a chance. I saw their status board. In addition to this battle-ship, there are only four more ships in the system. They have two battle-ships, two battlecruisers and a cruiser. That's it."

"That's all they have?" Farhome asked, wonder tinging his voice. "This is the front line. When we left Keppler 62, there were only two cruisers left in the system, and that is their other front line against the Mrowry. If what you say is true, they are down to their final seven ships."

"Yeah, that's it. If they lose this next battle here, they are pretty much done as a race. There won't be anything to keep the Shaitans from rolling up their last couple of systems and exterminating them."

"They need to mine the stargate," Farhome said. "Maybe tow an asteroid or 10 in front of it, too. They can't let the Shaitans into the system." He paused for a second, then asked, "How soon can we expect the *Vella Gulf* to get—"

The door to their room opened, and a low-ranking Ssselipsssiss entered. "It'sss started," he announced. "The enemy isss through the gate. Captain Skrelleth demandsss you attend him on the bridge."

Calvin turned back to Farhome. "Not soon enough."

CHAPTER
TWO

Emperor Yazhak the Third's Estate, Grrrnow, 61 Virginis, December 12, 2021

Emperor Yazhak turned away from the large bay window. Behind him, a large rock formation could be seen several miles away. The massive sandstone monolith glowed red in the morning sun.

"That is worse than I feared," the large felinoid finally said.

"Why is that?" Captain James Sheppard, the commanding officer of the Terran ship *Vella Gulf*, asked.

"We have guessed for some time the Ssselipsssiss were fighting another race, and they were probably losing. Although we have been at war with them for some time, they recently began pushing us hard. It was like they *had* to break through; there was a desperation we had never seen before. Then, all of a sudden, they stopped. Although a welcome respite, the absence of war was eerie; we wondered what new stratagem they might be working on."

"And now we know they stopped attacking because they're out of ships," Captain Sheppard interjected. When he had taken the *Vella Gulf* into their territory, the lizards only had three ships guarding their side of the stargate…and only one was battleship-sized.

"That worries me even more," the emperor continued. "If their enemy is strong enough to destroy their entire fleet, something we were never able to do, I am worried about who they will attack once they are finished with the Ssselipsssiss. Our territory is next, unless they advance on Terra."

"Which isn't a great choice in my book," Captain Sheppard said.

"Not only has their enemy destroyed the Ssselipsssiss fleet, they also seem to be taking the planets just as fast," Lieutenant Rrower added. The young Mrowry was his civilization's liaison to the *Vella Gulf*. "I saw one of their maps, grandfather, and they have lost their capital planet; they only have three systems remaining."

"Based on your conversation with them, you believe their enemy to be the Shaitans you fought at Golirion?" Emperor Yazhak asked.

"Yes, it sounds like them," Captain Sheppard answered. "Their ships can jump out of our universe, and they use time-based weapons. If it isn't the Shaitans, it is a race nearly identical to them. Personally, I hope it *is* them; I don't think we can afford to be fighting two of them at the same time; one is more than enough!"

"Truth," the emperor agreed. "So, what did the Ssselipsssiss want?"

"They want us to go to the Shaitans' home world and blow it up."

"Well, that seems simple enough," Emperor Yazhak said with a chuckle. "Did they have any information on where this planet might be, and how you were supposed to destroy it?"

"They have an idea where it is," Captain Sheppard replied. "It's a long way behind enemy lines, and getting further as the Shaitans advance. As for how we blow it up, I don't think they care; they just want it done. They are desperate for a little breathing room."

"What did they offer for taking on this mission?"

"They were very vague on what they would, or even what they could, do," Captain Sheppard replied. "We got an awful lot of 'maybes,' but nothing very definite." He shook his head. "We didn't see a replicator in the system where we met with them, and they have lost most of their other systems. Honestly, I don't think they have much to give. Our choice is pretty simple—we can either help them out of the goodness of our hearts, or we can watch them be exterminated."

"A few months ago, I'm not sure I would have minded watching them go," Captain Paul 'Night' Train interjected. The Terran Space Marine captain was the executive officer of the platoon Calvin commanded. "However, the Shaitans are a much worse enemy…and the Ssselipsssiss are holding Lieutenant Commander Hobbs hostage until we return."

"Ah, I see," the emperor said. "I wondered where he was but was afraid to ask in case he'd been killed."

"No, he was fine the last time we saw him," Captain Sheppard explained, "but the Ssselipsssiss held onto him for fear we would return with a large Mrowry fleet and wipe them out. I think they were worried you would attack from this side if you knew how poorly defended their side of the stargate was."

"There is something to be said for that," the emperor replied, scratching his chin. "I certainly would like to get Typhon back from them… Don't worry, I'm not going to," he added when he saw the Terrans bristle. "Calvin has done just as much for us; I am not going to blithely sacrifice him. Besides, you don't win wars by throwing away your hero spirits; you win wars by supporting them. Calvin must have approved of helping them, or he wouldn't have stayed with the Ssselipsssiss?"

"Yes, he did," Captain Sheppard replied. "He also believes the Shaitans are the greater enemy; he stayed both as a hostage and to help the Ssselipsssiss with their defenses. Although the lizzies have been fighting the Shaitans for a while, they don't really have much of a clue as to how to fight them. The enemy is so different from what they're used to, the only thing the Ssselipsssiss have been good at is losing. Calvin is going to try to shore up their defenses; maybe it will buy them some time."

Bridge, *Harvest of Flesh*, Ssellississ System, December 12, 2021

"The enemy is here, Terran," Captain Skrelleth announced as Calvin walked onto the bridge. Calvin had put on his aviator's space suit, but carried the helmet under an arm.

"What is the status, sir?"

"As you indicated would happen, the enemy vessels came through the portal and immediately disappeared."

"Yes sir, they jumped back to their own universe."

"Whatever. The fact remains that they are loose in this system. I have told the other ships' captains to return to orbit. We cannot allow this planet to fall. There are more of my race here than the other two systems combined. We must hold."

"How many enemy ships are there?"

"At least three of the cruiser-sized vessels and four of the destroyer-sized vessels entered the system. I know from experience all of them carry their time-based weapons."

"Damn," Calvin said, shaking his head. "That's more than I've seen at one time. What defenses does the planet have?"

"Not much," Captain Skrelleth said; "however, the moon has both missile and laser systems on its surface. We also have a few orbital missile pods we can use. By pulling all of our forces back to orbit, it will limit the number of directions from which the enemy can attack and will concentrate our defenses to where we can hopefully get some shots at them."

"Gate emergence!" one of the Ssselipsssiss technicians exclaimed. "It is a type of ship I haven't seen before. It is battleship-sized. There is a second one...now a third."

"Images on screen," the captain ordered.

"Coming up now, sir!" the same technician replied.

The front viewer changed to show a shape Calvin recognized. "That isn't a battleship," he advised; "it is a Jotunn *Raptor*-class battlecruiser."

"Jotunn?" Captain Skrelleth asked. "What is a Jotunn and what are the capabilities of their ships?"

"The Jotunn is a race of giant-sized humanoids, nearly three times my size. Their vessels are over-sized, as you can see. They are very strong, and their weapons are quite powerful."

"How will they attack?"

"I have fought a combined battlegroup of Shaitans and Jotunn before. The Jotunn don't believe in finesse; they will come straight at you and try to destroy your biggest vessels first. Meanwhile, the Shaitans will hover on the edges of the battle, picking off your most vulnerable ships. If they can separate a ship from the group, they will destroy it before coming back to pick off another one."

"Just like a pack of colvargs," the captain replied.

"I don't know what those are," Calvin replied, "but their tactics are very effective. It will be difficult to win this fight." Difficult? Calvin shook his head. This battle was unwinnable. After all he'd been through, he was going to die on a lizard ship.

"How can we defeat this joint assault?" Captain Skrelleth asked.

"As much as it hurts me to say it," Calvin said, "you need to write off this planet and pull back to the next one. That way, you can fight them one at a time as they come through the stargate—"

"Unacceptable," Captain Skrelleth interrupted. "The planet must be saved."

"You can't win this battle!" Calvin exclaimed. "You may destroy some of their ships, but you are outclassed; in the end, your ships will be destroyed, and the remaining enemy ships will have free rein to do whatever they wish with the planet. The only chance you have is to save the two planets you have remaining. Perhaps some of the civilians there can be pulled back to a Terran or Mrowry planet and resettled there, ensuring the continuity of your race. Whatever you do, though, you've *got* to withdraw. *You can't win this fight!*"

"If this fight is unwinnable, then we will die," the captain said. "This ship was built on the planet below, and most of us have families there. *We will not leave them behind.* We will stand and fight, dying if we must, but we *will* win in the end. We have to; our families are counting on us, and we can do no lessss." He pushed a button and the tactical plot reappeared on the front screen. "We will stand and fight."

ADMIRAL'S GAMBIT

(SPINEWARD SECTORS SERIES,

BOOK TWO OF TEN)

JOSHUA WACHTER

CHAPTER 1:
CATCHING UP

My name is Jason Montagne Vekna, although I'm not sure if my new wife agrees with that or thinks my new last name should be Zosime. It's a long story. I never really cared for the 'Vekna' part, so it wouldn't be any skin off my nose to switch it out but it might cause problems back on the home world, and we had plenty of those right now. So I was deliberately not asking her opinion.

Anyway, I'm currently the Admiral of the ever-so-proudly named Confederation Multi-Sector Patrol Fleet, or MSP as I like to call it. Of course, I'm only an Honorary Admiral in my home world's SDF or System Defense Force, and was forwarded to be the Acting Admiral of the MSP. But I try not to tell anyone about that little technicality.

One week ago, the Imperial Admiral in command of the MSP resigned on orders from his Triumvir, and the Empire as a whole abandoned the eight Confederation Sectors comprising what we natives like to call 'The Spine,' or 'The Spineward Sectors.'

Before becoming the official figurehead of the MSP nine months ago, I was a minor member of a nearly irrelevant Provincial Dynasty. The Royal Family on my home world answered to the Caprian Parliament, not the other way around, and the Parliament held our purse strings. So generally, we acted as some sort of glorified galactic butlers, wining and dining anyone Parliament needed to impress or fob off in an appropriately decedent style.

Before leaving, Rear Admiral Arnold Janeski of the Imperial Rim fleet turned command over to me and I proceeded to…well, I picked up a pirate ship or three - again, a long story.

I also saved a beautiful native woman from horrible space-faring Bugs. Unfortunately, I was busy ogling her half-naked neighbor and there was a cultural misunderstanding. She thought that by giving her a sword with which to cut herself and the rest of the Bug prisoners free (coincidentally, including her busty neighbor) that I was proposing some form of shotgun marriage wherein if she didn't take my sword and accept my offer of marriage, she and everyone else would die a gruesome death.

I, on the other hand, had no clue about this and was only trying to do the heroic thing. In other words, I had given her my only weapon and, as a result, was being slowly overwhelmed by ravenous insects. The very same ones that were trying to eat us all alive, regardless of potential or real wardrobe malfunctions.

It's safe to say that as far as romantic meetings go, it was hate at first sight. She wanted me dead, and as far as I was concerned, she had let other people die and even tried to kill me by deliberately not lifting a finger to help anyone, all after I gave her my only sword.

A series of further misunderstandings followed, but when I found out that a quarter of a million settlers I had rescued couldn't land on her planet without local permission, and couldn't stay in orbit without dying of suffocation…well, let's just say I decided to go through with the marriage anyway.

By this point, we were both generally aware of the situation, and still feeling things (if not each other) out. She was no longer trying to kill me, at least. Instead, she was now determined that I survive long enough to 'fulfill my obligations,' which I took to mean I needed to save the entire population of her world from being eaten by semi-intelligent (and officially non-sentient, according to the Empire's propaganda machine) space-faring Bugs in slow-drive ships.

After that, I assumed she planned to dump me like a bad habit. I was just hoping it happened before she met my mother so I could sweep the whole thing under the rug. As it was, she had recruited around eighteen hundred super-sized native warriors to my 'banner,' although they sure seemed to listen to her a lot more than me, and she was determined to stick to my side like glue at this point.

In the meantime, I had a Fleet consisting of one ship because, as far as I knew, in the two weeks since everything else had fallen apart, the fleet had fallen apart too and returned home, each ship determined to protect its own home world rather than uphold its obligations to the Confederacy's charter of mutual defense. This mass egress left no one to prevent piracy, or protect merchants and other civilian ships. Like the ones carrying the quarter of a million settlers we had rescued from pirates.

CHAPTER 5:
INTO THE FRAY!

Soon our plan was in motion and the pirate cruiser separated from our hull. Behind it was a small swarm of shuttles filled with newly minted Lancers; barely trained to walk in their power armor without falling down, hiding in its shadow and thirsty for blood. Who said putting a man that Parliament considered a Royalist Fanatic (like the Lancer Colonel) in command of a bunch of clueless but bloodthirsty natives was a bad idea?

As for myself, I was starting to have second thoughts. Particularly when word reached me that Akantha was on one of those shuttles.

I heard it was a feeding frenzy down there as Lancers argued over who should have the first chance at action. She must have gone down and gotten caught up in all the excitement. The longer I knew her, the more savage she seemed to become.

But there was no way to recall the shuttles without tipping our hand, so I was left with nothing but worry. I told myself it was only for the Settlers back on Tracto VI, the people who might lose their homes if she died. I even believed myself for once. But all of my rationalizations didn't get rid of the small aching pit in my stomach at the sight of her going into a battle I would be helpless to join. Not unless things went very wrong and I finished with the Imperials first.

We'd actually timed things so that even though we had the farthest to go, the *Lucky Clover* would get within range of the Imperial Cruiser first. Hopefully, the whole system would be focused on the little drama playing out around the fleet of Constructor ships, buying crucial seconds for the small fleet of shuttles carrying my wife and nearly six hundred armed and angry (did I mention power-armored?) Lancers.

Because there had been so many volunteers, the Lancer Colonel had stationed another group of six hundred Lancers on the hull of the pirate ship, just in case reinforcements were needed somewhere along the way. In total, about half my Lancer force of twenty four hundred was deployed on this little side mission.

I still had about twelve hundred untrained Lancers, many of them former Promethean settlers who weren't as enthusiastic about attacking their former countrymen. Even if those same countrymen had left their settler brothers and sisters to die in cold space.

I wouldn't say the new Promethean Lancers were particularly forgiving about the situation, but I think the thought of facing a cousin, friend or someone you knew, just because they happened to serve under an awful captain, probably made them less eager to get out there and mix it up than they otherwise might have been.

Now there was nothing to do but wait. Did I mention that I hate waiting? Watching our ship creep closer and closer to the Imperial, and switching back and forth to watch the same thing happen with the Promethean Medium Cruisers, was maddening.

"We're getting close enough to the Imperial that they are bound to notice-" Officer Tremblay started.

"We're being hailed by the Imperial Strike Cruiser," exclaimed the Ex-Com Tech. "They're demanding we back off or they'll blow the Constructors."

"Put the Imperials on screen," I instructed, ready for battle.

"You're live, Admiral," said the Ex-Com tech.

I straightened myself in the Throne. "Unidentified vessel, this is MSP *Lucky Clover*, Admiral Jason Montagne commanding. Identify yourself or be destroyed," I said in my most imperious tone.

The First Officer's head whipped around. "This isn't part of the script," he whispered hoarsely.

I smiled grimly, maintaining focus on the main screen's pickup point.

A tall, white-skinned man with well-bred Imperial features appeared on the screen. "Move that filthy old space bucket away from my ship or the Constructors get it," said the man, "Imperial Commander Marcus Cornwallis, out."

"Marcus Cornwallis, of the same Cornwallis's as Rear Admiral Charles Cornwallis," I demanded, deliberately hardening my face.

"I won't warn you again," said the Imperial Officer with cool professionalism.

"A man of the same family who bombarded my home world fifty years ago," I continued, deliberately raising my voice, "in the process, killing my father and most of my extended family? That Cornwallis," by this time, I was shouting at the screen.

The first crack appeared in the Imperial Commander's features. "I don't know what you are referring to but, let me assure you, familias inside the Empire do not direct the actions of its naval vessels."

"So you admit it," I exclaimed, finding myself dangerously close to the line between playing a character and becoming actually enraged. I suppose coming face-to-face with a member of the family directly responsible for my own's near-complete destruction was enough to blur certain lines.

The Imperial Commander looked nonplused, "Don't you understand? Back off, or I'll blow the Constructors to kingdom come," he said smugly, as though speaking to a child.

"To Hades with the Constructors!" I was absolutely livid, and leapt out of my chair. "Helmsman," I barked, turning to that section of the bridge, "set a course to put us between the Imperial Cruiser and the Constructor." I then turned toward the tactical section. "First Officer, instruct gunnery to fire as she bears. I want one broadside firing at the Imperials and another into the Constructors," I roared, feeling the veins in my neck and forehead bulging. Turning back to the Imperial Commander, who was looking at me like one would a crazy person, I sneered, "I'd rather see them destroyed than fall into the hands of a Cornwallis!"

"You're insane," exclaimed the Imperial Commander, turning to someone outside the main pick up. "Communications, get me System Command and tell that moron LeGodat to warn off this crazy person before I'm forced to destroy his ship," said the Imperial Commander, speaking quickly and looking suddenly red-faced.

"LeGodat and his simplistic, we-all-have-to-go-along-to-get-along protestations," I scoffed, thinking this was the perfect time to throw some more wood on the fire. "I outrank the man and have taken control of all mobile Confederation Forces in Easy Haven, for the duration."

"Demon Murphy take you for a fool," snarled the Imperial Command, "I won't let you ruin everything." The Imperial Commander turned to his bridge crew, "Light the engines and put us between the Constructors and this rogue warship."

The Ex-Com on my bridge chimed in, "Sir! System Command and the Imperials are both requesting we accept a conference call with LeGodat."

"Oh, whatever," I said, waving my hand in our patented royal dismissive way. "Put him on. I'm curious to know if he's scrounged up any more vessels for my fleet yet."

"You're going to get us all killed," said Tremblay, looking both pale and furious. Oh, how I love to see that man squirm.

"Death in the pursuit of Honor is no death all," I said, trying for my most pompous. Hanging around these bloodthirsty natives with their strange honor code was giving me some truly wild inspiration.

"Sir!" exclaimed Tremblay and LeGodat at the same time.

Seeing another person to carry the torch of reason, Tremblay stepped back they all looked at LeGodat.

The Imperial cut in. "Who is this stooge I see on my view screen, System Commander?" demanded the Imperial Commander. "Instruct him to vacate this area of space at once, or I will destroy more than just these Constructor ships," threatened the young Cornwallis.

"A moment, Commander, please," begged the System Commander, turning away from the Imperial and toward myself. "What is this, Admiral?" LeGodat demanded desperately. "You told me you would be restrained and when I questioned you after hearing the name of the Imperial Commander, you told me there was only some old, outdated family business from before you were born between you! You can't do this!" The System Commander looked like a man powerless to stop a train wreck, yet desperate to try anyway.

I drew myself up into my most Princely and regal pose, "Commodore LeGodat, let me assure you, I have been the height of reason," I said looking down my nose at the System Commander.

"It's just 'Lieutenant Commander,' not Commodore," said the Fleet Officer in charge of system command and the Corvette squadron, "and I'm sorry to have to say you've been anything but, Admiral." LeGodat looked like a man caught between a rock and hard place, a slight sheen of sweat growing on his forehead.

"Listen, Commodore," I repeated the title purposely.

"It's *Commander*," exclaimed the Fleet Officer.

I shook my head, trying for my most condescending bearing. "It's simply not proper for a 'Lieutenant Commander' to command a Star Base of this size and tactical importance. Commodore has a much nicer ring to it, wouldn't you say? So I've promoted you," I said grandly, accompanying this statement with a regal tilt of the head.

I then snapped my head around to face the Imperial Commander's image. "But neither is it proper for a member of the Caprian Blood Royal to let a Cornwallis slip through his fingers, not when the Imperial Commander has been caught red-handed in the act of piracy against the Confederacy!"

"I regret to have to inform you, Admiral," said the System Commander, looking grey-faced, "that if you engage the Imperial Strike Cruiser in combat, I will have no choice but to fulfill my mandate to protect this system and its inhabitants by firing on your vessel."

The Imperial Commander looked like a man who'd just swallowed something bitter.

"You'll do as you feel you have to, Commodore," I said in a sympathetic voice. "In the meantime, every Imperial vessel that hasn't pointed its nose to the hyper-limit and started a maximum burn will feel a taste of my wrath! Ex-Com, cut the transmission and redirect us to the Promethean Cruisers. Continue on the open frequency," I instructed.

The entire bridge staff sat rigidly in their chairs, fingers and hands clenched tight.

"What was that, Admiral?" Tremblay began in despair. "You've not only cast us as the aggressors in this conflict, but you've implicated the home world, not to mention potentially the entire Confederacy as well!"

I ignored him and turned to the tactical section instead. I caught the eye of the grey-haired individual manning the main console.

"If we actually pass between the Imperials and the Constructors, and we're within range of our weapons, instruct Gunnery to aim for non-critical areas and most importantly of all, they are instructed to miss their targets," I said firmly.

The Tactical Officer pursed his lips and then nodded.

Officer Tremblay looked angry and surprised, "Was this whole thing a ruse then," he demanded. "What's the big plan now? Bluff them until it's time for us to turn around and run away with our tail firmly between our legs, having made ourselves the laughing stock of civilized space?" I could imagine him envisioning his career's former projected trajectory, now watching it go down in flames, and had to stifle a smile.

I shook my head. "You and your insistence that everything I do is a bluff, up until I actually go and do it," I said warningly. "When will you learn, Mr. Tremblay? Now, on the other hand, threatening to fire on unarmed civilians? Unarmed Confederation Civilians? That was a legitimate ruse of warfare, not a bluff. Threatening to fire on and destroy an Imperial ship caught in the act of pirating Confederation vessels," I slammed my good fist into the bent side of the Throne. "No. That was no bluff, Mr. Tremblay, that was a stated fact. If they don't high-tail it out of here faster than we can catch them, that Strike Cruiser will soon know that they've been in a fight."

I deliberately turned my face away from the First Officer and back to the main screen. "Ex-Com, the Prometheans please," I said harshly.

The tech jumped, "Yes, Sir," said the person manning the Ex-Com section. "You're live now, Admiral."

"Members of Confederation Multi-Sector Patrol Fleet, *Pride of Prometheus* and *Prometheus Fire*, you are immediately instructed to heave to and prepare yourselves for inspection teams from the Confederation Flagship, MPF Lucky Clover," I said harshly. "Resistance will be met with overwhelming force. Put your power generators into shutdown mode and do not attempt to spin up your hyper drive systems. You are being detained on the suspicion of mutiny and piracy." I glared unmoving at the screen for several moments, making sure they had the opportunity to see my ruined face in all its terrifying glory.

"Ex-Com, cut transmission," I said when I felt an appropriate dose had been administered. I was really going now.

A saw a yeoman out of the corner of my eye. I leaned back in my chair and said "Yeoman, a spot of tea, if you'd be so kind. All of this reasonable communicating makes for an awfully dry throat." I couldn't help myself.

After the Tech indicated they were off the air, I leaned back and heaved a sigh of relief.

The signal, when it came back, was twofold.

A swarthy, medium-sized man neither fat nor slim, middle aged and with a haggard look to him appeared on the screen first. "The Medium Cruiser, *Prometheus Fire*, regrets to inform you that she has been voluntarily withdrawn from the Patrol Fleet, as per agreed upon protocol. The Fire stipulates that it has been, and continues to be, in compliance with all applicable Confederation and Confederated Empire statutes and ordinances. Costel Iorghu of *Prometheus Fire*, out," said what must have been the captain of the ship.

Then the transmission from Captain Stood came in. Grey hair slicked back and still as fat as ever, the older man jiggled as he slammed his hands down on the arms of his chair and leaned forward. "The Empire's all but gone and the Confederation dead and buried. I think you have more pressing worries than us and what happened to your fancy little prize ship, right this moment," he sneered before cutting the transmission.

I paused, uncertain for a moment. It was a good opportunity to take a sip of tea the yeoman had just delivered. "That went well," I commented in an off-handed fashion.

NO MIDDLE GROUND

(SPINEWARD SECTORS: MIDDLETON'S PRIDE, BOOK ONE OF FIVE)

CALEB WACHTER

PROLOGUE: THE BIG CHAIR

"Have a seat, Lieutenant Commander," the young Admiral, Jason Montagne, gestured to the seat opposite his own in the Admiral's office adjacent to the Flag Bridge.

Lieutenant Commander Tyrone 'Tim' Middleton was apprehensive about the nature of the meeting, but he was more intrigued than concerned. So he took his seat as indicated, acknowledging with a nod, "Thank you, Admiral."

After he had been seated, he felt the Little Admiral—a moniker which was far from respectful in its origins—pour the weight of his gaze over his features. The young man had absolutely zero military training, having been born into a relatively minor branch of his home planet's nobility and being placed aboard the *Lucky Clover* as little more than a face-saving piece of political theater. Just a few months earlier it would have been inconceivably ludicrous to suggest that he would be commanding one of the most powerful mobile assets in the entire Spineward Sectors. But, as is so often the case, reality turned out to be more incredible than the cheapest fiction.

"I've been going over our latest status reports," the young Admiral began, gesturing languidly to a neat stack of data slates on the desk before him, "and it seems that the *Lucky Clover* has no further use for you on her bridge."

"Sir?!" Middleton said in surprise. He had been the First Shift Tactical Officer ever since Admiral Montagne had fully assumed command of the aged battleship, and to his mind he had performed his duties precisely as needed.

Admiral Montagne nodded coolly, lacing his fingers before his face as he explained in his aggravating, Royalist manner. "The *Clover*'s crew, while still a tick or two below a proper military standard, have rounded into form nicely under the direction of her various department heads—your own department included."

"We've just been doing our jobs, Admiral," Middleton said guardedly. The truth of his own circumstances was that if the Imperial Navy had not withdrawn the entirety of its mobile assets from the Spineward Sectors just a few short weeks earlier, he likely would have already retired and moved on to the next phase of his life. He had no great wish to abandon the Multi-Sector Patrol Fleet—the peacekeeping force to which he had been attached for the past several years—but the time had come for him to move on from his twenty year military career.

"As have we all," Admiral Montagne agreed easily, but Middleton felt the younger man's gaze probe his eyes for some purpose of which he was uncertain. "And, in keeping with that particular sentiment," the Little Admiral continued, reaching to the top data slate on the pile and sliding it across the desk, "you have a new assignment."

Lieutenant Commander Middleton picked up the data slate, and within a few seconds his eyebrows rose in surprise—and then lowered darkly as he realized what those orders entailed. "Admiral—" he began to protest, but the younger man cut him off.

"You're the top bridge officer aboard this ship, Lieutenant Commander Middleton," the Admiral said smoothly, "or, at least, the top one with the necessary credentials to fulfill this particular duty."

Middleton shook his head dubiously, knowing there had been supposedly good reason why he had not advanced higher up the chain of command than he had already done. "My psych profile—"

"Is just one of several data points I've incorporated while making my decision," the Little Admiral interrupted with a dismissive wave of his hand. "I assure you, Lieutenant Commander, that this will be a simple 'wave the flag' mission. The people of the Spineward Sectors need to see friendly faces in light of the recent chaos caused by the Imperial withdrawal; a month-long patrol on the border of Sectors 24 & 25 should alleviate some portion of the anxiety felt by those citizens living there."

Middleton considered the younger man's words, and as he did so he realized he was probably right. The people of the Spineward Sectors needed a stabilizing force—or at least the appearance of one—and with that in mind he arrived at what most would deem an unnaturally quick decision. But as a Tactical Officer, it was Middleton's job to adapt to new variables as quickly as possible—and there were precious few TO's in the Multi-Sector Patrol Fleet who were as good at that particular part of the job as Lieutenant Commander Middleton.

"I'll need a few days to draw up a roster," Middleton said as he leaned back in the chair and considered possible crew for the mission.

"You've got forty eight hours to submit your transfer requests," Admiral Montagne said with what Middleton suspected was a false smile, and the young man stood to offer his hand across the desk. "Congratulations, Captain Middleton."

CHAPTER 3:
EARNING HAZARD PAY

Three weeks after the Pride of Prometheus *was seized by the Mult-Sector Patrol Fleet and sent on patrol by the order of Vice Admiral Jason Montagne*

"Airborne biohazard detected on decks four, five and six," the Comm. officer reported frantically, clarifying the nature of the alarm—and only then did Captain Tim Middleton understand the pirates' intentions in surrendering so quickly. "Emergency lockdown protocols are now in effect, sir."

Captain Middleton closed his eyes briefly and thought, *That's why the torpedo didn't destroy us when it impacted—it was carrying a bio-weapon instead of a ship-busting warhead.*

He punched up the ship's doctor on his chair's comm. unit and was quickly rewarded with the image of the aging doctor's face. "What is it, Doctor?" he asked, feeling an odd mixture of anxiety and serenity now that the final piece had fallen into place. It was terrifying to have a biological contagion aboard the ship, but he now fully understood the tactical situation and would no longer need to analyze and re-analyze each and every piece of new information. To Middleton, this was a more significant relief than anything.

"Computer's reading some kind of multi-part, auto-recombinant airborne virus," Doctor Milton replied grimly. "It beat the standard filters because it only recombines inside the host's body. Frankly, we're lucky it got detected by the outdated filters in here," he said with a hard look.

Middleton kept his features firm despite the roiling sensation in his abdomen. "Can you treat it?"

The Doctor shook his head as he rubbed the bridge of his nose. "Realistically the best thing we can do is lock the ship down, shut off the primary air circulation systems, and hope to Murphy it's been contained."

"Can we re-route the air circulation through the systems in Engineering and the Bridge?" Middleton pressed, knowing it was a long shot. The *Pride*'s critical areas—the bridge, Engineering, the gun deck and sickbay—had independent air re-circulation systems which, when activated, could keep those portions of the ship separate in the event of a contaminant like the one just discovered. They could also filter out and destroy any potential bio-contaminants for several days with no more than emergency power. Tapping into those filtration systems was a long shot, but Middleton had to do everything possible for his crew.

"If we do that, we risk exposing the crew that are already protected within the high-security sections," the Doctor shook his head firmly. "Protocols are clear on this situation, Captain; I've already initiated the lockdown, and now only you or I can override it. As Chief Medical Officer, it is my opinion that you should leave the lockdown in place until this contagion has been identified and treated, or run its course in containment."

Captain Middleton felt the urge to sit back in his chair but fought it, remaining precisely where he was so he could maintain eye contact with Milton. "How long, Doctor?" he asked after a lengthy pause which saw all activity on the bridge come to a grinding halt.

"If this is a high-grade bioweapon—and I've got no reason to believe it isn't—we've got no more than twelve hours, barring extreme luck with the available treatments," Doctor Milton replied matter-of-factly. "That still gives me a few hours here to determine what it is we're dealing with… in the event we don't have 'extreme luck.'"

Middleton could feel the eyes of the entire bridge crew on him as the reality of the situation sank in for them. But to him, Doctor Milton's report was just another piece of the puzzle which explained the second corvette captain's behavior perfectly. To Middleton's mind, the fact that the Liberator torpedo had carried a bioweapon rather than a ship-busting bomb was good news since it meant that at least some of the crew would survive. They were already in full lockdown containment mode, so there was little point in worrying about the inevitable aftermath of this weaponized virus just yet.

"I'll leave you to it then, Doctor," Middleton said with a short nod which Milton returned before cutting the com-link. Straightening himself in his chair, Captain Middleton turned deliberately toward Ensign Sarkozi. "Has Captain Raubach's vessel come to a full stop?"

Sarkozi stared blankly at him for a moment before snapping to and checking her console with a glance. "No, Captain," she said with a note of surprise, "she's cut her engines and stopped her acceleration, but the corvette's inertia is still carrying it forward with only the gravity of the gas giant slowing her down fractionally, and they've already gone well past orbit-breaking speed."

Middleton had expected such, so he continued calmly, "Are their shields still raised?"

Sarkozi glanced down and shook her head. "Negative, Captain; her shields are down and her primary generator is off-line. Aside from her forward momentum, she's dead in space."

Replaying the sequence of events in his mind, Captain Middleton shook his head at his own lack of experience. Foreseeing the presence of not one, but *two* banned weapons in the Liberator torpedo and the bioweapon it carried, required an unreasonable amount of foresight. But he now knew that he should not have accepted Captain Raubach's unconditional surrender as readily as he had.

"Tactical," he began evenly, feeling his face go red with anger, "have the gun deck transfer fire control of the forward batteries to my console."

"Captain—" Tactical Officer Sarkozi began, but the rest of her words caught in her throat at Middleton's hard, unyielding look. "Transferring now, sir," she said professionally before bracing to attention several seconds later and adding, "transfer complete, Captain."

"Comm.," the Captain said, his eyes fixed on the main viewer, "hail the corvette."

"Hailing now, Captain," Ensign Jardine replied after a brief pause.

A moment later, the screen was filled with Captain Meisha T. Raubach's smug features. "We are prepared to receive your boarding party,

Captain Middleton," she said officiously, but Middleton could plainly see the outright arrogance in her visage. She clearly knew that the *Pride of Prometheus* would catch her eventually, but she also just as clearly knew that the *Pride* would be in lockdown and that sending a boarding party would be next to impossible until that lockdown was over—which could either take hours or days.

Still, Middleton thought to himself bitterly as he leaned forward in his chair, *at least we won't have to worry about them sending a boarding party of their own*. "Captain Raubach," he began in an officious tone of his own, "you have deployed outlawed ordnance, including weapons of mass destruction in the form of an engineered bioweapon, delivered by a universally banned ship-to-ship delivery platform. Your crimes have been noted in my ship's log and are witnessed by the members of this crew and the ship's sensor feeds; under the Confederation War Crimes statute you are hereby sentenced to summary execution."

Captain Raubach stiffened visibly as she shook her head in negation, her curly hair bouncing around her oddly handsome features. "The Confederation War Crimes statutes are outdated, *Captain*," she said smugly. "As Imperial citizens, both I and my crew are to be afforded safe passage to an Imperial outpost—as stipulated under both the Union Treaty *and* the United Space Sectors and Provinces Act—where our legal status can be impartially determined. We have complied with your demands by powering down our fusion reactor and disabling our weaponry—as well as our engines," she added with a triumphant smirk, "and are even now awaiting your boarding party. I assure you we will cooperate fully with your inspection and seizure teams whenever they arrive."

"The Union Treaty has been dissolved, Captain Raubach," Middleton said evenly, "and with it your so-called 'protection.'"

"Even if that's true," she countered easily, "as an officer in the Imperial Navy, the United Space Sectors and Provinces Act stipulates that I be remanded into Imperial custody before any provincial legal action can proceed."

"Captain Raubach," Middleton began, feeling his collar begin to heat at the incessant back-and-forth wordplay but knowing he needed to keep calm, "are you saying that your actions here are condoned by the Imperial Navy?"

Raubach laughed in open derision. "Of course not," she spat with a piteous shake of her head, "I, and my crew, seized this ship and station in an act of piracy in order to take financial advantage of the political instability in the region. But, as a mutinous Imperial officer, my superiors will naturally want me remanded to their custody immediately following my arrest."

Middleton felt the urge to scream at the top of his lungs, but he kept his best poker face throughout the exchange. His mind raced as he tried to devise a way to outmaneuver this woman, but it was clear that she had the legal framework on her side—which meant this had been a well-coordinated effort, likely with significant backing. "Raubach," Middleton mused as he tried to buy time, "I've heard that name before. Your family's one of the most powerful in the Imperium, isn't it?"

"My *husband,* James', family," she corrected with a disdainful shake of her head, looking for all the world like the cat that got the cream. "My maiden name is Tate," she added in her insufferably smug tone.

Ensign Sarkozi approached Middleton's chair and leaned close to say under her breath, "In three minutes they will have left our heavy lasers' extreme range, Captain."

At Middleton's momentary hesitation, Captain Raubach snickered triumphantly. "Face it, Captain," she said, taking a triumphant step toward the viewer's pickup, "there's nothing you can do now; I've got complete legal immunity."

Middleton closed his eyes and his hand hung suspended over the arm console of his chair. He knew full well that what he was contemplating bordered on a capital offense in and of itself. But even assuming the *Pride* caught up to the corvette and secured both it and its crew, all that would do is buy more time for the merchantmen to conclude their business at the mining facility—and Captain Middleton was now certain that said business was far from legitimate.

Conversely, if he turned his back on the corvette to secure the gas facility and merchantmen, there was nothing to stop it from coasting further and further away until it was outside the *Pride*'s effective zone of control. And if there was even a half-reasonable possibility that the gas facility had been turned into a bioweapons manufacturing site—

His eyes snapped open after he had worked his way through the situation, and he knew what he had to do—no matter how much it might cost him personally.

"Your 'immunity,' Captain Raubach," he began coldly, his fingers tapping the Captain's fire control code into the console on his chair, "has just been revoked."

His finger rammed down on the firing icon, and the look on the pirate Captain's face was one of shocked incredulity as the *Pride*'s forward batteries fired in unison. Captain Raubach made to protest, but the connection was severed before any sound passed her lips.

The viewer shimmered to replace her smug visage with a real-time image of the corvette. Its superstructure buckled from the combined power of eight heavy lasers landing in concert on the drifting vessel's lightly-armored hull.

Seconds later there was a series of explosions which cascaded through the corvette's hull, sending sections of hull plating flying in every direction as the vessel began to topple end over end from the force of the internal ruptures. Debris went spinning off with every rotation, and after less than a minute all power signatures aboard the corvette went dark.

There was shocked silence on the bridge, into which Middleton smartly ordered, "Helm, best possible speed to the gas collection facility; I don't want a single ship escaping this system under any circumstances. Comm.," he continued, bracing himself against the arm of his chair, "transmit on all channels the order for vessels in system to heave to—or, if docked, to remain where they are—and await MSP inspection. Failure to comply will result in..." he cocked a cold grin in spite of the situation's severity, "further revocations."

APPENDIX:
GLOSSARY OF UK TERMS AND SLANG

[Author's Note: I've tried to define every incident of specifically UK slang in this glossary, but I can't promise to have spotted everything. If you spot something I've missed, please let me know and it will be included.]

Aggro - slang term for aggression or trouble, as in 'I don't want any aggro.'

Beasting/Beasted - military slang for anything from a chewing out by one's commander to outright corporal punishment or hazing. The latter two are now officially banned.

Binned - SAS slang for a prospective recruit being kicked from the course, then returned to unit (RTU).

Boffin - Scientist

Bootnecks - slang for Royal Marines. Loosely comparable to 'Jarhead.'

Bottle - slang for nerve, as in 'lost his bottle.'

Borstal - a school/prison for young offenders.

Donkey Wallopers - slang for the Royal Horse Artillery.

Fortnight - two weeks. (Hence the terrible pun, courtesy of the *Goon Show*, that Fort Knight cannot possibly last three weeks.)

'Get stuck into' - 'start fighting.'

'I should coco' - 'you're damned right.'

Kip - sleep.

Levies - native troops. The Ghurkhas are the last remnants of native troops from British India.

Lorries - trucks.

MOD - Ministry of Defence. (The UK's Pentagon.)

Panda Cola - Coke as supplied by the British Army to the troops.

RFA - Royal Fleet Auxiliary

Rumbled - discovered/spotted.

SAS - Special Air Service.

SBS - Special Boat Service

Spotted Dick - a traditional fruity sponge pudding with suet, citrus zest and currants served in thick slices with hot custard. The name always caused a snigger.

Squaddies - slang for British soldiers.

Stag - guard duty.

TAB (tab/tabbing) - Tactical Advance to Battle.

Tearaway - boisterous/badly behaved child, normally a teenager.

Walt - Poser, i.e. someone who claims to have served in the military and/or a very famous regiment. There's a joke about 22 SAS being the largest regiment in the British Army - it must be, because of all the people who claim to have served in it.

Wanker - Masturbator (jerk-off). Commonly used as an insult.

Wanking - Masturbating.

Yank/Yankee - Americans

CPSIA information can be obtained
at www.ICGtesting.com
Printed in the USA
LVOW08s1519250118
563986LV00021B/497/P